KU-736-579

CARRIE'S RUN

Also by Andrew Kaplan

HOMELAND™
CARRIE'S RUN

ANDREW KAPLAN

HARPER

This novel is entirely a work of fiction.
The names, characters and incidents portrayed in it are
the work of the author's imagination. Any resemblance to
actual persons, living or dead, events or localities is
entirely coincidental.

Harper
An imprint of HarperCollins*Publishers*
77–85 Fulham Palace Road,
Hammersmith, London W6 8JB

www.harpercollins.co.uk

This paperback edition 2013

1

First published in Great Britain by
HarperCollins*Publishers* 2013

Homeland: Carrie's Run. Copyright © 2013 by Twentieth Century Fox
Film Corporation. All rights reserved.

Artwork/Photographs © 2013 Showtime Networks, Inc., a CBS Company.
All rights reserved.

Designed by Diahann Sturge

Andrew Kaplan asserts the moral right to be identified as the author of this work

A catalogue record for this book is available from the British Library

ISBN: 978 0 00 794653 2

Printed and bound in Great Britain by
Clays Ltd, St Ives plc

All rights reserved. No part of this publication may be reproduced,
stored in a retrieval system, or transmitted, in any form or by any means,
electronic, mechanical, photocopying, recording or otherwise, without
the prior permission of the publishers.

This book is sold subject to the condition that it shall not, by way of
trade or otherwise, be lent, re-sold, hired out or otherwise circulated
without the publisher's prior consent in any form of binding or cover
other than that in which it is published and without a similar condition
including this condition being imposed on the subsequent purchaser.

MIX
Paper from
responsible sources
FSC
www.fsc.org **FSC C007454**

FSC™ is a non-profit international organisation established to promote
the responsible management of the world's forests. Products carrying the
FSC label are independently certified to assure consumers that they come
from forests that are managed to meet the social, economic and
ecological needs of present and future generations,
and other controlled sources.

Find out more about HarperCollins and the environment at
www.harpercollins.co.uk/green

To my son, Justin, who makes everything better,
and
to the men and women of the U.S. intelligence services,
who pursue in shadow the most elusive commodity on earth—truth

AUTHOR'S NOTE

For readers interested in additional information on the characters, organizations and agencies described in this novel, a glossary and a list of characters are provided at the back of the book.

"*You know how it is at Princeton on a dark winter morning, five* A.M., *before anyone else is up? Coming out of 1915 Hall in my sweats, because I was never the glamour girl. I was the serious girl, the one who didn't flirt with the boys but who maybe was going to do something. I would start my run without touching the stopwatch. The campus silent, no one anywhere, the air so cold it hurt to breathe. Running all the way to Nassau Street, shops shuttered, streetlights reflected on the icy pavement. Then right on Washington, back on campus, past Woodrow Wilson and Frist to Weaver Track.*

"*I would stop, my breath coming out in clouds, the sky breaking gray, then click the stopwatch and run the fifteen hundred as if my life depended on it, trying to remember the pacing, but I swear, Saul, there were times, even when it was killing me in the final two hundred, I thought I could run forever.*"

"*What do you want, Carrie? What the hell do you really want?*"

"*I don't know. To be that girl again. To feel the cleanness—is that a word? He's hiding something, Saul. I swear to God.*"

"*Everybody's hiding something. We're human.*"

"*No, something bad. Something that's going to really hurt us. We can't let it happen again.*"

"*Let's be clear, you're not just risking your life and both our careers; it's national security, the Agency itself. You sure you want to do this?*"

"*I just realized something. I'll never be that girl again, will I?*"

"*I'm not sure you ever were.*"

2006
BEFORE BRODY

CHAPTER 1

Ashrafieh, Beirut, Lebanon

Nightingale was late.

Sitting in the darkened movie theater, second seat, fourth row from the back, Carrie Mathison tried to decide whether to abort. It was supposed to be an initial contact only. "Passing ships," Saul Berenson, her boss and mentor, had called it during training back at the Farm, the CIA's training facility in Virginia. Get a close-up look at one Taha al-Douni, to whom they'd assigned the code name "Nightingale," let him get a quick look at her for the next time, whisper the time and location for the next meet and leave. Strictly by the book.

If the contact was late, Company protocol was to wait fifteen to twenty minutes, then abort and reschedule only if the contact provided a damn good reason why they hadn't shown. An everyday excuse such as Middle Eastern time, which could be anything from a half hour to a half day late, or the regular Friday-evening traffic mash-up on Boulevard Fouad Chehab during the *cinq á sept*, the hours between five and seven P.M. when businessmen met their mistresses in discreet little Hamra-district apartments wouldn't cut it.

Except Carrie wanted this one. According to her source,

Dima, a pretty Lebanese party girl from March 14, a Maronite Christian political group, whom you could find every night at the rooftop bar at Le Gray in the Central District, al-Douni had two things that made him someone the CIA would die to get their hands on: one, he was GSD, an officer in the General Security Directorate, the brutal Syrian secret intelligence agency, which gave him a direct pipeline into the Assad regime in Damascus; and two, he needed money. A foxy Egyptian girlfriend with expensive tastes was bleeding him dry, Dima said.

She checked her watch again. Twenty-nine minutes. Where the hell was he? She looked around the theater. It was more than three-quarters full. Since the movie started, no one had come in. On the screen, Harry Potter, Ron and Hermione were in Mad-eye Moody's class, watching him put an Imperius curse on a lethal-looking flying insect.

Her nerves felt taut as a violin string, though that didn't mean anything. She couldn't always trust her feelings, because there were times when she thought her nervous electrical system had been put together by the same idiots who built the Washington, DC, power grid. Bipolar disorder, the doctors called it. A psychiatric mood disorder characterized by episodes of hypomania alternating with depressive episodes, as a psychiatrist once recommended by the student health center back at Princeton, had described it. Her sister, Maggie, had a better definition for it: "Mood swings that cycle from 'I'm the smartest, prettiest, most fantastic girl in the universe' to 'I want to kill myself.'" Even so, everything about this contact felt wrong.

She couldn't wait any longer, she told herself. On the screen, Hermione was screaming at Moody, begging him to stop a curse that was torturing the poor insect to death. Perfect timing; lots of noise and special effects. No one would notice her, she decided, getting up and making her way out to the theater lobby.

She stepped outside to the street, feeling conspicuous, exposed. To a certain extent, it was always that way for a Western woman in the Middle East. You stood out. The only way to disguise yourself would be to wear a full-body-covering *abaya* and veil, and hope no one got close enough to get a good look. But with her slender build, long straight blond hair and all-American face, Carrie couldn't fool anyone except at a distance, and in any case, that wouldn't work in North Beirut, where women wore everything from *hijabs* to skintight designer jeans, and sometimes both at the same time.

It had grown dark while she had been in the theater. Traffic was heavy on Avenue Michel Bustros, the headlights of the cars and the lighted windows in tall office and apartment buildings making a mosaic of lights and shadows. She scanned the street looking for watchers. Broken contacts were always potentially dangerous. And then her heart almost stopped.

Nightingale was seated at a café table across the street looking right at her. Totally wrong. He couldn't have misunderstood the instructions passed to him by Dima at Le Gray last night. Was he crazy? And then he made it worse. He beckoned her with a hand gesture that in America means "go away" but in the Middle East means "come here." Instantly the pattern resolved itself, like one of those kaleidoscopes that you shake and suddenly all the pieces fall into place. It was an ambush. Al-Douni was supposed to be GSD. A seasoned intelligence professional. He couldn't be doing something so amateurish.

Whether it was GSD or Hezbollah, they weren't above killing a CIA agent or, better yet, taking one hostage for their own purposes. For them, grabbing an attractive blond female CIA spy would be like hitting the lottery. In her mind, she could already visualize the media circus as they paraded her before the camera, denouncing yet more American interference in the Middle East while they kept her locked in a closet for years, torturing and raping her because after all, she was a spy, not to mention that many men in the Middle East believed Western women were all sluts anyway. Nightingale motioned to her again and as he did so, out of the corner of her eye, she spotted two Arab men getting out of a van on her side of the street and moving toward her.

It was a snatch. She had to decide instantly; in a few seconds she would be a prisoner. She turned and walked back into the theater.

"I forgot something," she mumbled in Arabic, showing her *billet* to the ticket taker. She walked down the aisle, squinting to readjust her eyes to the dark. On the screen, Dumbledore was announcing that Hogwarts was to host the Triwizard Tournmanet as Carrie stepped out the side emergency exit into an alley. They would be coming in after her, she thought, heading back to the avenue. She peeked out from the side of the building. Nightingale was no longer at the café. The two men must have entered the theater.

She ran out onto the avenue, making a turn around the corner and down a narrow street away from the traffic. How many were there? she wondered, cursing herself for wearing high heels. Part of her cover. Unless she was in an *abaya*, no self-respecting woman in Beirut would be caught dead in flats. There wouldn't be just the two men, she thought, stopping to pull off her heels. Not if they were serious.

The street was dark, shaded with trees. Not many people around, not that having people around would stop them. The two Arab men from the van came around the corner. One of them pulled something out of his jacket. It looked like a pistol with an attached sound suppressor. She started to run. They had underestimated her, she thought. She had been a runner. She could outrun them.

Just then she heard a sharp ping and felt something sting her leg. She glanced down and back and saw a white scar on the sidewalk from a bullet. They were shooting at her. She dodged left, then right and touched her leg, feeling a tear in her jeans and a smear. Blood. A bit of sidewalk must have ricocheted and hit her, she thought, running for her life, the concrete hard on her bare feet. Turning the corner, she raced down an empty street. She had to do something and fast. On her left was a large gated house behind a wrought-iron fence; on the other side of the street, a Greek Orthodox church with a domed roof, spotlighted white in the darkness.

She raced to the side door of the church and yanked on the handle. It was locked. Looking behind her, her heart pounding, she could see the two Arab men running. They both had pistols with silencers now and were getting closer. Ahead at the corner, a Mercedes sedan screeched to a halt. Four men piled out. Shit! she thought, running as hard as she could for the main door to the church. She yanked it open and ran inside.

There were perhaps a dozen people, nearly all women dressed in black, in the church. They were walking around, lighting candles and kissing icons or just standing facing the altar with its arches and gold-backed icons. A bearded young man, a priest in a black robe, came down the aisle toward her.

"Christ is in our midst," he said in Arabic.

"Of course he is, Father. I need help. Is there a back way out?" she replied in Arabic.

Instinctively, he glanced to the side toward his shoulder. She ran that way, just as the main door burst open and the four men from the Mercedes ran in, two of them holding automatic rifles. A woman screamed and everyone began to scatter. Except the priest, who walked toward the men.

"*Bess!*" he shouted. *Stop!* "This is the house of our Lord!" One of the men bowled him aside as he ran down the aisle toward the alcove where Carrie had disappeared behind a curtain that led to a door.

She ran outside. A walkway led to an avenue, or she could cross the walkway to a parking lot surrounded by a hedge. She ran through the parking lot, jogging right at the muffled sound of a shot behind her, then dodged through a gap in a hedge and out onto Avenue Charles Malek, a broad main street thick with traffic and people. She ran into the middle of the street, dodging cars, horns honking. The light turned green and the traffic was moving all around her. Out of the corner of her eye, she looked back at the side street and saw three of the men from the Mercedes on the sidewalk looking around for her. They would spot her in seconds.

She was in the middle of traffic between two lanes of cars barely eight inches apart. She felt a hand groping her ass from a car moving in the opposite direction. She didn't waste time looking to see who had done it; she had to do something fast to get out of their line of sight.

A Service taxi was about to pass her. There was one seat in the back available. She waved her hand at the windshield in front of the driver's face and shouted "Hamra!" The Service was already heading that way, west, and there was a CIA safe house in the Ras Beirut neighborhood not far from Hamra if she could reach it undetected. The Service stopped in the middle of traffic, horns behind him honking, and she jumped into the backseat.

"*Salaam alaikum,*" she murmured to the other passengers, slipping the shoes she'd been carrying back on and pulling a black *hijab* from her pocket and putting it on her head to help change her image. She tossed one end of the scarf over her shoulder while looking around quickly. One of the men on the sidewalk was pointing at the Service and saying something. She leaned back, so she would be screened by the other two passengers in the backseat, an older woman in a gray suit staring at her with frank interest and a young man in sweats, probably a university student. In the front seat next to the driver was a young woman ignoring everyone and talking to someone on a cell phone.

"*Wa alaikum salaam*," the student and the older woman murmured back.

"Where in Hamra?" the driver asked, hitting the gas and swerving into a gap between the cars ahead to advance a few meters.

"Central Bank," she said, not wanting to give away the actual safe house location, especially if they were still following her. Close enough to where she wanted to go. She passed two thousand-livre bills to the driver, then pulled a makeup compact out of her handbag and tried to angle it so she could see out the rear window. Nothing but traffic behind. If the van or the Mercedes was behind her, they were too far back to be seen. But they were still after her. She was sure of it. Because of her, everyone in the Service was in danger. She had to get out as soon as she could, she thought. Brushing a strand of hair out of her eyes and looking around, she put the compact away.

"You shouldn't do that," the older woman said. "Standing in the middle of traffic like that."

"There's a lot I shouldn't do." Then, realizing the woman was taking too much interest in her, she added, "My husband tells me all the time," making sure the woman saw the wedding band she always wore for contact meetings even though she wasn't married, to help prevent what Virgil, her black-bag guy, called "Everest sex." Sex that was unwanted or with the wrong partners or the Everest part, "because it's there, Carrie."

They were on Boulevard General Fouad Chehab now, the main east-west street across northern Beirut, and the traffic was moving a little faster. If they were going to come at her in the Service, it would be now, she thought, eyes darting around. Cars and trucks all around and the teenage girl in front on the cell phone saying, "I know, *habibi*. Ciao." The girl hung up and immediately began texting.

The driver made the turn by the tall rectangular al-Mour building onto Boulevard Fakhreddine. All the buildings in this area were new; the old ones had been destroyed during the long civil war. Farther up the boulevard, she could see tall cranes where still more new buildings were going up. The Service made a left and after a few blocks, the driver slowed to find a place to let someone off.

Carrie glanced back out the rear window. They were still behind her. In traffic, four cars back in the Mercedes, looking to move over. They were waiting for her to get out, then they'd pick her up before she'd gone twenty feet. What could she do? The Service pulled over and stopped near a tall apartment building. Carrie tensed. Would they come at her now? They could stop by the Service, blocking it so it couldn't pull out in traffic. She'd be trapped. She had to do something and fast.

The older woman nodded to the other passengers and got out. After a second, Carrie got out on the street side, went around and took her arm.

"I thought you were going to Central Bank," the woman said.

"I'm in trouble. Please, madame," Carrie said.

The woman looked at her. "What kind of trouble?" she

asked as they walked toward the entrance to the apartment building. Carrie glanced over her shoulder. As the Service pulled away, the Mercedes was pulling up in its place at the curb.

"The worst kind. We have to run or they'll kill you too, madame," Carrie said, starting to run and pulling the woman with her. They ran inside the building, over to the elevators, and pushed the button.

"Don't push the button for your floor," Carrie said. "Pick a higher floor and walk down. Lock the door and don't open it for anyone for at least an hour. I'm so sorry." She touched the woman's arm.

"Wait," the woman said, digging in her handbag. "I have a red Renault in the parking lot." She held out the keys.

"Wait an hour before you report it stolen," Carrie said, taking the keys. "You know the Crowne Plaza, by the shopping mall?"

The woman nodded.

"If I can, I'll leave it there," Carrie said, already running to the side door near the parking lot. "*Shokran*," she called back to thank the woman as she stepped into the elevator.

She went out to the parking lot. The red Renault was parked in a row of cars near a low wall and hedge. She ran over, unlocked it, got in and started it up. As she was adjusting the mirrors, she saw them. Two men. The same two who had chased her into the church. She threw the car into reverse, backed out and drove toward the exit. The men ran after her; the one who had shot at her going into shooting position, aiming at the car. Instinctively she ducked as she swerved into the street, turning hard and accelerating as fast as the little car could go. A bullet smashed through the rear window, spreading a spider-web of cracks from the hole.

She swerved again, looking toward the parking lot, where the shooter was aiming right at her. She would have to come directly abreast of where he was standing. At the last second, she hit the brake and banged her head back against the headrest. Another bullet went through the side window, slicing the air in front of her face. She stomped on the gas again, a car horn honking loudly behind her, and raced down the street, looking for a gap in traffic. Checking the rearview mirror, she saw that for the moment, the Mercedes was still stopped at the curb. Someone was running on the sidewalk toward it. God, she hoped they hadn't hurt the older woman. Why had they shot at her? What was going on? A CIA hostage was valuable for Hezbollah or Syria or whoever the hell was behind this. A dead woman, even CIA, wasn't worth that much.

Suddenly, without signaling, she edged into the right lane and turned the corner, tires squealing as she raced up the narrow street. Ahead, a man was crossing in the middle of the street and instead of braking, she slammed the horn, not slowing for a second, and just managed to swing around him as he gave her a thumbs-up, the Middle Eastern equivalent of the middle finger. She didn't slow but made the next left, checking the rearview mirror again. For the moment, there was no one behind her.

She made another left onto Rome and back toward Rue Hamra, the narrow street dense with cars and people. If they were behind her with the Mercedes or another car, there was no way to catch up to her through the traffic. The sidewalks were thick with people of all ages, many stylish, a few women in *hijabs,* the cafés and restaurants bright with neon signs and sounds of hip-hop music from the open door of a club.

She drove west on Rue Hamra, checking mirrors while the city in all its colors swirled around her. She opened a window and heard the sounds of people and music and caught the smell of roast *shawarma* and apple tobacco smoke from the *shisha* cafés. No sign of tails. They might have switched off from the Mercedes or the van, but so far as she could tell, she had lost them. Still, she couldn't relax. They would be scouring the city for her. If they had grabbed the Service driver, he would have told them she was headed for Hamra. They might be anywhere. And she could only hope they hadn't gotten to the older woman. Time to get rid of the car.

She spotted the tall Crowne Plaza hotel up ahead, with its red electric sign at the top of the building. She drove past it into the mall entrance and, after fifteen minutes of circling, found a parking space. She left the car keys on the floor mat, got out and walked out of the parking structure into the mall and melted into the stream of shoppers, going out different exits and coming back in, looking in mirrors and going up and down stairs to ensure she wasn't followed, checking one last time as she exited the mall and walked away from the crowds and up Rue Gemayel in the direction of the American University campus.

She circled the block twice, then another block walking in the opposite direction to make completely sure she wasn't being followed. Doing it that way, even if they switched off, you could almost always spot a tail. She began to breathe a little easier. So far, it looked like she had lost them. But she had no illusions. They would be scouring Hamra, looking for her. She had to get to the safe house now.

The key was to stay away from the crowds on Rue Hamra. They might get lucky and spot her there. Instead, she headed toward the university. For cover, she fell in with a group of students, chattering about where to go for *manaeesh*, a kind of pizza. The two girls were Lebanese and one of the boys was from Jordan, and for a second it was like being back at college. They invited her to join them at a hole-in-the-wall storefront, but she shrugged and walked on. The safe house wasn't far. Twenty minutes later, she was on Rue Adonis, a narrow tree-lined residential street, going up in the elevator to the eighth-floor-apartment safe house.

Coming out of the elevator, she scanned the corridor and the stairwell, listening to the elevator continuing on up before approaching the apartment door. She studied the doorjamb and frame for any signs of tampering. It looked clean. The peephole held a recording camera, she knew. She looked into it and gave the agreed-upon signal, two double-knocks, ready to run if something happened. There was no answer. She knocked again, then took out the key from her handbag and opened the door.

The apartment appeared empty. That was wrong. There was always supposed to be someone there. What the hell was going on? Checking that the drapes were drawn, she locked the door behind her and explored the two bedrooms, one filled with cots, the other with equipment. She went to the chest of drawers where they kept an assortment of guns. She took out a Glock 28 pistol and four magazines. Perfect for her. Small, light, with low recoil, and the .380 cartridges would go through anything. She loaded the pistol and put it and the magazines in her handbag.

She went to the window and peeked from the side of the curtain at the street below, lit by a single streetlamp. If there were any watchers, they were hidden in the shadows of the trees and parked cars on the dark street.

"Hell, I need a drink," she said aloud to herself, and went to the living room liquor cabinet, glancing at the laptop on the coffee table showing multiple views from security cameras in the door peephole, the corridor and the street from the roof outside. It all looked okay. She found a half-full bottle of Grey Goose in the cabinet and poured herself a quarter glass, knowing she probably shouldn't and thinking that at this point, she really didn't give a damn; took out one of her clozapine pills from her handbag—she would have to get more from the black market pharmacy in Zarif, she thought with a frown; and washed it down with the vodka. She checked her watch: 7:41 P.M. Who would be manning the Beirut Station exchange at this hour? she asked herself. Linda, she thought. Linda Benitez; on till midnight.

Except before she called, she needed to think this through. What had just happened didn't add up. The contact with Nightingale had been arranged by Dima. The party girl wasn't one of the pigeons, the agents Carrie had recruited since she'd been in Beirut. She'd inherited her from Davis Fielding, the CIA Beirut Station chief. She was one of his. There'd be hell to pay, she thought angrily. Except she couldn't be sure if Dima was playing both sides or if she'd been duped by Nightingale too. In fact, she might be in danger or even dead already.

Except Carrie had no way of reaching her. She couldn't just call. The two safe house phones were off-limits. The normal one was for taking calls only. The scrambled one was strictly for communicating with the highly secure exchange at the U.S. embassy in Aoukar in the northernmost part of the city. And using a cell phone could give away her position if they were GPS-tracking her. Figure it out, she told herself. Assume either GSD or Hezbollah is behind this. How did they get onto her? Dima. It had to be Dima, and that could mean there was something Fielding didn't know. He'd encouraged her to make the contact.

"We'd kill for someone inside GSD," he'd told her. And

he'd also told her she didn't need any backup. "Dima's solid. She hasn't given us a lot, but what she has is strictly twenty-four-karat stuff." Son of a bitch, she thought. Was he doing her? Was sex the twenty-four karats she was giving him? She'd wanted to take Virgil Maravich, the station's resident black-bag genius, the best technical guy for surveillance, bugs and break-ins she'd ever met, but Fielding said he needed Virgil for something else. "Besides," Fielding had told her, "you're a big girl. You can handle it," implying that if she couldn't, she didn't belong in Beirut, the big leagues.

"Beirut Rules," Fielding had told her that first day in his office on the top floor of the U.S. embassy, slouched in a leather chair, behind him a window overlooking the Municipality building with its arched windows and entryway. He was big, fair haired, starting to go to fat. Touch of rosacea on his nose; someone who liked his food and booze. "No second chances. And no one cares that you're a girl in the Middle East. You screw up, you make a mistake, a hundred to one you die. Even if you don't, you're out of here. This looks like a civilized city—plenty of clubs, beautiful women in designer clothes, great food, the most sophisticated people on the planet—but don't be fooled. It's still the Middle East. Put one foot the wrong way and they'll kill you—and a minute later go on to the next party."

What the hell is going on? she thought. It was Fielding's Joe who set it up, Fielding who encouraged her to make the pitch and Fielding who'd made sure she went into it without backup. But Fielding was a longtime station chief in Beirut. It was a standard first contact. He hadn't expected anything to go wrong. She'd almost been kidnapped or killed. Clearly, he didn't want that. She took a deep breath. This was crazy.

Did she feel a little buzzy? Could it be that the clozapine, the medication for her bipolar, wasn't working?

She stood up. She felt she had to do something, anything, but she wasn't sure what. Her skin was tingling. Oh God, not that. She wasn't starting on one of her "flights"—what she called the manic phase of her bipolar—was she? She started to walk around the room, then went over to the window, feeling an irresistible urge to throw the curtains open and look out. Go ahead, take a look at me, you bastards! Don't be stupid, Carrie, she told herself. You're fine, just give the clozapine and the vodka a second to kick in. Although maybe it was crazy to mix the two. She reached for the curtain. Careful, careful, she told herself. She pulled the corner of the curtain and peeked out at the street.

The Mercedes sedan that had been chasing her was double-parked in front of the safe house building. Three men were walking to the front entrance. Fear shot through her like electricity. She felt a terrible urge to urinate and had to squeeze her thighs together to control it.

It was impossible. This was a safe house. How had they found her? She hadn't been followed. She was sure of it. She'd lost them in the red Renault and made doubly sure going around the city streets in Hamra. No one on foot; no one in a car. And what was she to do? They were coming into the building. She only had seconds to get away. She picked up the secure phone to the embassy and dialed. The phone was picked up on the second ring.

"Good evening. U.S. Cultural Services Offices," a voice said. Despite a faint distortion from the line encryption, Carrie recognized Linda Benitez's voice. She didn't know her well, just enough to say hello.

"Amarillo," Carrie said, using this week's code word. "Nightingale was a setup."

"Confirm opposition?"

"I don't have time. Achilles security has been breached. Do you copy, dammit?" Carrie almost shouted. Achilles was the safe house.

"Confirm Achilles. What is your location and status?" Linda said, and Carrie knew she was not only recording but following a memorized text and writing down every word, asking whether she was still mobile and operative, or whether she was calling under duress or capture.

"I'm on the move. Tell you-know-who I'll see him tomorrow," Carrie snapped, and hung up. For an instant, she stood poised on her toes like a dancer, trying to decide which way to go. She had to get out fast, but how? There were three of them. Plus at least one outside in the Mercedes sedan. They would be coming up both the stairs and the elevator.

How was she supposed to get out? There was no contingency for something like this. It wasn't supposed to happen in a safe house.

She couldn't stay where she was. They would find a way in. If not through a door, then through a window, a balcony or even a wall from an apartment next door. If they did come in, they would be shooting. She might be able to shoot one, maybe even two, but not three. There weren't going to be any shootouts at the OK Corral. Nor could she go out into the corridor, try for the stairs or the elevator. They would be waiting. In fact, they would likely be outside the door any second, she thought, crossing to the apartment door and throwing the dead bolt.

That left the window and the balcony. As she headed toward the bedroom, a shock went through her at sounds in the corridor. She went over to the laptop. The three Arab men were in the corridor, going methodically and listening at each apartment door with some kind of hearing device. They'd be at her door in seconds.

She ran back to the bedroom closet, where they kept the gear. She opened it and began tearing through it, looking for rope or anything she could use to let herself down with. No rope. Just changes of men's clothes. Some suits, shoes and leather belts. Belts! She grabbed three belts and hooked them together to make a single long belt, then ran back to the laptop.

The screen showed the three men right outside the safe house apartment door. They were affixing something to the door. Explosives! she thought. She raced to the bedroom and opened the door to the balcony, looping the belt to the wrought-iron railing. She peeked over the edge. The Mercedes was still there, but no one had gotten out or was looking up this way. She looked down at the balcony below, unable to tell if anyone was in that apartment or not. What does it matter? she screamed inside. They were going to blow the door and maybe the whole apartment. She could be dead any second.

She tightened the belt on the railing and pulled at it hard. It felt like it would hold. It would have to. Climbing over the edge, she let herself down hand over hand on the belt. The glass door to the balcony of the apartment on the floor below was dark. No one home. Arms straining, she reached with her toes for the lower balcony's railing. Don't look down, she told herself as her toes touched the railing. She pushed forward, letting go as she fell forward onto the balcony. A deafening explosion above shook the building.

They'd blown the safe house door. Ears ringing, she smashed the glass in the balcony door with the Glock, then put her hand through the jagged hole and opened the door.

Putting her shoes back on to avoid stepping on broken glass, she ran to the apartment's front door, unlocked it and raced out into the corridor and down the stairs to the ground floor. Another few seconds and she was out the service door to an alley in back. She went cautiously down the alley to a side street. It looked clear. No watchers from the Mercedes around the corner. Taking off her heels again, she ran as hard as she could, her slender figure disappearing into the darkness.

CHAPTER 2

Central District, Beirut, Lebanon

"What went wrong? And don't bullshit me. You're on very thin ice, Carrie," Davis Fielding said, rubbing his hands together as though he were cold. They were in his office in the old-fashioned building on Rue Maarad, near Nejmeh Square, with its iconic clock tower, where Beirut Station maintained a cover company, Middle East Maritime Insurance SA, a cover so solid they actually sold policies.

"You tell me. Nightingale was your idea. Dima was your agent. I just inherited her," Carrie answered, rubbing her eyes. She felt tired, grimy in the same clothes she had worn the previous day, having only slept a few hours on Virgil's living room couch after a night spent going all over Beirut, looking for Dima.

"Don't pull that shit on me," Fielding growled. "She was your bird. You ran her. You brought Nightingale to me and I okayed an approach. That's all. Toe in the water. Nothing more. Next thing I know, you're being chased all the hell over Beirut by so-called assassins and leading them right to our safe house door! You've jeopardized our position here, which, as you know, is damn delicate," he said, tapping the desk with his index finger.

"I didn't lead them anywhere," Carrie said, thinking, Why doesn't he see it? He should have been patting her on the back for escaping. How could he be so thick? "I got away. I was clean. I ditched a car at the Crowne Plaza and walked away a hundred percent clean, but just to be sure I spent an hour in the mall, walking around blocks, reversing, you name it. There was nothing. Not mobile, not on foot, not electronic, not with a telescope from twenty miles away. You better face up to it, Davis. We have a security breach."

"The hell we do. You screwed it up and now you're running for cover. I warned you, Mathison. We play Beirut Rules here. Now, let's go over it again. First of all, where's Dima?"

"You tell me. After the fiasco at the contact and again at the safe house, I spent half the night looking for her. Instead of yelling at me, how about considering that she might be a double? Maybe she set me up. Because if not, when did you become so trusting?"

"We don't even know that you were set up. Maybe you panicked because Nightingale got the contact location wrong. Maybe he was on Lebanese time. Maybe he was drunk. Shit, Carrie. This was supposed to be a fly-by, that's all. Get a look at him; let him get a look at your tits and set up the next one. You panicked. Admit it," Fielding said, face red as Santa Claus, but his eyes cold and blue as ice.

"Not true. You weren't there. I was. He motioned to me," she said, showing him. "He's supposed to be a senior intelligence officer and he motions to a contact he's never met to come right over like we're housewives in the park? Are you kidding?"

"Maybe that's how they do it in the GSD. Maybe he thought you got it wrong. You're a woman, for crying out loud. No man in the Middle East is going to take you seriously. Based on last night, they're probably right."

She could feel her heart pounding. What was going on here? There'd been a serious screw-up that nearly led to her capture or death. He should have been supporting her; not ripping her a new one. "There were two men in a van and four in a Mercedes. They tried to kidnap me, dammit! They shot at me. Here." She showed him the scab on her leg where the piece of sidewalk had hit her.

"Yes—and then you led them right to the safe house, which for all I know was the object of the exercise for them in the first place!" Fielding snapped. "This is going in your 201," he added, referring to the CIA's personnel file on each employee. "Don't think it isn't."

Carrie stood up.

"Listen, Davis," she said, trying to control herself. "There's something bigger going on here. Has it occurred to you to wonder why they wanted a CIA case officer when if Nightingale was a double, they could have fed us garbage for years and we'd have eaten it like pigs at a trough? Ask yourself why."

"Sit down," Fielding snapped. "Where do you think you're going? I'm not done with you."

She sat. Inside, she was shaking with anger. She could have ripped his eyeballs out, she was so furious. She was that strong, that powerful. Oh God, was she going on one of her flights? She could feel control slipping; she was almost on the verge of killing him. Control yourself, Carrie. You can do it.

"Dima set the contact up. We need to consider her," she said carefully, trying to hold it in.

"What about her cell phone?"

She shook her head. "Nothing in the dead drop either." For emergency contacts with Dima, she used the hollow of a tree in Sanayeh Park. When she'd gone there in the middle of the night after trawling the clubs, the hollow was empty. She had left a chalk mark on a branch, indicating that Dima should contact her ASAP, but she had a bad feeling about hearing from her.

"Where else did you look?"

"Le Gray, Whiskey, the Palais, her place—and you don't have to say it; I was careful—everywhere. No one's seen her. I picked the lock in her apartment. She hadn't been home. It looked like she hadn't been there for a couple of days."

"So she's shacked up with the latest hunk from Riyadh with cash in his pocket, so what?"

"Or she's being tortured or is already dead. There's been a security breach, Davis. You can't ignore the possibility."

"So you say," he said, biting his lip. "What else?"

"There was no one in the safe house," she said. "What was that about?"

"Budget. Bean counters in Washington." He shrugged. "They're running the universe. We had to cut back. So according to you, you were clean. They chased you. You got away. No one followed you to Achilles? What about this older woman you got the car from?" He steepled his index fingers, his blue eyes lasering into her. "She gives her car to a complete stranger. Why would she do that?"

She swallowed. "She was a decent person. Woman to woman. She could see I was in trouble." She could see I was desperate, she thought.

"Or maybe she was one of theirs and told them where to find you. Either that, or they persuaded her," he said, making a gesture like pulling out a fingernail.

Is he crazy? she wondered. Where does he come up with this crap?

"She had no idea where I was going. I told her I'd leave the car at the Crowne Plaza and I did. She knew nothing about the Achilles location."

"No, but like everyone in Beirut, she knew the Crowne was on Rue Hamra, so where you were going couldn't be far. All they had to do was blanket the area. Fifty watchers in the Friday-night crowd and you didn't even spot one." He shook his head disgustedly. "The only amateur in this whole ridiculous fiasco is sitting right across from me."

"I don't believe this. I manage to escape a deadly Hezbollah trap and it's my fault?" she said, standing again. She felt sick to her stomach. What was happening? Was he firing her? "What are you saying? Would you rather I'd died or been captured?"

"I'm saying you're done here. You're certainly compromised and we'll have to get a new safe house, thanks to you."

"What about my agents? They count on me," she said, her heartbeat pounding in her head like a drum. She'd never been fired before. It was the most sickening feeling she'd ever experienced.

"For the time being, I'll handle Dima and your other Joes. You're done. Talk to Carol about arrangements and your flight back," he said. "And I'll call Berenson. He's the one who foisted you on me in the first place."

"So that's it. All my work and I'm gone for something that isn't my fault?"

"Go pack, Carrie. I'm sending you back to Langley. Maybe they can find something useful for you. Not everybody's cut out for the field."

"You're wrong, Davis," she said, her jaw clenched, knowing

she was wasting her breath. "I wasn't followed. There's a security breach. You need to check it out."

"We'll look into it," he said, waving her off and picking up the phone.

On the way to the airport, Virgil Maravich made the turn off El Asad Road at the Boulevard El Sader roundabout. He kept glancing sideways at Carrie, who was dressed in a full head-to-foot black *abaya*.

"I shouldn't be doing this," he said. "Not to mention, Dahiyeh isn't exactly the safest place in the world for outsiders."

He was right, of course, Carrie thought. Dahiyeh, in southern Beirut, was poor, Shiite, and controlled by Hezbollah militia armed to the teeth, who might stop you at any intersection. Driving through, there were still plenty of bombed-out buildings and empty lots filled with weeds and rubble from past Israeli attacks and the long civil war.

"I appreciate it," she said, shaking her head. "What is his problem?"

"Fielding?" Virgil grinned. "He's one of the old-boy network, don't you get it? He knows the rules. Somebody's head had to roll over Nightingale and the breach at Achilles. He puts it on you, it's not on him."

"That's disgusting," she said, looking over at Virgil. Tall, thin, bald on top; she had met him on her first surveillance in Beirut. Then as now, they'd been talking about Fielding.

"Did he give you his 'Beirut Rules' speech? One mistake and they kill you and then they go and party. Asshole," he'd said with a grin that first time. It had been Virgil who'd given her the idea of wearing a wedding band when going out at night or on RDVs. "Your sex life is none of my business," he'd told her. "But unless you want it to be everybody's business or you enjoy being groped, in this part of the world it's a good idea to let men think you belong to another man, which is how they think of it. Breaking that is a bigger taboo than rape. At least the ring gives you the choice."

She'd never been attracted to Virgil. She didn't know how he felt about her and she never let it go there. He was married but didn't talk about it. It had nothing to do with her. They were colleagues, foxhole buddies. She respected him. She thought he felt the same about her. Even if she'd wanted to, they both knew that sex would only screw things up and the truth was, they'd come to rely on each other.

"Welcome to the real CIA," Virgil said with a grimace. He had the typical attitude of contempt that most field operatives had for the suits back at Langley. "We don't need enemy spies. We've got our own little organizational cesspool. I'm sorry you got caught up in it."

They drove to the Ghobeiry district, where they turned off into side streets filled with kids playing, kicking cans and using sticks for guns, and men playing *tawla*, a form of backgammon, and sipping tea outside storefronts. On the sides of buildings were the giant painted faces of martyrs, most of them bearded men so young their beards looked fake, and everywhere, yellow and green Hezbollah flags hanging like laundry.

Before she'd ever gone to Lebanon, Saul had told her, "Beirut is like Istanbul; it's on two continents. North Beirut is Paris with palm trees; Dahiyeh is the Middle East."

"Where are you meeting her?" Virgil asked.

"Supermarket," she said. "It's hard for her to sneak away."

"How do you want to play this?"

"You stay in the car, engine going, in case we need to get away. If anyone asks, you're my male guardian."

"Well, don't let anyone get too close. With that Irish-

American mug of yours, even with an *abaya* and veil, you're not fooling anyone." He grinned.

"Thanks, Virgil. I appreciate this. You're always there for me." She looked at him. "Why?"

He glanced over at her. The *abaya*, the *hijab* she was wearing; it was weird.

"You really want to know?"

"Yeah, I really do."

He nodded. "Don't let it get around, but you're the smartest damn person here. Oh, and you're not bad to look at either. No wonder Fielding hates your guts. Just do me one favor."

"Name it."

He drove the narrow street up the hill. Four young men with AK-47s, smoking water pipes outside a *shisha* café, watched them drive slowly by, Carrie pulling her *niqab*, her veil, across her face as they passed.

"This is nuts," he muttered, looking around.

"I have to do this. She only trusts me. I can't just leave her hanging."

"All I want is, don't push it. As soon as you're done, Fielding's orders, I've got to take you to the airport."

"I'll make it fast."

"Better be," he said, pulling into a narrow street with sandbags piled in front of a sand-colored mosque. "I don't know how long the welcome mat's going to be out around here," he added, eyes darting around.

Carrie nodded. She had to take this chance. Of all her assets, Fatima Ali, code-named "Julia"—because she and Carrie had first met in a movie theater and afterward, the two of them walking, Fatima had confided that she loved American movies and was a big fan of the movie star Julia Roberts—was the one she was closest to. Behind her *abaya* and *niqab*, Julia was a pretty, dark-haired, sharp-as-a-razor woman whose husband, Abbas, abused her nonstop because she had painful endometriosis that prevented her from having children.

He hit her almost every day, called her a *sharmuta*—a whore—and a useless piece of childless *khara,* and had once beaten her so badly with a tire iron, she'd had to drag herself to the hospital with six broken bones, including a smashed tibia, a skull fracture and a shattered jaw. He had taken a second wife, a gap-toothed teenage girl, and when she became pregnant, he made Julia subservient to her and allowed the young girl to slap her in the face and laugh whenever Julia did anything that displeased her.

She couldn't leave him because Abbas was commander of the Harakat al-Mahnum, the Organization of the Oppressed brigade, within Hezbollah. If she left, he'd track her down and kill her. Movies were her only escape. All Carrie had to do to recruit her was to listen. Only now, she was leaving Julia without a lifeline. She had to at least warn her face-to-face.

Virgil pulled into an unpaved parking area behind a small supermarket. As Carrie got out of the car, he pulled out a Sig Sauer automatic and said, "Make it quick. I think I'm outgunned around here."

She nodded and as she walked into the supermarket, she heard the loudspeaker from a nearby mosque with the call for the noon Dhuhr prayer and it tore at her in a way she didn't expect. She was going to miss Beirut.

Taking a basket, she walked over to the dry-goods section. Julia, also in an *abaya* and veil, was examining a box of Poppins, a popular Lebanese breakfast cereal. Carrie put a Poppins box in her basket too.

"So good to see you," Carrie said in Arabic. "And how is your husband and family?"

"Good, *alhamdulillah*"—*thank God*—Fatima said, pulling her aside, her eyes darting around. "What's happened?" she whispered. Carrie had left her a one-word note, *ya'ut,* the Arabic word for "ruby," their code for an emergency contact, under a potted urn in the Muslim cemetery near Boulevard Bayhoum. Julia's husband monitored all her calls and e-mails; the dead drop was the only way to communicate with her.

"I'm being pulled from Beirut. Another assignment," Carrie whispered as they pretended to shop together.

"Why?"

"I can't say." She took Julia's hand. They walked hand-in-hand like children. "I'll miss you. I wish I could take you with me."

"I wish too," Fatima said, looking away. "You go to real America, but for me it's like the movies. A made-up place."

"I'll come back, I swear."

"What will happen to me?"

"They'll assign you to someone else. Not me." Julia's eyes welled up. She shook her head and wiped her eyes with her sleeve. "They'll be okay. I promise," Carrie said.

"No they won't. I won't talk to anyone else. They'll have to send you back."

"You have to listen," Carrie said. "They won't do that."

"Then, *inshallah*"—*God willing*—"they'll never get another word from me."

"If there's an emergency, use the cemetery. I'll have someone monitor the dead drop," she whispered.

"There is something I have to tell you." She looked around to make sure they weren't overheard and pulled Carrie close. "There's going to be an attack against America. A big one."

"How do you know?"

Fatima's eyes darted around like a trapped animal's. She

took a few steps and motioned for Carrie to follow. She glanced around the corner of the aisle to make sure there was no one near.

"I overheard Abbas talking on his special cell phone. The one he only uses when it is important," she whispered.

"Who was he talking to?"

"I don't know. But the way he stood and listened, someone of importance."

"What about the attack?" Carrie whispered. "Any details? Time? Place? Method?"

"I don't think they told him. I'm not even sure it's Hezbollah. But it's soon."

"How soon?"

"I don't know. But he said '*khaliban zhada,*' you understand?"

"I understand," Carrie said. *Very soon.* She leaned close to Fatima's ear. "Any idea how big or where?"

She shook her head. "But when he heard, Abbas said something. *Allahu akbar.*" *God is great,* Carrie translated automatically. "We say this all the time." She shrugged. "But it was the way he said it. I can't explain, but it scared me. I wish I could help you more. Something very bad is going to happen."

"This helps a lot. Truly. Are you okay?"

"No." She looked around again. "I can't stay. Someone might see us."

"I know. *Shokran.*" *Thank you.* Carrie squeezed her hand. "I have to go too. Be careful."

"Carrie," Fatima said. "You're my only friend. Think of me. Otherwise, I think I'm lost forever."

A horn honked outside. Virgil. Carrie took Fatima's hand and put it to her own cheek.

"Me too," she said.

CHAPTER 3

After four years in Beirut, plus time in Iraq, it felt strange driving the woodsy George Washington Memorial Parkway, handing the badge she'd gotten out of her safe-deposit box to the guard at the gate like an everyday commuter. Coming into the George Bush headquarters building, she was struck by how many people she didn't know. No one gave her a second glance in the elevator. In a skirt, blouse, jacket and makeup for the office, she felt like she was wearing a disguise. *I don't belong here,* she thought. *Maybe I never did.*

She'd been up all night, unable to sleep. When she closed her eyes to try to sleep she saw her father, Frank Mathison. Not as he was now, but how he was when she was a child back in Michigan. He'd lost his job at Ford Motor Company when she was six. She remembered her mother coming into her sister's and her room to sleep with them, the three of them huddled under the covers while her father paced the house all night, saying nonstop that there was a miracle coming; he had seen the sign in computer code.

She remembered her father driving them up to New Baltimore on Lake St. Clair when she was in first grade in the middle of De-

cember, talking about the miracle and how they were to be witnesses, and sitting there on a dock near the water tower, away from the center of the town decorated for Christmas, all of them shivering, freezing cold, looking out at the gray waters of the lake for two days while her father kept saying, "It's coming. Just you wait. It's coming."

And her mother shouting at him, "What's coming, Frank? What's the big miracle? Is Jesus gonna come strolling toward us across Anchor Bay? Because if he is and if the angels are coming with him, tell 'em to bring us some heaters, because me and the kids are freezing to death."

"Do you see the water tower, Emma. It's mathematics. Don't you get it? The universe is mathematics. Computers are mathematics. Everything is math. And look where it sits. Right by the water."

"What has math got to do with it? What are you talking about?"

"I measured it. It's thirty-seven miles exactly from our front door to the water tower. This is where the miracle is going to happen. Thirty-seven."

"What has thirty-seven miles got to do with anything?"

"It's a prime number, Emma. It was in the computer code. And water is life. Moses struck the rock for water. Christ turned water into wine at Cana. Look at it. It's coming. This is where it's going to happen. Don't you see?"

"It's a damn water tower, Frank!"

Until finally they drove back to Dearborn, her father not saying anything, just driving like he wanted to kill someone, her mother yelling, "Slow down, Frank! Do you want to kill us?" and her big sister, Maggie, next to her, crying and screaming, "Stop, Daddy! Stop! Stop!" And when she got ready to go to school the next day, her mother telling her, "Don't say anything about your father, understand?"

It wasn't till later that she realized that whatever strange thing had taken her father over had taken them over too when she heard *her parents arguing with each other at the top of their lungs in the middle of the night. Maggie told her to stay in bed, but she tiptoed out of their room and saw them in the kitchen, the walls and floor smeared with food and broken plates and her mother screaming:*

"Three weeks! They said you haven't been at work in three weeks without telling anyone! Of course they fired you! What the hell did you expect them to do? Give you a promotion?"

"I was busy. You'll see, Emma. It'll be good. They'll be begging for me to come back. Don't you see? It's all about the miracle. That's where everyone gets it wrong. They don't understand. Remember those license plate numbers on the cars we passed coming back from New Baltimore? They were a code. I just have to figure out the numbers," her father said.

"What are you talking about? Does anybody know what you're talking about? What are we going to do? How are we going to live?"

"For God's sakes, Emma. You think they can run those servers without me? Trust me, they'll call me back any time now. They'll be begging for me to come back."

"Oh God, oh God, oh God! What are we going to do?"

And now she'd been fired. Just like her father.

Saul Berenson, Middle East Division chief, NCS, was expecting her in his office on the fourth floor. She took a deep breath, knocked and went in.

Saul, big rumpled bearded teddy bear of a man, was working on his computer. Rabbi Saul, as she sometimes thought of him. He'd been the one who'd first recruited her for the CIA, on a cold March day in her senior year at the Career Center at Princeton.

The office was the usual messy disorder that only Saul could find his way through. As always, a stuffed Winnie the Pooh sat slumped on a shelf next to two photographs: one of Saul with the first President Bush, the one they'd named the building after; the second of Saul with CIA director James Woolsey and President Clinton.

Saul looked up from the computer as she sat down.

"You found someplace?" he asked, tilting his glasses so he could see her better.

"A one-bedroom in Reston," she said.

"Convenient?"

"It's not far from the Dulles Toll Road. Is that what we're going to talk about?"

"What do you want to talk about?"

"You saw the information from Julia. You need to send me back to Beirut."

"Not gonna happen, Carrie. I don't think you realize how many people you've pissed off or how high it goes."

"I escaped a Hezbollah trap, Saul. Would you have preferred that they captured me, paraded me on al-Jazeera as a CIA spy? Because the way I've been treated, I'm beginning to think that's what you and Davis wanted."

"Don't be an idiot. It's not that simple," he said, scratching his beard. "It's never that simple."

"You're wrong. It's exactly that simple. I was set up—and now Beirut Station's security is compromised and you've got a dick for a station chief who only wants to kill the messenger."

Saul took off his glasses. Without them, his eyes were softer, less focused.

"You're not making this easy, Carrie," he said. He wiped his glasses on his shirt and put them back on.

"Did I ever?" she said.

"No." He smiled wryly. "I'll give you that. You were a pain in the ass right from the beginning."

"So why did you hire me? I'm not the only woman in America who speaks Arabic," she said, leaning back in her chair and looking at his Winnie the Pooh in its red "Pooh" shirt. He had once told her Pooh was a perfect metaphor for the human condition. All it took was a single letter change to describe our obsession; just change "honey" to "money."

"Look, Carrie, a CIA station chief is like the captain of a ship. It's one of the last pure dictatorships on earth. If he doesn't think he can trust you, your judgment, there isn't a lot I can do."

She sat straight up in her chair, tense, knees tightly together, as if it were a job interview. "You're his boss. Fire him, not me." Please, she thought. Please Saul. Please believe me. Saul was the only one she could trust, the only one who believed in her. If he turned against her, she had nothing; was nothing.

"I can't," he said. "Think about it. My job's like being the admiral of a fleet. If I start firing captains for using their judgment, they'll be second-guessing themselves all over the place. They'll be of no use to me or anyone else. I have to look at the bigger picture."

"Bullshit!" she said, standing up, thinking, why couldn't he understand? It was Saul. He was supposed to be on her side. "This is total bullshit. This isn't about morale or security or some other bullshit. This is politics. And it stinks." She stared at him. "When did you become one of them, Saul? The people who are ready to sell this country out in the interest of their own pathetic careers?"

Saul slammed his hand hard on the desk, making her jump.

"Don't you dare talk to me that way! You know me better than that. If that's the way you spoke to Fielding, it's no wonder he threw your sorry ass out of Beirut. And you know the worst part, Carrie? You know the worst? The intel you just brought back from your little jaybird, Julia, is so critical that I was trying to think of a way to send you back to Beirut before you walked in here."

Wonderful, thank you, she thought, relief flooding through her. Saul still believed in her. He knew she was right. He was on her side. It was just a matter of trying to find a way to maneuver the bureaucracy. All she had to do was show him she was still Carrie; she still knew how to mix it up with anyone, including him.

"Are you taking it to the Director? Are we going to act on it?"

"I've sent it upstairs," he said, glancing at the ceiling. "But it's not up to me. We get threats like this every day."

"Her stuff has always been grade A. You know it. Remember what she gave us on the Hariri assassination? This is actionable, Saul."

"Is it? Is it really? Your Julia gave us no particulars. Nothing. An attack soon. We don't know where. We don't know how. We don't know when. We don't know the target. We don't even know if it's Hezbollah or maybe somebody who just passed it along to Hezbollah to distract us from something else. What the hell are we supposed to do with it?"

"So that's it? We just pass it along and hope for the best? That's how we protect the country these days?"

"Don't give me crap, Carrie. I told both Estes and the deputy director that we had a very high degree of confidence this is actionable intel. The ball's in their court. I've also alerted Fielding in Beirut to keep digging."

"Fielding," she said disgustedly. She got up and walked over to the window and looked out over the green lawn and the back parking lot. "We have a security crisis in Beirut. What about Achilles?"

"Fielding says you led them to it." He clicked his mouse till he found what he was looking for on his computer and read out loud: "'Mathison displayed amateurish tradecraft in resorting in desperation to an unknown, unvetted female Lebanese contact, who—if this case officer is to be believed—out of the presumed goodness of her heart gave her car to a complete stranger. Then, after leaving the car in highly public parking venue, Mathison failed to lose her presumed pursuers, leading them directly to the safe house location on Rue Adonis, which in turn led to the elimination of this safe house and the total breach of security at that location and compromise of our operations.'"

Saul looked at her over his glasses.

"What am I supposed to do with that?"

He couldn't believe that about her, she thought. Not Saul.

"Tell Fielding to wipe his ass with it," Carrie snapped. "I was clean. I was clean in Hamra and I was sure as hell clean on foot in Ras Beirut. There was no one there, inside or out. Then all of a sudden they're breaking in like they've known about the location all along. Someone set me up."

"Who?" Saul said, raising a hand. "Where do you start?"

"Nightingale for openers," Carrie said, leaning forward on his desk with both hands like a runner getting set. "Dima too. Let me go back, Saul. I'll nail them both. And I'll find the leak."

He shook his head.

"Impossible. Look, Carrie, even if I believed you're right and assumed that Fielding is a hundred percent wrong, I can't."

"Why not? What's he got on you?" This wasn't like Saul, she thought.

"He's connected, okay?" Saul said disgustedly. "He and

David Estes, director of the Counterterrorism Center, are both protégés of Bill Walden."

"The DCIA?"

"The big man himself. It's the old-boy network right down the line. And Walden has political ambitions. He's no one to mess with. You? You're just a female officer in a compromising situation. For the people upstairs, that's not a hard decision. Not to mention, we've reorganized for the four millionth time. Nowadays, I've got a dotted line reporting to Estes. It's not so simple."

"What do we do?"

Saul nodded. "Fielding put it on you and for the time being, I have to leave it there. You try to fight this, and I won't be able to help you. That's how it is," he said, raising his hands.

"So I'm supposed to be the good little girl. Shut up, bend over and let 'em do whatever they want?"

"And live to fight another day." Saul nodded. "Look, for what it's worth, I agree with you about one thing. This whole thing with Nightingale smells fishy as hell. At a minimum, Fielding should've sent you in there with a support team. I'm not going to let you sit around wasted." He got up and came around the desk; the two of them were side by side, leaning back on it. He believed her. He was still behind her, she thought, breathing a sigh of relief.

"So?" she said.

"Do you remember what I told you when I pulled you early from your training at the Farm? My beautiful golden girl with a brain like Stephen Hawking." He smiled. "Do you remember what I said?"

"About how I could learn the rest of tradecraft in the field— and the pond?"

"That you were too big a fish for this pond. We needed you in the ocean."

"But that sometimes the only way to swim with the sharks is to be a shark. I remember. What do you want me to do?"

"I want you to get Nightingale. And find out about this attack. But we're going to do it here."

"I don't understand."

"You'll be liaising between us, the Middle East Division and the Counterterrorism Center. They're unofficially absorbing Alec Station." Alec Station was CIA-speak for the only CIA station assigned not a locale but a specific target: the al-Qaeda terrorist network. "You'll report to Estes." He leaned close and she could smell his aftershave. Polo, Ralph Lauren. "But you'll work for me."

"So now we're spying on ourselves?"

"Who better? It's what we do," he said.

"What about Julia's intel? There's an attack coming, Saul. Something big, and we both know it."

He took a breath and exhaled.

"How much time have we got?" he asked.

"A couple of weeks maybe. Julia's husband said soon. His exact words were '*khaliban zhada*.' Very soon."

CHAPTER 4

Georgetown, Washington, DC

It was the song that brought it back. Shania Twain's "You're Still the One." 1998. Her junior year at Princeton. The year of *Saving Private Ryan* and *Shakespeare in Love,* and her first big sexual relationship—beyond fumbling when your parents and sister weren't home and getting your thighs sticky wet in high school—an almost-crush on John, her tall, unbelievably bright poly sci professor, who introduced her to tequila shots, oral sex and jazz music.

"When I was a kid it was all Madonna, Mariah, Luther Vandross, Boyz II Men. The closest to jazz was my dad once in a while maybe listening to a little Dave Brubeck."

"You're joking, right? You don't know jazz? Miles Davis, Charlie 'Yardbird' Parker, Dizzy Gillespie, Coltrane, Louis Armstrong? The greatest music ever invented or that ever will be. The one truly original thing we Americans gave the world, and you don't know? In a way, I envy you."

"Why?"

"You've got a whole new continent to explore, better than anything you can imagine."

"Better than sex?"

"*That's the beauty of it, gorgeous. We can do both at the same time.*"

Nineteen ninety-eight: the last time she ever ran the fifteen hundred. A long time ago, she thought.

She was sitting in a pub on M Street in Georgetown, downing her third Patrón Silver margarita, when the Shania video came on the TV perched behind the bar.

"Remember this? Nineteen ninety-eight. I was in college," she said, indicating the song to Dave, the guy nursing a Heineken on the bar stool next to her. He was a curly-haired early-forties DOJ attorney in an off-the-rack suit and a Rolex watch that he made sure you caught a glimpse of, his finger brushing her forearm as though neither of them knew it was there or what he was thinking. There was a white band of skin on his ring finger where he'd taken off his wedding ring, so he was either divorced or out trolling, she thought.

"I was a law intern. For me it was Puff Daddy. *Been around the world, uh-huh, uh-huh,*" he half-sang, moving his shoulders in a manner that was midway between hopeless and semisexy. He wasn't terrible looking. She hadn't decided whether to let him get her into bed or not.

She had to force herself not to think about work. That was why she had gone out. Her inquiries were going nowhere. If anything, instead of finding answers, the questions were multiplying and getting more troubling.

For three days straight, she'd been working the computer. Going nonstop. Sleeping at her desk, living on crackers from the vending machine. She went over everything the Counterterrorism Center had on contacts between the Syrian GSD and Hezbollah in Lebanon. Reported contacts. Sightings. Cell phone and e-mail records. Most of it pure data, the everyday sludge of intelligence work. Saul had once compared it to mining for diamonds. "You have to go through tons of debris to every once in a while spot something that glitters. Something that might actually be useful."

Interestingly, some of the best of it was intel that she herself had supplied, obtained from her source, Julia.

Other than the lead from Dima, there wasn't much on Nightingale, a.k.a. Taha al-Douni. A graduate of Damascus University in mechanical engineering, he'd first attracted attention from Moscow Station, nine years ago, trying to do business with the big Russian arms company Rosoboronexport. She studied the surveillance photo. It had been taken on a wide snowy street in Moscow, lots of traffic, maybe Tverskaya Street, she thought. Although he was younger, thinner and in an overcoat and big floppy-eared fur hat, it was Nightingale all right, the man who had beckoned to her from the café across the street in Beirut.

No information on where he lived, wife, kids, his work in the GSD. Talk to me, Nightingale, she thought. Where do you work? How high up are you? Where do you fit between the GSD and Hezbollah? Who do you care about? Who do you put your dick in? But combing through everything at CTC, there was just the Moscow surveillance.

And nothing on a possible major terrorist attack on the U.S. What Julia had told her was a lone indicator, completely unsubstantiated. Otherwise nothing. No wonder no one had gotten back to her on it.

And then on the third day, late, she found something. A single photo the NSA had lifted from an Israeli spy satellite download stream, showing Nightingale sitting at a *shisha* café table. There was a partial tile wall sign in Arabic. She magnified it on the computer screen, then popped it into Photoshop to try to clarify the writing on the sign. It looked like the image could have been taken in either Amman or Cairo, she thought. In a *souk*, maybe.

Much more important than where the photo was taken was the man Nightingale was sitting with. She didn't need the identification the Israelis had attached to tell her who it was. It was someone that everyone at Beirut Station, including her, had had in their sights for a long time but almost never actually sighted: Ahmed Haidar, a member of al-Majlis al-Markazis, the Hezbollah Central Council, their inner circle.

So Nightingale, a.k.a. al-Douni, was real. Dima had at least given them solid intel. A bona fide link between the GSD and Hezbollah. She wished she were back in Beirut so she could talk to Julia about Nightingale. Had her husband, Abbas, ever met him? Did he know anything about him? Was he involved in the Hariri assassination?

And then there was another unanswered question: Where was Dima? The link between Nightingale and Ahmed Haidar made that even more critical. This was insane. And there was piss-all from Beirut Station. Just a cryptic note from Fielding to Saul that he had followed up and no one had seen Dima since the break-in at Achilles. And nothing about a terrorist attack in the United States. If he was doing any further follow-up, he didn't say. Asshole, she thought.

She began tearing through every record from Damascus Station on the GSD. Every reference. Like Saul said, most of it was garbage.

Then she came across something interesting. In the 1990s, a senior CIA case officer, Dar Adal, had run a mole, Nabeel Abdul-Amir, code-named Pineapple, who was supposedly midlevel GSD. Adal had supposedly confirmed the mole's bona fides. Pineapple was Alawite, Ba'athist, and related to the

Assad clan. For more than forty years, the Assads—the father, Hafez al-Assad, and son, Bashar—members of the small minority Alawite Shiite Muslim sect and the pan-Arab nationalistic Ba'athist party, had ruthlessly ruled Syria. Pineapple, a distant cousin, also Alawite and Ba'athist, seemed a perfect choice for a mole. Too perfect, maybe, she mused.

Adal had fed Pineapple tidbits about Israel's negotiating position on the Golan Heights from a supposed Israeli mole with whom he would have clandestine meetings in Cyprus but who was actually a Hebrew-speaking New York Jew, all in order to get Pineapple promoted within the GSD. When Pineapple tried to expand his Israeli contacts on his own and was about to expose the CIA operation to the Israeli Shin Bet, Adal had apparently—here the record was redacted and got pretty murky—arranged to feed Pineapple to either the Mossad or an outside contractor, who assassinated him, along with his mistress and her child. The three bodies were found on a boat tied to a slip in the Limassol Marina in Cyprus.

Carrie sat up straight, staring at nothing. Who redacted all this? she wondered. How and why? This was old intel. What was going on?

If it came to that, why was there so little on the GSD? Damascus Station was apparently pretty useless, but Fielding had been running Beirut Station for a long time. At least since the early 1990s. Yet, everyone knew the GSD was linked to Hezbollah in Lebanon. The Rafik Hariri assassination last year and the Israeli photograph of Nightingale with Ahmed Haidar proved it. What the hell was going on at Beirut Station? It didn't add up.

It was late, well after eight P.M. As she worked on the file, Estes, the big African-American who was the director of the

Counterterrorism Center, came out of his office and headed toward the elevator, spotted her light still on and came over to her cubicle.

"What are you working on?" he said.

"Syrian GSD. After the nineties, we don't seem to have a lot."

"I thought you were working on AQAP." Estes frowned. Al-Qaeda in the Arabian Peninsula, which mostly meant Yemen, was supposed to be her official assignment for CTC since coming back to Langley. "Is there a link?"

"Not sure," she said, heart beating. She wasn't supposed to be doing this. "Just vague stuff."

"Not likely. Syrian Alawites and AQAP? They're on opposite sides of the Sunni-Shiite divide. You're not still on Beirut, are you, Carrie?" he said.

Christ, he's quick, she thought. There was a split that divided the Muslim world between Sunnis and Shiites that went back centuries over who was supposed to be the Prophet Muhammad's successor. Shiites believed that only Ali, the fourth caliph, and his heirs were legitimate successors to the Prophet. Syrian Alawites were a branch of Shiites, hardly likely to ally themselves with al-Qaeda, extremist Salafist Sunni Muslims. Estes, a Stanford undergrad and Harvard MBA, had picked up on it instantly. She had to keep that in mind. She was slipping, she thought. Running out of meds since coming back from Beirut. It had been a day since she'd taken a clozapine pill and she could feel herself getting ragged around the edges. Keep it together, Carrie, she told herself.

"Sometimes the lines cross. When it's in their interest," she said.

He thought for a moment. "That's true."

"What about the possible attack on the U.S.? Hear anything?"

"We've found nothing to corroborate what your bird said, Carrie. You've got to give us more."

It was on the tip of her tongue to tell him, *Send me back to Beirut*, but she didn't say it.

"I'm still looking."

"I know. Let me know if you find something," he said, continuing on toward the elevator.

She watched him walk away. She liked the bigness of him, the color of his skin, the grace in his movement despite his size. For a second she fantasized about what sex with him would be like. Slow, strong, intense; she squeezed her thighs together. Her reaction caught her by surprise. This was getting crazy. Masturbation wasn't going to do it. Maybe it was time she had a man. Real sex. But simple. No complications.

Forget Pineapple, she told herself. Forget Nightingale and Dima for a second. Get away and let the subconscious brain work on the problem. There was a connection she was missing. Nightingale and Ahmed Haidar and the Hezbollah Central Council and suddenly, Nightingale wants to kill or capture a CIA girl?

Why? Who for? GSD? Hezbollah? Somebody else? And after the Achilles break-in, why didn't Beirut Station go into fire-drill mode? And key files from Damascus Station were redacted? And what did this have to do with an attack? There were too many pieces missing, she thought, turning off her computer and her desk light.

She went back to her apartment in Reston and changed clothes. What am I going to do about my meds? she wondered. *Walla*, she missed the pharmacy in Beirut, the one on

Rue Nakhle in Zarif across from the Doctors Hospital. She could go in there, wave a prescription at them that she'd gotten from an old Lebanese doctor who'd write one for anything so long as you paid him cash in dollars or euros. She could get any drug in the universe there, no questions asked. In the Middle East, her Joe, Julia, had told her, "There are rules and then there are necessities. Allah understands everything. There's always a way."

She'd have to go see her sister. Not looking forward to that little conversation, she thought. Maggie was a physician, with a practice in West End, and a house in Seminary Hill in Alexandria, Virginia. The problem was, she couldn't see a psychiatrist who could write her a prescription. The minute it was on the record, if anyone checked, she, Carrie, could lose her security clearance. Her career at the CIA would be over. It had to be done without a prescription. Off the record. She could call Maggie and go over tomorrow, she decided. Tonight, she needed to get out.

She picked out a silky red top revealing a bit of cleavage and a short black skirt and matching jacket that always made her feel sexy. It was while she was changing clothes and putting on her makeup, Coltrane and Miles Davis on the CD doing "Round Midnight," the greatest track ever, the one that spoke of night and New York and sex and loneliness and longing and everything there was, that she started to fly.

It began with her looking in the mirror and thinking she looked good, with the makeup and eyelashes, and realizing that she was at her peak. Nature was working to make her as attractive as she would ever be in her life, because nature wanted procreation, and studying herself, she realized she was beautiful, that if she wanted, she could have any man, a hundred men, a thousand. The thought of it, of getting any man anytime, that they were powerless, that she could decide, was like an aphrodisiac. All she had to do was let them get close to her and they would follow like sheep. Nature.

Oh God, the music. Davis and Coltrane. It couldn't get any better. She felt warm and happy and invincible. She would solve what had happened in Beirut. She would find out about Dima and get Nightingale. She would stop the terror attack and Fielding would have to eat it. Saul would be proud. She was sure of it, her body tingling.

The music went inside you right down your spine. Running out of the house, getting into the car, she drove Reston Parkway to VA 267, then into town across the Key Bridge and into Georgetown; Lester Young's "She's Funny That Way" on the CD player, and she felt better, sexier, more irresistible than she'd ever felt in her life.

Now, sitting next to Lawyer Dave at the bar, she leaned forward so he could get a peek at her boobs. Tiny, but the perfect size for a man's hand to cup, and God knew the guys didn't seem to care. They would paw at you, the idiots not knowing that if they just touched them the right way, squeezing gently but firmly with just the right amount of pressure, taking their time, they could have any woman they wanted.

"So what do you do?" he was asking.

"Why do you give a shit about what I do?" she said. "Let's be honest. All you really want to do is have sex with me, right? I mean, stop me if I'm wrong here, because ten-to-one you're married. Taking the ring off doesn't fool that many girls except the stupid ones—and even they figure it out eventually, right, Lawyer Dave? So let's cut to the chase, shall we? Do you want to take me out of here and screw my brains out or don't you?"

He stared at her, stunned, cautious.

"You're wearing a ring too," he said.

"Damn right, I'm taken. Don't fall in love with me. Don't even fall in like with me. Don't get obsessed with me. There's no future, no romance, no bullshit. There's just tonight. Take it or leave it. You don't want to, you want to think about your sweet little wife and kiddies back at the other end of your commute, get off that bar stool and free it up for someone a little more honest about what he really wants in this screwed-up world," she said.

"You're really something," he said.

"You have no idea."

He put down his beer and stood up.

"Let's go," he said.

"Where?"

"Your place."

"Uh-uh. You don't get to find out where I live." She shook her head and downed the rest of her margarita. "Besides, hotshot. You trying to tell me you can afford a Rolex and you can't afford condoms and a hotel room?"

He held her jacket for her and put on his coat. They went outside. The night was clear and cool and windy; the two-story buildings along M Street stretched as far as could be seen. He put his arm around her as they walked to his car. A Lincoln. Bullshit lawyer's car, she thought, getting in.

"Where do you want to go?" he asked.

"Ritz-Carlton's not too far." The radio was tuned to hip-hop. He's trying to be cool, she thought. "Put on jazz. WPFW, 89.3." He tweaked the radio button till she heard the sound of Brubeck and Paul Desmond. "The two Daves," she said out loud. "You and Dave Brubeck."

He grimaced. Thinking of money, she thought. How's he going to explain it on the credit card at his firm or to his wife?

"How about the Latham, just down M Street?" he said.

"A room at the Latham sounds perfect. They should advertise. 'Come to the Latham. We won't tell if you don't,'" she said, leaning over and kissing his crotch, nearly causing him to swerve into oncoming traffic. "Careful, cowboy. We don't want an accident now." She exhaled, her breath warm on his pants, her lips feeling him rock-hard under the fabric, then looked up.

The neon lights from the bars and shuttered stores and from the street and traffic lights made patterns on the windows. The patterns merged with the jazz. Nonrepresentational, but a repetitious pattern, like Islamic art. It means something. Something important—then, Oh no! she thought, massaging his crotch, realizing she was starting to lose it.

Bipolar disorder. She'd won the genetic lottery; she'd gotten it from her father. The same thing that had caused him to lose his job and eventually forced them to move from Michigan to Maryland. Not now, she thought. Please not now.

"Take it easy," he said. She sat up and let him call on his cell to reserve the room. Soon, they were walking through the arched entryway into the hotel lobby. They stopped at the desk, went into the elevator and a minute later, they were in the room, tearing off each other's clothes. Kissing, tongues fencing inside each other's mouths and then on the bed.

He reached over to his pants on the floor beside the bed to put on a condom, and as he turned out the light, something about the wallpaper pattern struck her. It was like a grid, only in the darkness, this guy Dave's outline was like a space. Oh no, she thought. Her bipolar. Get control, Carrie. A space in a grid like the space where Dima was missing. They were all connected, Dima and Nightingale and Ahmed Haidar of Hezbollah in that empty space. It was a grid. And it was the wrong color. The wallpaper was gray, but it should be blue. She needed it to be blue. That's all she could think of. Spaces in a blue grid, only the color was wrong.

"So beautiful," Dave said, nuzzling at her breasts, his fingers between her legs, stroking and probing inside her. She smelled his breath. It smelled of beer and, suddenly, something bad, something from the space in the grid. She jerked her head back, almost gagging. He rubbed against her, then took his penis in his hand and guided it inside her. She gasped at the first sensation of him sliding in and looked at the wall. The wallpaper was grid that was moving—and the wrong color.

"Stop! Stop!" she cried, pushing him away.

He pressed in harder. Pumping, moving in and out.

"Stop it! Get off me! Get off me now or so help me, you'll be sorry, you son of a bitch!"

He stopped. Pulled out.

"What the hell is this? What kind of a tease are you?" he snapped.

"I'm sorry. I can't. I want to, but I can't. I can't, I can't, I can't, I can't, I can't. It's because, don't you see, it isn't the sex. I want the sex. I want you inside me, but I can't and I don't know why. It's my meds. Something I took. It's the grid. There's a space. It's the wrong color. I can't look at it."

"Turn over," he said, pushing at her hips to turn her on her stomach. "We'll do it that way. You don't have to look."

"I can't, dammit! Don't you understand? I don't have to see it to see it! We can't do this. You have to get out. I'm just a crazy lady, okay? A crazy blonde you met in a bar. A crazy blonde whore in a bar. That's all I am. I'm so sorry, Dave or whatever your name is. I'm so sorry. Please, there's something wrong with me. I wanted you. I did, but I can't do it." The wallpaper was a moving pattern, geometrically repeating into infinity like the inside of a mosque. "I can't. Not this way."

He stood up and started to pull on his clothes.

"You're crazy, you know that? I'm sorry I met you, stupid crazy bitch."

"Go to hell!" she shouted back. "Go back to your wife. Tell her you were working late at the office, you lying cheat!" she screamed. "Better yet, do her and pretend it's me. That way you can have both of us!"

He smacked her hard across the cheek.

"Shut up. You want to get us arrested? I'm leaving. Here." He threw down a twenty-dollar bill. "Call a cab," he said, pulling on his coat. He checked his pockets to make sure he hadn't left anything behind.

"Crazy bitch," he muttered, opening the door and closing it behind him. As he did so, Carrie stumbled like a drunk to the bathroom sink and threw up.

CHAPTER 5

Alexandria, Virginia

"When did it start?" her older sister, Maggie, asked.

They were sitting in Maggie's SUV near the Van Dorn Metro station, not far from the Landmark Mall in Alexandria. They'd met there instead of Maggie's office or her house so no one would see them. Maggie was the only person in her family who knew she worked for the CIA.

"Last night," Carrie said. "I could feel it coming a little earlier, but it really started last night. The margaritas probably didn't help," she added.

"Why didn't you call me sooner?"

"I was working. Something important."

"Nonstop? No sleep? Little food, either Chinese or maybe just a few crackers?"

"Well, I was at my desk. I was digging into something. I didn't want to stop."

"Come on, Carrie. You know perfectly well that all of those are prodromal symptoms of a manic onset for you. You're my sister and I love you," she said, brushing Carrie's hair from her eyes, "but I wish you would let me get you some treatment. You could live a normal life. You really could."

"Mag, we've been through this. The minute I get treatment, whether it's you or a shrink, or there's record of a prescription, I lose my security clearance. My job is over. And since, as we both know, or at least you've told me often enough, I don't have a personal life, that doesn't leave me with anything else."

Maggie looked at her, squinting slightly against the sun on the car window. The weather was fair, unusually warm for March. People going to their cars had their jackets open or even no jackets.

"Maybe you should do something else. This isn't a life. We worry about you. Dad, me, the kids."

"Don't start on that. And I wouldn't mention Dad. He's hardly the one to talk about 'normal.'"

"How does the lithium feel?"

"I hate it. It makes me stupid, logy. It's like I'm looking at the world through a thick window. A thick, dirty, fifty-IQ-points-lower window. Did I mention thick? I'm like a zombie. I hate it."

"At least you're coherent. When I saw you last night, you weren't. God, Carrie, you can't go on like this."

"You know I was fine in—where I was. I was able to get all the meds I wanted. Clozapine works just fine. I can function. I'm a normal person. You'd be surprised. I'm actually good at what I do. Just get me a big supply of clozapine and I'll be Aunt Carrie and everyone'll be happy. The kids'll love it." Maggie had two small daughters, Ruby, seven, and Josie, five.

"If you think self-medicating, getting all the meds you want, is good practice, you're crazier than you think."

Carrie put her hand on her sister's arm. "I know. I know you're right. Look, I know you don't like or understand what I do, but it's important. Believe me, you and your children sleep safer in bed at night because of what I do. You've got to help me. There's no one else. Otherwise, I'm up the creek."

"Have you any idea what a risk I'm taking? I could lose my license. Bad enough I'm prescribing for Dad. But at least he's in therapy. I coordinate with his psychiatrist. Between the therapy and me watching him, he's been good for two years now. You should spend some time with him. I know he'd like it. You wouldn't know there was a problem."

"Tell that to Mom," Carrie said.

Neither of them spoke. That was a family black hole. The wound that didn't heal. Their mother, Emma, had disappeared.

"If I can't meet your father, what about your mother?" her lover at Princeton, *John, the professor, had asked her one night in bed.*

"I don't know where she is."

"What do you mean you don't know where she is? Is she dead?"

"I don't know that either."

"I don't understand."

"That's the one thing I do know. I do understand."

"Well, explain it to me and then there'll be two of us," he'd said.

"She left. Just like that. One day she said she was going to CVS. The drugstore. She'd be right back. We never saw her again."

"Did your family look for her? The police? Did she ever try to make contact?"

"Yes. Yes. And no."

"Wow! No wonder you don't talk about your family."

"That was the day I left for Princeton. She just disappeared and off I went. Just me and a suitcase and my happy childhood memories. Don't you see? She was free. I was her youngest. The baby. And I was leaving. I could take care of myself. Now do you get an inkling of how screwed up I am? I'm the cute blond undergraduate you want to have sex with, but tell the truth, John. Am I really the girl you want to be with?"

"At least let me get you tested," Maggie said. "Clozapine has potential side effects that are not good. Hypoglycemia. Agranulocytosis. You understand? Lowered white blood cell count can be really serious. At least let me do that."

"Listen," Carrie said, grabbing Maggie's arms. "Don't you get it? I can't do it. Just give me the damn pills and let me get back to work. You don't understand. I have to get back. It's important."

"Here's three weeks' worth of samples," Maggie said, handing them to her in a plastic bag. "It'll help stabilize you and hold you over, but that's it. I mean it, Carrie. I can't keep doing this. It'll ruin both of us. I want you to seriously consider going into therapy. A psychiatrist can prescribe enough of this for you to walk to the moon on."

"Shhhh! Be quiet," Carrie said, turning up the car radio. She'd heard something.

" . . . reports that five U.S. servicemen from the Five Hundred and Second Infantry Regiment stationed at a checkpoint outside the city of Abbasiyah, south of Baghdad in the so-called Iraqi Triangle of Death, entered the home of a local Iraqi family, where they are charged by Iraqi authorities with raping a fourteen-year-old girl, then killing her and her entire family and setting the bodies on fire. The soldiers being accused claim that the attack was done by Sunni militants. U.S. military and Coalition government spokesmen have stated that the incident is under investigation. A spokesman for General Casey, commander of the Multi-National Force–Iraq, stated, 'We will get to the bottom of this deplorable act,'" the announcer said.

Carrie turned the radio down.

"Shit, this is going to blow things up. I've got to go. Thanks for this, Maggie," she said, indicating the pills. "Thanks for coming to get me. I'll come see the girls as soon as I can. I promise."

"Is this Iraq thing something you're involved in?" Maggie asked.

Carrie looked at her.

"We do . . . everything. People don't have a clue. I'll call," she said, getting out of the car.

"What about Dad?" Maggie asked. Carrie squinted at her in the sun. "You have to talk to him sometime."

"Good old Mag, you never give up. I will. Sometime," she said.

She got back to Langley just in time for an all-hands meeting called by David Estes for everyone in the Counterterrorism Center unit. He told them that they could expect a significant rise in terrorism against Americans both within and outside Iraq as a result of what had happened in Abbasiyah.

"So, just when you think we couldn't possibly come up with anything that could make us even more unpopular with the Arab street or make the Iraqi population hate us even more, some asshole grunts in Iraq have managed to come up with the best recruiting ad for al-Qaeda since they decided to fly into buildings in lower Manhattan!" Estes snapped angrily. "American targets in the Middle East and Europe are of particular concern.

"And I would remind everyone that we have a threat, from an unsubstantiated but previously credible source, of a major attack on American soil," he added, not looking at Carrie as he said it. "All of you start combing through every piece of intel we've got from anywhere in the Middle East and South Asia. I mean everything. Any threats, no matter how iffy, should be brought directly to me immediately.

"We're going to have to deploy additional resources to Baghdad Station. Saul, you'll handle it," he said to Saul, who nodded. "There's going to be a ton of fallout. The media is going to have a field day with this and I've already told the DCIA we can expect a significant increase in U.S. casualties, both military and civilian, both inside and outside the Green Zone, but I want more-detailed projections. I need to let the Joint Chiefs and the White House know what they're in for.

"In addition, I want a complete analysis of all Sunni activity in the Triangle of Death zone, from IA, but also from you, Saul, on my desk by seventeen hundred today. If somebody farts anywhere from Baghdad to al-Hillah, I want to know about it. Those of you not being reassigned to support Baghdad Station will have to pick up the extra slack from the people we're pulling away. Now get to work. We're wasting time," Estes said, dismissing them.

An hour later, Carrie caught Saul in the corridor on his way to the elevator. She'd been waiting for him.

"Not now, Carrie. I've got a meeting on the seventh floor," he told her, meaning with the top directors in the CIA.

"Nightingale met with Ahmed Haidar. Fielding must've known about it but never said a word," she said.

He stood there, blinking behind his glasses like an owl in the daytime.

"How do you know?"

"There was a photo. NSA picked it up from an Israeli satellite stream. In a café. I couldn't tell where. Possibly Cairo or Amman."

"What does that tell you?"

"GSD and Hezbollah are in bed. Maybe the Hariri assassination. Maybe something coming up, like Julia said, using something juicy like Abbasiyah to cover it up. You tell me, Saul. What the hell is going on?"

"I don't know. That's why I hired you. What do you want?"

"I need Fort Meade. Who can I talk to there?" The National Security Agency was headquartered at the Fort Meade, Maryland, army base.

"Out of the question. We have established procedures for this kind of thing and they don't include you charging off on your own like a bull in a china shop. You're already on thin ice." He looked at his watch. "I've got to go deal with this latest screw-up. What the hell did they expect?" he said, stabbing his finger at the elevator button half a dozen times. "You send young men over in multiple deployments, half of them from National Guard units, lousy civilians, many of them with post-traumatic stress, dealing with headless corpses, IEDs on every street corner, allies you can't turn your back on and millions of women you can look at but can't touch. What did they think was going to happen? Christ!" he said, and entered the elevator. "You don't go near Fort Meade. I mean it," he added as the elevator door closed.

Bullshit, she thought to herself. There wasn't enough to go on without the NSA. She'd find someone.

CHAPTER 6

Fort Meade, Maryland

Driving up I-295 in Maryland, she thought if she took 495 instead of continuing north, she could stop in Kensington, where she'd grown up after her family had moved from Michigan because her dad got a job in Bethesda.

Holy Trinity High, she remembered. All girls, all Catholic. Nuns, field hockey and short plaid skirts. "The masturbation center of the universe," Maggie called it. Before her bipolar disorder, which didn't hit her till her sophomore year in college, she was the ultimate little overachiever: Class president. Second place in the state fifteen-hundred-meter championships. Valedictorian on a solid Ivy trajectory; Princeton and Columbia talking scholarships. And her mother growing bleaker by the minute.

"It's the state championship, Mom. I'd like you to come."

"Talk to your father, Carrie. I know he wants to go."

"You know I can't do that. There are college scouts there. He'll ruin it for me. He always ruins it for me."

"You go, Carrie. You'll be fine."

"What's the matter, Mom? Afraid I might win?"

"Why do you say that? I do hope you win. Not that it matters."

"Because I might actually amount to something? Is that what you're afraid of? That one of us might actually escape from this lunatic asylum and it won't be you?"

"You're such a little fool, Carrie. The game is rigged. Even winners don't win."

Man oh man, she thought. It's a wonder I didn't end up even crazier than I already am. She turned off the highway and went on to the sentry gate. From the gate she could see the big rectangular black glass building, the National Security Agency headquarters, a.k.a. the Black House.

It took a half hour for them to vet her identity, give her a visitor's badge and lead her to an empty conference room with a long mahogany table. A thin man in shirtsleeves and a bow tie, looking like a throwback to the fifties, came in.

"Jerry Bishop," he said, sitting across from her. "This is an occasion. We usually don't get folks from McLean making the 295 trek. What's the occasion? Abbasiyah?"

"Well, if you had something on that that was interesting, or any new al-Qaeda ops, you could make me a superstar. I wouldn't argue." She smiled at him, wafting just the vaguest whiff of seduction at him, like perfume.

"We're not seeing any real increase in traffic, apart from the usual *jihadi* Web crap. Poisoning the New York City water supply, attacking refineries, chemical plants in the U.S., and that perennial favorite: flying a private plane loaded with explosives into the Capitol building, although why anyone would think that getting rid of some congressmen would cause any harm to America is beyond me." He grinned. "Other than that, a bit of a surge in cell phone traffic with some Salafi tribesmen in El Arish in Sinai. Maybe something for the Israelis." He shrugged. "That's about it."

"There are tourist resorts in southern Sinai. You'd get all

kinds of tourists: Israelis, Americans, Europeans, scuba divers. And the Egyptian government doesn't have much control there. Might be something."

"It might. I'll give it to you." He nodded. "But that's not why you're here, is it?"

She took photographs of Taha al-Douni, a.k.a. Nightingale; Ahmed Haidar; Dima; and Davis Fielding out of her laptop case and put them on the table. Touching each one, she identified each of them in turn.

"These three are from Beirut," she said, indicating Nightingale, Dima and Davis Fielding. Tapping the Haidar photograph, she added, "This one we got from you guys from an Israeli satellite download stream."

"What do you want?"

"Everything you've got on all four of these guys. Cell phone conversations, e-mails, tweets, surveillance, Hallmark cards from their grandmothers. Anything."

He snorted a quick laugh. "Look, you realize we deal in quantity, not quality, right? We pull in everything. Public, private, cell phones, a text from Abu What's-his-name to his mother. We decrypt, we translate, we run algorithms to try to separate out some of the more obvious garbage. Then we send it to you CIA types. Also to DIA, NSC, FBI, the whole alphabet soup. That's it. You're the ones who are supposed to put the pieces together."

"I'll narrow it for you. Focus just on these people and except for al-Douni and Haidar, just on Beirut."

He looked at her speculatively.

"You work for Estes, right?"

"I report directly to David Estes. For what it's worth, Saul Berenson, Middle East chief, National Clandestine Service, also knows I'm here," she lied.

He picked up Fielding's photograph, then looked directly at her. "We don't usually decrypt a CIA station chief's stuff. What's going on?"

"I can't tell you."

"But something's going down in Beirut? Is that it?"

"I can't tell you that either. But you do the math. Do you think I'd be talking like this to you now if we didn't have a problem?"

"But you don't want me to tell anyone?"

"You can't. It would compromise what we're doing."

"Wait," he breathed. "Are you suggesting we have a mole in Beirut Station?"

"I'm not saying anything of the kind," she snapped. "Don't read into this. I'm asking you to keep this inquiry secret. That's what you and I do every day, Jerry. It's our job. That's all."

"How do you want it? An e-mail via JWICS?" he said, referring to the government's Joint Worldwide Intelligence Communications System, the special computer network designed for highly secure encrypted top secret communications, the highest secrecy level in the U.S. government.

"No. On this," she said, taking an external hard drive and handing it to him along with the photographs.

"Jesus, you really do want to keep this thing quiet. C'mon," he said, and led her down the hallway to the elevator and down to one of a number of subterranean levels.

They walked down a windowless corridor and through a sequence of locked offices, all with heavy security-camera surveillance, some opening to a badge swipe, some requiring a badge and a keypad code entry, the last one requiring a badge, keypad and hand-vein print to open. Inside was a room with a vast wall of monitors showing satellite images from locales around the world. Prominent among them was a bank of screens showing live feeds from key street locations in Iraq.

The room was also filled with analysts in cubicles working at computers. Bishop led her to a group of analysts at a partitioned section near the wall.

"Some folks from the Middle East section," he said. "You may not know them, but you've seen their work."

"Hi," Carrie said. One of the male analysts, a tousle-haired, freckle-faced redhead with a trim beard, gave her a once-over, then went back to his screen. He was in a wheelchair. Bishop told his people what she was looking for. He handed out the photographs to four of them and gave them instructions.

"Do you want to come sit next to me while I look it up?" the redhead in the wheelchair, who'd been given Fielding's photograph, said.

"Sure, if it'll get me what I want," Carrie said.

"Makes two of us," the redhead said, and grinned. He was attractive, in a preppy way, she thought.

"I'd like to see how this works. Do you mind?" Carrie said to Bishop, and sat next to the redhead. She couldn't help noticing his pencil-thin legs in skinny jeans.

"I'm James. James Abdel-Shawafi. Call me Jimbo," the redhead said.

"You don't look Arabic," Carrie said.

"Egyptian father. Irish-American mother." He grinned.

"*Hal tatakalam Arabiya?*" Asking him if he spoke Arabic.

"*Aiwa, dekubah,*" he said. *Yes, of course.* "Where do you want to start? Phone messages? E-mails?"

"You read my mind. Phones," she said, showing him a list of Fielding's numbers at the embassy, the secure scrambled phone, his cell phone, etc. She had five numbers in all.

"Don't need that. Watch," Jimbo said, bringing up a database and querying it for Fielding. The query brought up eleven phone numbers. She sat up straight. Most CIA personnel had one or two private cell phones, but this was surprising.

"How far back do you want to go?" he asked.

"Years. But let's just start with the last three months."

"No problem, but there'll be a lot," he said, typing in the query operators and pressing Enter.

They waited a bit. Then a string of database statements and numbers and dates and times filled the screen. Jimbo stared at it.

"Jesus. Can't be," he said, shaking his head.

"What?"

"Look," he said, pointing at the screen. "See the gap?"

"Show me."

He highlighted a part of the screen.

"According to this, your Mr. Fielding made no calls on these three cell phones for approximately the past five months."

"Maybe he didn't need them. He had eight other phones."

"No, there was limited but active usage on these three till this past October. See? This is bullshit," he said. "Wait a minute." He glanced at her. "I've got DBA admin privileges." He opened another window and typed a DBA_SOURCE database string. "This gives me access to the entire database. I mean everything. This is the whole universe."

They waited and the screen filled with similar results to what they had seen before.

"This is impossible," he muttered. He entered a series of computer shell commands. "Son of a bitch," he breathed.

"What is it?"

"It's been deleted. See there?" he said, pointing at what was to her an incomprehensible string of characters.

"Is that something that happens? Deletion from an NSA database?" she asked.

He looked at her. "I've never seen it before. Ever," he said.

"When was it deleted?"

He studied the screen.

"That's odd too. Two weeks ago, he said.

It rang a bell. She thought for a moment, then it hit her. The same day she left Beirut. Rule Two, she thought, remembering something Saul Berenson had said back in her training days at the Farm. "There are only two rules," he'd told them. "One: This business can kill you. So never ever trust a source—or anyone else. And two: There are no, I repeat, no coincidences." She looked at Jimbo.

"Who can authorize something like that?" she asked.

"I don't know." He leaned closer and whispered to her. "It has to be at the highest level."

CHAPTER 7

George Bush Center for Intelligence, Langley, Virginia

Going through the files on Dima she'd brought back on the hard drive from the NSA, Carrie saw that Dima's last cell phone call had been to a hair salon in Ras Beirut at 3:47 P.M. the day she disappeared. After that, nothing. She started to backtrack, looking to identify every cell phone contact. Was the hair salon a cutout or did she just want to get her hair blown out? A call from Estes interrupted her.

"Come up to my office. Now," Estes said, and rang off.

Good. Finally, she thought, wondering whether it was about the e-mail she'd sent him on the Sawarka, a Salafist Bedouin tribe in northern Sinai, and the possibility of a terrorist strike against tourists in Sharm el-Sheikh and Dahab. Stuff she'd gotten from the Black House. She was thinking about that and Dima as she headed up to Estes's office. Why hadn't she surfaced—or at least some news about her? If a body had been found, she was sure Virgil would've contacted her.

When she knocked on the door and saw Saul, looking worried, in the office with Estes, she realized it was something else.

Estes didn't smile, just gestured for her to sit. Saul, seated on another chair, didn't look at her. Oh boy, she thought.

The afternoon sun was bright on the window behind him, its reflection nearly obscuring the view of the courtyard between the George Bush Center and the old headquarters building, a few staffers sitting outside in shirtsleeves. Strange weather, she thought, her mind suddenly noticing everything. Something is about to happen. She could feel her crazy electrical circuits firing.

"What the hell were you thinking?" Estes said. "Are you completely out of your mind?"

"Thinking about what? What are we talking about?" she said.

"Don't pretend you didn't go to the NSA. On your own. Without authorization. Do you have any idea how many procedures you broke?" Estes snapped.

"I told you not to, Carrie," Saul said softly.

"How'd you find out?" she asked Estes.

"I had a very nice e-mail from some midlevel manager named Jerry Bishop over there. He appreciated you coming over, bridging the interagency-rivalry thing and all that. Just letting me know—nicely—that it happened despite the rules. Thinks it's a good idea. We should do more of it. The only thing missing was a suggestion that we toast marshmallows around the old campfire together. Except I don't want to do more of it, Carrie. We are consumers of theirs, nothing more. And we don't have the time or resources to sort through their shit as it is. I can't have it. More importantly"—he gestured vaguely at the ceiling—"neither can our masters upstairs."

"Even when it's productive? I came up with something. The tribesmen in Sinai. You said you wanted everything. I sent you an e-mail," she said to Estes, afraid to look over at Saul.

"Terrific. Tribesmen in Sinai. I'll alert Lawrence of Arabia. What the hell were you thinking, Carrie? Do you have any idea where we are in terms of budget? Do you know that the Senate is dying to cut our balls off if they see a spark of redundancy— and here you go, traipsing up to Fort Meade, violating understandings it's taken us years to come up with." He shook his head. "Beirut Station said you were out of control, but Saul convinced me otherwise. I can't have this."

"What about the Sawarka?" she said. It was on the tip of her tongue to raise the missing NSA database records and the redacted CTC material, but something told her not to. Just stick to the *jihadis*.

"Saul gave a heads-up to the Egyptian SSI. They said they'd look into it. Also the Israelis. That's not the issue."

"Then you tell me what the issue is, David," she said, standing up to confront him. "Because I got pulled from Beirut in the middle of an op, where we've got a female agent who's disappeared off the face of the earth after Hezbollah and the GSD made a move against one of your case officers, me"—she tapped her chest—"and not only has nobody even looked at it, but nobody's had the brains to ask the question 'Why?' Plus I gave you actionable intel from a highly credible source on a possible major terrorist attack on the U.S. and so far nobody seems to give a shit except me. So you tell me what the damn issue is."

This time she did look at Saul and he looked green, like he was sick to his stomach.

"Sit down. I mean it," Estes said, biting off the words.

She sat. He took a breath, then another.

"Look, Carrie. We're not the military here. We don't just give orders. Our people are expected to act independently, to think for themselves. Management-wise, it's like herding cats.

But that's the price you pay for good people who dig things up in places no one would expect that can save an entire nation. So we give you a lot of leeway, but this crossed the line.

"You went outside the Agency completely on your own. You were way beyond the parameters of 'need to know,' which is why we only allow authorized interagency contacts through normal channels. The NSA's job is to provide us with data. Period. They don't have the intelligence-analysis experts to turn raw data into useful intel. We do. Most of the people on this entire campus do nothing else but analyze data. If we get the NSA into our business, then Congress has the right to ask what the hell they're paying us for. And if you want me to do something about this so-called actionable intel about an attack, you better damn well give me something to work with.

"Furthermore, while you're busy playing in your sandbox with Sinai and Beirut, you are not paying attention to al-Qaeda, especially in Iraq, which is what I needed you to concentrate on and the only reason you're still here."

"I'm looking at Iraq too. I—"

"Cut the crap, Carrie. We don't have time for this. What just happened in Abbasiyah is a gift to the bad guys. I can't have you off doing whatever the hell you want. It doesn't work that way." He shook his head. "Anyway, I've notified HR. I'm removing you from CTC. In fact, not just from CTC, from the National Clandestine Service. You're done here. Saul?" he said, looking at Berenson.

Carrie felt like she'd been punched in the stomach. She wanted to throw up. This couldn't be happening. Didn't they see what was going on? Missing files, a possible terrorist attack, and she was the only one who'd spotted it and now they were getting rid of her?

"Carrie, you're a great talent. Your language skills, your

instincts," Saul said, leaning forward, hands clasped, almost as if he were praying. "But you forced our hand. You're being reassigned."

Relief flooded her. It was bad, but she wasn't being fired.

"I thought I'm out of NCS," she said.

"You are," Saul said, glancing at Estes, "being transferred to the Intelligence Analysis Division. The Office of Collection Strategies and Analysis."

"Effective immediately," Estes said. "No more fieldwork, Mathison. You're done."

Who did you piss off?" her workmate in the next cubicle, Joanne Dayton, said. Blond, blue-eyed, a little overweight and pretty enough to have been a cheerleader in high school, but according to Joanne, she'd been a doper, not one of the cool kids. "Otherwise, I'd've never ended up here," she'd whispered, rolling her eyes.

"David Estes," Carrie said.

"Really?" Joanne said, looking at her with greater interest. "I'm surprised you're still working here." She moved closer. Just girls. "What'd you do?"

What did I do? Carrie thought. She hadn't let them kidnap or kill her. Since she'd started running for her life on Avenue Michel Bustros, she hadn't really stopped.

"Oddly enough, my job," she said.

Her new boss was a tall, odd-looking long-haired man of Russian descent, with arms and legs disproportionately larger than his torso, as if his body had been assembled from cast-off odds and ends of other people somehow welded together like one of the Watts Towers. Someone said he'd been wounded in Bosnia, but no one would speak about it. His name was Yerushenko. Alan Yerushenko.

"I don't know why they moved you over from NCS and I don't care," Yerushenko told her, looking at her through tinted glasses. "We may not be the glamour boys of the business like on the other side of the house, but don't think what we do is not important. And I'll expect a daily report of your progress."

The hell with you, she thought.

"What's with Yerushenko?" she asked Joanne.

"He's a stickler, but it could be worse. He's not entirely an idiot. Just mostly." She grinned.

Yerushenko put her on Iraq data analysis from NCS core collectors, CIA officers who collected data from case officers and forwarded the intel to Langley for analysis and evaluation. "You have to assign probabilities for credibility and accuracy," he told her. "The rule of thumb is that most are barely credible and the rest are even worse."

She started to work on reports on AQI, al-Qaeda in Iraq. Their leader was a mysterious figure who used the nom de guerre Abu Nazir. She'd first heard about him while following up on a lead in Baghdad last year. But he was like a ghost; there was hardly anything real on him. There was little known about him personally too, although he was suspected of being in Anbar Province, where he had cowed local tribal leaders by cutting off the heads of everyone who got in his way. Sometimes, they were left stuck on poles along the roads like gruesome signposts. There was also mention of an equally ruthless lieutenant of his, about whom even less was known, codenamed Abu Ubaida.

But she couldn't concentrate. She felt humiliated, sick to her stomach. Why had they done this to her? Why had Saul abandoned her? And why didn't they listen? There was an attack planned against America that might happen in a few days or weeks and nobody seemed to care. She went to the ladies' room, into a stall, and closed the door. Sitting on the lid, her face in her hands, it was all she could do to keep from screaming at the top of her lungs.

What was happening? Her skin was tingling. Prickling, like when your foot falls asleep. It's stress. An emotional jolt of hormones, she told herself. The stress was sideswiping her meds, knocking out the circuits. She rubbed the skin on her arms to try to make it stop tingling. It didn't work. Then she understood. She'd been running low on clozapine, so she had started taking them every other day. Her bipolar was kicking in. She was going into a depressive episode.

She looked around the stall like a trapped animal. She had to get home.

CHAPTER 8

For a week and a half, she'd managed to drag herself to work, to get dressed, to put on makeup, to pretend she gave a shit. She had stopped taking the few meds she had left from Maggie altogether. It felt like she'd fallen into a black hole, abandoned, exiled. She read reports about AQI but had to reread everything three or four times. It was impossible to concentrate.

The bastards, she thought. All this time she'd thought Saul was like the father she'd never had, or more like the wise, funny Jewish uncle everybody wished they had. And Estes. She'd thought he appreciated what she did, how hard she worked, how good she was at her job.

But even when she brought them actionable intel, they not only did nothing, they punished her. They destroyed her career. It was over, she thought, and spent more and more time in the ladies' room at work. She had nothing. She was nothing.

She stopped going to work. She knew she needed to try to find out about the pending attack Julia had told her about, but she couldn't make herself do anything.

Sitting on the floor in a corner of her bedroom, the apartment in Reston completely dark and silent. She hadn't eaten in how many days? Two? Three? Some part of her brain told her, This is not you. This is the disease, but she couldn't make herself care. What difference did it make?

She had to pee but couldn't make herself get up to go to the bathroom. When was the last time she had gone? What did it matter? She was alone in the darkness. A failure. Like her father.

Her father.

Thanksgiving. Her freshman year at Princeton. Her sister, Maggie, was a senior at NYU in New York. She'd called Carrie to let her know she was having Thanksgiving in Connecticut with her boyfriend Todd's family.

"Dad's alone. You have to go, Carrie," Maggie said.

"Why me? You need to come too. He needs us." Thinking, It's Thanksgiving. Maybe Mom will finally call. She was married to him all those years. Didn't that count for something? And what about her and Maggie? What did they do wrong? If she didn't want to call Frank, she could have at least called her or Maggie. She knew Maggie's phone number at her apartment in Morningside Heights. And she knew Carrie was at Butler at Princeton. If she wanted to, she could have gotten hold of them. Their father, Frank, need never have known. Oh God, was her entire family crazy?

Her father called two days before Thanksgiving.

"Your sister's not coming," he said.

"I know, Dad. It's her boyfriend. I think it's getting serious, her and Todd. But I'm coming. I'll be there Wednesday. I'm looking forward to seeing you," she lied, thinking it was going to be deadly in that house, just the two of them.

"You don't have to come, Caroline. I know you have things you'd rather . . ." His voice trailed off.

"Dad, don't be silly. It's Thanksgiving. Look, you buy the turkey.

I'll be there Wednesday afternoon. I'll cook it. I'll do the whole thing, okay?"

"It's all right. Maybe it's better you don't come," he said.

"Dad, please! Don't do this. I said I'll be home. I'll be home."

"You were always a good girl, Carrie. Your sister too. She wasn't as smart or as pretty as you, but a good girl too. We should have done better by you. I'm sorry."

"Dad! Don't talk like that. I'll see you Wednesday."

"I know. Good-bye, Carrie," he said, and hung up, leaving her staring at the phone in her hand.

She thought about calling Maggie and insisting, then decided against it. Maggie was with Todd. Let it be. But he sounded strange. Like he was down. She calculated. There was a midterm on Tuesday morning, but after that, nothing as the college started to close down for the holiday. She could surprise him. Leave Tuesday right after the exam and get home by Tuesday afternoon.

That Tuesday, she caught a Greyhound bus in Mount Laurel and connected to Silver Spring. She got to Kensington in the afternoon. It was sunny and clear and cool, the leaves turning brown and red and gold. She caught the local bus and was dropped off near the small frame house she'd grown up in. It looked shabbier in the sunlight than she remembered. He hasn't been keeping it up, she thought, unlocking the door.

A minute later, she was on the phone calling 911.

Happy Thanksgiving, Dad, she remembered thinking as she rode with him in the ambulance to the hospital.

Only now, Maggie had taken in her father, Frank, to live with her nice all-American husband and her nice all-American children, and she, Carrie, was a failure and a crazy like her father. Like him, she had nothing.

No man, no kids, no life, a total failure at work. Alone.

Totally alone. Even Saul had abandoned her. She could have been on the far side of the moon, she was so alone. The exact opposite of someone like Dima. The party girl. The girl who couldn't stand being alone, who was never without a man, although the men in her life went through the endless revolving door that passed for relationships among single women in North Beirut.

Dima was never alone. It was a clue, but to what? She had disappeared off the face of the earth.

"Maybe," Carrie said out loud in what she realized was her first rational moment in days, "the bitch is with my mother."

CHAPTER 9

McLean, Virginia

The next day, she managed to make herself go to work. There was something about Dima, how she could never be alone. Carrie was determined to have it out with Saul. But not at headquarters, she thought. She needed to get him someplace they could talk.

Putting on her makeup, she thought she looked like a ghost. That's what I am, she decided. The ghost at the party. But before she disappeared into the darkness, she'd make Saul listen. He had to listen, she thought.

She drove in to work. Joanne was all concerned.

"Where've you been?" she asked. "Yerushenko's ready to dump you. You're lucky he's at an all-day meeting on the threat post-Abbasiyah."

Yeah, boy am I lucky, Carrie thought.

The day lasted forever. It moved so slowly she could have sworn at times the clock moved backward. In her mind, she kept going back to the same questions. Who had deleted the NSA database records? And redacted the details about Beirut? Who was Dar Adal? What did he have to do with anything?

An even better question was, why? What were they protecting? What had gone wrong? Why wasn't anything happening on Beirut or on the intel she'd given them from Julia? There were only questions and no answers—and time, moving slower than the traffic on I-95.

That evening, she waited in the parking lot until Saul came out, around eleven P.M. She followed his car, tailing him back to his house in McLean. It was a white colonial on a dark tree-shaded street without sidewalks. She'd been there once a long time ago for lunch. She watched him go in, waited twenty minutes, then got out and rang the doorbell.

Saul's wife, Mira, an Indian woman from Mumbai whom Saul had met in Africa and whom Carrie had met once before, answered the door in a nightdress and robe.

"Hi, Mira. Remember me? I need to see Saul."

"I remember," Mira said, not moving from the doorway. "He just got home."

"I'm sorry," Carrie said. "It's important."

"It's always important," Mira said, moving aside so Carrie could come in. "Someday you people are going to realize it's what's not important that really matters." She motioned with her head. "He's upstairs."

"Thanks," Carrie said, going up the stairs. A bedroom door was half-open. She knocked and went in. Saul was still in his trousers but had changed into his pajama top. He was eating out of a yogurt container. The bed was made and looked small to her. It made her wonder if they slept together. He put the yogurt down.

"Who's Dar Adal?" she asked.

"Where'd you get that from?" he said.

"Going through CTC files. The work you and David put me on when I came back. Only there's a bunch of it redacted—and piss-all on the Syrian GSD out of either Damascus or

Beirut Station. Plenty of reports, but once you squeeze the air out of it, there's nothing there. So you tell me what's going on."

"Go home, Carrie," he said. "It's been a long day."

"Who is he?"

"Ancient history. Not our finest hour," he said, looking away. "I can't get you back. I know that's what you want, but I can't. Go home."

"Not till you talk to me."

He shook his head. "Grow up, Carrie! It's done. I've done all I can."

"It isn't fair."

"You're just finding out that the world isn't fair? Get used to it; you'll be a lot less disappointed in life. Look, this is my home. You have no right to be here. I mean it. I want you to leave," he said, his face set like it had been carved in stone.

"Listen to me, dammit!"

"I'm listening, Carrie, but you're not saying anything, just whining."

"There were records deleted from the NSA database. They said they'd never seen that before. Ever. They were deleted the day I was sent from Beirut," she said. "Who can do that?"

For a moment, neither of them spoke. There was the sound of a TV from the master bedroom down the hall. Jay Leno. They really don't sleep together, she thought, feeling like an intruder. She really didn't belong here in his house.

"What were the records on?" he asked finally.

"Cell phone records from three of Davis Fielding's eleven phones. Goes back months," she said.

"Shit," he said, and sat down on the edge of the bed.

She sat next to him.

"Why does Estes hate me?" she asked.

Saul took off his glasses and wiped them with his pajama

top. "I don't think he does. I once caught him watching you walk away. He just looked at me. I assumed it was just a male thing, but whatever it is, he's aware of you."

"So he likes my ass. That doesn't mean he likes me."

"For some reason, he didn't want you poking around where you've been poking." He put his glasses back on. "Also, I think he really wanted you on Iraq. A smart, good-looking female CO who speaks Arabic like you do, I think he was trying to aim you at something, but this NSA thing fouled it up. I'm not sure why."

"So you don't believe this Senate budget bullshit either?"

"Not really." He frowned. "What you said about the NSA data being deleted is a game changer. I have no choice now. We've got to look at Beirut."

"C'mon, Saul, send me back. Virgil and me, we'll find out what's going on."

"I can't. I've got Estes looking over my shoulder, and what's on his mind—and he's not wrong—is Iraq, and whatever the hell al-Qaeda's cooking up against the U.S. And trust me"—he looked at her—"there's something coming at us soon. Very soon. And it won't be Sinai, although you're probably right about that too, not that anybody gives a shit. This is AQI, al-Qaeda in Iraq, and Abu Nazir, and when they come at us, it'll be Washington or New York."

"Could it have anything to do with what my Joe Julia told me?"

He frowned. "It's hard to link Abu Nazir and Hezbollah. Sunni versus Shiite, plus they really don't like each other."

"But it's possible?"

"Maybe. You have good instincts. But don't force it. Only if that's where it leads."

"What do you want me to do?"

"Two things," he said, patting her hand. "First, we need to convert Estes. If he's protecting Fielding, it's because of the DCIA, Bill Walden. You need to turn Estes. Second, don't underestimate OCSA. Or Yerushenko. I didn't move you there by accident."

"I thought it was a punishment."

Saul grinned. "Yeah, like throwing Brer Rabbit into the briar patch. The patch he was born in, the place he's most comfortable. Listen." He touched her arm. "As an analyst in the Office of Collection Strategies and Analysis, you have a right to see anything. I mean anything. It's the Holy Grail, the most general mandate in the whole Agency. And trust me, Yerushenko may be a weird son of a bitch, but if you dig up something, he'll back you all the way to Jesus Christ himself if he has to."

"Did David Estes understand that when you reassigned me?"

"I think so." He nodded. "When I recommended it, he gave me a look. Don't underestimate Estes. There's a lot going on. He's playing three-dimensional chess. He could've terminated you, ended your career over this NSA bullshit. Instead, he didn't say a word about me moving you over to OCSA. More importantly, he could've cut you off. Told this Bishop character over at the Black House never to communicate with you again. He didn't. Plus, by transferring you, he's covered both our asses, his and mine. If anyone asks, he can say we disciplined you and prove it."

She put her face in her hands. "You could tell a girl," she said. "I've been sick for two weeks." It took every bit of her self-control not to break down sobbing. She wanted to throw her arms around him and hug him forever. Saul hadn't abandoned her. He still believed in her, a relief shuddering through her.

"No, I couldn't," he said. "I really couldn't. Besides, he might have had another reason to want to transfer you."

She looked at him, confused. Then it hit her.

"You're not suggesting . . . ," she said.

"It's possible. There are plenty of men who might take advantage of an attractive woman working under them. David's human, but he's a by-the-book kind of guy. He would never do that."

"So you think . . ."

"I don't know. I hear his marriage is in trouble, but whose isn't?" Saul shrugged, looking away, and she suspected he was talking about his own marriage as well. Was Estes sleeping in a separate bed too? Did this job destroy everybody's personal life?

"So you want me to find something and then use it to turn David?"

"ASAP. You're a good Catholic girl. You can, what's the saying, 'bring him to the light.'"

"I haven't been either of those things, good or Catholic, for a long time," she said thoughtfully. "Besides"—she smiled wistfully—"that sounds funny coming from a Jew."

"Well, we're a funny people," Saul said.

CHAPTER 10

Glen Burnie, Maryland

She met Jimbo Abdel-Shawafi for an early lunch at a Chick-fil-A in a mall in Glen Burnie, just outside Baltimore. He had texted her: "ever had disabled sex?"

"can u get it up?" she'd texted back.

"4 u, I can try harder."

"hard is the word im looking 4."

"c u anyway? something u need 2 c."

The redhead was waiting for her in his wheelchair at a table in the mall food court. It was early enough that the tables weren't too crowded with shoppers grabbing a quick bite.

"Why here?" she asked.

"Far enough away from both our shops so we won't run into anyone," he said, leaning toward her. "Plus, access." He indicated a wheelchair sign. "Besides, it's cheap and I like the chicken sandwich," he said, taking a bite.

"What've you got?" she asked, poking at a salad with a plastic fork.

"We reactivated tracking COMINT on all the phone numbers. I programmed my input streams to alert me if anything popped up. There were no messages of particular interest, so I decided just for the hell of it to run face-recognition software, especially on anyone taking interest in the U.S., and look what popped up." He showed her a passport photo on a DS-160 online application form for a visitor's visa, the kind foreigners use to come to the United States, on his laptop computer. She stared at it.

The hair was different. Instead of being long, black and sleek, it was short and streaked, but Carrie recognized her immediately. It was Dima. She's alive, she thought excitedly.

"Is it her?" Jimbo asked, holding the original photo of Dima she'd given him next to the photo on the screen to compare.

"It's her," Carrie said, her heart beating fast.

"And this," he said, showing her on his laptop. Displayed in another window on the screen was an airline reservation entry from Beirut to New York on British Airways with a stopover in London. Also, a Lebanese passport page and the DS-160. "As you can see by the passport and reservation, she's using the cover name Jihan Miradi."

"God," she said. "I could kiss you."

"Who's stopping you?" He grinned.

She got up, came around the table and kissed him on the cheek.

"I think you missed the target," he said.

"I like you, Jimbo. And I owe you, big-time. But I don't want you to get the wrong idea."

"Well, at least I got a peck on the cheek," he said.

"For stuff like this, anytime. Any idea where she's staying?"

He winked at her. "The reservation was made by a travel agency. Seems she's alone."

"Trust me, she's not alone," Carrie said. She said it without thinking, but now that she thought about it, it was true.

"Have a look," he said, showing her a copy of the airline

reservation. It was made by Unicorn Travel on Rue Pasteur. She knew roughly where that was. In Beirut's Central District, not far from the harbor. "She's staying at the Waldorf Astoria in New York. She must have money."

"Not her own. She knows how to get men to spend it on her," she said.

"Not the only woman in the world who knows that trick."

She looked at him sharply. "We're not all like that," she said. "Not even close."

"Sorry. Didn't mean that the way it came out." Then he brightened. "Would I like her?" He grinned.

"You like anything in a skirt." She smiled. "But yes, you'd like her. Definitely."

Suddenly, it was as if all the cylinders in a slot machine stopped on sevens. Dima had set her up with Nightingale, who tried to grab or kill her. Dima had disappeared and now was suddenly surfacing in New York right after the rape and killings in Abbasiyah. Dima was here on an op. But for whom? GSD? Hezbollah? That didn't make sense. If anyone was going to avenge Abbasiyah, it would be al-Qaeda. This had to have been set up before then. There's a missing piece somewhere, she thought. And it's in Beirut.

She looked at the airline and hotel reservations again. Dima was due in New York in four days. Estes had mobilized the entire CTC in anticipation of something aimed at the U.S. Saul had said the target would be either Washington or New York. Was this it?

What was happening at the Waldorf or anywhere in New York this week? She had to get back to her OCSA computer fast.

"Jimbo, thanks," she said, putting her hand on his arm. "This is a big deal. Really."

He looked at her. Blue eyes. He really did have beautiful eyes, she thought.

"Maybe we could get together sometime?" he asked.

She hesitated. "No."

He took a deep breath and let it out. "It's the chair, isn't it?" He put both hands on the wheelchair's armrests.

"Maybe a little," she said, ducking her head. "Maybe more than a little. But that's not it."

"I don't do it for you?" he said, looking away.

"I don't know. I hate being put in this situation. That's always a problem for a woman—and anyway, it's beside the point." She took a breath. "I like you, Jimbo. Thing is, I like you too much to screw you up—and that's what I do. I know you think it's bullshit, but trust me, I'm doing you a big favor."

"Sounds like bullshit." He frowned.

"It's not. I'm not kidding. Besides, I'm kind of involved with someone," she said, thinking of Estes.

"You're a fantasy girl, you know, Carrie? You should let someone in. Here." He handed her a flash drive with the data he'd shown her on it.

"I will, someday. But not today. This," she said, getting up and showing him the flash drive, "is going to save lives. You did something important, cowboy."

"Listen, there's something else on the flash drive."

"What?"

"I reinstituted tracking on those three cell phones of Fielding's that had been deleted. Those are all the calls he's made on them since. There are a bunch to a single number. A woman. I put the data on the flash."

"You really are something," she said, and kissed him on the forehead. "Thanks."

"Glad to help. Listen, you be careful," he said. "Not everybody likes this cross-agency communication. I've been warned."

"Makes two of us," she said, every fiber in her screaming to get back to Langley. She had to figure a way to turn Estes. What was it Saul had said with his vaguely Catholic turn of phrase? God, he knew her. Shades of Holy Trinity High. "Bring him to the light," he'd said.

Dima was on her way, courtesy of British Airways, and if she couldn't figure out a way to stop her, she was bringing death.

CHAPTER 11

F Street, Washington, DC

David Estes was already seated when Carrie walked into the brasserie at the Monaco, a boutique hotel with a columned façade and red awnings across the street from the National Portrait Gallery. The maître d' looked at her, but she shook her head and went over to the bar. Estes was having dinner with a man who had the well-fed look of a congressman from a safe district, the kind who didn't have to bottom-feed on K Street because the lobbyists would come to him.

She'd worn her sexiest outfit, a form-fitting sleeveless embroidered Terani, a midthigh minidress with a plunging neckline that left as little to the imagination as she could get away with. The second she walked over to the modernistic bar, three men jumped off their stools to make room for her. Nice little ego boost; guess the dress worked, she thought.

Back at Langley after lunch with Jimbo, it hadn't taken thirty seconds to figure it out. There was a Republican Party fund-raiser at the Waldorf the day after tomorrow. The Vice-President, the governor of New Jersey and the mayor were the name draws. The obvious targets.

She couldn't just turn it over to the FBI. They'd have to

be briefed and in any case, she would have to be there in New York, she thought. For her, Dima wasn't just a photo. She knew her. The problem was Estes and bringing him to the light.

The man whose stool she'd taken in the brasserie bar was distinguished, fortyish and graying, in an Armani suit. Odds-on a lobbyist. Ten-to-one he made his living selling something—or someone, she thought.

"K Street?" she asked.

He nodded, grinning like he'd just pulled the third ace to turn a high two pair into a full house.

"What are you drinking?" he said.

"Margarita, with Patrón Silver."

He motioned to the bartender and gave him the order.

"Where do you work?" he asked.

"Foggy Bottom," she said, meaning the State Department. "Just another paper pusher." She shrugged and looked over at Estes's table. "Who's that man with the black guy? He looks like somebody I should know. Maybe from TV or something?" she said. Sometimes playing dumb was the smartest thing a girl could do, she thought.

"You don't recognize him? That's Congressman Riley. Hal Riley, chairman of the House Appropriations Committee. He's a heavy hitter on the Hill." He winked.

"You know him?" she asked, thinking if this guy's ego got any bigger, he'd start to rise like the Goodyear blimp.

"Played golf with him on Tuesday," Armani Suit said. "Good guy, but"—he leaned closer to whisper in her ear—"with him, every other shot is a Mulligan. What does that tell you?"

"That he cheats, like half the people in this town. I guess you really do know him," she said, wondering how long it would be before Estes came over.

"Don't know the African-American though," Armani Suit said. "Probably deputy director of some bullshit agency."

"I guess," she said, watching Estes out of the corner of her eye, wondering if he'd spotted her yet. She hoped he would soon. Another twenty minutes and she'd have Armani Suit's hand on her ass, whispering sweet nothings about a weekend in the Bahamas.

Estes looked up, spotted her, leaned over and said something to the congressman. He got up and came over to her at the bar.

"I was just telling the little lady—" Armani Suit started to say.

"What do you want?" Estes said to her, ignoring him. "Are you following me?"

"We need to talk," she said.

He frowned. "This is unprofessional. We'll talk tomorrow. At my office." He turned away.

She grabbed at his sleeve. "No, now," she said. "It's urgent."

"I'm with Congressman Riley. He's—"

"I know who the hell he is," Carrie interrupted. "Get rid of him."

Estes looked at her, a muscle in his jaw twitching. He turned, went back to his table, said something to the congressman and the waiter, then came back to her.

"We can't talk here. Let's go," he said, glancing at Armani Suit, then went to the rack and grabbed his coat. Carrie got hers and the two of them walked out of the restaurant into the hotel lobby. They walked over to one of the square columns near the gas-burning fireplace.

"This better be important," he said. "I'm trying to convince that asshole that the bad guys are still around and not to gut us."

"We can't talk here either," she said, glancing around. "Washington's like a small town. I booked a room upstairs. We can talk there."

Estes looked startled, then his features hardened. "Are you insane? What the hell is this?"

"This is business," she said. "What do you think it is?"

"You better not be jerking me around, Carrie. I want to know what this is about. Are you stalking me?"

"Don't be stupid. Why would I stalk you? I know where you work. C'mon," she said, heading for the elevator. He watched her go, then, after a moment, followed.

They didn't say anything in the elevator or in the corridor with its elegant patterned rugs and striped wallpaper. She unlocked the room and they went inside. He turned on the light, but she turned on a single lamp and clicked the ceiling light off.

"Now what the hell is this all—" he started to say, but couldn't finish because she threw herself into his arms and kissed him.

He pulled her arms from around him. "If this is a setup, you are in more trouble than you can believe," he said.

"Two things. Just two—and then you can fire me or do whatever the hell you want," she said, holding up two fingers. "One. Dima, the contact who set me up for the snatch in Beirut, is alive. Dima who connected me with Nightingale, who by the way is in bed with Hezbollah, something your buddy Fielding didn't tell you, and who tried to kill or kidnap me. Are you listening, David? I got that information from NSA, the people you ripped me a new one for just talking to. And she's headed our way, right after Abbasiyah? Do the math." She didn't tell him where Dima was headed in case he tried to stop her.

"And two," she said, coming close, pressing herself against

him. "I want you. And this has nothing to do with work. You can have me and fire me afterward. I don't care."

"You know I'm married?"

"I don't care if I burn in hell. I want you and as sure as I know anything, I know you want me too."

She tried to kiss him, but he turned his face away, so she kissed his face again and again, reaching for his lips.

"Tell me you don't want me," she murmured. "Tell me you never once thought about this and I'll stop and I'll never come near you again, I swear."

Her lips found his and they kissed long and hard. She bit his lower lip, tasting blood, and he pushed her away.

"Bitch!" he said, hand to his lip to wipe off the blood.

"I am. What are you going to do about it?" She leaped at him and kissed him hard, putting his hand on her breast. He was so much bigger that she had to stretch to reach, and she loved that about him. Pressing against him, she could feel his erection hard against her. "Tell me you haven't wanted this," she murmured.

"I admit it. I thought about it," he whispered. She reached behind her to unzip her dress. She pulled the zipper down from the top, then reversed and pulled the zipper down the rest of the way and pulled off her dress. She stood before him in just her bra and bikini panties. She touched herself.

"My God, I'm wet. Do something," she whispered, pulling him toward the bed. Through the window, they could see the museum lit up at night, white as an iceberg.

"This is a bad idea," he said, starting to undress.

"Terrible," she said in agreement.

"I'm going to regret this. We both are," he said, his tie and shirt half-off.

"I know."

"I won't do it. I can't," he said, stopping, standing there, staring at the window.

"If you don't want me, say the word and we'll stop now," she said, unhooking her bra and freeing her breasts. She lay on top of the bed, raised her hips, and pulled down her panties. "But I'm sick of being only half-alive," she whispered. "Aren't you? Or is the view so perfect from the good seats?"

"You're a devil," he said, pulling off his pants and jockey shorts and getting on top of her.

"Last chance to say no," she whispered, reaching down for his penis to put it inside her. Heavy as he was, she wrapped her legs around his hips and pressed herself up against him. "Oh God," she gasped as he pushed inside. "It's been forever."

CHAPTER 12

Amtrak Acela Express, New Jersey

The Amtrak Acela Express, Washington to New York, four days later. Through the window, she watched the flatlands of New Jersey rushing by as they headed for Penn Station in Manhattan. Saul Berenson sat in the seat next to her, working on his laptop computer. Carrie was lost in thought, her mind wandering somewhere between Beirut and David Estes. Every time she thought of him, she had fantasies of the two of them naked.

She liked the bigness of him, on top of her and inside her. He'd been a football player in college and he still had that athleticism that was part of the sex. She liked the feel of him and the contrast of their skins against each other, black and white, like piano keys. It made her think of great jazz chords. Thelonious Monk, Bud Powell—and memories of Princeton and the night she learned who she was.

Her junior year. *The year of Near East studies and learning Arabic and John, her professor-lover. They had spent the night at his apartment, smoking weed and listening to his jazz CDs and having sex in every position they could twist themselves into. In the morn-*

ing, breakfast was espresso, potato chips, chocolate chip cookies and Billie Holiday.

"I was a kid," he told her. "This was the sixties in upstate New York, right? Vietnam. Rock 'n' roll. The Stones. Creedence Clearwater. I was a lonely kid, up late at night listening to the radio in my room. They were playing Billie Holiday. This song, "Strange Fruit," which I swear, Carrie, says more about being black in America than all the books and documentaries you'll ever see, and I realized it was all in the music. All you had to do was listen."

Only she wasn't listening because it had already started. She was feeling light, like she was made of helium and if something didn't hold her down, she would float straight up into the sky and never come down.

That night, he was supposed to take her to a party, but he didn't show. Pissed, she went alone. Everybody was drinking and dancing and she was downing tequila and feeling like nothing could hurt her. They were talking about The X-Files, *the TV show, and Dolly, a sheep that had been cloned from another sheep.*

A good-looking Ivy guy in a preppy sweater who made sure she knew in the first three seconds that he belonged to the Colonial, one of Princeton's elite Eating Clubs, asked her if she thought people would be cloned and she just opened like a grenade exploding. Talking about how infinite repetition is impossible so cloning would inevitably degenerate and how it all started with Charlie Parker and jazz and you could see it in Islamic art in mosque mosaics. Talking nonstop, feeling beautiful and charming and to hell with John and not noticing how Colonial Club and all the other people were edging away from her. Until she saw two girls talking to each other and looking at her and their look wasn't like wow, she was finally the pretty girl who was charming and funny, but what the hell is going on with her, mingled with a touch of pity, and she just got up and ran back to the dorm as fast as she could.

Back in her room, she ripped off all her clothes, everything. Sit-

ting stark naked on her bed, she started writing furiously in a note-book. Page after page, as fast as she could. It was about the music and how the laws that underpinned the universe were a musical score. By the time she was finished, nearly seven hours later, it was morning and she had a forty-five-page manifesto she'd titled "How I Reinvented Music," explaining the connections between jazz notes and Jackson Pollock and mathematics and quantum mechanics and Einstein's Theory of General Relativity. Because it was all connected. Like John, that shit, had said: "All you had to do was listen."

And when she was done, she grabbed her jacket and the notebook and, still naked except for the jacket, ran out into the hallway and down the stairs and into the street. She ran barefoot in the snow, nearly knocking over a small Hispanic-looking man with glasses she'd never seen before. But he was obviously a professor. She grabbed his coat, thrusting her manifesto at him.

"You have to read this, publish it. It'll change the world. Everything is music, but the old way is hopeless. It's a dead end. I've reinvented it. Don't you see? It's all connected. This is the mind of God, damn it," she said.

"Are you all right, miss? Are you from Butler?" the little man said, looking around. There were students who had stopped to watch.

"You have to read this, now! It's the most important document in the world. Look!" she said, showing him the first page.

"Does anybody know this young woman?" the professor asked. Nobody moved or said anything.

"She's naked," a girl said.

"And barefoot," a male student added.

"What are you talking about?" Carrie shouted. "Don't you understand? What Charlie Parker and Thelonious Monk did for music was free it from the dead hand of European bullshit. They got a glimpse of the underlying mathematics. This is the damn universe you're holding!"

"I'm Professor Sanchez. Some of you help me," the professor said to the students. "Let's get her to McCosh."

They took her, still babbling nonstop, to the Student Health Center, where they gave her carbamazepine, which didn't do anything except make her throw up. Then they sedated her big-time, wiping the rest of the day and almost two weeks from her memory forever.

Afterward, lithium in a private hospital brought her back. Time had gone by. She was at home in Maryland.

"You flew," her father said to her. "I'm sorry, Caroline. Maybe now you understand. Sometimes I think it's the best and worst thing in the world."

"I got it from you, you son of a bitch," she said. "I don't ever want to see you or feel that way again."

"What makes you think you have a choice?" he said.

A few days after she came back to Princeton, John called her.

"What happened? I heard you had a breakdown," he said. "I want to see you."

"Go away. I don't want to see you."

"What's going on? Let me come over."

"No. Don't call again. Please."

"Why? At least tell me. You owe me that at least."

"That girl, the nice-looking girl you can have sex with and feel how smart you are, forget her. She's gone."

"Carrie, talk to me. What's happened? Is it your family?"

"In a way. Genetics. Look, John. You've got your routine down pat. You'll find another cute undergraduate girl to impress the shit out of. Tell your stories about Billie Holiday and Charlie Parker to. Do us both a favor. Forget about me."

"I think I'm in love with you."

"Bullshit! You loved how I made you feel about yourself. It was all about you, a kind of masturbation, not me."

"You had fun too, didn't you?" he snapped. "Admit it."

"Yes, I did. Now leave me alone. I mean it," she said, and hung up.

Back in her cubicle, she started with a single realization that hadn't left her: Dima wouldn't be alone. So the question was, who was coming with her and how did they plan to take out the Veep and the people at the fund-raiser?

First she got Joanne to help her, but that wasn't enough. They were running out of time. The attack could come any day. She marched into Yerushenko's office.

"What is it?" he said, looking up.

She told him. All of it. Dima and Nightingale in Beirut. Julia's warning. The missing files. Dima coming to the Waldorf under the cover name of Jihan Miradi and the fund-raiser for the veep and the others. They talked for two hours and when they finished, he mobilized his entire department and allowed her to use his office to start sticking up photos and notes on a big whiteboard.

"You surprised me," she told him. "I thought after the way I was transferred and everything, you wouldn't support me."

"It has nothing to do with you," Yerushenko said. "The math added up. A female double agent connected to GSD and, possibly, Hezbollah, who may have been a part of an attack or possible kidnapping of a CIA C.O., one who happens to work for me now—and by the way, I don't take anyone else's evaluation as gospel; I can judge my people for myself, thank you—and all of a sudden, this double agent who apparently went to ground after the attempt on you now suddenly reappears and is coming to the States right after Abbasiyah. Books herself into the Waldorf just before a fancy shindig with the Vice-President of the United States. I'd be derelict if I didn't take it seriously."

She set herself and the others in the department to checking every single male—"Trust me, with Dima, it's always going to be men," she told them—from any Middle Eastern country who had either come to the U.S. in the last two months or was scheduled to arrive before the fund-raiser. There were thousands. They got the full lists from the U.S. Department of State and Customs and Border Protection and began going through them.

"What we're looking for is a connection," she told her OCSA coworkers. "Anyone flying from Beirut or who's been in Beirut but may be flying from somewhere else. Anyone with any connection to the Syrian GSD or Damascus. Anyone who might have any kind of a connection to Nightingale or Dima of any kind, any kind of communications or who's been in the same city as either Nightingale or Dima at the same time. Any link, even indirect, of any kind."

With only a few days left before the fund-raiser, they worked in shifts around the clock. Eating cafeteria food and making midnight raids on the vending machines, Joanne dragging her in for company while she sneaked a quick cigarette in the ladies' room.

After three days, they'd narrowed it down to four possibles: Mohamed Hegazy, an Egyptian doctor visiting a brother in Manhattan; Ziad Ghaddar, a Lebanese businessman staying at the Best Western near JFK; Bassam al-Shakran, a Jordanian pharmaceutical salesman who had been to both Baghdad and Beirut within the last two months, had arrived three days ago from Amman and was staying with a cousin in Brooklyn; and Abdel Yassin, a Jordanian college student, also from Amman, coming in on a student visa for Brooklyn College.

"If you had to pick one, who would it be?" Saul asked her on the third day. They were with Yerushenko in his office, the entire wall covered with notes, papers, photos and screen captures with colored marker lines connecting them like a web created by an insane spider.

"The two Jordanians," she said, tapping their photos on the wall. "The salesman's cousin lives in Gravesend." She indicated the neighborhood in Brooklyn on a map of New York City. "The other one's going to Brooklyn College, which is in the Midwood-Flatbush area. They're not that far apart. I asked Joanne to check and see what the cousin does."

"And?" Yerushenko asked.

"You're going to love this. He has a fitness equipment company. Treadmills, weight machines, that kind of thing. They sell and service."

"Does the Waldorf have a fitness center?" Saul asked.

She nodded. The two men looked at each other.

"Don't tell me," Yerushenko said. "The Waldorf is one of his customers."

"Head of the class," she said. "They have access to the hotel."

They studied the connections on the wall. There were two line links, mostly because they were both from Amman, between the two Jordanians. Only the salesman had been in Beirut, but that had been three times that they knew about. The last one was just two weeks ago, according to NSA cell phone intercepts.

"Anything else on the Jordanians?" Saul asked.

"This," she said, pointing to a screen capture of a newspaper article in Arabic with a photograph of a young man with a single marker line to al-Shakran's DS-160 photo. "It's an obituary. Al-Shakran's brother. Killed in Iraq."

"Damn," Saul breathed. "Were American troops involved?"

"Don't know. The article doesn't say and Amman Station

hasn't had time to get back to me yet with anything on the brother. We have to assume it's a possibility."

"And a motive." Saul grimaced.

"So how are they going to do it?" Yerushenko asked. "Explosives?"

"Possible. Guns more likely." Saul shrugged. "Assault rifles would be best."

"Where would they get them? New York has pretty strict laws," Yerushenko said.

"Anywhere," Carrie said. "Vermont is not that far and it has the most liberal gun laws in the country. But it's not that hard really. Ten-to-one, they've already got everything they need now."

"What about the security at the fund-raiser? Secret Service for the veep. Metal detectors in the ballroom. They'd have to know they need to deal with it."

"Once they're inside the hotel, the venue's nothing. They could just shoot their way in. With assault rifles you can kill a bunch of people before even the Secret Service could start to react," she said.

"The Secret Service will kill them," Yerushenko said.

Saul and Carrie smiled.

"Sure. But they don't care. And it only takes getting off one or two good shots at the start to get the Veep. Anybody else they kill is just icing on the cake," Saul said.

"What about CTC and David Estes?" she asked.

Saul looked at her curiously. "Whatever you said did the trick. He's a hundred percent behind us. He's even got the director on board."

She glanced past Saul at the window as they pulled into the Trenton station. She watched people get off the train and crowds on the platform surging on. People living their lives with no idea what was coming at them unless they could stop it.

"Who's meeting us?" she asked.

"Captain Koslowski, NYPD Intelligence Division and Counter-Terrorism Bureau. He said he'll either be at Penn Station or he'll have someone waiting for us."

"Not the FBI?"

"Can't keep them out. But I want New York to handle this as much as possible," he said.

Carrie nodded. She wanted to tell Saul about her conversation last night with Virgil but decided against it. She'd only had a few quick hours with David at the Hilton in Tysons Corner before she left at six A.M. to get ready to leave for New York.

"My wife is leaving me," he'd told her. "She didn't even ask me about you or ask me to stop seeing you. She just said I can go back to my whore. She's done."

"Where does that leave us?" she asked.

"I don't know," he said. "What about you?"

"I don't know either," she said.

When she got back to Reston to pack, she'd contacted Virgil in Beirut to see if he'd come up with anything on Dima or Nightingale since she'd left, but he told her there'd been nothing. In any case, Fielding had him doing a black-bag job on some Bahraini diplomat throwing money around Ras Beirut like it was confetti.

"If you're interested in the sex life of Bahrainis away from home, I've got plenty of footage," he told her.

"Send it to Fielding. Give him something he understands," she'd responded.

"Yeah, well the line between porn and tradecraft is getting pretty thin around here," Virgil groused, ending the call.

So Beirut had nothing. How was that possible? Where

had Dima been all this time? It couldn't have been in Beirut. Dima wasn't the sort of girl who went unnoticed, especially in Beirut, where everyone notices everything. And who was she working for? March 14, the Maronite Christian faction? Hezbollah? The Syrians? The Iranians? After Abbasiyah, everyone assumed that if there was an attack, it would be the Sunnis. Al-Qaeda. But maybe it was the Iranians planning to blame it on the Sunnis.

Then a thought hit her. She sat up ramrod straight as the train pulled out of Trenton station. Maybe it was the other way around.

What if AQI, al-Qaeda in Iraq, was using Dima and her connections to the Syrians to hit the Waldorf and blame it on the Iranians?

Hell, it was possible. For part of the time she'd been in OCSA, when she wasn't working Beirut, her official assignment was al-Qaeda. And then last year, when she'd been stationed in Baghdad, she'd spent a lot of her time studying AQI, especially the tiny bits and pieces of intel they had on Abu Nazir, the leader of AQI, and the one thing she'd come away with was that he was devious. He never did anything simple or straightforward. Ever. An attack on the Waldorf with Syrian-Iranian connections would be just the sort of thing he'd do and then leverage it in Baghdad.

There's something else going on, she thought. She just couldn't put her finger on it, watching Saul packing up his laptop as they went underground into Penn Station.

CHAPTER 13

New York, New York

Koslowski and one of his men were waiting for them on the platform. Koslowski was a stocky six-footer with sandy hair, wearing jeans and a leather jacket. The man with him, Gillespie, was in a windbreaker and a Yankees baseball cap. Despite the casual clothes, they both had "cop" written all over them.

"Saul, good to see you again. You must be Mathison," Koslowski said to Carrie, showing her his badge. "You know this woman Dima? We're calling her by her cover name, Jihan. We're concerned she might change her look. Put on a wig. Could you spot her in a crowd like this?" he asked, indicating the people filling the platform from the train. "All we've got is the DS-160 photo."

"I could spot her in Yankee Stadium, Captain," Carrie said.

"I guess we've got the right people then," Koslowski said, grinning to his partner. "Glad you're here."

"Where are we going?" Saul asked as they walked into the main hall in Penn Station.

"We've set up on Forty-Eighth near the UN Plaza. We'll coordinate from there. Our headquarters is out in Queens, too far from the bull's-eye, the Waldorf." He frowned. "We'll have four Hercules teams, plus normal NYPD security details on the outside, with increasing security the closer we get to the bull's-eye."

"Lot of firepower. You're taking this seriously. Good," Saul said. "What about surveillance on the Jordanians?"

"Nothing, as we discussed. We don't want to spook 'em. And we're covering all four of the ones you sent us. But we have a warrant and we've bugged their land phones and the cell towers near their locations. We've got ears on every call."

"Arabic-speaking?" Carrie asked. Unless the monitors listening in on the calls spoke Arabic, they wouldn't be of much use.

"Yes," he nodded.

"What about Dima—sorry, Jihan? When does she get in?" Carrie asked.

"Her plane just landed. She's already through customs at JFK. Something interesting with her luggage," Koslowski added.

"Oh?" Saul said.

"She brought in a cello. Big case," he said.

"She doesn't play an instrument," Carrie said.

Koslowski nodded grimly. "That's what we thought. This little lady," he said, indicating Carrie to Saul, "definitely got our attention."

"What else?" Saul asked.

"FBI'll be coming. Special Agent Sanders. Also, we'll have to coordinate with the Secret Service because of the Veep. We're holding off notifying them for the moment," Koslowski said.

"Good. We want you guys to take the lead, not the Bureau. And we don't want Vice-President Chasen or the governor or anyone else canceling anything till the very last second," Saul said.

Koslowski and Gillespie exchanged cop looks as they came out on Seventh Avenue. Traffic, people, a cool, crisp afternoon.

"Our thinking exactly. Get them inside the killing box, then shut it down. Of course, once the Feds show up and the pissing contest over jurisdiction starts . . ." Koslowski shrugged. He led them to a police squad car parked illegally in front of Penn Station, being watched over by a uniformed policeman.

"I'll deal with Agent Sanders. Director Estes, Counterterrorism Center back at Langley, is on it," Saul said as they got into the squad car.

Gillespie got behind the wheel. They drove around the block to Eighth Avenue, then up to Forty-Second Street and across town.

The office was on the thirty-seventh floor of a steel and glass building overlooking the UN Plaza and the East River. The building housed a number of corporations and several foreign consulates. Gillespie told them there was a direct, highly secure link to their headquarters in Queens. There were some forty people in the office, some in plainclothes, most wearing blue NYPD Counter-Terrorism Bureau T-shirts working computers and banks of flat-screen TV monitors showing street views of Manhattan, including a five-block radius in every direction around the Waldorf Astoria, plus interior security camera views inside the hotel.

"How much street video surveillance have you got?" Saul asked after he and Carrie had set up their laptops at a big conference table.

"A lot of people don't realize we've got virtually every inch of lower Manhattan from Battery Park to midtown covered with surveillance cameras. Obviously, we're holding off on the suspects' locations, though at some point we'll try to kick that in," Koslowski said.

"Is there anybody on Dim—Jihan?" Carrie asked him.

"We've got a plainclothes team driving an unmarked car. Last I heard," he said, looking at Gillespie, "they're on the Van Wyck. One thing," he added. "We'll need you on Jihan. Make sure we've got her covered."

Carrie nodded. "But she can't see me. Use cameras or something. The instant she sees me, she knows she's blown. Also . . ." She looked at them and at a heavy-set older man in a suit who joined them. By his age and suit, she assumed he was a senior person in the New York Counter-Terrorism Bureau. "I need your men to understand. We don't want her killed. I can't get intel from a corpse."

The three men, Koslowski, Gillespie and the older man, frowned.

"You understand, our primary concern is the safety of our officers and the civilians—not to mention the Vice-President and the others," the older man said.

"This is Deputy Commissioner Cassani. He's our boss," Koslowski said.

Saul jumped in. "We understand perfectly. It's your call. But we also understand how it is when the adrenaline is pumping in a situation with a bunch of gung-ho guys. We want to make sure that if you have to take her and the others out, the decision is made at your level and not by some wannabe Rambo trying to save the world. There's information in that woman's head that will make this country safer if you can keep her alive for us to interrogate."

"We'll do our best," Cassani said, nodding at the two policemen. "But safety first."

A black female officer came over and whispered something to Koslowski.

"Okay," he said. "She's through the Midtown Tunnel. She'll be at the Waldorf in minutes. Cello and all." He pointed at one of the screens showing traffic emerging from the tunnel on Thirty-Seventh Street. There was a taxi with someone in it with a cello case. Carrie strained but she couldn't see Dima. After a second, the taxi passed out of view.

"What's the cello for?" Cassani asked.

"Best guess?" Saul asked, looking at Koslowski. "Keep assault rifles in the case till just before the party."

Koslowski nodded. "Exactly. We've spoken with the hotel manager. We've arranged a room for her on the twenty-sixth floor. Needless to say, it's completely bugged, with full interior and corridor surveillance."

"No good," Carrie said. "She's March 14, possibly GSD. She's not some stupid amateur. She'll spot the cameras and phone bugs in a New York second. You have to change the room. Now! And don't worry about bugging the land phones. She won't use them, except for room service or something. Give her an hour or two and she'll have a couple of prepaid cell phones. Those are the ones we want to pick up."

Koslowski nodded. He got up and hurried off, pulling out his cell phone. Gillespie and Cassani looked at her appraisingly, as if they were art dealers and she was a piece of art up for auction. Then Cassani grinned.

"Well, Miss Mathison. Welcome to the party."

CHAPTER 14

Lexington and Forty-ninth, New York City

The call came at 9:46 P.M. A voice message left on the answering machine at the Petra Fitness Equipment Company in Brooklyn.

"*Hada ho Jihan. Mataa takun baladiya aneyvan gahiza?*" Dima's voice saying, "This is Jihan. How long will my order take?"

They captured the number of the calling phone from the cell tower in Brooklyn nearest the fitness company that handled the call. It took Koslowski's team only fifteen minutes to track it to a prepaid cell phone Jihan had purchased at an AT&T store on Thirty-Seventh Street. The store was only minutes by cab from the hotel. They had two female Counter-Terrorism Bureau officers working undercover as hotel maids in the Waldorf and three male officers acting as hotel security. They confirmed with the on-site team that Jihan was not in the hotel at that time. When it was forwarded to Koslowski, Carrie translated it for him.

Koslowski nodded.

"We have lift-off," he said.

When one of the undercover maids inspected Jihan's room,

she reported that the cello was standing against the wall and its case was empty. She said she saw no weapons or explosives or anything suspicious.

"When do you start surveillance on the suspects?" Saul asked Koslowski.

"A little after midnight," he said, checking his watch. "We're totally passive. Two hidden cameras. One on the roof of the building across the street from the fitness company, the other across from the Jordanian salesman's cousin's apartment in Gravesend. Two of the Hercules teams go into the hotel at oh three hundred hours. They'll stay in suites until we decide to move."

"You'll take them in Jihan's room just before they go operational?" Saul asked.

"That's the plan," Koslowski said, pouring himself a cup of coffee.

Less than an hour later, the whole thing began to unravel. It started with a call from NYPD Counter-Terrorism's Queens headquarters. Koslowski came over to Carrie and Saul, looking grim.

"We had a helicopter do a fly-by to do an infrared scan on the Jordanians. Just to cover our asses before we put in the surveillance cameras. The college kid, Abdel Yassin, isn't in his apartment. We don't know where he is."

"College kid my ass. He's thirty years old," Gillespie growled.

"That's not all," Koslowski said, putting two satellite photographs on the table. They were of the same location: the Petra Fitness Equipment Company building and parking lot. "Do you see it?"

Saul and Carrie studied the photos. Then she saw it.

"Shit," she said.

"What's shit?" Saul said.

"One of the trucks is missing."

"All right, but what does it mean?" Gillespie asked. "We always assumed the guns would be fitted inside some fitness machine and delivered to the hotel. So they use another truck. What's the problem?"

"The problem is that we don't know what's going on or why they would do that. The problem is that there's an unknown operating here. It obviously has something to do with Yassin and the truck," Carrie said.

"What are you doing about it?" Saul asked.

"We wanted to run it by you two. See if you had any ideas," Koslowski said. "We're thinking of doing an APB on Yassin and the truck with a 'Do Not Approach or Attempt to Apprehend.'"

"Don't," Carrie said sharply. "You have ordinary cops who don't know what this is about and if they get too close, even inadvertently, they'll spook Yassin. The situation goes from unknown to uncontrollable in a nanosecond. I repeat, we don't know what this is about yet."

"She's right," Saul said.

"It's my fault," she said.

"How's it your fault?" Koslowski asked, looking at her.

"There's something else going on here. I've sensed it all along because the pieces don't fit. If Dima—sorry, Jihan is GSD or Hezbollah, I can see Syria involved, I can see Hezbollah, I can see Iran, but for the life of me, I can't see the Sunnis in this. And it has nothing to do with Abbasiyah. I should have figured it out," she said, shoving the laptop away from her. She looked out the window at the lights of the buildings on First Avenue. This is where September 11 happened, she thought, not far from here.

"Don't beat yourself up. None of the rest of us figured it out either," Koslowski said.

"What are you going to do?" Saul said to Koslowski.

"Start the surveillance on the three sites: the cousin's apartment in Gravesend, the factory and the college guy's apartment. We know where they're going. The Waldorf. We'll be waiting," he said grimly.

Carrie got up. "I need to change, shower. I can't stay here. I need to think," she said.

Saul looked at her, concerned. "You've been going nonstop for days," he said. "Take a breather."

"We booked rooms for you guys at the Marriott," Koslowski said. "On Lexington and Forty-Ninth. You can walk from here. Clean up. Grab a bite."

"Saul, I'll see you later," she said, grabbing her jacket.

"Wait," Koslowski said. "I'm sending Sergeant Watson with you. Leonora," he called over to the young black woman officer who had spoken to him earlier.

Carrie made a face. "I'm a big girl, Captain. I won't get lost in the big bad city."

"It's not that," he said as the woman, Leonora, came over. "You're critical to us. Out there"—he gestured at the window— "anything can happen. You could accidently run into Jihan on the street. I can't let you go without one of ours. Besides," he said, smiling, "she can keep you company. You can both grab a bite on the department. When you're ready, come back."

She and the policewoman, Leonora, walked to the hotel. The night was cool, crisp, people on the streets hurrying along, traffic normal for a weekday evening in Manhattan. Carrie checked in to the Marriott. They went up and after Leonora checked out the room, Carrie undressed. Leonora turned on the TV.

"He seems like a good guy, Koslowski," Carrie said, heading for the shower.

"He's one of the good ones." Leonora nodded. "Don't be fooled. He never does things simply."

It was while she was taking her shower, letting the warm water run over her, eyes closed, feeling everything that had happened over the past few weeks since Beirut start to drain away, that she found herself thinking about what Leonora had said about Koslowski. Not simple.

Simple.

And then she had it. Son of a bitch! The thing that had been bothering her all along. The thought jolted her so much she nearly ran out of the shower naked. She stood under the water, forcing herself to breathe.

Take it easy, she told herself. Think it through. She was good. Her mind was clear, meds okay. She was onto something.

He never does things simply. Abu Nazir. Damn him! What if the thought she'd had on the train was right? All along they'd assumed because of Dima and what had happened to her with Nightingale in Beirut that it was a Hezbollah or an Iranian operation. But what if it wasn't? What if it was AQI?

If it was Abu Nazir, he wouldn't do it simple. Never. That wasn't his style. There would be more than one attack. It wasn't just the Waldorf, which could be just a diversion! What was it Julia had said about her husband Abbas's reaction: "It was the way he said it . . . It scared me." There was going to be a second, separate attack. Something big. Even bigger than taking out the Vice-President. Something Abu Nazir could say to the Sunnis was retaliation for Abbasiyah. If he pulled it off, the Sunnis would flock to him. He could take all of Anbar Province. And it involved Abdel Yassin and the missing truck!

They had to find that missing truck—and fast. And do the

same thing they were doing with Dima and the Waldorf: wait till the last second, trap it, and kill it.

She got out of the shower, put on a fresh pair of jeans, a top and jacket. Her hair was still wet and she looked like a drowned rat, but that didn't matter.

"Come on," she told Leonora. "We have to go back to the office."

"What about dinner?" the policewoman said, getting up. "Believe me, it isn't often the department pays."

"I don't care," Carrie said, heading for the door. "We can order Chinese."

"Why? What's up?"

"I think I know how to find that truck," she said.

CHAPTER 15

Red Hook, Brooklyn, New York

"Back so soon?" Saul said over his shoulder. He and Koslowski and a handful of others were looking at security camera videos from sites around Brooklyn.

"I think I know how to find the truck," Carrie said, taking off her jacket and sitting at the table. Leonora sat next to her. Saul, Koslowski, Gillespie and a couple of other officers joined them.

"Well, Mathison, you certainly know how to get our attention," Koslowski said. "What've you got?"

"I'm an idiot," she said. "It was right in front of us. We knew Bassam al-Shakran, the Jordanian pharmaceutical salesman, had been in Iraq, and his brother was killed there. All along, because of Dima, and Nightingale in Beirut, we assumed the attack was coming from Hezbollah or the Iranians. But the Jordanians are Sunnis, not Shiites. Like al-Qaeda. What if the attack is coming from Abu Nazir in Iraq?"

"Suppose it is. So what?" Gillespie said.

"He never does just one attack."

"Never?" Gillespie asked.

"Listen, I was in Iraq. I studied this guy there and I've

looked at everything we have on him in Langley. He's never done anything like a single attack. Not ever," she said.

"Are you suggesting the Waldorf's a diversion?" Koslowski said, lasering in on her.

She nodded. "For something bigger."

"Like what?" Gillespie said.

"You tell me. I'm sure NYPD counterintelligence has a list of potential targets and probabilities."

"Sure. The Empire State Building, the Chrysler Building, the B of A Tower, the Statue of Liberty, Times Square, Grand Central Station, the UN, the Stock Exchange, the Federal Reserve, Lincoln Center, Yankee Stadium—although it's out of season—Madison Square Garden, bridges, tunnels. Take your pick. This is New York; the list is endless," Gillespie said.

"These guys are in Brooklyn. Anything there?" Saul asked.

"The Brooklyn Bridge," Leonora suggested.

"Interesting," Carrie said.

"Why interesting?" Koslowski said.

"On 9/11, there was a photograph of people fleeing from Manhattan on foot across the Brooklyn Bridge."

"Yeah, it was a famous picture. Among others. What about it?"

"It became iconic in the Middle East," she said. "At the time, Ayman al-Zawahiri was reported to have said, 'Next time we'll eliminate their means of escape too.'"

For a moment, no one spoke. They were New Yorkers, she realized. She had brought memories of the day back to them.

"What about the truck?" Saul said. "You said you thought of something."

"Yes," she said. "Suppose it is the Empire State Building or the Brooklyn Bridge or whatever. They're not flying planes, so it means a truck filled with explosives. Think. What explosive would they use?"

"Of course," Saul said, slapping the table. "HMTD. They flew in. Had to go through security. They didn't bring anything in with them."

"HMTD," Koslowski said. "Hexamethylene triperoxide diamine. We've always figured that would be what they would use. It's cheap. Powerful. You can make it from three ordinary household products that are all perfectly legal and that you can purchase anywhere without ever attracting the slightest attention. HMTD and, of course, fertilizer have always been our assumptions." He looked around the table, where the others of his team were nodding.

"Except it has a drawback," Carrie put in.

"We know. It's super unstable. Very volatile. The slightest jar, or if the temperature gets a little too warm, and—pow!" Gillespie said, snapping his fingers. "Dealing with it at room temperature is extremely dangerous."

"I see what she's getting at," Koslowski said. "The only way to be sure it won't go off until you need it is to refrigerate it."

"Exactly. We check every refrigerated storage facility in New York City, starting with Brooklyn," Saul said. "We'll find the truck nearby."

"There's another possibility," Koslowski added. "The explosive could be in one of their apartments or inside the fitness company building."

"I thought of that," Carrie said. "If they're using a number of refrigerators—and they'll need a lot because it'll take a ton of explosives to take something like the Brooklyn Bridge down—they'll have to be burning electricity like crazy. Check with the power company on the usage at the fitness company and their apartments. If it's gone up a whole lot recently at one of them, that's where it is."

"I'll get right on it. Wake the bastards up. Everyone hates Con Ed anyway," Gillespie said, getting up and going over to a phone. Carrie checked her watch. It was after three in the morning. When she looked up, Koslowski was watching her.

"Not bad, Carrie," he said, grinning widely. "If you ever decide to leave the CIA, you've got a job in New York if you want it."

"I'll keep it in mind, Captain," she said, glancing sideways at Saul, who was focused on his laptop screen.

Forty minutes later, one of the male officers jumped up.

"Got it," he called out, coming over. "The truck's parked in a lot one block from a refrigerated storage warehouse in Red Hook. We told our guys to look for it but leave it alone. Just drive on by and don't go back. Rookie patrol officer spotted it. Said they painted over the Petra Fitness company logo on the side of the truck and replaced it with a pizza restaurant, but he said the paint job was easy to spot."

"Where's Red Hook?" Saul asked.

"From where that location is you can go up the Brooklyn-Queens Expressway and be on the Brooklyn Bridge in less than five minutes. Manhattan in ten minutes," the officer said.

Saul looked at Koslowski. "Now what?"

"We're gonna need more resources," Koslowski said, getting up and taking out his cell phone. "I need to call the commissioner."

"Did somebody say 'resources'?" said a man in a gray business suit who was just coming in, followed by a half dozen men in suits and about twenty men in military-style SWAT gear with the acronym "HRT" in Day-Glo paint on their jackets.

"I'm Supervisory Special Agent Sanders," he said to Carrie and Saul.

"Great," Gillespie muttered under his breath. "The Feds are here."

Sanders came over to Carrie.

"You must be Mathison. I guess you're the little lady who got us all down here. I hope to hell you know what you're doing," he said.

"I could say the same about you," she said.

"They're on the move," Leonora said, indicating one of the TV monitors. The screen showed the Petra Fitness Equipment Company building and parking lot as viewed from the hidden video camera they'd installed on the roof of the building across the street. On the screen, two men—one of whom they'd identified as Bassam al-Shakran, the Jordanian salesman, from a frozen image that, though blurry and enlarged, appeared to be of him, and the other, the driver, an Arab-looking man they didn't know—had gotten into one of the Petra company's panel trucks.

It was 9:46 A.M. Carrie rubbed her eyes. They'd been up all night and they had a long day ahead of them. She'd just come back from the restroom, where she'd stepped inside a stall to take her meds before going to the sink and splashing her face with water.

"Assuming they're going to the Waldorf, how will they go?" Saul asked.

Gillespie shrugged. "Fastest would be Shore Parkway to the Gowanus Expressway to the Brooklyn Bridge," he said.

"So we don't know if they're going to hit the bridge or the hotel," one of the FBI men with Sanders said.

"Yes, we do," Carrie said as the truck passed out of the camera's view. "It's the wrong truck to hit the bridge. They're headed for the Waldorf."

"Do we have air surveillance?" Sanders asked.

"Over here," Koslowski said, pointing to one of the monitors that showed traffic on a Brooklyn street as seen from above. "We've got one of our AW119 helicopters flying high enough so they won't hear it. See the truck?" He pointed out the white panel truck in the traffic flow.

"They can't follow continuously," Saul said. "We don't want it spotted."

They watched the truck make a right turn onto a highway.

"They know. There it is. They're on the Belt Parkway. Looks like they're headed for Manhattan all right."

"We could take them out now," Sanders said. "Set up a roadblock. My sharpshooters. Never let them get near the Waldorf."

Koslowski made a face. "I don't think—"

"The minute you do you alert the other team. You think there are no media in New York City?" Carrie said, jumping in. "Once that happens you don't know what they'll do. And if they spot your roadblock and start improvising, what then? How many dead civilians do you want? Not to mention we don't know what's in that truck. A couple of pounds of C-4 would make one hell of a hole in Park Avenue. We want them contained."

Sanders stared at her. "You understand, Miss Mathison, you're here to observe," he said.

"Well, you just heard my damn observation, Special Agent," she said, and heard Gillespie snort, stifling a laugh.

"Easy, boys and girls," Koslowski said. "We've got two full Hercules teams, all of them ex–Navy SEALs, Delta, CIA, who spent the night in suites inside the Waldorf, just two floors above Jihan's room. We've got another Hercules team set up in the UBS office on Forty-Ninth across the street and another team inside the FedEx on Park Avenue. Plus, we'll have plenty of regular NYPD to lock down the block completely before the main event. Once we close it, we won't let a mosquito in or out."

"What about this woman, this Jihan? Are we sure she's in the hotel?" Sanders asked.

"We're monitoring the hotel corridor security camera. Here's the feed," Gillespie said, pointing out another of the monitors, showing the hotel corridor. "She went into the room at 12:17 P.M. and hasn't come out."

"Let's look at her going in," Koslowski said.

"Go to double oh sixteen hours," Gillespie said to one of his officers, who typed on his computer. They watched the corridor flash back in time to sixteen minutes after midnight. They waited, then saw a slim, stylish woman with long blond hair get out of the elevator and walk to one of the rooms. "Freeze it."

"You know this woman?" Sanders asked Carrie.

"As a double agent in Beirut. Yes," she said.

"Triple," Saul muttered.

"And that's her? No question?" Sanders said persistently.

"She's wearing a blond wig, but yes, that's Dima, a.k.a. Jihan."

"And nothing since?" Koslowski asked the officer.

"Nothing. Yesterday she requested room service for breakfast for after eleven A.M. We suspect she gets up late," the officer said.

"Okay. You keep your eyes peeled on her corridor. Nothing else. And let's keep monitoring her phones and the room phone, everyone," Koslowski called out. "Anything she does, let me know ASAP. Don't be afraid to interrupt me."

"What about the other two possibles we came up with? The Egyptian doctor and Ghaddar, the Lebanese businessman. Anything?" Saul asked, looking up from his laptop.

"We put front and back surveillance on them. Apart from the fact that our Egyptian doctor seems to have a fascination with the hookers on Tenth Avenue, they seem to be who they say they are," Gillespie said.

"And the truck? Where is it now?" Carrie asked.

Gillespie looked at the monitor showing the view from the helicopter camera.

"Looks like Fort Hamilton. See the water?" he said, referring to the bay. "They'll be coming up on the Verrazano Bridge shortly."

"What about the other truck? This refrigerated storage facility? The HMTD?" Sanders asked.

"That's where we'd like your Hostage Rescue Team," Koslowski said. "The problem is, we don't know who's watching. If we did, we could set up and the minute this Abdel Yassin shows up, take the son of a bitch down."

"We have no idea where he is right now?" Saul asked.

Koslowski shook his head. "We're checking to see if he bought a cell phone and we've been monitoring all the calls in the Midwood-Flatbush section of Brooklyn for the past two days. So far nothing."

"When do you think he'll move?" Sanders asked Carrie.

"Late afternoon. Early evening. They don't want to do something that will alert the authorities before their Waldorf operation is in motion. The Veep is scheduled to arrive at the Waldorf at eight thirty-five P.M. Figure Yassin and whoever else is with him will be at the storage place probably after six P.M.," she said.

"Where is this place?" Sanders asked.

"Red Hook in Brooklyn. Mostly an industrial area right near the waterfront," Koslowski said.

"We'll move our people in undercover this morning," Sanders said. "Set up so we can close it down."

"No uniforms, no badges, nothing that attracts attention of any kind, especially from locals. If they send an alert, we could blow the whole thing," Carrie said.

"Why are you so worried about locals? Won't they cooperate?" Sanders said.

Koslowski half-smiled. "Listen, you remember the movie *Casablanca*? You know the part where Humphrey Bogart tells the Nazi that there are certain sections in New York he advised even the German army not to try to enter?"

"What about it?"

"He was talking about Red Hook," Koslowski said.

CHAPTER 16

Park Avenue, New York City

There were two of them: Bassam al-Shakran, the Jordanian pharmaceutical salesman, and another man, whom they couldn't immediately identify. They watched on the monitor showing the view from the hidden camera across the street from the hotel as two men brought what looked like a treadmill machine wrapped in plastic off their panel truck and into the service entrance of the Waldorf Astoria on a dolly.

"That's him. That's Bassam," Carrie said.

"Who's the other guy? Is it the cousin?" Gillespie asked.

"It's the cousin. Mohammad al-Salman. Take a look," Leonora said. They went over to her computer. On the screen was a photograph with an article from a local newspaper showing two Arab men in suits with an imam. The article was about a donation they had made to the local mosque, the Islamic Foundation Masjid. "That's Mohammad." She pointed.

"You were right on the money," Koslowski said to Carrie.

They switched to a security camera video feed inside the hotel to watch the two men take the treadmill into the service elevator, but the monitor for the security camera on the nineteenth floor showed only one of the men getting out of the elevator to wheel the machine into the fitness center.

"I see Mohammad," Koslowski said. "Where's Bassam?"

"Look. The plastic covering on the machine's been cut." Carrie pointed.

They all turned to the monitor showing the hotel corridor outside Dima's room.

"Look, Bassam," Gillespie said, pointing. They watched al-Shakran walk down the corridor to Dima's room and knock on the door. "What's he carrying? A duffel bag?"

"A duffel bag," Gillespie said grimly. "What'll you bet is in it?"

They watched the hotel room door open and caught a brief glimpse of the woman in the blond wig letting him in. She put a "Do Not Disturb" hanger on the door and closed it. The corridor was empty.

"Now what?" Agent Sanders said, getting off the phone with the HRT team he had dispatched to Red Hook.

"We wait," Carrie said.

"For what?"

"For Mohammad to come back," she said.

"If he's coming back," Sanders said.

"He'll be back," she said. All along she had thought that to try to get through the Secret Service—even with the element of surprise—to the Vice-President wasn't a one-man job. And Dima wasn't going to be doing any of the shooting. Not Dima. So the cousin would have to come back to the hotel.

Koslowski was on his phone with Tom Raeden, the NYPD Hercules team leader. He and his men were in their Waldorf suites. One of the monitors showed them with their gear in the suite. Raeden was a six-footer with buzz-cut blond hair and the shoulders of a linebacker. Koslowski told them to get ready. With any luck, they would move in a few hours.

"What's happening in Red Hook?" Koslowski asked Sanders.

"We contacted a Mrs. Perez, who owns the storage facility. We've got two men inside. There's an auto-parts warehouse across the street. Our men went in as construction workers. They're setting up hidden cameras now, with ex-SEAL or -Delta snipers on the roofs. They'll be out of sight till the last second. We'll be able to see the feed any minute," Sanders said. "We've also notified the Secret Service. Part of our protocol with them," he explained. "They're keeping the Vice-President to his schedule until further notice."

"What about blocking the route just in case?" Koslowski asked.

"Once they show up with the truck, they'll never get out of that street," Sanders responded. "We've got two big armored trucks that will block off either end of the street at the same time we move in."

"Good." Koslowski nodded. "We need to see the feeds ASAP."

"What about when your people go into the hotel room?" Saul asked. "Will we be able to see anything?"

"Hopefully," Koslowski said. "Two of them will be wearing helmet cameras. It'll be jumpy, but we should see what they see."

"There's our surveillance," Sanders said, pointing at two monitors. One showed the front door to the refrigerated storage facility from a camera across the street. It was in a concrete building with no windows and barbed wire on the roof.

"Like a fortress," one of the Counter-Terrorism Bureau officers muttered.

The other monitor showed the parked panel truck with a

hastily painted sign for Giovanni's Pizza on the side, viewed from a height looking down at an angle from across the street.

"Where'd you put the camera for that one?" Koslowski asked.

"On a telephone pole," one of Sanders's FBI men said.

"What time is it?" someone asked.

"A little after noon," Gillespie said, looking at his watch.

"Going to be a long day," Sanders said.

Two officers, a man and a woman, from the counterterrorism team brought in boxes of deli sandwiches and soft drinks. Everyone grabbed something and started to eat. There was a murmur of conversation.

"There he is," Carrie said, her mouth full, pointing at the monitor showing the view from the FedEx office on Park Avenue.

"Who?"

"Mohammad. The cousin."

They watched a man in a brown suit walk toward the entrance to the Waldorf.

"Good eyes. He changed clothes," Koslowski said.

They watched Mohammad go into the hotel. On another monitor from normal hotel security surveillance they watched him walk across the ornate lobby into the elevator. A minute later, the corridor monitor showed him exit from the elevator, walk past a hotel maid—she was actually one of Koslowski's female officers—knock and enter the hotel room.

"Now all they have to do is wait," Koslowski said.

"Like us," Saul said.

"Where'd he leave the truck?" Sanders asked.

"Probably in a parking structure, then took the subway back," Koslowski said. "I've got plainclothes checking all the midtown parking structures for the truck."

"Tell them to be careful approaching. It's likely to be booby-trapped," Saul said.

"We assumed as much," Koslowski said. "We'll have to evacuate and get the bomb squad."

A half hour later he fielded a call from one of the plain-clothes officers.

"We found the truck. It's in a Quik Park on West Fifty-Sixth near Ninth," he announced, and said something on the phone.

"Tell them not to go near it. To wait to evacuate the entire structure and approach only after we take down the Waldorf and Red Hook," Saul said.

"I just did," Koslowski said.

"Son of a bitch, there it is," one of the FBI men said, pointing at one of the monitors.

"Is that him?" Gillespie asked.

"That's him," Koslowski said, glancing at the photograph on the table. "Abdel Yassin. Welcome back to the party. Who's that with him?"

"I don't know," Carrie said, "but tell your people to try not to kill him. If he's from a local cell, once this is over you're going to want to take them all down."

"There they go," Gillespie said as the truck drove away and out of the frame of the hidden camera, coming east, out of the sun, low on the horizon, hovering just above the building line. In a little while, it would be dark.

"Time?" Koslowski called out.

"Seventeen eleven hours," Leonora said, checking her watch.

"Tell your people to get ready," Koslowski said to Sanders.

"Yours too," Sanders said, talking on the phone.

Koslowski alerted Raeden and his team and the undercover operatives inside the Waldorf. He told Gillespie to get the outside perimeters ready to completely close off several city blocks around the hotel but not to move until the Hercules teams did.

"Once we say 'go,' no one, I mean no one, gets into or out of the Waldorf Astoria," he said.

All eyes were on two monitors: one showing the view from across the street from the refrigerated storage facility in Red Hook, the other showing the corridor security camera view where Dima and the two Jordanians were still in the room. They hadn't stirred all day. They had attached sound sensors on the floor of the room above Dima's, but there had been surprisingly little conversation or movement, although the technician did report a number of clicklike sounds that suggested they were loading and checking their weapons.

They watched on the monitor as the truck with the pizza restaurant name on its side drove up to the refrigeration facility and parked in the curbside loading space. The two men, Yassin and the unknown man who looked Middle Eastern, both dressed in white coveralls, got out of the truck. They took a steel flatbed handcart out of the truck into the storage building.

"Move into position," Sanders said into his phone. "Take 'em down."

They saw a squad of ten men, now dressed in full SWAT gear with HK33 assault rifles, the backs of their jackets marked "FBI HRT" in yellow Day-Glo letters, come out of the building across the way and split into two teams, deployed against the refrigeration building on either side of the door.

Watching, Carrie knew there were also at least two snipers who would now position themselves for firing on the roof of the building from which the team had emerged. She couldn't see the armored trucks and the rest of the team deploying to block off both sides of the street, but from Sanders's conversation on his cell phone, she assumed they were moving into position.

Koslowski and Gillespie looked at each other and nodded.

Koslowski called Raeden.

"Go," he said. "It's all yours, Tom."

"We're on," Gillespie said into his cell phone to the NYPD commander outside the Waldorf.

The two Hercules teams inside the Waldorf were now in motion, Carrie knew. They would be making their way down the stairs to the floor where Dima and the Jordanians were. Anyone they encountered on the stairs or in the hallway from this point on would be taken into custody. Then, on the monitor, she saw first one, then a number of the Hercules team members emerge into the corridor and move toward the room. One of the undercover maids was with them. In her hand was a Beretta nine-millimeter pistol.

The team positioned themselves on both sides of the room door. They wore Kevlar vests and were armed with M4A1 assault rifles and snub-nosed shotguns.

"Captain, tell them not to kill her," Carrie said to Koslowski. He didn't answer, his eyes riveted on the screen. They watched the maid knock on the door.

At that moment on the other TV, the two Arab men emerged from the refrigeration facility pushing the handcart stacked six rows high with large cartons.

It was the largest amount of HMTD Carrie had ever seen. There had to be a good thousand pounds there. The largest amount of it she'd ever even heard of. They really were going to take something serious down.

The HRT teams swarmed toward them, rifles aimed,

shouting for them to put the boxes down and raise their hands in the air. For an instant, the two men hesitated.

The Jordanian, Yassin, started to reach into his pocket. Cell phone! He's going to detonate, Carrie thought. Shoot! Now!

Instantly a bullet ripped into his head from across the street. The cart started to roll. It's going to tip over! she thought, instinctively tensing for the explosion. They're all going to die! As Yassin's body hit the pavement, the cart started to tip. It was like watching a disaster in slow motion. Her mind screamed, It's going to blow! At the same time, two HRT men opened fire on the second man, who crumpled to the pavement.

Don't hit the cartons! she thought, cringing in anticipation of the explosion. If just one of those bullets hit . . . They watched in horror as the handcart tipped over, the cartons spilling into the street, one of them bursting open to show something white inside. The HMTD.

Nothing happened.

They lucked out, Carrie thought, breathing again. The HMTD was still cold enough to keep it stable, otherwise they would have all been killed. The HRT team swarmed around the cartons and the two downed men.

"Both dead," Sanders announced to the room.

They'd been incredibly lucky. They'd have to get the HMTD back into refrigeration right away. It was just lying out there in the street. She barely had time to complete the thought.

"Housecleaning service," the undercover maid in the hotel corridor on the other monitor said, and then stepped away and out of range of the door.

"Come back later," said Dima's voice from behind the door.

Raeden, the Hercules team leader, nodded. A second man put a card key—Carrie assumed it was a master key—into the door slot, grabbed the handle when it turned green and pushed the door open.

"I said come back later," a woman said. It was Dima. Carrie could see her coming toward the door. Only one of the men, Bassam al-Shakran, was visible as the team barged into the room. He was holding what looked like an AR-15. Dima screamed as the Hercules team charged into the room.

The helmet camera of the lead Hercules team member showed a jumpy image as Bassam dived to the side and fired his rifle. The cousin fired a second AR-15 at Raeden as a storm of shooting erupted inside the room, loud popping shots sounding dense as hail. The helmet camera dropped to floor level, showing the room sideways. Raeden. Is he dead? she wondered. Are they all down? What's going on? All she could see from the helmet camera were legs moving; hard to tell whose.

It was over in seconds.

"I can't see. What about Dima? Is she alive?" Carrie cried out.

Gillespie was shouting into his phone to secure the site. Sanders was barking into the phone, calling the Secret Service. Koslowski was looking at the monitor and listening to someone on his cell phone. Probably one of his team inside the room.

"Is she alive, dammit?" Carrie shouted.

Koslowski turned to her, his face a mask.

CHAPTER 17

Lenox Hill, New York City

They took Dima to Lenox Hill, the nearest hospital trauma emergency room. Carrie, Saul and Koslowski raced straight up Park Avenue to Seventy-Seventh Street in a squad car. By the time they got there, several other members of the Hercules team were with Raeden, who'd been knocked down by a round from an AR-15.

Carrie raced past them and found a group of doctors and police around a curtained space. Two NYPD patrolmen stopped her.

"Is Jihan in there?" she asked.

"Let her through," Koslowski said, and they pushed past the police. A youngish doctor and a nurse were making notes on a computer screen. Dima was lying motionless on a gurney, her eyes open.

"Is she dead?" Carrie asked.

"She was already dead when she arrived," the doctor said over his shoulder. "Are you a relative?"

"No, nothing like that," she said, looking at Dima, her blouse open, her chest unbelievably bloody between her breasts, and thinking, Why did you do it? You were the party girl, not a true believer. What were you playing at this time? Who put you up to this? She hated seeing her exposed like that. Looking around, she found a folded sheet at the foot of the gurney and pulled it up over Dima's body and face.

She backed out and went over to Raeden, surrounded by his team. His shirt was off and there was a red bruise the size of a man's hand on his chest right over his heart.

"You okay?" she asked him.

He nodded. "Thank God for Kevlar. Saved my ass."

"It wasn't your ass that round hit," one of his teammates said, and the others sniggered.

"You Mathison?" Raeden asked her.

"Yes."

"We had to take her down. I'm sorry," he said.

"So am I," she said. "I had questions only she could answer."

When she came out of the curtained-off area they'd put Raeden in, she saw David Estes standing with Saul, Koslowski and Sanders. They were watching a television news conference on a TV mounted on the wall near the nurses' station. Deputy Commissioner Cassani was standing there, along with the mayor and the police commissioner. The mayor was doing the talking.

"I want to stress again that thanks to the excellent work of New York's Counter-Terrorism Bureau in close cooperation with their counterparts in the FBI, this terrorist plot against our city was completely foiled without a single officer or innocent civilian being harmed. There was no loss of life and no damage done to property. This was a superb example of what we do every day to protect our citizens," the mayor said.

"Acts like he did it single-handed," Sanders muttered.

"He's a politician. Taking credit for something they had nothing to do with is what they do best," Saul said.

"He didn't even know about it till about an hour ago," Sanders said with a grimace. He looked at Carrie. "By the way, you were right. They were going after the Brooklyn Bridge. We found a schematic in the truck."

"How?" Saul asked.

"Looks like they were going to park the truck right next to one of the suspension towers," Sanders said.

"Would it have worked?"

"I have no idea. Probably take a team of structural engineers to figure that one out, but maybe." He shrugged. "Right in the middle of evening rush hour. They would've killed a lot of people."

Estes looked away from the TV and directly at Carrie.

"You okay?" he asked.

"Dima's dead," she said. "I needed to interrogate her. I have a lot of questions, David," she said, looking into his eyes. "A lot."

He looked around.

"Is there a place we can talk?" he asked one of the nurses.

"There's a chapel down the hall," she said.

"C'mon," he said to Carrie.

"Maybe I should come," Saul said, watching them.

"Give us a minute, Saul," Estes said, and walked down the hall. After a second, Carrie followed. They walked into an empty room with folding chairs and, on a sideboard against the far wall, a cross and a menorah.

"I needed to see you," he said. "We left a lot unsaid."

"I can't think about that now, David. I really can't. I knew this woman. I knew her. She was a stupid, pretty party girl who liked to drink and seduce men, and the only reason she was working with us was the money. Her fantasy wasn't some *jihadi* paradise bullshit, it was a rich good-looking guy who would take care of her. So what in the hell was she doing here? How did that happen? You tell me."

"I don't know, but I think we both know you're not going to let it go till you find out."

She took a breath. "You got that right. Why did you come?"

"I had to see you." He looked around the room. "But not here. I'm at the New York Palace on Madison. Room 4208. You can see Saint Patrick's and Rockefeller Center."

"I'm not a damn tourist, David. I don't care."

"Look," he said, glancing at his watch. "I have to meet with Cassani and the mayor and the Secret Service guys. My job is such bullshit sometimes. Don't think there aren't times when I envy the people under me who do the real work. Come by tonight and we'll talk."

"Am I still in exile to Intel Analysis? Maybe you don't like me, but Yerushenko does."

"We'll talk," he said, heading for the door.

She and Saul were sitting at a table in the Marriott's modernistic bar. Although it was almost midnight, the bar was crowded with businessmen and sleek, unbelievably slim women. The noise level was high, too high to hear the TV behind the bar showing NBA highlights.

"You want to tell me about it?" Saul asked.

"No," she said, poking the lime slice in her margarita with her fingernail. "Because then you might feel you had to do something about it."

"And you don't want me to?"

"No," she said. "I don't."

At the bar, there was a sound of loud laughter. Someone called out, "Did you see Dwyane Wade's lay-up, man? Effing unbelievable."

"Come on, Carrie. I told you to enlighten him," Saul said. "I didn't say have an affair."

"I'm not having an affair," she said, still toying with her drink.

"Then what is happening?"

She looked directly at him. "None of your damn business. Besides, whatever I did, or whatever you think I did, there are people alive today in New York, maybe even some of the people in this room, because of what I did. So don't lecture me, Saul. I don't deserve it."

"No," he said softly. "You don't." He took a long sip of his single-malt Scotch. "You did a helluva job. Everyone did."

She shook her head, setting her long blond hair moving. "We were lucky. When those FBI guys started shooting around the HMTD, I cringed. One bullet in that stuff and they'd've blown up half of Brooklyn."

"Luck counts too. Napoleon said he'd rather have lucky generals than smart ones."

"Good for Napoleon," she said, and put her hand on his arm. "Don't try to be my father, Saul. I have a father and believe me, one is way more than enough. You know, if I had to choose between being captured and tortured by the Taliban or reliving my childhood, I'd have to think about it a really long time."

"I didn't know," he said. "And you're right. I am a little protective of you. I'm the one who recruited you. I'm not sure I did you any favors." He stared up at the TV screen. Basketball images flashed, something about LeBron James. "Do you care about him?"

"Do you mean am I sexually attracted to David? Yes, but give me some credit. There's a little more to me than that," she said, finishing her drink.

"I give you a lot of credit. What happened today was your doing. I'm not just protective of you because of guilt. You're good, Carrie. Damn good."

She looked around and grabbed her jacket. "This thing isn't over. There are too many questions that need answering. You know what I have to do?" she said.

He nodded.

"Beirut," he said.

"You see?" she said, getting up and squeezing his shoulder. "You do understand me."

"And Estes?"

"That," she said, "is the sixty-four-million-dollar question."

"Be careful," he said, motioning to the waitress for another Scotch.

"Why? What should I be afraid of?"

"Getting what you want."

She took a cab from the Marriott to the New York Palace, the trees in its courtyard strung with lights. I'm like a hooker, going from hotel to hotel, she thought, entering the lobby with its ornate grand staircase. They should have hookers review hotels, she thought, smiling to herself. They spend more time in them than anyone.

She walked straight to the elevator and took it up to the forty-second floor. When she knocked, David Estes opened the door. He had taken off his suit jacket and tie and was holding a glass of red wine.

"You're right," she said, walking in and taking off her jacket. "You can see Rockefeller Center."

"What are you drinking?" he asked.

"Do they have tequila in those little bottles in the courtesy bar?" she asked.

"Lemme look," he said, and went over to the console. He came back with a mini bottle of Jose Cuervo and a glass. "You want ice?"

She grimaced. "Cuervo. You'd think in a fancy place like this, it'd be a little more interesting. Cheers," she said, opening the top and drinking it straight from the bottle.

"Cheers," he said, taking a sip and putting down his wine. He put his arms around her. Pulling her close, he kissed her hard, his hands sliding down to her bottom and pulling her tight against him. She kissed him back, then pushed him away.

"Is this what you wanted to talk about? Maybe you should just put the money on the dresser first," she said.

"You know I didn't mean it like that. I can't stop thinking about you. My marriage ended because of you. Whatever you are to me, believe me, it's not a whore," he said.

She sat on the sofa. From where she was, she could see the tall office buildings, some of their windows still lit up at night, even though it was late.

"Look, David, I'm attracted to you. I want to have sex with you. Maybe I'd like even more. But we're not just people, we're coworkers in a business where everyone around us is a spy. It's not like we're going to be able to keep this secret. So what are you proposing?"

He sat in the chair opposite, leaning toward her, his hands on his knees.

"I'm not sure. I want you. And it's not just sex. I don't know where this is going. Do you?"

"I do." She nodded. "And it doesn't have a happy ending.

Not for me. Not for you either. It won't work. I'm not the housewife type. Trust me, you wouldn't like me. I'm a CIA case officer with a lot of unanswered questions. It's time we cleared the air, you and me."

He took a deep breath and sat back.

"Maybe I'd better have another drink," he said.

"Both of us," she said.

He got up, went over to the minibar and came back with mini bottles of Grey Goose. He poured them into glasses with ice and gave her one.

"What are we drinking to?" he said.

"The truth."

"Well, I did my master's at Harvard. '*Veritas,*'" he said, and they drank. "Let's have it."

"Before we get to us, I have to tell you, there's so much shit going on I don't even know where to start," she said. "Beginning with Beirut."

"Beirut." He nodded. "What about it?"

"Dammit, David, you're smart as hell. You didn't believe Fielding's bullshit any more than Saul did, yet you exiled me from NCS. What was that about? And then I discover redacted material in our files from both Beirut Station and Damascus Station. But to make matters worse, Fielding had eleven phone numbers, three of which had months of calls deleted from NSA files. And you know what day they were deleted?"

"Was it around the same time you left Beirut?"

She looked at him sharply. "How'd you know?"

"I didn't," he said, looking into her eyes. "But I suspected something. This is bad. Really bad."

"Why? Who could have done something like that?"

"Not just who. The more important question is, why?" he said.

"Do you believe me?" she whispered, putting her hand on his knee.

"Yes," he said, putting his hand over hers. "Shit." He grimaced and looked away.

"Who is it?"

"I don't know. But Fielding and the director himself, Bill Walden, go back a long way."

"Better to slap me on the wrist. Was that it?"

"But keep you in the game. Saul believes in you, Carrie. With me it was more complicated."

"Because you're attracted to me?" she said.

He looked away. For a moment, neither of them spoke. They sat there, the view of the skyline between them.

"There's something else," she said.

"What?"

"The girl, Dima. She was Fielding's originally, but I ran her."

"What about her?"

"Let's forget the anomaly about Sunni versus Shiite, al-Qaeda versus Hezbollah, two groups who should never come together. Let's forget about the Syrians and the Iranians and all that coming after Abbasiyah, because none of that makes any sense. Even putting that aside, I knew her better than Fielding ever did. I've been with her when she was so drunk she couldn't stand up. She was fun and sexy, but like every woman alive, she knew she had a sell-by date. She was desperate, do you understand? But for a man. If she ever got her hands on someone rich enough and at least not physically repulsive enough to make her ill, she told me she'd suck his brains out through his dick. So you tell me. What turns her into a red-hot *jihadi*? It doesn't compute."

"No, it doesn't," he said in agreement. "You want to go back to Beirut?"

"I have to," she said. "It's where the answers are."

"What about us?"

"It's impossible. We're impossible. One of us would have to quit the Company. I won't and"—she took his hand—"you shouldn't, David."

"You shouldn't either," he said, making a face.

"So here we are. Two orphans in the storm."

"You didn't kill my marriage, Carrie. I did. The job did. I did."

"*Veritas*," she said, and drank the vodka.

"So here we are." He looked around the room. "Nice room."

"Perfect for cheating wives and husbands," she nodded.

"It wasn't just sex, you know. Not for me. Flattering, that an attractive young woman like you would find me . . ." He hesitated. "I felt alive for the first time in years. Hell of a thing, isn't it?"

"Me too." She came over, wriggled onto his lap and kissed him.

CHAPTER 18

Verdun, Beirut, Lebanon

"I knew you'd be back. Never doubted it for a second. Wait a minute, there," Virgil said, disabling the security alarm. He inserted his Peterson universal key into the door lock, tapped and opened the door. He inched it open a crack, inspected for any secondary alarms and, holding a handheld RF scanner before him like a candle, entered the apartment.

They were on the fourteenth floor of a high-rise on Leonardo da Vinci in the trendy Verdun section of Beirut. The apartment belonged to Rana Saadi, a Lebanese actress and model known in the Middle East for her role in a movie about the love lives of women working in a Beirut beauty salon. Fielding called her cell phone at least twice a week according to the COMINT intercepts on the flash drive Jimbo had given Carrie. Yet, they never went anywhere together, although according to Virgil, they sometimes showed up at the same social function or party.

She followed Virgil into the apartment. Holding his finger to his lips, he began checking for hidden cameras and bugs, using the scanner and studying light fixtures and land phones and removing the plastic plates over electrical outlets. While he checked the rooms, Carrie, her hands in latex gloves, checked the drawers and desk in the bedroom, going through Rana's expensive Huit and Aubade lingerie and, in the closet, her clothes and shoes, being careful to put each thing she touched back in exactly the same position.

"It's clear," he whispered. "But don't talk," he mouthed.

She nodded. She felt with her fingertips along the closet's top shelf and found a photo album. Noting its exact position, she carefully lifted it up and brought it down. She sat on the floor and opened it, while Virgil went about the apartment installing electronic listening devices and hidden cameras. Every room from every angle was to be covered. In CIA parlance, it was a "360 black-bag job."

She pored through the photo album. Mostly pictures of Rana throughout her career, starting as a teenage model on up to her roles on television and in movies. In the pages she went from a thin gawky teenager with long chestnut hair posing with a puppy to a sexy black-haired bombshell in a low-cut dress on the cover of *Spécial* magazine and in promo stills from her films.

Then a picture stopped her cold.

It was a photo of Rana in a magazine ad for Aishti, an upscale women's clothing chain. She was with two other models in what looked like the ABC mall, all of them looking impossibly stylish and slim. One of them was Dima. There was no credit on the front of the photograph, but it was a studio print, the photo pasted on the page. She carefully separated the edge of the print from the page and lifted it up to see the back. A name had been stamped on it: François Abou Murad, Rue Gouraud. She knew where that was, in the Gemmayzeh section of the Ashrafieh district. She pressed it back down and took a photo of the print with her cell phone.

So Dima and Rana knew each other. Were they working together? She raced through the rest of the album, but nothing else caught her eye. She put the album back in the same position on the closet shelf and began rummaging through the pockets of all the clothes hanging in the closet. It was near the end, in the pocket of a short velveteen jacket, that she found a cell phone. She took it out and showed it to Virgil.

He nodded and did a "swipe," NSA-based technology that enabled him to hack someone's cell phone with another appropriately configured cell phone just by coming within a few meters of it. Rana's cell phone was now "slaved," so that via NSA SIGINT satellite communications, Virgil could eavesdrop on everything said or done with it. He tapped the screen and checked the cell number. He and Carrie looked at each other. This wasn't the one that Fielding had called and since Rana wasn't here, it wasn't the one she carried. So what was it for? Carrie wondered.

He looked at his watch. They'd been there almost forty minutes. There wasn't much time left. Carrie put the cell phone back into the jacket pocket, went to a writing table in the dining area that Rana apparently used as a desk and started going through the drawers. It was while she was going through Rana's checkbook and bills that she got the text message from the third person on their team, Ziad Atawi. A member of Les Forces Libanaises, a Maronite Christian militia affiliated with the March 14 group, Ziad had been one of Carrie's old assets in Beirut. Now she had formed a team with him and Virgil without the knowledge of anyone else in the CIA's Beirut Station, especially Fielding.

It read, "leaving bobs." Bob's Easy Diner was a popular Armenian lunchtime spot on Rue Sassine, only a few blocks away. It meant that Rana was leaving the restaurant and might be home any minute. She went over and showed it to Virgil, who nodded. They had to go.

They left the apartment, Virgil carefully resetting the alarm and locking the door. A few minutes later, they parted on a crowded avenue. He was heading back to Iroquois, the new safe house on Independence, near the Muslim cemetery, to monitor Rana from there. Carrie caught a Service to the Corniche, the palm-lined promenade along the sea front, to meet Julia/Fatima. Getting out of the Service, she placed a black *hijab* over her hair.

She spotted Fatima waiting in her black *abaya* and veil near the Mövenpick, not far from where the tourists gathered to take photos of waves crashing against Pigeon Rocks, jutting up out of the water.

"Dearest friend, *afdal sadeeqa*, petals of a chamomile cooled by the night," Carrie said in Arabic, taking Fatima's hand in both of hers.

"Ibn 'Arabi. You quote Ibn 'Arabi," Fatima said, her eyes glistening.

"She is the cure, she the disease," they said, reciting the poem's famous refrain together.

"I missed you. I'm so sorry," Carrie said.

"I thought you were never coming back."

"I would always come back. And I must tell you, what you told me saved lives. Many lives. Whatever anyone else says, what you did was wonderful." Holding hands like schoolgirls, they walked side by side on the promenade, the breeze off the water rustling the palm trees, the sun shining on the sea.

"Was it?" she asked. "Do they believe me now?"

"For them, you are solid gold. So . . ." Carrie hesitated. "How goes it with you?"

"Not good," Fatima said. "Sometimes I think he wants to

kill me. There are days I think it is better to be a dog than a woman."

"Don't, *habibi*. Don't say this. Just tell me, how can I help you?"

Fatima stopped walking and looked at her; only her eyes were not hidden by her veil.

"I want to go to America and get a divorce. That's what I want."

"*Inshallah*, I'll do what I can. I swear."

"Don't swear, Carrie. If you say it will be done, then I know it will be so. How is it they let you back?"

"Because of you," Carrie said, squeezing her hand. "Truly."

"Then I'm glad I did it."

They walked along the Corniche, stopping at a kiosk for ice cream cones that they ate as they walked.

"Anything new?" Carrie asked.

Fatima stopped and tilted her head close to Carrie's. "There's something that's going to happen in the south. On the Israeli side of the border," she said.

"A terrorist incident?"

The woman shook her head. "More than an incident. A provocation." She looked around again. "They think they're ready for war. Soon."

"Where will the incident be?"

"I'm not sure. But Abbas is being deployed in the south to a Lebanese town near the border, Bint Jbeil. Only underground, the entire town is a fortress. A trap for the Zionists. That's all I know."

"Good. There's something else," Carrie said, taking out her iPhone. "Something I want you to look at." They stepped over by the seawall. She brought up Dima's passport photograph. "Do you know her? Have you ever seen her?"

Fatima shook her head. Carrie closed Dima's photo and brought up Rana's picture.

"What about her?"

"That's Rana Saadi. Everyone knows her," Fatima said.

"Have you ever met her? Has Abbas ever spoken about her?" She shook her head again. "I can't help. I'm sorry," she said.

"No matter. I'm so glad to see you," Carrie said.

Fatima looked at her sharply. "You won't forget about America?"

"I won't forget," Carrie said.

She went up the stairs to the studio on Rue Gouraud. It was on the second floor of an old-fashioned colonial-era building. Behind the glass door, a young, very pretty female receptionist sat behind a sleek, ultra-modernistic desk in a tiny reception area.

"*Bonjour.* Do you have an appointment?" the pretty receptionist asked.

"I called earlier. I'm from al-Jadeed, the TV station," Carrie said, handing her a business card with the Jadeed logo she'd had made up yesterday.

"I remember. François—that is, Monsieur Abou Murad is in the studio. I'll let him know you're here."

Carrie looked at the photographs displayed on the walls. Fashion shoots and magazine covers, including a series of female models shot from behind wearing only striped bikini bottoms. After letting her wait fifteen minutes to make sure she knew how important and busy he was, Abou Murad came out and apologized as he led her back to his studio.

"I thought you would bring a crew," he said as they walked into a space with screens, drop cloths and lights, tall windows revealing old colonial-style buildings across the street. He was unbelievably short, not quite a little person, but less than five feet tall. He wore his hair long, like an old-fashioned rock musician.

"We always do a preliminary first. Saves time," she said.

They sat in director's chairs. There were glasses and bottles of Sohat water on a tiny table between them.

"I've had an amazing career," he said.

"I can see. You like women?"

"Very much." He smirked, looking pointedly at her breasts. "They like me back too."

"At least the short ones—or maybe just the ones you get magazine layouts for," she said, and put her laptop, its screen showing the Aishti ad photograph of Rana, Dima and a third model, on the little table.

"What's this?" he said sharply.

"You know these women? Rana and Dima? Who's the third?"

"Marielle Hilal. A wannabe model," he replied, shaking his head.

"Why only a wannabe? She's pretty enough."

"She doesn't *taneek*," he said, deliberately using "*neek*," the Arabic vulgarity for sex. "You won't get much work that way." He shrugged.

"And the others?"

"Rana, of course. I've done thirty-two covers with her. Publicity stills too. Of course I know her. Better than her own mother."

"What about Dima?" She pointed at her on the screen. "You knew her, didn't you? And don't tell me you didn't sleep with her. I knew her too—and when it came to getting ahead, she wasn't so picky."

"Dima Hamdan. What about her?"

"You took that shot?"

"You know I did," he said, eyeing her like she had grown a second, very ugly head. "What do you want?"

"How close were she and Rana?"

"They knew each other. What do you mean I *knew* her? What's happened?"

"She's dead," Carrie said.

"Who the *neek* are you? You're not the police. Are you Sûreté Générale?" He stood up, although standing he was no taller than she was sitting. "You better leave, mademoiselle."

"If I leave, you're going to get visitors you'll like a whole lot less," she said, opening her handbag and putting her hand inside. "Best get it over with."

Neither of them spoke or moved. Carrie could see motes of dust in the light coming from the windows. It was almost quiet enough to imagine she could hear the dust settle.

"Like a visit to the dentist," he said finally.

"Those are usually for your own good," she said. He looked at her hand in the handbag and sat back down.

"Are you threatening me?" he asked.

"I don't have to. You're Lebanese. Surely you understand what can happen here." The implication was obvious. Lebanese politics was volatile and dangerous. Being in the wrong place at the wrong time could get you killed.

"What do you want?" He frowned.

"Tell me about Dima and Rana. How close were they?"

"They knew each other. Are you asking if they slept together?"

This was new, Carrie thought. Dima liked men. "Did they?"

"For a short time. *Pour de rire.* For fun. They both liked men better. They knew each other from before Beirut."

"Really," Carrie said, her heart speeding up. That Dima

hadn't come from Beirut had never been mentioned in the 201 file Fielding had given her when she first took over as Dima's case officer. "Where did they come from?"

"They were both from the North. Dima was from Halba, the Akkar; Rana from Tripoli. Said she grew up in sight of the Clock Tower," he said.

Those were both Sunni Muslim areas, not Christian, she thought. So what the hell was Dima doing with the Alawite Syrian Nightingale? She was ostensibly a March 14 Maronite Christian, but it still didn't make sense even if she had been lying about that and was actually a Sunni Muslim. The Alawites, like Hezbollah, were both Shiite groups. Either way, whether she was a Christian or a Sunni Muslim, she would have seen Nightingale as an enemy. In Lebanon, to cross sectarian lines was about as safe as crossing a California freeway blindfolded.

"Those are Sunni areas," she said carefully.

The little man nodded.

"What are you saying? That Dima and Rana were Sunni?" she asked.

"Me? I say nothing." He shrugged. "I take pictures of women. Beautiful women. *C'est tout.*"

"They never discussed it?"

"Not with me. No," he said, taking out a bright red pack of Gauloises Blondes and lighting one.

"But you suspected they were Sunnis. Did you know that Dima was involved with March 14?"

He shrugged. "I didn't talk politics with them. Just fashion, photos and"—he picked a shred of tobacco from the tip of his tongue—"*enculer.*" French for screwing.

"Dima dropped out of sight more than a month ago. Where'd she go?"

"You're the Sûreté or the CIA or whoever the hell you are. You tell me."

"You have no idea?"

"*La adri*," he shrugged. *No idea*. "Ask Rana. She might know."

"Tell me about Rana. Is she affiliated with any group?"

"Don't know. Wouldn't tell you if I did." He smirked.

"Trust me, if I want I can make you tell me," she said. She leaned over, ripped the lit cigarette from his lips and stubbed the lighted end hard against his cheek.

"Yeoww!" he howled, and jumped away. "Crazy bitch!" he shouted in Arabic. He poured water from the bottle onto his hand and rubbed it on his burned cheek. The receptionist ran in and looked at them.

"Tell her to leave," Carrie said. "And not do anything stupid."

"*C'est* okay, Yasmine. Just go back to the front. Truly," he said to the girl, who waited for a moment, then left.

"Bitch! Don't do that again," he said, wincing as he touched the burn mark on his cheek with his finger.

"Don't make me," she said. "Is Rana affiliated with any group?"

"I don't know. Ask her," he said sulkily.

"Is she seeing anyone?"

He hesitated. "Are you looking into Dima's death? Is that what this is about?"

Carrie nodded. He looked at the window, then back at her.

"I can't believe she's dead. I liked her," he said.

"So did I."

"*La pauvre*." He frowned. *The poor thing*. "Dima had a new boyfriend. I never saw him. He was from Dubai," he said, rubbing his thumb against his fingers in the universal sign for money. "I figured that's where she went, because you're right, nobody saw her in weeks. Poor Dima."

"And Rana has a boyfriend too?"

He nodded. "An American. He must have money." He smirked again. "Rana is high-priced goods."

"Do you know who he is?"

His answer shocked her to her core. It told her the entire mission in Beirut had been blown.

"What are you asking me for? You should know. He's with the CIA," he said.

CHAPTER 19

Halba, Lebanon

The house was an old-fashioned stone building on a hill looking out toward the town of Bebnine and the sea. Asking around at the *salon tagmil*, the local hair salon, the one place in the Middle East where it was an advantage to be a woman because you could find out everything about everybody, Carrie learned that Dima's parents were deceased. But she found an uncle of the Hamdan family and soon she was sitting in the parlor with an older woman, Khala Majida, Aunt Majida, sipping iced tea, Lebanese-style, made with rose water and pine nuts. They sat on a sofa facing the balcony, the French doors open to the sun. Carrie, in jeans and a sweater, wore her *hijab*. She told Aunt Majida she was a friend of Dima's from America. She didn't tell her Dima was dead; the FBI was still keeping the attackers' identities from the media.

"Did she tell you her father, Hamid Ali Hamdan, was with al-Murabitun?" the aunt said in Arabic.

"She told me," Carrie lied. The Murabitun was the most powerful of the Sunni militias during the long Lebanese civil war. None of this had been in Dima's file and she had never revealed any of this to Carrie or anyone else.

"He fought side by side with Ibrahim Kulaylat. The Israelis

killed him in '82, to Allah we belong, and may those sons of apes and pigs rot in hell. Dima was an infant. It was hard for her, a girl without a father," Aunt Majida said.

"Of course," Carrie murmured, looking around. It seemed inconceivable that sophisticated, party-girl Dima, the girl who knew everyone who was anyone in Christian North Beirut, came from this conservative Sunni Muslim setting.

"And no money. And then her mother got the cancer." The aunt shook her head.

"How did she survive?"

"Her grandmother. And me. We helped, but then she went to Beirut and we didn't see her after that."

"How did she come to leave Halba?"

"You know the famous actress Rana? The one who's on the television?"

"Rana Saadi?" Carrie said, her mind racing. It wasn't just the magazine photo!

"That's the one. Rana's father and poor Hamid Ali, to Allah we belong, were friends in al-Murabitun. Rana came from Tripoli and took her to Beirut. They were going to become models there. I warned her against it. There are many Christians and unbelievers in Beirut. Much that is *haram*, I told her. But she said, 'I have nothing but my looks, Khala. It's the only chance I have. And I'll be with my father's friend's daughter.'"

"Why would Rana take her?"

"*Ikram*. A debt of honor. Hamid Ali had saved Rana's father's life in the civil war."

"*Min fathleki*, excuse me, I understand her father, to Allah we belong, was a hero, but Dima didn't strike me as political—or religious. Not to say she wasn't a good Muslim girl, but you know what I mean," Carrie said.

The aunt looked at her sharply. "She knew who her

father was and who she was, *alhamdulillah*," Aunt Majida said. *Thank God.*

"Of course, *Allahu akbar*," Carrie murmured. *God is great.*

"*Allahu akbar*," the aunt said sternly.

So Dima was a Sunni Muslim who had moved a long way from her roots, Carrie thought on the way back to Beirut in Virgil's Peugeot. She was driving south on the coast road. To her left were fields and clusters of houses and on her right, beyond the houses, the sea. Well, haven't we all? A point Saul had made when she spoke with him on an encrypted cell phone call last night.

"Beirut Station's blown. This place is a shambles," she told him.

"How bad is it?" Saul asked, his voice a bit blurry from the encryption.

"Listen, if a fashion photographer in Gemmayzeh knows Fielding is CIA, everybody knows. That's how bad."

"And Dima?"

"She comes from Halba. That little tidbit wasn't in her 201," Carrie said.

Saul caught it right away. She loved that about him. "Is it possible she's Sunni?" he said.

"I'm checking it out. Kind of leaves us nowhere in figuring out how New York happened. A Sunni op set up by Shiites? And according to Fielding, Dima was supposed to be March 14, which is Christian. Makes no sense. Not in Lebanon."

"There's something else going on. We're not seeing it," he said. "What about this other woman, Rana?"

"She's from the north too. Tripoli. Also probably Sunni. She and Dima knew each other. Their fathers did too. Interesting, huh?"

"What does it tell you?" he said.

"Maybe Rana is part of it."

"Obviously. What else?"

"They were outsiders. Both of them."

"Aren't we all?" he said, reminding her of their conversation just before she left.

Saul had come over to drive her the short distance from her apartment in Reston to Dulles International for the flight to Beirut.

"Keep clear of Beirut Station, especially Fielding," he warned her. "Otherwise you'll never find out what's going on."

"What if we run into each other? Beirut's a small town sometimes."

"Tell him you're on a Special Access op." Special Access operations were the CIA's highest-level operations that could only be authorized directly by the director of the CIA and were on a strict need-to-know basis, including those with top secret clearance, even station chiefs. "If he makes a fuss, refer him to me or to David. Remember, no one from Beirut Station is to even know you're in Lebanon."

"Except Virgil."

"No one else. You can't come to Langley for help either. You're on your own."

"Story of my life," she said.

Saying it, she remembered the little white house on Farragut Avenue in Kensington and how none of their neighbors spoke to them after her father bought a big RV trailer and parked it in the driveway, and when the neighbors asked where he was going, her father told them it was so he could take the family to the Great Lakes to see the miracle. And how she and Maggie had no friends because playdates at their house were unimaginable and they couldn't go to other kids' houses either because their father might call. Her mother was of no help and her sister, Maggie, only wanted out. Theirs was a house of silence, each of them hiding from the others as if madness was contagious like the flu.

"Sometimes I think you prefer it alone," Saul said.

"I've always been an outsider."

"All of us. This is a business for outsiders," he said.

"You too?"

"Are you kidding? Can you even begin to imagine what it was like growing up as the only Orthodox Jewish kid in tiny white-bread Calliope, Indiana? In the fifties and early sixties? My parents were Holocaust survivors. It made them ultra-Orthodox. They clung to God as if to the side of a cliff. My father owned the local drugstore. But there was no one like us in that town. We were like Martians in that place.

"I couldn't participate in anything like Christmas pageants at school. Anything goyish or that even smacked of what they considered idolatry. I had to fight with my parents just to say the Pledge of Allegiance because there was a metal eagle at the top of the flagpole. I couldn't even play Little League even though I loved baseball, because they began the games with a prayer that mentioned Jesus. We're all outsiders, Carrie. The reason we do this is because this is the only profession that'll let us in."

She was driving south, approaching Byblos, the town where the word "bible" came from, when she got the call from Virgil. Ahead, she could see Byblos's old city, crowded along the Mediterranean coast, and in clusters on the hills white houses, churches and a mosque.

"We got a hit," Virgil said.

"I'm listening."

"She made a call on that cell phone, our little actress. I tracked who it went to via the No Such database. Your pal

Jimbo. You do collect admirers, Sweet Pea." Virgil called the NSA "No Such" because for a long time the joke in Washington had been that the acronym for the super-secret National Security Agency stood for "No Such Agency." "Sweet Pea," his sarcastic nickname for her, rhymed with "Sweet C," for "Sweet Caroline," the Neil Diamond song.

"Cut the crap, Vee. Who was it?"

"An old friend of yours. A certain singing little birdie?"

Oh my God! Nightingale, she thought excitedly. Taha al-Douni. It closed the circle: Dima—Nightingale—Rana. And don't forget the third woman in the photo, she reminded herself. Marielle.

"What'd they say?"

"I'll tell you tonight. The usual place? Twenty fifteen?" That meant he didn't want to speak about it over a cell phone connection. The usual place was the circular Khalil Gibran Garden, opposite the UN House in the Hamra district. Subtracting forty-five minutes from 2015 hours meant to meet him at 1930 hours. Seven thirty P.M.

"Okay, bye."

"*Ma'al salaama,*" he said mockingly, and ended the call.

Driving along the coast, the sun shining on the sea, she had never felt better, almost as if she were gliding unmoving on the air like a hawk. Although she couldn't see all the pieces in the puzzle, she could sense them falling into place. Everything was perfect. A feeling of well-being enveloped her, like slipping into a warm bathtub. She was closing in on what had happened and who was behind it. They were just out of sight, behind a curtain that rose behind Beirut like the mountains. It was all coming together. Like sex at that moment when it starts to build and you're not there yet, but you can feel it coming and it's getting better and better.

She drove past farm fields on the coastal highway that divided Byblos's old city from the more modern part of town, thinking maybe she should take some time off. Do a little sightseeing. See the Crusader castle or the Roman ruins or maybe stop off at one of the seaside hotels. Wouldn't that be good? Go out on the beach, let her bare feet feel the sand. Sit in a beach lounge and have a waiter bring her a margarita and watch the seabirds fly and dip toward the water as they spotted a fish and—

Pay attention! she thought, sitting up and focusing on the road. When was the last time she'd had her pill? Was she really feeling this way or was it one of her flights coming on?

Shit!

Focus, Carrie. It's the bipolar doing the thinking, not you, she told herself. Think. Rana, who was both Fielding's girl-friend and Dima's friend, had called Nightingale. It was like closing an electrical circuit. She needed to be sharp now. She couldn't drift. That bullshit about the beach. It's the missing clozapine that's talking. Time to get more at the pharmacy on Rue Nakhle. She needed to get back to Beirut before they closed. She had to get her meds. And she had to pay atten-tion. The last time she'd dealt with Nightingale he'd nearly kidnapped or killed her. He wasn't someone she could take on without having her wits about her.

And then there was the third woman in the photograph. Another mystery. She checked her watch.

If she stepped on it, she just had time to get back to Beirut, get to the Rue Nakhle pharmacy, then meet Virgil. And find Marielle Hilal, the third woman in the photograph. She shook her head to clear it and, going around a slow-moving car, pressed her foot down on the accelerator.

CHAPTER 20

Karantina, Beirut, Lebanon

It was late; the pharmacy was just about to close when she got there, the shop windows along the street glowing with neon in the night. She handed the pharmacist, a bald middle-aged Lebanese man with a fringe of white hair, her old prescription. He barely glanced at it.

"This is out of date, mademoiselle," he said.

"Here's my new one," she said, putting two hundred dollars U.S. on the counter. He looked at it but didn't pick it up. "*Min fathleki*," she added. *Please.* She didn't have to fake the desperation in her voice; it was already there.

He glanced the door, then swept the money into his pocket. He went in back and while she waited she thought about Virgil's news. Rana was to meet Nightingale tomorrow in Baalbek, the town with the famous Roman ruins in the Beqaa Valley, about eighty-five kilometers northeast of Beirut. The three of them, her, Virgil and Ziad, would also be there.

The pharmacist came back. He was holding two containers of pills.

"You understand these are serious?" he said.

"I know, *shokran*," she said, thanking him.

"You should be tested. The side effects can be very bad."

"I know. But I've been taking them for years without any problems," she said, thinking, Just give it to me, dammit. Her heart was beating a mile a minute; the street was already becoming a maze of moving patterns and if she didn't get one inside her soon, she didn't know what she would do. Murder the bastard.

"No more old prescriptions, mademoiselle. Next time, I will insist," he said.

"I understand, *assayid*. Thank you so much." She was thinking, What does he want, a blow job? Please, just give them to me.

"Good night, mademoiselle," he said, handing them to her in a little plastic bag.

"Bye," she said, not looking back as she headed out the door. She stopped at a neighborhood grocery *bakkal* a few doors down just as he was shuttering for the night, bought a bottle of water and washed a pill down. She checked her watch. Just after nine. The nighttime city was coming alive. The streets were clogged with traffic and noisy horns from drivers.

The question now was whether she could find Marielle. The third woman.

The address she had from the photographer, Abou Murad, for Marielle Hilal was on Rue Mar Yousef in Bourj Hammoud, the Armenian quarter. It was in a six-story building on a crowded street just a few blocks from the Municipality building. There was a hole-in-the-wall kebab restaurant on the ground floor with the building door right next to it. Someone had strung a red-blue-and-yellow-striped Armenian flag over the street. She used a credit card slipped between the door lock and the jamb to unlock the apartment building's front door.

Going up the stairs—there was no elevator—she could smell the roast kebabs from the restaurant. The hallway was dark and there was no timed light. She found the apartment and lit her cell phone to see the name handwritten in Arabic on a piece of tape pasted on the doorpost of the apartment door. It wasn't "Hilal" or anything like it. She listened at the door. Someone was watching television. It sounded like a popular show about a beautiful woman journalist in the middle of a divorce. She knocked. No answer. After a minute, she knocked again and the door opened.

A thin woman with streaked blond hair, in jeans and a red B018 Club T-shirt—she must have been in her forties—opened the door.

"*Aiwa,* what is it?" the woman asked in Arabic.

"I'm looking for Marielle," Carrie said.

"I don't know what you're talking about. There's no Marielle here," the woman said.

"Please, madame. I'm a friend of hers and Dima Hamdan's. I have to see her. It's urgent."

"I told you. There's no such person here," the woman said.

"Is that *Kinda*?" Carrie asked, talking about the TV show. "I like that show."

The woman nodded. "It's good," she said, and started to close the door. "Sorry, I can't help you."

"Wait! Could you at least give her a message? Her life is in danger," Carrie said, stepping into the doorway so the woman couldn't close the door.

"Whoever you are, go away! I don't know any Marielle Hilal!" the woman snapped.

Carrie looked at her. I've got you, she thought, thinking, thank God she'd gotten her meds or she wouldn't have caught it.

"How did you know her family name was Hilal? I didn't say it," she said.

The woman stood there, her face working. She looked around as if for a weapon.

"If you don't leave, I'll call the police," she said.

"Go ahead." Carrie crossed her arms. "You're hiding something. I think we both know the last thing you want is the police."

The woman hesitated, stepped out into the hallway to make sure Carrie was alone, then let her in. They stood awkwardly in the foyer; after a moment the woman led her into the living room.

"How do you know Marielle?" the woman asked, turning to confront her.

"I know Rana and Dima," Carrie said.

"How do you know Dima?"

"From Le Gray and the fashion photographer François Abou Murad—and other places."

The woman stood there, calculating.

"You said Marielle's life was in danger. What did you mean?"

"You know exactly what I mean or you wouldn't be trying to protect her. I have to talk to her." She decided to take a chance. "Dima is dead, madame."

The woman stared at her, stunned. "Dead? What are you saying?"

"I have to talk to Marielle. It is unbelievably urgent."

"You're American?" she asked, studying her.

"Yes. I'm Carrie. A friend."

"Wait here," she said, and went to a bedroom. Carrie assumed she was calling Marielle. It was puzzling. The woman—she assumed she was a relative of Marielle's—didn't look Armenian, and looking around, there was no sign of a cross or pictures of Mount Ararat or anything Armenian, so why did she live in Bourj Hammoud? Except, Carrie thought, everyone knew everyone here. They were aware of outsiders. Maybe Marielle lived near here for safety. On the TV, Kinda was being threatened by a man in a business suit. The woman came back.

"She'll meet you tonight after midnight at B Dix-Huit. Come alone or you won't get to talk to her." The woman frowned. "I'm sorry for all the precaution."

"No, she's right. She may be in great danger," Carrie said.

B018 was in the Karantina district, sandwiched between the Beirut River in its narrow concrete channel and the harbor. In times past, the area was called La Quarantaine and had been a refugee camp for survivors of the Armenian massacre in Turkey during World War I. Later, during the Lebanese civil war, it was a camp for Palestinians. Now it was a working-class industrial area that, as an oddity, housed the most exclusive club in town.

From the outside, the B018 Club looked like a concrete spaceship, and going down the narrow inclined ramp to the underground entrance, Carrie, who'd gone home and changed into her Terani and highest heels, wondered if her midthigh minidress was short enough. It was that kind of place. Coming down to the front-door area, she could hear the music throbbing loud enough to make the walls vibrate.

Even before she got past the six-foot bouncers at the door, a man in a Hugo Boss jacket put his arm around her waist and asked her if she wanted a Johnnie Walker Blue. At club prices, a drink like that could go for five hundred dollars.

"Maybe later," she said, disentangling herself. After the

bouncers gave her a once-over that lasted only a few seconds but felt as probing as a gynecological exam and waved her through—thanks to the Terani and her Jimmy Choos, she thought—she went inside. The main club, with its hangarlike space and endlessly long bar, was jammed with people, many of them dancing for all they were worth to Chris Brown's "Run It." A half dozen beautiful women in ultratight miniskirts were writhing to the music on top of the bar to raucous cheers.

Someone shoved a cocktail into her hand, nearly spilling it, while a drop-dead gorgeous girl with gold eye shadow and purple lipstick stared at her and said, "What a pretty face, *cherie*. Can I kiss you?" Without waiting for an answer, she kissed Carrie full on the lips, her tongue darting in like a little fish. So different than kissing a man, Carrie thought. Softer, the sensation oddly disconcerting and interesting.

"Come with me," the girl said, putting her hand on Carrie's breast.

"Maybe later," Carrie said—it was fast becoming her new mantra—and moved quickly away.

She weaved her way around the dance floor and along the walls, looking for Marielle. All she had to go on was the photograph; she hoped the woman hadn't changed her hairstyle too much. A man grabbed her free hand and kissed it.

"Have a drink, *habibi*," he said. She freed her hand and moved on. The music was deafening and someone shouted in Arabic that things were just getting started, you *kahleteen*! Laserlike lights flashed and someone said they were going to open the retractable roof to the stars, but nothing happened. The music had changed and everyone was going wild to the Finnish heavy metal band Nightwish.

Carrie spotted someone who could have been Marielle seated near the far end of the bar. Crossing the dance floor, she was groped twice and barely escaped getting pulled into a group of three girls dancing so hard their bouncing breasts threatened to escape their décolletage.

When she got closer, she saw that it was Marielle. She'd dyed her hair red, wore a low-cut al-Ansar Sporting Club tank top that showed her cleavage and Escada jeans so tight they could've been spray-painted on. She wasn't as pretty as her photo, but her face was more interesting, Carrie thought, squeezing in next to her.

"Where can we talk?" Carrie asked in Arabic.

"You Carrie?" Marielle said, leaning closer.

"It's too loud. Let's go somewhere."

"I'm not moving till I know you are who you say you are. Where was Dima from? Really from?" the redhead said into her ear.

"The Akkar. Halba."

"Come," Marielle said, getting off her stool and marching away. Carrie followed. After a long walk out of the main club to a hallway, they found a line snaking out of the women's bathroom. Marielle walked past it and, taking out a key, unlocked a side door at the end of the corridor. It opened to an empty storage space. Looking behind them to make sure no one was paying attention, they stepped inside. Except for a single light-bulb, the room was dark, with cartons stacked at the back. They could hear the music throbbing through the walls.

"Is Dima dead?" Marielle asked.

Carrie nodded.

"I knew it. These people . . . ," Marielle said, shaking her head bitterly.

"Which people?"

"I don't know. I don't know them. I don't know you. All I know is that it's dangerous. I knew she was in trouble."

"How'd you know?"

"Dima and Rana were always playing with fire. Rana is with some guy we think is CIA."

"Fielding?" Carrie put in.

"American." She nodded. "Like you. Did you come from him?"

"What do you think?"

"I don't know what to think. I'm scared, that's what I think. If they killed Dima, they can kill me. Look at me. My hand is shaking." She held out her hand in the dim light.

"Less than two months ago, Dima disappeared out of sight. What happened?"

"It was him," Marielle said.

"Who?"

"Her new boyfriend. Mohammed. Mohammed Siddiqi. She was with him."

"The one from Dubai?"

"Where'd you hear Dubai?"

"The photographer, François."

"He's such a *khara* liar. Mohammed's Iraqi. From Baghdad. He claimed to be from Qatar, but I knew he lied, the dog." She made a face. "At first, she was in love. It was all about how wonderful he was. He had all this money. How good-looking he was. What an incredible lover. They walked on the beach at Saint Georges and watched the sun come up. All that *khara*."

"What happened?"

"It was an act. Once he had her, he changed. She was afraid of him. She showed me the bruises. Cigarette burns on the inside of her thighs where no one would see. One time he shoved her face into a toilet and held her under the water till she promised she would do anything he said. I told her to run. Or talk to Rana's CIA guy, but she was too terrified. All he had to do was look at her and she would go white. She told me there was a woman, someone she thought she could trust. American." Her eyes searched Carrie's face, shadowed by the lightbulb in the darkness. "Was that you?"

Carrie nodded. "I failed her," she said. "I'm sorry. I might've helped her, but she disappeared. I couldn't find her."

"She was in Doha. In Qatar. With him," she said, spitting the words out. "I don't know what they were doing, but before she left, she warned me to stay away. He said I'd be next."

"So you went to ground in Bourj Hammoud? Is that why? For safety? You're not Armenian," Carrie said.

"The people there notice outsiders. They protect us. You won't tell anyone?"

Carrie shook her head. "This Mohammed Siddiqi. You say he's Iraqi?" she asked.

Marielle nodded, a grim smile on her face. "He claimed to be Qatari, but he lied."

"How do you know?"

"My mother's family spent time in Qatar. I asked him where he went to school. The Doha Academy on B Ring Road? Everyone who's anyone goes there. He said yes. Liar! Everyone in Qatar knows Doha Academy is in al-Khalifa al-Jadeeda, nowhere near the B Ring. And his slang was Iraqi Arabic, not Qatari or Lebanese."

"Do you know where he is now?"

She shook her head.

It's a dead end. We don't have enough, Carrie thought, casting around desperately for something else. This Mohammed was part of the attack on New York. She was sure of it.

"Were you ever together with them? Did anybody ever take any photos?" she asked.

"He didn't want pictures. One time Dima asked me to take

a snapshot of the two of them on the Corniche and before I could do anything, he took the camera out of my hand and smashed it."

"So there are no photos at all?"

Marielle hesitated, then shook her head no. She's lying, Carrie thought.

"There is a photo, isn't there?" she asked, her heart beating wildly. It was as if her hearing was ultra-acute. She could hear the beating of her heart and Marielle's heart and the music and conversations outside and thought, Oh God, it's the meds. Please, not now. Everything is hanging by a thread.

Marielle didn't answer. She looked away.

"*Min fathleki.*" *Please.* "Don't let Dima's death be for nothing. It matters more than you can imagine," Carrie pleaded. Some instinct—she prayed it wasn't her damned bipolar—told her what Marielle said now would change everything. Like Saint Paul on the road to Damascus—kicking back to her Catholic childhood—his world trembling, waiting for what his night visitor would say next.

Marielle's eyes searched hers as if she could see into her soul, then she opened her purse, took out her cell phone and, after a minute, found what she was looking for.

"I took this when he wasn't looking. I don't know why," she said, then bit her lip. "No, that's not true. I thought he might kill her and I might need it for the police."

She showed Carrie the photo on her cell phone. It was a snapshot of Dima, in tight shorts and a tee, on the Corniche, looking tense, her arm around a lean coppery-skinned man with curly hair and a three-day stubble squinting slightly in the sun, facing three-quarters to the camera. Carrie could hardly believe it, a sensation close to orgasm thrilling through her. I've got you, you bastard! she thought wildly.

"I need that picture," she said. "If you need money, help . . ." She left it open.

Neither of them spoke. They could hear the beat of the music and the sounds of the crowd from outside the room like the sound of the ocean in a seashell.

"Give me an e-mail address and I'll send it," Marielle said, suddenly nervous. "Anything else? I risked coming here to meet you in a public place. I have to go."

Carrie touched her arm. "What about Rana? Did she know him?"

Marielle stepped back, her face hard to see in the dim light coming from behind her. "I don't know. I don't know anything. I don't want to know."

"But she knows the Syrian, Taha al-Douni?"

"Rana's famous. Either she knows everybody or they know her or pretend they do. Ask her," she said with a shrug.

"It's dangerous for her too, isn't it?" Carrie asked.

"It's Beirut," she said. "We live on a bridge over an abyss made of explosives and lies."

CHAPTER 21

Baalbek, Lebanon

The lobby of the Palmyra Hotel in Baalbek was filled with palms, antiquities and dusty furniture left over from the French colonial era. It smelled of mold and could have been lifted intact from an Agatha Christie novel, but the hotel's upper rooms had an incredible view of the Roman ruins. After they checked in, Virgil and Ziad set up the equipment and the guns in a room that opened to a balcony that overlooked the columns of the Temple of Jupiter towering over the Beqaa plain.

Driving up the mountain road in a rented Honda Odyssey, they had few illusions about where they were. The road and town were festooned with yellow Hezbollah flags hanging from every building and lamppost. Since they were GPS-tracking Rana's cell phone, they didn't have to follow closely, so she had no way of suspecting they were following her. The only question, as Virgil put it, was firepower.

How many men was Nightingale bringing with him?

From inside the room, they scanned the ruins with binoculars, making sure no glint of the sun on the lenses gave them away.

"Do you see her?" Carrie asked.

"Not yet," Virgil said, moving the binoculars inch by inch in a back-and-forth sweep. "There she is, by the Temple of Bacchus. On the left. See her?"

Carrie trained her binoculars on the virtually intact temple. The ruins were staggering; it was the biggest, best-preserved complex of Roman ruins in the Middle East, possibly anywhere. They dated from when Baalbek was known as Heliopolis and served as an important temple center for worship of the Roman gods Jupiter, Venus, and Bacchus, the first two of which had been merged with the local deities Baal and Astarte. The temple complex was organized around the Grand Court, a vast rectangular space where Carrie spotted Rana, talking to someone beside a column near the steps to the Temple of Bacchus.

"I see her. Who's she talking to?" Carrie said.

"Can't see from here. But he's brought armed men with him," Virgil said, nudging her arm. "Over there, by that big stone at an angle and over by the Temple of Venus."

She saw them. A man with what looked like an AK-47 on top of a giant stone lying sideways at an angle, another on the steps to the Grand Court and two more by the Temple of Venus.

"I see four," Carrie said.

"What the hell," Virgil muttered. "How'd they get into the museum complex with guns?"

"They're Hezbollah. How do you think?" Ziad said.

"Can we hear what they're saying?" she asked Ziad, who had unpacked a suitcase and set up a parabolic microphone dish with multichannel equalizers aimed through the open balcony door at Rana.

"Maybe." Ziad shrugged. "They're about four hundred meters from us. I've adjusted the equalizers for conversation at that distance. It's fifty-fifty." He handed her the earphones and set up the video camera to record what they were watching.

Carrie listened intently. She heard a woman, Rana, talking in Arabic, saying something—the words were unclear—about "him," whoever that was, telling her they'd have to be more circumspect after (something unclear) about New York. Someone, a man, was saying (something unclear) about "focus on Anbar."

She sat up straight. That couldn't be right. What the hell would an actress screwing an American CIA station chief in Beirut have to do with Anbar province in Iraq? Why would Hezbollah care? They had nothing to do with Iraq. But Iran, Hezbollah's sponsor, did, she thought. Still, that couldn't be right. Both Rana and Dima were Sunnis from the North pretending to be Christians. Why would they be feeding intel to Hezbollah or the Syrian GSD, which was Alawite?

At that moment, the man stepped away from the column. She focused the binoculars on him.

"Is that Nightingale?" Virgil asked her.

Although at this distance identification was iffy, she was almost certain it was Nightingale.

"It's him. Fielding's girlfriend is a nasty little mole," she said.

"Man oh man! He's a station chief. He's got the keys to the kingdom. What has he given her?" Virgil breathed.

No, Carrie thought. The question wasn't what he'd given, but to whom he had given it. Who was he really working for? And suddenly, she had it.

What if Nightingale was a double?

Then the question became, who was actually running him? The Iranians via Syria and Hezbollah, or al-Qaeda in Iraq? There was only one way to find out. They had to take Rana, she thought, straining to hear through the headphones.

"Anything on Iraq is [the words were broken up] top priority, do you understand? If you can get to his laptop computer," she heard Nightingale say.

"It isn't easy," Rana said. "What about Dima?"

"We've heard only that the action failed. We have to assume the worst. And your other friend, Marielle?" She and Marielle had both been right, she thought. They were after her too. He said something more, but she couldn't catch it. Through the binoculars, she could see they were walking farther away, behind some stones. Shit, she thought.

"How'd Nightingale get here?" she asked Virgil.

"I spotted two black Toyota SUVs parked near the souk," Virgil said. There was an outdoor market with *shawarma* stalls and souvenir vendors just outside the temple complex grounds. "There were two Hezbollah fighters keeping guard."

"Could we distract them long enough to get bugs in them?" Carrie said.

"Not unless you've got a harem of Hezbollah girls available," he said, and Ziad turned and grinned, showing them his gold tooth.

"No, and I'm not volunteering," Carrie said. She watched through the binoculars as Rana and Nightingale went inside the Temple of Bacchus. It was impossible to hear anything they said through the thick ancient marble walls. "We need to take Rana."

"You want to do it here?" Virgil said, a slight gesture taking in the entire Beqaa Valley. She understood what he meant. They were in solid Hezbollah country. If it went wrong, they didn't stand a snowball's chance in hell of coming out alive.

"She came in her own car," Carrie said. Rana had driven here alone in a pale blue BMW sedan. They had spotted it parked on a side street leading to the souk and the entrance to the temple complex.

"What if she's not alone?" Ziad asked.

"She came alone. That's how she'll go back. Why do you think they came all the hell the way to Baalbek? She didn't want anyone to know about this little tête-à-tête," she said.

"You better be right. Once the shooting starts, we'll have a thousand dicks in our ass," Ziad replied, using an Arabic vulgarity.

"If she's in trouble, Nightingale or his people might step in," Virgil said.

"I'll delay her," Carrie said. "Once their meet is over, he's not going to hang around for *shawarma*. We just have to make sure she leaves after he does."

"Are we done here?" Virgil said.

"Let's pack up. You two get into costume and disable her BMW. I'll see she's late to the party."

The two men nodded. They pulled out green berets with the Hezbollah insignia on them, camouflage fatigues and assault rifles; put them on; and started to pack up the rest of the gear. In this environment, everyone would assume they were on legitimate Hezbollah business and if anyone stopped them, Ziad would speak Arabic to them and let them know to mind their own business. Carrie would follow based on what was happening with Rana and Nightingale in the ruins.

Virgil and Ziad left a few minutes later. They packed up the listening gear and the headphones and left her with only a pair of mini-binoculars.

She checked the Glock 26, the small nine-millimeter pistol Virgil had given her, and put it back into her handbag. She hoped to God she wouldn't need it, then trained the binoculars on the Temple of Bacchus.

Nightingale came hurrying out of the temple. He glanced

at his men and they headed toward the Grand Court and the entrance steps. A minute later, wearing a green *hijab*, a Hezbollah-friendly color, Carrie thought, Rana came out of the temple and followed.

Carrie put the binoculars in her handbag and went out of the room and down to the street. She rushed to the *souk* and pretended to shop on a lane near the gateway that Rana would be coming out of. She just had to make sure Nightingale didn't see her; she pulled one end of her *hijab* over her face like a veil. She knew that Virgil and Ziad were heading to disable the BMW and get the Honda minivan into position.

"If we have to, how will you do it?" she'd asked him on the ride from Beirut.

"Lead wire from the coil pack." He shrugged. "Just disconnect it. She won't be able to start the car."

"Then just reattach it and she's ready to go?"

He nodded. And with them wearing the Hezbollah berets, hopefully no one should stop them, she thought. Hopefully.

Nightingale and his men were coming. She stepped into a recessed stall selling antiquities. Coins, pottery, amber and silver jewelry. All presumably from the Roman and Phoenician periods. Ten-to-one made in China, she thought.

"These are all genuine?" she asked the shopkeeper, a round man with a mustache, in Arabic.

"I will give you a certificate of authenticity from the Bureau of Antiquities myself, madame," he replied as Nightingale and his men went by. One of them glanced toward her and a shiver went down her spine.

"Look, madame, Roman jewelry," said the shopkeeper, showing her a silver and colored glass bracelet.

"Authentic?" she asked, stepping away to check the lane. It was clear.

"One hundred fifty thousand livres, madame. Or if you pay in U.S. dollars, eighty-five."

"Let me think about it," she said, putting down the bracelet and walking out.

"Seventy-five thousand, madame," he called after her as she headed down the lane. "Fifty thousand! Twenty-five American!"

She saw two little Arab girls, aged about ten and seven, standing by a stall selling prayer beads and went up to them.

"You know Rana Saadi, the television star?" she said in Arabic.

They both nodded.

"She's here! She'll be here any second. You should get her autograph. At least say hello to her," she said, guiding them into the lane, just as Rana came down the ancient stone steps to the exit from the temple complex. "See, look!" she said, nudging them toward the actress. And as Rana approached, she called out loudly, "Look! It's Rana, the famous star! *Onzor!*"

People in the *souk* looked up, and a half dozen women and the two girls crowded around Rana, who at first looked startled, then began to smile and wave at everyone as though she was on a Rose Parade float. As she started to sign autographs, Carrie turned and walked away. She found Virgil and Ziad eating *shawarma* in pita bread at a stand across the street from Rana's BMW.

"Where's the van?" she asked.

"Around the corner," Virgil said, indicating the direction with his chin.

"And Nightingale?"

"Gone. Both SUVs."

A few minutes later, they watched Rana come down the street and get into the BMW.

"Go bring the van," Virgil told Ziad, who left.

They watched her try to start the car and heard it whine and not turn over.

"When do we move?" Carrie asked.

"Wait till she gets out of the car," Virgil said as Ziad came around the corner in the minivan. Ziad stopped the minivan about five meters back.

They watched Rana try to start the BMW, then just sit there in frustration. As she sat there trying to figure it out, every second making it more dangerous, Virgil took the syringe out of his pocket, removed the tip and hid it in his hand.

"C'mon, get out of the damn car," he muttered.

As she started to get out, Carrie and Virgil walked over, Ziad inching closer in the minivan.

"*Ahlan*, do you need help?" Carrie asked her in Arabic.

"It's this stupid car—" Rana started to say, but didn't finish because Virgil grabbed her and stabbed the needle into her arm. "What is—" she tried to call out, but she had already started to slump as Carrie opened the minivan door and Virgil bundled her into the seat. Carrie put a plastic tie around her wrists even though she could see it was redundant. Rana was out cold. The ketamine worked fast, Carrie thought, putting the seat belt on the slumped woman as Virgil opened the BMW's hood and reattached the coil lead.

"Key's in the ignition. Go," he told her as he went around and got into the minivan next to Rana. Within seconds, the minivan was moving, Carrie following in the BMW.

By the time Rana came to, they would be back in Beirut. One way or another, Carrie thought, she would get some answers.

CHAPTER 22

Bashoura, Beirut, Lebanon

Carrie watched Rana open her eyes. They were in a basement storage room of the safe house building near the Bashoura Cemetery that Beirut Station had code-named Iroquois. The room was empty, lit by a single lightbulb; its walls were sound-proofed and the door locked. The actress had been tied to a chair with plastic ties. The only other furniture was the chair that Carrie sat in, a stool and a wooden bench on which they'd put a bucket of water and a towel. On a stool next to her, Carrie had put her Glock 26 with a sound suppressor attached.

"You can scream your head off, no one will hear," Carrie told her in Arabic.

"Not my style," Rana said. "Not unless they pay me. I did a great scream in a horror movie once. *Evil Cannibal Streets*. As opposed to *Good Cannibal Streets*, I suppose. Do you want to hear?"

"I don't care about your credits. This isn't an audition," Carrie said.

"Do you want money? I'm not rich," Rana said.

"You're famous."

"Not the same thing."

"It's not money. Let's talk about Taha al-Douni."

"Who?"

Carrie looked down at the floor, then up at Rana.

"I need you to tell me the truth. If you do, you'll be back to your old life in a few hours. If not, you'll never leave this room," she said.

For a long moment, neither spoke. Rana looked around, as if seeking a way out.

"What is this about?" she asked, only a slight tremor in her voice betraying her nervousness. She's an actress, Carrie reminded herself. She lies for a living. Like the rest of us.

"Listen, there's already a lot you don't have to tell us. We know about you. And about Dima and Marielle and that you're Davis Fielding's, the CIA station chief in Beirut's, little whore. We'll get to that in a minute." She could see that Rana was shocked by what she had said, that she knew all that.

Interrogation 101, she thought. Let the subject think you know about him and what he's doing and he'll assume you know more than you are letting on. Amazing the things he'll let slip because he thinks you already know them. "You met with Taha al-Douni in Baalbek. What was the meeting about?"

"I don't know what you mean," Rana said.

"Yes, you do." Carrie frowned and took out the video camera and showed her the playback of her and Nightingale talking in the ruins. "*Min fathleki*, let's not make this unpleasant. Actually, even before we get to that, I've a better question. What's a nice Sunni Muslim girl from Tripoli doing with a Shiite spy for the GSD and Hezbollah?"

Rana stared at her, wide-eyed.

"Who are you? What do you want from me?" she whispered.

"The truth. The Christian Bible says it'll set you free. In this case, that's the literal truth. But if you lie to me"—she looked at the bench and the bucket of water—"trust me, you won't like it."

"How do you know about me? About Tripoli? Was it Dima, that bitch? She couldn't keep her mouth closed any more than she could keep her legs together."

"Did you really imagine you could be the mistress of a CIA station chief and meet with Syrian spies and not attract attention?" Carrie said. "Who are you working for?"

"Don't you know?" Rana moistened her lips. Dark hair, dark eyes. An attractive woman, Carrie thought. One who thought that her looks would always get her out of a tough spot. "God, I would kill for a cigarette."

"Later." Carrie frowned. "You're going to have to start answering my questions or it's not going to go well for you. Who are you working for? Hezbollah?"

Rana shook her head, the faintest hint of a smile on her lips. "*Kos emek* Hezbollah," she said, using the worst Arabic vulgarity. "Neither Hezbollah nor the Syrians."

"Who then? Al-Douni is GSD."

"Who told you that? Dima? Are you CIA? Do you have her? Has she been talking?"

Carrie thought for a moment, deciding. Was Rana was trying to play her? They'd see who played whom.

"Dima's dead. Right now, your chances don't look so good either," she said. That got her. She could see Rana go pale. She shook her head, her famous brown hair tossing back and forth. "Last chance. Then the men come. They're dying to jump in. Work on a good-looking woman like you. Something we women know," Carrie said, crossing her legs. "Beauty is such a fragile thing, isn't it? Who are you and al-Douni working for?"

Rana shook her head. Carrie decided to try a little more truth.

"Is al-Douni a double agent? The only way I can help you is if you'll let me. All you have to do is nod."

Almost unwillingly, Rana nodded.

Carrie's mind raced. If al-Douni was a double, who was he doubling for? Who was running him? Dima's boyfriend, Mohammed Siddiqi? The Iraqi pretending to be a Qatari, according to Marielle. Or was Rana just telling her what she thought Carrie wanted to hear?

"Who's he really working for?"

"I'm not sure. But he was the one who introduced Dima to her boyfriend, the Qatari," Rana said.

"Mohammed Siddiqi? I heard he wasn't a real Qatari," Carrie said.

"You've been talking to Marielle." Rana frowned. "*Inshallah*, give me a cigarette and I'll tell you anything you want to know."

Carrie went to the door, went out and came back with a lit Marlboro cigarette. She put it between Rana's lips. She'd find out now if Rana had really decided to cooperate.

"Okay," Rana said, taking a drag and exhaling a stream of smoke. "You're right. I work for Taha. I mean al-Douni. I recruited Dima too, though she pretended to be a Maronite for March 14. As you obviously know, we're both from the north, both Sunni, both daughters of fathers in the Murabitun."

"Taha al-Douni recruited you to become Davis Fielding's mistress?"

"I'm not his mistress," she said, taking a deep drag and letting Carrie take the cigarette from between her lips so she could exhale.

"What do you mean? You're not saying you don't have sex? You're a beautiful woman. Famous even."

"It's not that simple. At first we did, but now I'm mostly just for show. We meet at parties, diplomatic receptions, things like that." She shrugged.

"But you spy on him?"

Rana nodded.

"Does he know?"

"I don't know what he knows." She shrugged. "Lately, with the arrival of Dima's Mohammed, the emphasis shifted."

"From what to what?"

"From anything we could get on CIA activities in Lebanon and Syria to Iraq. They want to know about what the Americans know and don't know and what their plans in Iraq are."

"Is Mohammed, Dima's boyfriend, running al-Douni?"

She snorted with derision. "That *ibn el himar*?" *Son of a donkey.* "He's a courier, a delivery boy. A nobody."

"Dima was afraid of him?"

She nodded. "The bastard abused her, the pig. She was terrified of him. All he had to do was look at her."

That's what Marielle said, Carrie thought. So that's how they got Dima, the Sunni party girl, to become a terrorist. If Nightingale wasn't running the show and Mohammed was just a messenger boy, whose op was it? And what was their interest in American intel about Iraq? The answer was obvious.

"Does Mohammed work for al-Qaeda? Is he in contact with Abu Nazir?"

"I don't know. No one talks to Abu Nazir. No one knows who his contacts are. Taha once spoke about Abu Nazir's deputy, Abu Ubaida."

"What did he say?"

"He said he was Abu Nazir's executioner."

CHAPTER 23

Le Hippodrome, Beirut, Lebanon

They set up in the trees behind the grandstand at the Hippodrome racetrack, the sunset casting the shadow of the grandstand across the track and the trees. There were seven of them: her, Virgil, Ziad and four men of the Forces Libanaises he had brought with him. They were well armed, all four with M4 carbines; one of them had an M4 with an M203 grenade launcher attached.

Carrie didn't like using the FLs, but there wasn't much choice. Things were moving too fast. She believed Saul was on his way to Beirut, but he wouldn't get there in time and there wasn't time to put an SOG, a CIA Special Operations Group team, in place.

There were a hundred reasons not to use the FLs. They weren't trained, they weren't under her control, they were sectarian to their core and they would be dealing with their Shiite enemies. A total wild-card scenario.

There was only one reason to use them. Nightingale /al-Douni never went anywhere without armed Hezbollah guards, so she needed some kind of muscle. Saul had agreed, reluctantly, during their texting interaction earlier that day.

She had gone to an Internet café on Rue Makhoul in Hamra, near the American University, getting onto a computer against the wall next to a teenage Arab boy gaming with online friends. As previously agreed, to keep what she was doing separate from normal channels that Davis Fielding would have access to, she and Saul communicated via a chat room for teenagers so heavily trafficked, there was little chance of their conversation being hacked. The volume was simply too great for even powerful intelligence-agency search-engine algorithms to find an individual conversation.

The way they'd set the chat up, Carrie was supposedly a high school senior from Bloomington, Illinois, named Bradley, and Saul was a girl named Tiffany from nearby Normal Community High School. She sent him her report and the photo of Mohammed Siddiqi as attachments.

"hey qt pie. u got everyl in nesa going loco," Saul typed. NESA was the CIA's Office of Near Eastern and South Asian Analysis, an elite group that included the Agency's best Middle East experts.

"ctc?" she typed back. Was David Estes's Counterterrorism Center unit also involved?

"24/7. im jealous. u got all the girls attention." About time Langley paid attention, she grumped to herself.

"do u no the real ms? who she is dating?" That was the big question. The one she absolutely had to know. Who was Mohammed Siddiqi really? What did the Company know about him? And who was he working for?

"not yet," Saul typed back. "but yr fmr bff, allie, is working on it like its her sats." So her former best friend forever, "allie," Alan Yerushenko, and her colleagues at the Office of Collection Strategies and Analysis were working on it nonstop too.

"mary L thinks she's baggy, not cutter." Hoping he would catch that she meant Marielle thought Siddiqi was an Iraqi from Baghdad, "baggy," and not from Qatar, which Saul pronounced "Cutter." That plus the fact Nightingale wanted Rana to get intel on Iraq was pointing everything that had happened in Beirut and New York like a compass needle right at Abu Nazir.

"shes looking at a boo n friends," Saul typed back, showing he got it. They were looking at "a boo n," Abu Nazir.

"r u coming to c me?" she responded.

"c u soon. what about our lil birdie?" So Saul was on his way to Beirut. Thank God. The little birdie was Nightingale.

"big date 2nite. ok use fls?"

There was a pause so long, she wasn't sure Saul was still there. And she had to remember the time difference, she thought, checking her watch. It was 2:47 p.m. in Beirut, before 8:00 a.m. in Langley.

"only if u have 2. Be crful," he sent. He obviously didn't like it. Well, she wasn't crazy about it herself. All this dancing around, she thought, because Fielding was having an affair with a double agent he wasn't even screwing.

"bye," she replied, and logged off.

Which had led her and Virgil and Ziad here to the Hippodrome and the meet she'd had Rana set with Nightingale in the grandstand of the race track. Races were only run once a week, on Sundays, so today, Thursday, and at this hour, the grandstand would be empty. Hopefully, it would make Nightingale confident about coming and would give her FLs a clear field of fire if things went south.

"Where will they be coming from?" she asked in Arabic.

"There." Ziad pointed. "From Avenue Abdallah El Yafi

into the parking area. I can put two men in the trees near the French embassy compound to take care of whoever is with the car."

Carrie turned to the two men he indicated. The other two were already in position in the stables, from which they could get to the grandstand within thirty seconds.

"You understand, we need this man, Taha al-Douni, alive? Even if they start shooting. Dead he's of no use to us."

"He's a *hatha neek* Hezbollah piece of *khara*," one of them cursed.

"This is no good." She turned to Virgil. These crazy guys would just start shooting. "We need to abort."

"Too late," he said, pointing. "There's Rana's BMW." She saw the blue sedan stopped at the gate. The Hippodrome was closed, but Rana had bribed the gatekeeper in advance so they could meet here.

Carrie raised her binoculars and saw it was Rana, alone, in the BMW. She watched it drive into the parking area, then turned to the two FL men.

"If shooting starts, take out the SUVs so they can't leave. Take out the guards for the SUVs. But don't kill anyone else, understood?" she said.

"Okay, *la mashkilah*." He shrugged. *No problem.*

She didn't believe him, watching as the two men moved through the trees toward the parking area.

"Let's go," Virgil said, his eyes scanning the grandstand. He started to jog toward it, his M4 held ready. Carrie and Ziad followed, every cell in her body screaming that this was all wrong.

She had told Rana she would be running her until further notice. There would be money and she was to say nothing to either Davis Fielding or al-Douni or anyone else, and she might not be seeing Fielding much anymore.

Her first instruction to Rana had been to set up the meet with Nightingale/al-Douni by telling him she had urgent intel on American actions against al-Qaeda in Iraq. As expected, al-Douni had agreed immediately. As Carrie listened in on Rana's call, he was the one who set the RDV at the Hippodrome.

"What are you really after?" Rana had asked her.

"For you to feed al-Douni what I want him to know, not what he wants to know," Carrie said. "And find out where it goes after he gets it."

"You mean, who is he really working for? You don't believe it's the Syrians?" Rana said.

"He's working more than one side."

"Aren't we all? This is Beirut," Rana said.

The way she said it, that fatalism, reminded Carrie of Marielle as she ran into the grandstand and hid, lying flat behind the seats, in the fourth row. The other two FLs were waiting, hidden in the jockeys' restroom near the passageway from the stables to the track. Were they all like that? Doomed? Was that Beirut?

Through the gap between the seats, she saw Rana walk toward the paddock to wait by the railing. The sun was setting over the racetrack, the sky pink and gold, really lovely, she thought, the shadows lengthening, making it harder to see. In a little while, it would be dark.

A few minutes later, her cell phone buzzed. A signal from the FLs near the parking area. Nightingale had arrived.

Carrie waited, every nerve ending screaming as if an electrical current was surging through them. Any second now, Nightingale would be coming up to Rana. It was critical that she hear what he said before they moved. Whatever happened, they shouldn't move too soon. They had wired Rana and set it to a receiver connected with Carrie's earbud.

She spotted Nightingale through the gap in the seats. He was accompanied by three of his Hezbollah guards. The son of a bitch really never went anywhere unprotected. She'd had no choice but to bring the extra firepower.

"Salaam. We just met. This better be good," she heard him say to Rana.

"Judge for yourself. I was with the American yesterday when I came back from Baalbek," she said.

"In his bed?"

"Of course. When he was asleep, I got to his computer. Here are the files," she said, handing him a flash drive that Carrie had given her.

"Is that all?"

She shook her head. "There's more. It's about the Americans doing something in Iraq."

"Tell me," he demanded.

"Mohammed Siddiqi. They've learned about him. They know he's Iraqi, not Qatari," Rana said.

Carrie strained to hear; every syllable was critical.

"*Khara*," Nightingale cursed. "What else?"

"They know about you too. They think—" she started to say, but never finished because at that instant, the two FLs from the passageway emerged, one of them firing at Nightingale's men. One of the Hezbollah guards toppled face-forward; the second swiveled and returned fire.

Oh God, no, Carrie thought. Before she could say or do anything, Nightingale had pulled a pistol from his jacket. Don't! Not Rana! her mind screamed. Don't!

"You whore!" he shouted, firing the gun point-blank into Rana's face.

Suddenly, there was an explosion from the parking area. The grenade launcher, Carrie thought, cringing as she half-stood and shouted in Arabic: "Don't kill him!"

Near her, Virgil and Ziad rose up, firing their M4s into the darkness, streaked with flashes of gunfire.

CHAPTER 24

Basta Tahta, Beirut, Lebanon

She and Virgil split up by the French embassy next to the race-track to ensure one of them would make it back. Taking buses and Services back and forth across the northern part of the city to make sure she was clean, she headed for Iroquois, the safe-house apartment on Avenue Independence in the Basta Tahta quarter. When she knocked on the apartment door using the code, three knocks, then two, Davis Fielding opened it, a Beretta pistol pointed at her.

"I've been waiting for you," Fielding said.

"Have you got any tequila? I need a drink," she said.

"Just vodka. Belvedere," he said, gesturing at a cupboard.

She went over and poured herself a glass of vodka and took a gulp, then flopped into an armchair. It didn't feel like there was anyone else in the apartment, which surprised her. Fielding rarely went anywhere without a couple of CIA operations personnel with him. And he never went to the safe house except for interrogations. So why was he here? she wondered.

Fielding sat on a sofa, framed by a curtain that completely covered the window behind him. He was still holding the gun, she noticed.

"Planning on shooting me, Davis?" she asked.

"Might not be the worst idea in the world. How many did you kill this time, Mathison?" he said, making a face.

"That's right, Davis," she said, taking another drink, feeling it burn going down and thinking, Thank God for the alcohol, at this moment not caring how it reacted with her meds. "People die. Tonight it was your girlfriend, Rana. Nightingale shot her in the face. She's not pretty anymore. Cheers," she said, and took another sip.

The blood drained from his face. She could see how shocked he was. His hand clenched the pistol so tightly his knuckles turned white. She wondered if he really was going to shoot her.

"This time you're finished. Saul's little pinup girl," he said, his voice hoarse. "Before I'm done with you, you'll be in a federal prison." He stood up and began pacing as he talked. "I've been onto you all along. Did you really think you could come to my station, my city, and me not know about it? You stupid amateur. I was matching wits in Moscow with the real professionals, the KGB, while you were still crapping in your diapers."

"Missed a few beats since then though, haven't you?" she said. "Like how your prize pigeon, Dima Hamdan, came to New York to kill the Vice-President of the United States and blow up the Brooklyn Bridge, and not a peep out of Beirut Station. Or that she was Sunni, not Christian. Or that your mistress was a double agent for Nightingale, who was himself doubling for both Hezbollah and al-Qaeda in Iraq, and nothing, not one word, from the great Davis Fielding, King of Beirut, just a great big pile of nothing!"

He stopped pacing and stared at her, his mouth working like he was trying to swallow but couldn't.

"We looked for Dima. She disappeared," he said.

"Is that so?" she said. "She filed a DS-160 using the cover

name Jihan Miradi, right through your own lousy embassy, and you didn't catch it. Not to mention that your mistress was passing on everything you touched via Nightingale to Abu Nazir in Iraq. So the only question is, are you totally incompetent or a traitor, you son of a bitch?"

He looked at the pistol in his hand like it was some kind of alien object he had never seen before. His finger, she noticed, was on the trigger.

"Rana wasn't my girlfriend," he said finally. "I barely knew her."

"Bullshit!" she snapped. "You telephoned her multiple times a week for months. Then you had the messages deleted from Company files and the NSA database. It was done the same day you ordered me out of Beirut—and by the way, I'd really like to know how you managed that little trick."

"I don't know what you're talking about," he said.

"Sure you do, Davis. You didn't think anybody would ever find out, did you? Well guess what, asshole? I know. And I'm not the only one."

He looked at her strangely, with a sick little smile. She wondered if he was mentally stable. *Funny, coming from me,* she thought.

"You think you know something, Mathison, but you don't. There are things going on; you don't have a clue," he said, straightening. "Tell me about your latest screwup. How did Rana die?"

"We were going to snatch Nightingale. He was both a double and a bridge agent between Hezbollah and, we think, al-Qaeda in Iraq. He's linked with Abu Ubaida and possibly Abu Nazir. We especially wanted to know about Dima's boyfriend, Mohammed Siddiqi, who, by the way, you also never mentioned to anyone back at Langley and who may have been the link. Only the Forces Libanaises jumped the gun. Nightingale shot her."

He looked bleakly at the window curtain, as if he could see through it. It made the room feel closed, like a prison cell.

"Poor Rana," he said, letting the gun hang by his side. He went back to the sofa and sat down. "She was such a beautiful woman. Smart. When you were with her, people noticed you."

"She was your mistress?"

"She was a contact. We may have had sex a few times, but . . ." He hesitated.

"What's the matter, Davis? She wouldn't let you have any? Or was it you who couldn't get it up?"

He looked at her as if seeing her for the first time.

"You really are a bitch, aren't you?"

"But not a traitor," she said, looking around. "There's nobody here. Just between us girls, you didn't have a clue what she was? Who she was working for?"

He almost imperceptibly shook his head. "What about Nightingale?" he asked.

"He's dead too. Damned FLs. Two of his Hezbollah guards got away. We had one wounded FL."

"So you got nothing?"

"Not exactly," she said, taking a cell phone out of her pocket. "This is Nightingale's."

He held out his free hand. "Let me see it," he said.

She shook her head no, her blond hair swaying. "I'm curious, Davis. How did you know about tonight's meet? Who told you? It wasn't me and it wasn't Virgil. Was it Ziad? One of the FL guys? Did they jump the gun because of you?"

He pointed the pistol at her.

"You seem to be confused, Mathison. In case you've forgotten, I'm the station chief, not you. If I can give the cell phone to Langley, maybe the mess you've made won't be a total fiasco. Give it here." He held out his free hand.

She put the cell phone back into her pocket. "What are you going to do, Davis? Shoot me?" she said.

"You really don't have a clue, do you?" He smiled. "This is a midterm election year. No one is going to screw with the Agency. You're done here. We're doing extraordinary renditions of Islamist extremists. You're being reassigned. You can interrogate bad guys in northeastern Poland, middle of piss-all nowhere. I suggest you dress warm, Mathison. I hear it's cold there this time of year."

"I'm not going anywhere. And you'll have to take this from me," she said, tapping the pocket where she'd put the cell phone.

"I have people coming. When they get here, they'll take you to the airport," he said, leaning back. "Before that's done, you'll of course give me the cell phone."

"I won't go."

"In that case, you're done," he said, looking as smug as a fraternity president watching a pledge make a fool of himself. "Your career's over. And I will press charges, Carrie. I guarantee we'll get something to stick. Truth is, it's impossible to be in this business and not break some law or congressional rule or other."

They sat not speaking, Carrie thinking that shits like him always got away with it, but she'd nail him somehow if it was the last thing she did. The apartment was silent, not even the sounds of Beirut evening traffic breaking through. She wondered if her career really was over. It would end when Fielding's people came. Just like her father, she thought.

There was a knock at the door.

CHAPTER 25

Ouzai, Beirut, Lebanon

Fielding answered the door, gun in hand. It was Saul Berenson, pulling a wheeled suitcase, obviously having come straight from the airport. Virgil was with him, carrying his assault rifle in a rigid plastic gun case.

"Hello, Davis. Expecting an invasion?" Saul asked, coming in, eyes on the gun. Virgil followed.

"Mathison blew Achilles, our last safe house. I wouldn't put it past her to blow this one," Fielding said, putting the gun into his pocket.

Saul took off his jacket and sat opposite Carrie. He looked at Fielding, who, after a moment, put the gun away.

"I understand Nightingale's dead," he said to Carrie.

"Rana too," she muttered, looking away. "Fielding says she was just a contact."

Saul rubbed his hands as if it were cold. "Pity we couldn't interrogate him. Might've nailed it down a thousand percent."

"What did you expect?" Fielding said. "I told you she's too new to run an op like this. You should have given it to me."

Saul looked at Fielding. "What would you have done differently, Davis? For the record," he said quietly.

"I would've used our people, not Forces Libanaises. And I would've picked the spot," Fielding said.

"There wasn't time—and he was already susp—" Carrie started to say, but Saul held his hand up to stop her.

"She had my authorization," he said.

"Look, Saul, I know she's your protégé, but this is my station. Do you want me to run it or don't you?" Fielding said.

"Wait," Carrie said, taking the cell phone out and handing it to Saul. "It wasn't a total loss. This is Nightingale's."

Saul tossed it to Virgil.

"I want every damn nitpicky little thing that's ever been on that phone," he told Virgil, who nodded; then he turned to Fielding. "I need to talk to Carrie alone, Davis. But you'll be glad to know she's leaving Beirut."

"But, Saul—" she said, then stopped at a look from him.

Saul turned to Fielding, who was smiling broadly.

"You're doing the right th—" Fielding started to say, but Saul interrupted.

"You're leaving too, Davis. I need to talk to you too. I'll meet you at your office, the one on Rue Maarad, in"—he glanced at his watch—"about an hour."

"What are you talking about? Leaving?" Fielding said, standing up.

"Langley. We need you back there." Saul smiled. "It's all fine. I'll explain everything. Now I need to straighten Carrie out first, okay?" He looked at Carrie. "What are you drinking?"

"Vodka. Belvedere."

"May I?" he said, reaching for her glass. "It's been a hell of a long flight."

Fielding looked at Carrie grimly and got his jacket. He watched Saul finish the vodka in the glass.

"What about the station? Who's going to be in charge?" Fielding asked.

"We're bringing in Saunders from Ankara. Don't worry. It's just temporary," Saul said reassuringly, making a gesture like it was no big deal.

"Jeez, Saul. Can you give me a hint?" Fielding asked.

Saul shook his head. "Your ears only. I don't want these two"—he indicated Carrie and Virgil—"to know. I'll be by shortly. I promise."

Fielding studied Saul for a moment as if trying to decide whether to believe him. "So you know, I've got some of my guys coming," he said. "We didn't want a repeat of Achilles."

"Call 'em off. We won't need them," Saul said, waving him away. "I'll brief you in an hour, okay?"

Fielding nodded and, not taking his eyes off Saul, left the apartment.

"Are you completely insane? Do you know what that asshole—" she started to say, but Saul put his finger to his lips to stop her and looked at Virgil, who went to the door and opened it to make sure Fielding was gone. "What's going on? Why'd you want to see me alone?"

Saul broke into a grin. Virgil, looking at the two of them, smiled.

"Do you know what you did? Have you any idea?" Saul said.

"What are you talking about?"

"That picture you sent. The one from the contact you tracked down, that Marielle."

"The man, Mohammed Siddiqi. What about him?"

Saul leaned forward and touched her arm. "Well, according to your former boss Alan Yerushenko and his entire team, plus everyone at NESA, they are telling us with a seventy-plus percent probability that what you sent, the person you identi-fied as one Mohammed Siddiqi, a so-called Qatari, who, by the way, according to Doha doesn't exist, is the only known photograph of Abu Ubaida, right-hand man and number two of Abu Nazir, head of al-Qaeda in Iraq and the person in all likelihood behind the attacks in New York."

She rocked back, stunned. Unbelievable, she thought. One minute she was being shipped off to Poland and now suddenly she had just hit a home run to win a World Series game.

"What about Fielding?" she asked.

"When he gets off the plane, Langley'll handle it." He frowned. "It won't be pleasant. I don't know what in the name of God he was thinking. Or how deep he's in, or with whom."

"What about Langley? Am I off the shit list?"

Saul grinned. "Are you kidding? As far as the director's concerned, you are the prom queen, Wonder Woman and the female James Bond rolled into one. Yerushenko said if he wasn't already married and a grandfather, he'd marry you. We finally have a shot at getting this son of a bitch."

"What about David?" she asked, not looking at him.

"Estes too."

"So why'd you say I was leaving? I've got a lot more to do here."

He shook his head. "You're going to Baghdad. Your flight leaves in four hours. You have a new mission. It's all yours. You're running it."

"Which is?"

"This is from Bill Walden himself. Bring us the heads of Abu Ubaida and Abu Nazir. Al-Qaeda's on the verge of taking over all of Anbar Province in Iraq. The country's about to ex-plode into civil war. Our troops are caught in the middle. It'll be a bloodbath. The Defense Intelligence guys've got casualty estimates you wouldn't believe. The only way to stop it is to stop those two."

"Why me?"

"I understand. This is big. But you found him. You have a better feel for him than any of us. You speak Arabic like a native. Who better? You were born for this, Carrie."

"And maybe a little justice for Dima. And Rana," she murmured.

"Ah, Carrie," he sighed. "Don't look for justice in this life. You'll be a whole lot less disappointed."

"The targets. How do you want 'em? Dead or alive?" she asked.

"In a million pieces for all I care. Just get the bastards," Saul said through gritted teeth.

She and Virgil were in a taxi heading down Rue Ouzai toward the airport. The road was crowded and noisy, even this late at night. The buildings near the coast were old and cracked, with washing and black banners with white lettering proclaiming, "Death to Israel," hanging from their balconies.

She'd gone back to Virgil's place to pack. When she started to fold her Terani dress, Virgil just shook his head.

"Won't have much use for that in Baghdad," he said.

"Probably not," she said, folding it and putting it in the suitcase, not knowing what else to do with it.

When they were ready, they headed for the cemetery near Boulevard Bayhoum so she could leave a message in the dead drop letting Julia/Fatima know she had to leave again. She told her to stay safe. She didn't have to mention what they both knew: that the bombs were coming.

"What about Julia's warning about Hezbollah and the Israelis?" she'd asked Saul when they were still at the safe house apartment. "She's been solid gold. There's a war coming. It's only a matter of weeks or months."

"We've kicked it upstairs. It was in the President's Daily Brief. Estes made sure the president saw it," Saul said.

"Are they warning the Israelis?"

Saul raised his hands in a gesture that somehow inexplicably encompassed two thousand years of Jewish history. "That's up to the administration. Sharing with other countries isn't intelligence, it's politics," he said.

"Even allies?" she asked.

"Especially allies."

"If it happens, Lebanon will get the worst of it," she said, pouring the last of the Belvedere into glasses for the three of them.

"Always. *L'chaim*," he said, raising his glass.

"Up yours," Virgil said, and drank.

Looking out the window, she saw the outline of a palm tree silhouetted against the ugly slum buildings in the headlights of passing traffic and she felt something tug at her.

"I'm going to miss Beirut," she said to Virgil. There was something about this life, these people. A kind of gallant madness. What was it Marielle had said? That they lived on "a bridge over an abyss."

"It's not Virginia," he nodded. A road sign indicated the airport was up ahead.

Her cell phone rang. It was Saul.

"Carrie?" he said.

"We're almost at the airport," she responded.

"Fielding's dead."

She felt a sudden vacuum, a hole open in the pit of her stomach. She'd hated him, but still. Unable to stop herself, she thought about her father, feeling sick at the memory of finding him the day before Thanksgiving, seeing what he had done to himself and rushing him to the hospital in an ambulance, thinking I'm sorry, Dad, so sorry, and in a horrible awful way, wishing she hadn't come home early at the same time.

"What happened?" she asked.

"Gunshot to the head. Looks like suicide."

Virgil glanced over at her, wondering what was happening, then straight ahead, squinting against the headlights from oncoming cars.

"We're coming back," she said. "We need to get to the bottom of this."

"Carrie, he wasn't stupid. He knew what was coming."

"Saul, listen to me. He was a lying piece of shit, a pathetic excuse for a human being, but he wouldn't do this. Not this. He wasn't the type."

"What type do you think he was?"

"The kind who thought he was smarter than anybody. That no one could touch him. He would always come out on top." She tapped Virgil's arm. "Listen, just wait for me. We're coming back."

"Don't. That's an order. Iraq's too important. Besides, whatever caused this, the answers are in Baghdad," he said.

CHAPTER 26

Route Irish, Baghdad, Iraq

Demon was talking under the metal arches in the waiting area at Baghdad International Airport. A stocky ex-military type with an Alfred E. Neuman gap between his front teeth, he was dressed in desert BDUs with a pirate skull and crossbones painted on his armored vest and the word "Demon" on his military helmet. He wore no shirt under the vest and his gym-built arms and neck were covered with cobra and devil-face tattoos. Like the other members of their Blackwater company escort team, he wore an ammo belt with extra magazines and a pair of hand grenades hanging like deadly fruit across his chest, an M4 carbine cradled in the crook of his arm.

Although it was before nine in the morning, Carrie was already sweating. The temperature was over ninety degrees on this early April day and it felt like it was going to get a lot hotter. Like the others, she was wearing an armor vest and Kevlar helmet and awkwardly carried a Blackwater-issued M4, a weapon she had never touched before. Virgil, next to her, looking equally uncomfortable, wiped the sweat off his forehead with his sleeve.

It had been seven months since she had been in Iraq, but

the heat, the private military companies, the sense of war the minute you flew in brought it all back almost as if she had never left, as if Beirut had never happened. Hard to believe it had been less than two months since it had all started with Nightingale's attempt to kidnap her in Beirut. The ninth of April now. Back in the States, spring break, April Fool's, tax season and the end of March Madness. As if she were on a run, where time seemed both compressed and endless simultaneously. Back in Iraq now, she thought grimly. Only this time she had a lead.

During the layover in Amman, she'd gone to the ladies' room in the airport, where a female agent from Amman Station, an attractive young Arab-American woman, had slipped her an encrypted cell phone under the stall partition and she'd used it to call Saul.

"What about the thing I gave you?" she'd asked him. Nightingale's cell phone.

"Still working on it. After every time he met Rana, he called the same cell number in Iraq."

"Where?"

"All over. Baghdad, Fallujah, Ramadi. Last one was Ramadi."

"So do we think that's where Abu you-know-who is?" she whispered into the phone.

"Ubaida? Yes. Carrie?"

"I'm here."

"Watch yourself. You're in the red zone." Things must really be bad if he thought he had to warn her, she thought. From the news on TV she knew the war, which had been bad when she had left Iraq, was amping up. Or was he warning her about something else? Like a major escalation or AQI op?

"Saul, is something coming?"

"It usually is," he said.

Demon was briefing them on what to expect on the drive into Baghdad's Green Zone from the airport. They stood with a group of contractors for Blackwater and other security companies and a pair of CNN reporters who'd just flown in with them from Amman.

"Listen up. I'm only gonna say this once and I don't give a shit if you listen because you may not be alive long enough for it to matter," Demon said in a way that let Carrie understand he'd given this speech plenty of times before. "It's only six miles from here to the Green Zone. It's a flat, mostly straight route on the Airport Road, a.k.a. 'Route Irish' for you newbies, a.k.a. 'RPG Alley' for those of you who are actually paying attention. We'll be there in ten minutes. No big deal, right?" He grinned, showing the gap in his teeth.

"We'll be in two convoys of five vehicles each. Each will have three armored Chevy Suburbans and an armored Blackwater Mamba truck with an M240 machine gun on the roof in the lead and another Mamba to bring up the rear. Now, some of you new people," he said, looking around at them, "may be thinking this is all a bit of overkill. Some of you may look at our big fat-ass American vehicles and feel a little safer with all that steel plate welded on them. Trust me, with the amount of RDX explosive our little *jihadi* brothers use, the armor around you is about as effective as tissue paper.

"Each of you will be assigned a field of vision to watch as we go. Keep your eyes open. Do not fire your weapon unless I yell 'Fire!' I mean it. If I do tell you to shoot, you better do it or I'll shoot you myself. Now, at this point, some smartass might be saying to himself, 'This is bullshit, Jack.'

"Okay, bullshit. But just for the record, yesterday there were twenty-one attacks on American convoys on this same road. We had two fatalities. But today, you lucky people, is the day before the big Mawlid al-Nabi holiday. The birthday of the Prophet Muhammad. So we can expect the ragheads to up the ante. By the way, it's the Sunni holiday, so in addition to attacks on us, we can expect explosions and car bombs at Sunni mosques and markets. Five days from now is the Shiite version of Mawlid al-Nabi and we get to do the whole damn thing all over again. Briefing's over. We'll either get through or we won't. Any questions?"

He looked at them. A couple of the contractors shuffled their feet, but no one said anything.

"Okay, boys and girl"—he nodded to Carrie, the only woman—"get ready for the longest ten minutes of your life. Let's get the hell outta here," he said, and turned and walked away. After a moment, they followed him outside the terminal. The gray Mambas and black SUVs were lined up at the curb in the blazing sun.

Rabbit, an ex-marine with cropped peach-fuzz hair, told Carrie and Virgil which SUV to get into and where to sit and gave them their field-of-fire assignments. They were in the second convoy. Carrie's seat was in the middle row, right side.

"What are we looking for?" she asked Rabbit. She'd done this before, last time she had been here, but from everything around her, it was clear things had changed.

"Any vehicle that doesn't stay the hell away from us. Anything. Women, kids, a pile of garbage where it shouldn't be," he said. "If anyone comes close, yell '*imshi*.' It means—"

"I know what it means," she snapped.

"I'll bet you do." He nodded.

She checked her M4. It was loaded with a standard thirty-round magazine. The safety selector lever on the left side was on "Safe." She brushed a fly off her face and hoped to God she wouldn't have to use it.

Waiting at Beirut airport and on the flight to Amman and the second flight to Baghdad, Virgil next to her reading a paperback, she'd mostly listened to John Coltrane on her iPod, cool romantic tracks like "Body and Soul," and thought about Fielding's suicide. The question was why. It couldn't have been because of what was waiting for him at Langley. Fielding was the kind of asshole who had always gotten away with things his whole life. He would've figured he'd find a way out of this too. So why had he done it? What was he hiding? And what did it have to do with Abu Ubaida and Abu Nazir?

The SUV and the Mambas were loaded up and waiting. Rabbit was sitting in front of her in the "shotgun" passenger seat. Although the air-conditioning was on, the SUV was hot with the windows partially rolled down, their weapons poking out. The radio crackled. She heard Demon's voice say, "Keep your eyes open and your sphincters tight. Let's roll."

The lead Mamba started to move forward and their SUV followed right behind it, the Mamba's Blackwater company flag, black with a white bear's paw, flying from the open roof-hatch cover. The convoy circled on the access road and headed for the airport gate. Carrie could see it up ahead through the windshield. The gate was heavily sandbagged, with concrete barriers that forced vehicles to make sharp back-and-forth turns before they could enter the airport. It was operated by Blackwater guards in full body armor manning machine guns.

A sign next to the gate read, "Leaving Airport Zone. Condition Red." Virgil leaned over and whispered in her ear that "Condition Red" meant weapons ready to fire. As they approached the barrier arm across the road, Demon's voice crackled over the radio:

"Lock and load, people. Safeties off. No tourists on this bus."

There was a sound of clacking as everyone racked the

charging handles on their weapons. Carrie moved the lever from "Safe" to "Semi" instead of "Burst" as she'd been shown. This is insane, she thought. She had no idea how to use this weapon and she wasn't sure she could hit anything.

They drove out of the airport onto a highway surrounded by desert. Right out of the gate she saw palm trees, trunks blackened and tops sheared off by explosions. Along the side of the highway was a long column of twisted wreckage, the charred and blackened remains of SUVs and trucks. Just by the amount of debris, it was clear that things had gotten a lot worse since she had been here last. A wide highway divider with flat ground, scrub and palm trees separated them from oncoming traffic.

Their SUV sped up. They were moving faster now, about sixty miles per hour. Carrie wiped the sweat out of her eyes. Along her side of the road was more of the same. Charred chassis of vehicles, mangled palm trees and scrub. In front of them was the lead Mamba, with someone on top manning the machine gun and ahead, the road, partially obscured in the distance by a yellow veil of dust. Stirred up, she assumed, from the first convoy, a couple of minutes ahead of theirs.

"Overpass ahead," Rabbit said over his shoulder. "Get ready. The *hajis* like to drop grenades and IEDs down on us. Eyes open. You won't see them till they pop up."

"Mother," Virgil muttered, throwing a look at Carrie indicating he didn't like this any more than she did.

They drove under the overpass, every nerve in her body expecting something to come down on them. As they came out of the shadow, she looked back but didn't see anyone. She was about to draw a breath when the radio crackled again.

"Get ready, people. IED Junction. Here's where the fun starts," Demon's voice said.

"Always something at least once a day here," Rabbit said, hunching over his weapon.

Carrie saw what he meant. A number of cars entered onto the highway from a feeder road. One of them, a taxi with two Arab men wearing checked *kaffiyehs* in the front seat, pulled toward them.

"*Imshi!* Get away, dammit!" Rabbit shouted, and fired a warning burst right in front of the taxi's front bumper, gesturing for them to back off. The taxi driver glared at them, but slowed and pulled away. Ahead, the lead Mamba was honking its horn constantly, but she couldn't see at what. Then she saw the Mamba deliberately bump into the rear of a car in front of it and watched as the car pulled over to the side of the road to get out of the way.

Now she saw that one car after another was pulling over to the side of the highway to let their convoy by, the Iraqis in them watching them from the side of the road, their expressions unreadable.

They passed under another overpass, training their weapons up at it, and then another. There was a crater in the road from a past IED explosion and the convoy slowed to go around it.

Suddenly a woman in a black *abaya* with two little boys appeared on the side of the highway ahead of them, near the wreckage of a car that hadn't been cleared away yet. She was holding a basket. They were in Carrie's field of fire.

"Two o'clock! Woman with a basket and children!" she called out. The woman beckoned at them, holding the basket toward them. My God! she thought. Was there an IED in the basket? She didn't know what to do.

"Don't fire yet," Rabbit shouted as they trained their weapons on the woman and the two children. What is going on here? Carrie thought. What are we doing?

"*Balah!*" the woman cried, waving at them as they slowed to go around the wrecked car.

"Wait!" Carrie cried. "She's selling dates!"

"Don't shoot!" Rabbit shouted.

Carrie moved her finger away from the trigger. As they passed, the smaller of the boys waved at them. This place is surreal, she thought, her heart beating like a snare drum.

They slowed again at a highway checkpoint formed by APCs and manned by Iraqi Army soldiers watched over by a pair of U.S. Marines. The Iraqi soldiers waved them through with hardly a glance and they sped up again. A highway sign read, "Qadisaya Expressway."

Suddenly, she heard an incredibly loud explosion and saw a massive orange fireball blossom a few hundred yards ahead of them. A blast of heat and a whiff of explosive came back at them like a hot wind.

"Shit," Rabbit murmured.

"What is it?" Carrie asked.

"Convoy ahead of us," he muttered through clenched teeth.

A minute later, they had to slow to drive around the shattered hulk of an SUV exactly like theirs, completely engulfed in flames, emitting a thick, acrid column of black smoke hundreds of feet into the air. Next to it was the smoldering hulk of another destroyed vehicle, nothing left of it but the chassis. Car bomb, Carrie thought automatically as they maneuvered past. She could feel the heat of the flames on her skin. The air was thick with smoke and the smell of explosive.

Because of the flames, she couldn't see anyone inside, but there was a man's arm lying yards away on the highway. They were going to drive right past it, maybe over it. Nauseous, she forced herself to swallow to keep from throwing up. As they drove by, she couldn't take her eyes off the severed arm. It lay there, palm up, the fingers perfect, untouched, even relaxed looking. Two Blackwater men were carrying a third man, his upper body drenched in blood. They brought him to an SUV stopped in the middle of the highway, its door open.

It must've just happened, she thought, sickened and suddenly reminded of the way it had been for her in Iraq before, that this place was for real; she could die any second. She was suddenly terrified. And yet, she felt more alive than she had ever felt in her life. Each pore of her skin was like a receptor sensing every atom in the air around her.

This is like one of my flights, she thought. This was true insanity. And yet. And yet. This was who she truly was.

As they started to speed up, the M240 and the M4s from the right side of the Mamba in front of them opened up. Everyone on the right side of the Mamba, her side, was shooting. Following the flight of the machine gun's tracers, it looked like they were firing at the roof of a sandstone-colored building about a hundred meters from the highway. God, she thought, seeing a flash of fire from there. Someone was shooting at them.

"Snipers. Fire, dammit!" Rabbit shouted, firing his M4 at the roof of the building as well.

Carrie tried, but she couldn't see who was shooting at them, though her nerves screamed in expectation of a bullet hitting her at any second. The harsh rip of M4 bursts from Rabbit and the man behind her sounded unbelievably loud in her ears. She put her finger on the trigger, not knowing what to do as they drew opposite the building. Then she saw it.

She could see the outline of someone up there and before

she realized what she was doing, she squeezed the trigger blindly, feeling the M4 move in her hands. She squeezed off another, the shots sounding very loud, although she was positive she hadn't come near hitting whoever it was. Before she could even see what happened, they were speeding away. She felt a terrible urge to urinate and tightened to hold it in. She put the safety selector back to "Safe."

After what seemed like an hour but must've been barely a minute later, they exited the highway, the lead Mamba honking and bumping into Iraqi cars to get them out of their way as they headed toward the Green Zone checkpoint. The streets were crowded with cars and motorbikes and people. Through the window came a smell of dust and diesel and rotting garbage.

The checkpoint was ahead of them: concertina wire; concrete blast walls, some decorated with graffiti; sandbags; concrete turn barriers in the roadway; a queue of cars and a long line of people going through inspection and metal detectors to get in, watched over by an M1 Abrams tank and a detachment of U.S. Army soldiers. They snaked their way around the serpentine turn barriers and stopped briefly at the checkpoint, where a contractor who looked exactly like a soldier except for the Blackwater shoulder patch on his shirt waved them on through.

Passing by the blast walls, it was as if they had landed on another planet. They were on a wide avenue lined with palm trees, villas with green lawns and gardens, monumental buildings with pointed domes like something out of *The Arabian Nights* and, in the distance, the sun shining on the Tigris River. They drove past a monument with giant crossed curved swords over the entrance to what looked like a vast parade ground. Near it was what looked like a big concrete flying saucer with its hatch open. She remembered it from her last trip, but Rabbit, assuming she was a newbie, pointed it out.

"Monument to the Unknown Soldier," Rabbit said as they continued on down the avenue, finally turning left past some government buildings in grassy open spaces, then right onto Yafa Street and pulling up at the entrance to a tall building with a dry fountain with statues in front that sooner or later, every foreigner who wasn't tied down in the military got to know: the Al-Rasheed Hotel.

"Do you want to check in or go over to the Convention Center?" Virgil asked as they unloaded. The Convention Center was where the Iraqi Provisional Government and U.S. government agencies had offices.

"Convention Center," she said, checking the safety was back on and handing her M4 to Rabbit.

"You did good," he said.

"I was scared to death," she said.

"Me too." He grinned and waved.

She and Virgil, pulling their rolling suitcases behind them, walked across the wide boulevard and showed their IDs to U.S. Marines stationed behind sandbags outside the Convention Center building's wrought-iron and concrete fence. The Convention Center was a giant fortresslike building made of gray concrete. It looked like a fortification from World War I.

They showed their IDs again to American MPs manning the entrance and went inside. Instantly, they were hit by the air-conditioning, and after asking, they eventually found an office with a sign on the door that said "USAID Baghdad," the U.S. government aid agency. They knocked and went inside.

They were shown to an office waiting room, where they sat and waited while a young American man in a Marine Service

C uniform shirt and tie, military written all over him, went to get someone. A U.S. Marine captain, also in Service Cs, came out of an inner office.

He was about six feet tall, athletic, good-looking, with dark wavy hair longer than the normal Marine's, blue eyes and a Tom Cruise smile.

"I'm Ryan Dempsey. You must be Virgil and Carrie. Welcome to the Sandbox," he said, shaking their hands. When he touched her hand she felt a tingle like nothing she'd experienced since the first time she'd met her poly sci professor, John, at Princeton so long ago. It's the adrenaline, she told herself, the thrill of surviving the drive, of being alive. But taking a good look at Captain Dempsey, she knew it wasn't true.

Oh shit, she thought. I'm in trouble.

CHAPTER 27

Green Zone, Baghdad, Iraq

They were at a small table at the BCC, the Baghdad Country Club. A white cinder-block house with blue trim on a residential street near the river, it was one of the few places in Baghdad where the booze flowed freely. The club was packed with Green Zone expats who came here instead of the bars at the Al-Rasheed or the Palestine Hotel because with the Shiites trying to form a government, the hotels didn't openly serve alcohol.

There were men in uniforms from a dozen different Coalition countries—Brits, Canadians, Aussies, Poles, Georgians, U.S. embassy and Provisional Government officials—and contractors from private military companies like Blackwater, DynCorp, KBR-Halliburton and a hundred others. More and more, the war had been subcontracted to these private companies and they had practically taken over. The bar and adjoining rooms were crammed with their employees, hired from every corner of the earth at Wall Street–like wages, speaking dozens of languages and spending money like it was going out of style. Jet planes taking off couldn't have matched the noise level, and female waitresses who didn't mind a pat on the butt could make a thousand dollars a night.

Carrie was sitting with Virgil and Dempsey, who was really a Marine captain on loan to the CIA, using the USAID office cover, from Task Force 145, a shadowy outfit fighting the insurgency.

Joining them was an Iraqi national, Warzer Zafir, officially a translator for the U.S. embassy, unofficially also from Task Force 145. The Iraqi was mid-thirties with dark hair, a three-day stubble, a straight nose sharp as an ax blade. Also attractive, Carrie thought. At the table next to them, a trio of Aussies was loudly celebrating an Australian cricket victory over "those donger South African whackers, mate."

"I speak Arabic. I don't need a translator," Carrie had told Dempsey back in his office.

"Warzer has other virtues," he said.

"Like what?"

"He's from Ramadi," Dempsey said.

"What about Ramadi?" Carrie asked.

Now, at the BCC, draining a Heineken, Dempsey told them: "You guys need to understand what's going on. Iraq's changed since you were here last. Over the past two weeks, more than three hundred bodies, most burned, tortured beyond recognition, have shown up here in Baghdad alone. Our troops are getting it from all sides. IEDs and snipers on every block. It's hard to tell who the Iraqis hate more, us or each other.

"The Sunnis will never accept Jaafari as prime minister." He leaned closer. "This insurgency has legs. AQI is getting stronger. They're on the verge of taking over Anbar. We're talking from the outskirts of Baghdad all the way to the Syrian border. People are scared shitless. Last week, two U.S. Army Rangers from the Seventy-Fifth went missing in Ramadi. An hour later they turned up minus their heads."

"That's why I'm here," Carrie said. "You've seen the photo. Do we have anybody who's seen him?"

Both Dempsey and Warzer shook their heads.

"Even if somebody did recognize him, they'd never talk. What you Americans don't understand," Warzer said, "is that it's not like Democrats and Republicans. If the Shiites take over, they'll kill all the Sunnis. They fear if we take over, we'll do the same. Saddam was a pig," he said, his face contorted, "and I'm glad he's been caught. But when he ran things, only some people died. Not everyone."

"I need someone from AQI. I heard you had a prisoner," she said to Dempsey.

Dempsey nodded. "While I was with the Seventh Marines, before all this spook shit, we captured an AQI commander in Fallujah. But they're tough to interrogate. They're not only not afraid to die, they want to die."

"What's his name?"

"He goes by Abu Ammar," Dempsey said.

"That's his *kunya*, his nom de guerre, not his name. Interesting he chose Abu Ammar," Carrie said.

"Why?"

"Yasser Arafat used it. Ammar was a companion of the Prophet. Maybe our 'Father of Ammar' has delusions of grandeur. Where do you have him?"

"Abu Ghraib."

"The same place they did all the tortures and stuff?" Virgil asked. Two years earlier, leaked photographs of U.S. servicemen and women torturing and sexually humiliating inmates at Abu Ghraib prison had been a worldwide political disaster for the United States.

"When you've seen what I've seen . . . ," Dempsey said,

then shrugged, as if Iraq were quantum physics, impossible to explain to laymen.

"Have you bugged his cell?" Carrie asked.

Dempsey shook his head.

"Shit." She frowned. "Does anyone have a clue what his real name is?"

"We have a snitch in there. Swears our Ammar is from Ramadi, which makes sense, and that his real name is Walid. We don't know his last name."

"Why does Ramadi make sense?" she asked.

"Because it's the heart of the insurgency. It's rumored that's where Abu Nazir is." He leaned closer. "I have to tell you, CENTCOM is planning a major operation in Ramadi," he whispered in her ear.

"When?" she whispered back.

"Soon. You don't have much time."

"So no one's seen Abu Nazir or Abu Ubaida?" Virgil asked.

"They say if you see them," Warzer put in, "it's the last thing your eyes ever see."

Dempsey looked around and motioned them closer. They all leaned in.

"So what's next? We go to Abu Ghraib for you to interrogate Ammar?" he said.

"No," she said. "Ramadi."

"Forgive me, al-Anesah Carrie," Warzer said. "But you are a little new in Iraq. Ramadi is . . ." He searched for the word. "You cannot imagine how dangerous."

"We've already seen how dangerous Baghdad is," Virgil said.

Warzer looked at Carrie and Virgil with his dark brown eyes. "Baghdad is nothing. Ramadi is death," he said quietly.

"We have no choice. I need to talk to his family," she said.

Dempsey grinned. "There's one born every minute," he said.

"What? A fool?" Virgil asked.

"Worse," he said, still grinning. "An optimist."

From the open door to her balcony at the Al-Rasheed Hotel, she could see the lights atop the Fourteenth of July Bridge over the Tigris River. The half of the city on the other side of the river was in pitch darkness, the power more often off than on, the curving river a silver ribbon in the moonlight.

From beyond the Green Zone she heard the crump of an explosion and the rattle of automatic weapons. Looking that way, she saw a line of red tracer bullets, trailing dreamlike across the darkness. The shooting stopped, then it started again, as much a part of the night sounds of this city as police sirens and cleaning trucks in an American city.

She went back in her mind to the same old question: What was Fielding's secret? What had he been hiding? Why did he kill himself?

Why does anyone? Why did her father try? Where in this night was her mother? Wasn't her leaving also a kind of suicide, a killing of her old life? Was that why she had never tried to contact any of them, not even her own children? Saul was right, she thought. We're all hiding something.

When her father finally got on clozapine, he tried to reconnect. It was as if she had never really known Frank Mathison, the Frank Mathison who had been in Vietnam—and she hadn't even known that about him till she found a photograph in a box in his closet, him shirtless, looking incredibly young and skinny, cradling an M14 in a jungle clearing with two friends, all of them grinning at the camera, shitfaced on whatever they were smoking, the Frank Mathison her mother had married before it all got really bad. He had moved in with her sister, Maggie, and Maggie's husband, Todd. He was in therapy, basically normal now, according to Maggie.

"He wants to see you," Maggie had said. "He needs to reconnect. It's important for his process."

"His process? What about mine?" she'd snapped.

She wouldn't let him get close. If she saw him at Maggie's house, she'd say, "Hello, Dad," "Good-bye, Dad," and that was all. Because she couldn't forget; her bizarre childhood a Ping-Pong match between gibberish and silence. And because he might seem normal, but she knew the craziness was hiding in him, waiting to get out the second you turned your head away.

And what about her? Her craziness?

Son of a bitch, she needed a drink. And jazz. She got her iPod ready. Just then, there was a knock on the door.

It was Dempsey, filling the doorway. Still in his service shirt and pants, a few drinks further to the wind than he had been at the Baghdad Country Club. The way he looked at her thrilled her to her core— Damn, he was a good-looking man.

"I want the truth. Are you married?" she asked.

"What difference does it make?" he said, not taking his blue eyes off her.

"I don't know, but it does. Are you?"

"I'm between," he said, as if marriages were military assignments, temporary postings, and then you moved on to the next.

"Oh shit," she said, the two of them coming together like atoms smashing, tearing off their clothes as he came into the room, kissing each other like the world was ending. They stumbled to the bed and as she wrapped her legs around his hips, feeling him push himself inside her, some part of her heard a pair of loud explosions this side of the river followed by a renewed outburst of automatic-weapons fire.

CHAPTER 28

Abu Ghraib Prison, Anbar Province, Iraq

They brought Abu Ammar, a.k.a. Walid, in manacles into the interrogation room where Carrie was waiting. The room was bare: concrete walls and two wooden chairs facing each other, nothing else. She gestured for him to sit down and after a moment, he did.

"*Salaam alaikum,*" she said to him, gesturing to the two U.S. soldiers who had brought him to leave. Walid didn't respond with "*Wa alaikum salaam*" as Arab courtesy demanded. He was a thin man with close-cropped hair and a ragged beard in an orange prisoner's jumpsuit with a nervous tick that caused him to jerk his head slightly sideways every few seconds. She wondered if it was natural or a result of his imprisonment and past interrogations.

His eyes flicked over her for less than a second, taking in her blue *hijab*, jeans and USMC hoodie, then moving away. He didn't have to say anything. She understood. She was the enemy. For several minutes, neither of them spoke. She made sure to sit still so the recording equipment and hidden miniature video camera she was wearing got a good image.

"You know the *hadith* of Abu 'Isa al-Tirmidhi reporting of

the Messenger of Allah, peace be upon him, who said, 'The best of you is he who is best to his family,'" she said in Arabic.

He twitched his head, but he never stopped watching her. His eyes blinked multiple times like a bird's.

"So, no electrics or waterboarding this time. You must be 'the good policeman,'" he said in Iraqi Arabic.

"Something like that." She smiled. "I need your help, Assayid Walid Karim. I know you would rather die than do this, but think. A word from me—and you will be free of this place." She waved vaguely at the walls.

"I don't believe you. Even if I did, I would rather die than help you. In fact, I think"—he twitched—"I prefer the electrics and waterboarding to your stupidity," he said.

"You will believe me, Walid Karim. That is your name, isn't it?" Although he tried not to show it, she could see he was shocked that she knew his name.

"I am Abu Ammar," he said.

"And what of poor Yasser Arafat, who wants his *kunya* back?" She grimaced sarcastically. "Listen, this will go much better if we tell the truth to each other. You are Walid Karim of the Abu Risha tribe and a commander in the Tanzim Qaidat al-Jihad fi Bilad al-Rafidayn, known to us poor American infidels as al-Qaeda in Iraq. You come from Ramadi, from al-Thaela'a al-Sharqiya, south of the river, near the hospital."

Karim stared intently at her, barely breathing, twitching. It had taken her and Warzer, using all his family and tribal connections, three difficult, secretive days hiding in Warzer's uncle's house in Ramadi, Carrie in a full *abaya*, her eyebrows colored brunette, wearing brown contact lenses and never breaking her disguise, to uncover Karim's real name and the house where his family lived. Then she visited Karim's family, bringing Warzer, who claimed to have been imprisoned in Abu Ghraib with Karim, so they would trust her.

"I've been to your house," she said. "I've spoken with your mother, Aasera. Your wife, Shada. I held your children, your daughter, Farah, your boy, Gabir, with these hands." She held up her hands. With every word, she could see how appalled he was that she knew so much. "Your son, Gabir, is beautiful but too young to understand what it is to be a *shahid*, a martyr. He misses his father. Say the word, and I promise, you will be home and holding him yourself in a couple of hours."

"You lie," he said. Twitch. "And even if not, I would rather see you kill them than help you."

"God is great. I would never kill them, *ya* Walid. But you will," she said.

His face twisted with disgust. "How do you say such a thing? What kind of a woman are you?"

"Remember the *hadith* of Abu 'Isa. I'm trying to save your family." She bit her lip. "I'm trying to save you, *sadiqi*."

"Don't call me that. We're not friends. We'll never be friends," he said, his eyes fierce like those of an Old Testament prophet.

"No, but we're both human. If you don't help me, the Tanzim will cut off your children's heads—and I won't be able to stop it, may Allah forbid it," she said, holding up her right hand.

"My brothers would never—"

"And what will they do to a traitor, a *murtadd*?" She spat out the word, "apostate," into his horrified expression. "What would they do to his family? His poor mother? His wife and children?"

"They won't believe it," he snapped.

"They will." She nodded. "They will when they see the American Marines bringing gifts, new big flat-screen televisions, and money, fixing and painting the house. When we have members of the Dulaimi and Abu Risha tribes whispering across the Anbar how you helped the Americans and are even thinking of becoming a Christian. They won't want to believe, but they will see the gifts and the protection from the Americans and they will know. And then, one day, the Americans will suddenly be gone. Then the Taksim will come to administer justice."

"You whore," he muttered.

"What of the *hadith* of the Prophet of Allah on that day? Or you can go free of this terrible place today. Go home, Walid. Be a husband to your wife and a father to Farah and Gabir and never worry about money or safety again for as long as you live. You need to choose," she said, looking at her watch. "In a little while I'll leave—and whatever you decide, there's no going back."

For a long time, he didn't speak. She looked around at the bare walls and thought about the things that had been done in this room. Perhaps he did too, she thought.

"This is evil," he said finally, twitching.

"For a greater good. You cut off innocent people's heads, Walid. Don't talk to me about evil," she said.

He looked at her, his eyes narrowed. "There are no innocent people," he said. "Not me. You?"

She hesitated, then shook her head no.

He twitched his head and exhaled. "What do you want, woman?"

Carrie took a photograph of Dima's boyfriend Mohammed Siddiqi, a.k.a. Abu Ubaida, out of her pocket.

"You know this man?" she asked. By the expression on his face, she could see that he did.

"Abu Ubaida." He nodded. "You must know or you wouldn't ask me."

"What's his real name?"

"I don't know."

"Yes you do," she said, crossing her arms in front of her chest.

"*La*, truly. I don't know."

"What do you know about him? You must know something. Someone must've called him something."

"He is not Anbari, not even Iraqi. Once I heard someone call him 'Kaden.'"

"Where's he from?"

His face hardened, and he looked at her suspiciously. "You will let me go? Today?"

"But secretly, you will work for me," she said. "Where did he come from?"

"Palestine, like—" He stopped suddenly.

He had slipped. She jumped at it. "Like whom? Like Abu Nazir? Both Palestinians?" When he didn't answer, she added, "Your son Gabir's life hangs by a thread, Walid."

"As do we all. We are all in Allah's hands," he said.

"And in your own. Tell me, they're Palestinians? Both of them? Is that why they're so close?"

He twitched and nodded, then: "Maybe not so close anymore."

"Why? What's happened?"

"I don't know. How could I? I'm locked up in here like an animal," he snapped.

"Then go free. Where is Abu Nazir now?"

"I don't know. He moves all the time anyway. They say he never spends two nights in the same bed. Like Saddam." He grinned, showing yellowing teeth.

"And Abu Ubaida? Where is he? Ramadi?"

He nodded, almost imperceptibly. "But not for long," he said.

"Why? Where is he going?"

He shook his head. For a moment she was afraid he was done talking. Walid was the best shot they had. If she couldn't get him to commit now—with a major battle for Ramadi coming, according to Dempsey—they would fail. Roll the damn dice, Carrie, she told herself, and stood up.

"Stay or go, Walid. This is the moment," she said, holding her breath. From somewhere in the prison came the faint sound of someone screaming, but she couldn't make out the words. Walid must be hearing it, she thought.

"What's your name?" he asked.

CHAPTER 29

Ramadi, Anbar Province, Iraq

They drove into Ramadi in a Humvee behind a Marine LAV armored personnel carrier, going on the bridge over the Euphrates River to the checkpoint by the electrical power station, the four of them, Carrie, Virgil, Warzer and Dempsey, in U.S. Marine desert combat utility uniforms. The sun was high, the day hot; the temperature was in the nineties, with a fine grit in the air from the desert wind.

They stopped at the checkpoint, a pile of sandbags and concrete. Dempsey got out and briefly talked with the Marines manning it. He came back and slid in behind the wheel.

"Not good," he told them. "Two police stations got hit last night. Jarheads on IED Avenue got plastered with heavy mortars. Bet they didn't tell you that at Langley, that AQI has hundred-and-twenty-millimeter mortars and Russian AT-13 Saxhorn missiles? Serious shit. And the *hajis* have upped the ante. They're offering two months' wages to anyone who plants an IED on Route Michigan, the main drag in the city. Three months if it kills any Americans."

"What do we do?" Carrie asked.

"Have to use RPG Alley," he grimaced and started driving.

On the way in from Abu Ghraib, Warzer and Dempsey had briefed them. Ramadi was, Warzer had explained, a city of a half million under siege, caught between three forces: al-Qaeda, the Sunni insurgents, and the Marines. A hundred kilometers west of Baghdad on the main highway across the desert, it was, in Dempsey's words, "easily the most dangerous place on the planet."

Now, driving onto the main street behind the LAV, Carrie could see what he meant. The street was bordered by rubble from where buildings used to be; the few buildings and power-line poles left standing were Swiss-cheesed with bullet holes. Except for a few mosques and rusted water towers still upright, the city looked like photographs of Germany after World War II, she thought. They passed a deep bomb crater in the road and Virgil glanced at Carrie over the Humvee's center console, then went back to scanning the street, his M4 ready.

In the distance off to the right, in the direction of a mosque about a quarter of a mile away, its minaret poking up over the buildings, they heard the sound of automatic-weapon fire, followed by staccato bursts from a heavy machine gun. Dempsey turned off the main street, no longer following the LAV.

"He's going to the Glass Factory," he explained. A Marine FOB—forward operating base—had been set up there. They on the other hand were headed for a police station in al-Andalus district, where they could set up. As they drove down a narrow street, two Iraqi men dressed in white *thaub* robes and *kaffiyehs* and holding AK-47s came out of a café doorway, then sat at a metal table outside over thimble-sized coffee cups and watched the Americans drive by. Dempsey started to speed up, then almost immediately slowed down.

"Shit," he said.

"What?" Virgil asked.

"Pile of stones on the sidewalk by that corner ahead," he said.

"What about it?"

"I don't know. IED maybe." Dempsey looked left, right, then behind them. "No good way around. Hold on to your favorite body parts, people," he said, gunning the engine as he raced toward the corner, aiming the Humvee so it would be scraping against the building on the opposite side of the street, as far away as they could get from the pile of stones.

Carrie held her breath, unable to take her eyes from the pile of stones, expecting an explosion as they raced by it. They made the turn onto the next street, where, incredibly, a handful of young boys were kicking a bundle of rags fashioned into a soccer ball in the dusty street.

"Wow," she said, exhaling.

Unlike children elsewhere in Iraq, none of the boys waved at them or even stopped playing, though the sudden stopping of chatter among them let Carrie know they were aware of the Humvee. After they passed the boys, Dempsey gunned the engine, raising a storm of dust.

Finally, they pulled up to the police station, surrounded by sandbags and manned by Iraqi policemen with AKM assault rifles. Carrie spotted another Iraqi on the roof behind a light machine gun. They got out of the Humvee and went inside, where Dempsey introduced them to Hakim Gassid, the police commander.

"Have you been hit yet?" Dempsey asked him. Police stations were a prime al-Qaeda target, since the Iraqi police and the U.S. Marines were the only forces standing between al-Qaeda and complete control of the city. Not a day went by that policemen weren't killed and stations attacked, typically with mortars, RPGs and IEDs, and sometimes with attempts to overrun them.

"Twice, but nothing this week, thanks to Allah," Gassid said.

A few minutes later, Carrie, in full black *abaya*, and Warzer, wearing a white *thaub* and a *kaffiyeh* with the checked pattern of the Dulaimi tribe, left the police station by the back door, taking a motor scooter to Warzer's cousin's house on the other side of the river.

The problem was how to run Walid Karim, to whom they'd assigned the code name "Romeo," in a city under siege. Normal tradecraft like dead drops, coded messages, hidden radios and disposable cell phones wouldn't work in a place where al-Qaeda checked every cell phone, even those of people they supposedly trusted, and you could get killed crossing any street in the city at the wrong time. Especially someone so embedded within al-Qaeda as Romeo.

The solution she and Warzer came up with was a teahouse in the *souk*, the downtown market near the central bus station, and a staggered set of prearranged days and times when Romeo would be there. The teahouse belonged to Falah Khadim, the uncle of a cousin of Warzer's. For ten thousand American dollars cash and no questions asked, he was willing to risk it. Abu Nazir had cut people's heads off for doing a lot less.

It was getting late in the day, after the loudspeaker call of the *muezzin* from a nearby minaret for the afternoon Asr prayer. Riding on the scooter to the *souk* on streets that were crowded despite the sound of gunfire and explosions coming from al-Thuba't district near the Euphrates Canal, the waterway that branched from the main Euphrates River on the western side of the city, they went to meet the uncle, Falah.

Warzer went into the teahouse to get Falah, because as a woman, Carrie could not enter. In conservative Ramadi, the teahouse was where men went to drink strong Iraqi tea, smoke *shisha* hubble-bubble pipes and play dominos or *tawla*.

A group of men came walking toward her as she stood outside a shop selling *hijabs* and other women's clothes. They were moving quickly, all of them with AKM assault rifles, and before she could move aside—thinking she needed to take cover and warn Warzer there was about to be shooting—one of them bumped into her.

"*Alma'derah,*" he apologized.

"*La mashkila,*" she said—*It's nothing*—and then her heart stopped.

It was Abu Ubaida himself. She recognized him instantly from the photograph. He was attractive in an Arab male way and she could see why Dima had been drawn to him. He looked at her strangely and she turned away, pulling the edge of her *hijab* modestly across her face. Despite her dyed eyebrows and brown contact lenses, she could tell she looked odd to him. He was starting to say something when one of his men called and they ran off.

A moment later, she understood when there was the sound of an IED explosion near the entrance to the *souk,* followed a minute later by the roar of an American F/A-18 fighter jet overhead, making the awnings and the goods in the *souk* vendors' stands rattle.

He's here, she thought, hardly breathing as she moved to find Warzer. People were running everywhere. Some to get away from the blast scene, others to go to help. She ran to the teahouse just as Warzer and a short, fat Iraqi with a Saddam-style mustache came outside.

"I saw him," she told them. "Abu Ubaida. He's here."

"Come inside, quick," Warzer said, looking around. "It's not good to talk out here."

"I thought I couldn't," she said.

"There's a storage room with a back door. Come," the uncle said in Arabic, looking at her the same way Abu Ubaida just had. Her disguise wasn't worth shit, she warned herself. They went around and into the storage room through a back door that had a padlock that the uncle, Falah, unlocked.

The room was small and piled high with boxes of tea and sugar and weapons of every kind.

"*Salaam*. You sell guns?" Carrie asked Falah.

"Every teahouse and half the shops in Ramadi sell guns," Falah said, looking at her as though he had never seen anyone like her. The disguise wasn't working, but what the hell was she supposed to do? Walk around in a miniskirt and halter top? "You're American, yes?"

"I appreciate you doing this," she told him.

"Just give me the money and don't tell anyone," Falah said. She opened the plastic bag she was carrying and handed him the money from a stash of hundred-dollar bills Dempsey had in a safe in the USAID office. "When is he coming, this man?"

Carrie checked her watch. "In about twenty minutes. Can I meet him back here?"

"I don't like to sell guns in front of my customers. Usually, I do it in back, but we can't have a woman in a teahouse. You hide here. If someone wants to buy, I'll tell him to come back later."

"How's business?" Carrie asked him.

"Not too bad, thanks to Allah," Falah said. "Even though the supply is good, the prices keep going up. It's cutting into my margins. If you're interested"—he looked at her—"I can get you anything you want."

"What are the ordinary guns going for?" she asked.

"Depends." He shrugged. "For a brand-new American Glock 19, four hundred fifty dollars. For an AKM, Kalashnikov, never used, one hundred fifty to two hundred fifty dollars." He studied her, then asked, "Will they execute Saddam?" Saddam Hussein, now in Abu Ghraib prison, had just been charged with war crimes against the Kurds and Shiites.

"I don't know. It's up to the Iraqis," she said.

"Nothing is up to the Iraqis," he said, motioning to Warzer. The two men left, Falah back to his business and Warzer to keep watch while she waited for Romeo to show. The storage area was hot, claustrophobic; a thin blade of sunlight came from a crack between the back door and the sagging lintel.

After Romeo's release from Abu Ghraib, using the cover story of an amnesty for a score of Sunni prisoners called for by al-Waliki, the new candidate of the Shiites after Jaafari had been rejected, they had gone back to the Green Zone. There Virgil tracked Romeo via the cell phone they had given him. As expected, they saw that he had gone back to Ramadi. But she had no illusions. She and Romeo didn't trust each other. He could get rid of the cell phone and slip the leash any time he wanted. The only hold she had on him was the threat against his family.

"We're threatening to kill his family with kindness, literally," she told Virgil and Dempsey. Romeo was completely untrustworthy, but yet they were so close. Only minutes ago, she had literally touched Abu Ubaida. She thought about Dima and Rana and admitted to herself how badly she wanted him dead. And Abu Nazir.

Falah, followed by Walid/Romeo, came into the storage room.

"Not too long," Falah said, and left.

"You have the money?" Walid said. She showed him the money in the plastic bag.

"Did the Tanzim accept the amnesty story?"

"I told my brothers that since they could never get real information no matter what they did to me, they never knew who they had. To the infidels, I was just another Sunni prisoner. They released me without knowing anything." He twitched. His nervous tic.

"And they accepted it?"

"The news about al-Waliki and the amnesty was on the television. It seemed reasonable."

"Tell me about Abu Ubaida. Is he in Ramadi?" She was testing him, not revealing she'd seen him.

"He's here but may be leaving very soon," he said, looking around as if they might be overheard.

"What about Abu Nazir?"

"No one knows. Some say here. Some say Haditha." He twitched. "Or Fallujah. No one sees him. He is a *jinn*." He twitched again and looked away. Something in the way he did it made her feel he was holding something back or had made a mistake.

"'But those who swerve away, they are fuel for hellfire,'" she recited from the Koran, the *sura* on the *jinn*.

He stared at her. "So, you know the Holy Koran," he said, as if something completely new had been added to the equation. "A woman no less."

"Only as a woman knows such things," she said, playing to his ego. "There's something else. What aren't you telling me?"

He motioned her closer. "Abu Ubaida is acting more independently. There are those who say Abu Nazir is no longer in control. Abu Ubaida is here in Ramadi where the battle is. As for Abu Nazir, who can say?" He shrugged. "Some of the Tanzim are choosing sides."

"Are you choosing?"

"Not yet. But it may come to that." He twitched. "Abu

Ubaida doesn't trust me. He doesn't trust anyone. Anyone he doesn't trust, he kills."

"Unless someone kills him first," she said. For a moment, neither spoke. She could hear the clack of domino tiles and smell the apple tobacco smoke from the *shisha* hubble-bubbles coming from the teahouse. "I need to know a time and place where he's going to be. Can you tell me?"

"No." He leaned almost close enough to kiss her. "There is something. But before I say, I need to know my family will be safe."

"I can't guarantee that in Ramadi. Not even in the Green Zone. You know this."

"I need to know my son will be safe."

"If something happens, *inshallah,* I will do my best. If you want, we can take them to America. Farah and Gabir will be safe," she said.

"Not America. There are only infidels in America. Syria— but with money." He twitched. Now she understood. He was telling her he did not expect to survive. He was making his last will and testament with her.

"How much money?" she said.

"One hundred thousand dollars U.S."

"Only if what you tell me is worth it," she snapped. "And only if they are in danger." She took a breath. "*Inshallah.*" God willing.

He twitched again. She remembered Saul telling her once, "Don't force it. When the asset is ready to drop his pants, you have to wait for him to realize he doesn't have a lot of choices. He has to talk himself into it. Just wait for it. All night if you have to." She waited.

"There is going to be an attack against the new Shiite prime minister. Something big," he said.

"In the Green Zone?" she asked. "How? Where will it come?"

"No one says. But we have men training on attacking a narrow street. They are told there is an arch."

"You know what it is, don't you?"

"I think Assassin's Gate. Very soon. Maybe a week. They are getting everything ready," he said.

"That's it? Just break into the Green Zone and attack the prime minister's office? Nothing else? That's not his style."

He stared at her, twitching, with his dark eyes. "I think you are a most dangerous person, Zahaba." The code name they had agreed on for her. Gold, for the color of her hair. "Perhaps not every American is a fool."

"Are you trying to provoke me? It won't work," she said. "There's another attack, isn't there? Abu Nazir and Abu Ubaida, they never do just one, do they?"

"It is their signature," he said in agreement. "There is another one. This against the Americans. Someone important."

Her mind raced. The Assassin's Gate was a big sandstone arch topped by a dome spanning one of the main entry points into the Green Zone in Baghdad. If Abu Ubaida managed to assassinate the new Shiite leader, al-Waliki, it would trigger a civil war that would lead to the destruction of Iraq and the complete failure of the American mission. The casualties, including Americans, would be enormous.

On top of that, there was another assassination planned. Of an important American. She had to find out from Saul who was coming in from Washington and where. Ten-to-one, the second attack would be on Camp Victory, near the airport. It was where all the VIPs came in. Having failed in New York, Abu Ubaida was making his bid for the leadership of AQI. It all fit.

She had to get this intel back to Saul immediately.

"Do you know who the American is?" she asked.

"Only that Abu Ubaida said he would cut off both heads of the two-headed snake."

"Were you in the room with him when he said this?"

"Not in a room. Last night. We were dropping off four policemen on the road to what the Americans call Hurricane Point. This is Saddam's old palace where the Euphrates divides into the main river and the canal, but first"—he twitched, never taking his eyes off her—"we cut off their hands and heads. We put the heads on stakes in the ground, like signs along the side of the road. Go drive there; you can see them." He smiled oddly. "If he knew we were speaking, what do you think he would do to me?"

CHAPTER 30

Fallujah, Anbar Province, Iraq

As the sun set, the sky a stunning pink and purple, calls to prayer from the minarets of dozens of mosques echoed over the city. Riding on the motor scooter, they could hear gunfire and explosions from mortars to the west as Warzer drove her back to al-Andalus police station. They were running out of time. Dangerous at any time, after dark, the city was a no-man's-land.

She and Warzer had gone to Romeo's house to take Romeo's wife and family to a nearby *souk*. They ate kebabs from a charcoal grill and bought Harry Potter toys for the children at market stalls. While she was with them, Virgil, disguised with a false beard and a Kurdish-style turban, snuck into Romeo's house to black-bag it, installing listening devices and hidden cameras.

Now, driving past a mosque in the fading light, they spotted a Marine LAV APC followed by two Humvees with mounted machine guns.

"Shit, a patrol," Warzer said.

They were in disguise, Carrie thought. To the Marines, they were Iraqis on a scooter on an empty street at night.

"Their fingers are on their triggers. Do as they say," she reminded him.

The LAV stopped. The turret gun pointed right at them. The Humvees stopped and a loudspeaker voice from the front Humvee said, "*Kiff!*" *Halt!*

Warzer stopped. He and Carrie got off the scooter, Warzer setting the scooter on its stand, then raising his hands in the air. So did Carrie, removing the veil and head-covering portion of her *abaya* so they could see her blond hair. She raised her hands high. A Marine got out of the Humvee and gestured for them to come closer.

"Let me go first," she told Warzer, and, hands held high, approached closer.

The Marine, a young corporal, stared at her, eyes like saucers. With her blond hair and all-American face, she must've been a completely surreal sight, but he kept his M4 still pointed at her.

"I'm American," she told him in English. "We're with Task Force One Forty-Five. We need to get to al-Andalus police station."

"An American woman? Here?" the Marine said.

"I know. Our mission is classified. We're working with Marine Captain Ryan Dempsey from the Two Twenty-Eighth. Can you help us?"

"Excuse me, ma'am, but are you out of your mind?" the Marine said, squinting at her as if to make sure she was real. "This is Sniper Alley. I don't know how you're still alive. Are you really American?"

"I live in Reston, Virginia, if that helps," she said. "This is Warzer," she said, gesturing with a tilt of her head. "He's with me. Could you escort us back to the police station?"

"Let me check with the lieutenant, ma'am. You can put your

hands down, just don't move," he said, backing away from her as though she were still dangerous. He spoke into the Humvee and after a minute, came back.

"That's a negative, ma'am. We have our sector to do. To tell you the truth, it's a mother—sorry, miracle someone hasn't shot at us already. You better get going," he said, eyeing Warzer as if he'd like to shoot him anyway.

"Thanks, Corporal. We'll do that," she said, and, putting her *abaya* head covering and veil back on, tugged at Warzer.

They got back on the scooter and drove past the LAV and Humvees, Carrie conscious of every eye on her even though she couldn't see them. The street they were driving on was completely dark now, the only light the headlight on the scooter.

We left it too late, she thought, feeling a twinge in her spine as if a bullet might come ripping into her back any second. A minute later, one almost did. Driving down the narrow street, she saw a flash of light and the loud crack of a shot rang out. Instinctively, Warzer swerved to the side, then straightened and turned the accelerator as far as it could go. He swerved again, slaloming left, then right. She could see the lights of the police station up ahead, surrounded by sandbags and concertina wire, its flat roof silhouetted against the stars.

Warzer raced straight at it, the scooter bouncing on the potholes in the road. She heard another shot coming from behind that by some miracle missed them. They swerved sharply and turned into a gap in the sandbags to the front of the police station, Iraqi policemen pointing their AKMs at them, shouting in Arabic for them to stop. They stopped and got off the scooter. The instant she pulled off her *abaya* head covering, revealing her long blond hair, the Iraqis relaxed and waved them inside.

"We left it too late," she told Warzer, going into the police station.

"We managed. You're good luck, Carrie," he said.

"I don't believe in luck. It better not happen again."

The intel she had for Saul was critical. She had to get it back to him ASAP, she thought, finding the police commander, Hakim Gassid. "Impossible, *al-anesah*." He shook his head. "No cell phones are working."

"What about land phones, the Internet?" she asked.

He shook his head.

"I have to communicate with my superiors. It's life or death, *Makayib*." She called him "Captain."

"Maybe in Fallujah, *inshallah*, there is some way. In Ramadi, *al-anesah*, is only destruction. You have no idea how beautiful our city was, *al-anesah*. We would have picnics by the river," he said wistfully.

It was insane, Carrie thought. She had one of the most important actionable pieces of intel she'd ever come up with, and suddenly, she was in the eighteenth century, with no way to communicate it back to Langley. She had to come up with something fast.

"Have you ever made love in a jail before?" Dempsey asked her. They were on a cot in Hakim Gassid's office on the second floor of the police station. Outside, they could hear the sound of gunfire and the crump of RPGs answered by the rattle of the machine gun on the roof and the AKM automatic fire from the policemen around the perimeter of the building.

"Have you?" Carrie asked.

"No, but I have, in worse."

"Where?"

"Back pew of a Baptist church in the middle of a sermon.

Her daddy was the preacher. Stella Mae. Great-looking girl. I'm not sure whether she was doing it to get back at Daddy or she just didn't give a shit, but the pew was about as comfortable as concrete and I kept thinking, They're going to catch us any second and every dick here has a gun in their car or truck. You?"

"Never did this. Sneaking in a little sex while people are trying to kill me. The Iraqi cops must think I'm a whore."

"They probably wish their own women were half as sexy. Sorry about the setting," he said, kissing her neck. "You have no idea what you do to me."

"Don't talk so much. Speaking of which, I need to talk to Langley."

"While we're doing it?" he said, sliding his hand between her legs, making her crazy.

"Stop it. We can't use cell phones."

"I know. The last local cell tower was blown up last week. Even if it was up, they monitor cell traffic just like us. I don't think anybody back home has a clue how sophisticated the enemy is here. Our best bet is to use the encrypted line back at the embassy in the Green Zone. Touch me right there."

"Won't work. I need to be here to run Romeo. Stop, wait a second. Wait a second."

"Write a report. I'll take it to Baghdad and send it from there."

"No good. You don't have my security clearance level. Oh God, that feels good. Wait. Romeo mentioned a VIP coming in next week. An attempted assassination. Any idea who's coming in?"

"Me, in just a minute," he said.

"Asshole." She pulled his head up by the hair. "Do you know?"

"Secretary of State Bryce," he said. "Her trip's supposed to be a secret, but if the *hajis* already know, we're blown."

"I need you to go to Baghdad to stop her from coming. Can you do that?"

"Do this first," he said, making her arch her back in delight. "Like that?"

"Shut up and pay attention to your work," she said.

At dawn, Dempsey left the police station for Baghdad in his Humvee. Carrie had made him memorize Saul's phone number at Langley. Regardless of whether his report got sufficient attention from whatever DIA–CIA liaison he reported to or not, Saul had to know what she'd learned. They had to get Secretary Bryce to cancel her trip to Baghdad. In addition, arrangements had to be made to protect the Iraqi prime minister at the government offices in the Green Zone and to prepare for an attempt to breach the Assassin's Gate. If there were any problems, Dempsey was to contact her ASAP somehow. Someone said there was a repair crew working on a cell tower, but if he had to, he was to drive all the way back from Baghdad if necessary.

Carrie watched him go. There had been shooting all through the night, and sometime around three in the morning, they'd heard a massive explosion over toward the hospital by the canal. Someone said it was a car bomb at the Iraqi police station in the Mua'almeen District. There was a rumor that more than thirty policemen had been killed. As he drove off, she thought, I shouldn't have sent him. It's too dangerous. Every *mujahideen* in Ramadi has got to be watching him drive toward Route Michigan and the highway back to Baghdad.

Watching the Humvee drive away, she tried calling him on the cell phone on the wild chance it was working, already missing him. But there was nothing. No reception of any kind. Not to mention, her cell battery was nearly dead, with hardly any place to recharge it because electricity in the city was so sporadic.

It was crazy calling him anyway; she felt like a total idiot. What the hell was she doing acting like a teenager? She felt strange, disconnected from herself. Was it her bipolar? Or was it that everything they did here was so dangerous you had to live not just day by day but second by second? She felt out-of-body, like she was watching the dusty trash-strewn street where he drove away and watching herself watching.

A shiver went through her for no reason she could understand. She was never going to see him again, something told her. She shook her head to try to clear it. This was crazy. She still had pills from Beirut, but when she got back to Baghdad, she'd find someplace and arrange for more. She couldn't shake the uneasy feeling, looking at the area around the police station. Forget bipolar; this place was making her crazy in all kinds of ways.

Although it was still early in the morning, the sun barely clearing the tops of the buildings, she could feel the heat coming. Except for the debris and death, Ramadi could have been anywhere in the Middle East. Strange, she thought. Decisions we make for the most arbitrary of reasons end up changing our lives forever. For her, a decision she had made almost casually at Princeton years ago to study Near East Studies because the geometric patterns in Islamic art had fascinated her had brought her to this.

And then there was Romeo. He was giving her actionable intel, but she could trust him about as far as she could throw the Brooklyn Bridge, the last thing Abu Ubaida had tried to destroy.

She went back inside to an open jail cell where Warzer and Virgil had spent the night. They were getting up, and in a little while, they were all sitting in the cell, drinking glasses of strong Iraqi tea with plenty of sugar and eating *kahi*, phyllo-dough pastries dipped in honey, that one of the Iraqi police-men had brought them.

"Now what?" Virgil said, brushing a fly off his *kahi*, then taking a bite.

"Anything on the bugs you planted at Romeo's house?" Carrie asked.

"The women were talking. Arabic." He grimaced. "Need you or Warzer to translate, but Romeo didn't show."

"Which means he's with Abu Ubaida. He's inside. That's what we want," she told them.

"What about the intel on the attack in Baghdad?" Virgil asked.

"We wait till we hear what Langley wants to do. Dempsey'll tell us tomorrow when he gets back," she said.

"You, wait?" Virgil grinned. "Doesn't sound like you. Get-ting cold feet, Carrie?"

"I'll admit it," she said. "This place scares the shit out of me."

"It should," Warzer said. "I moved my family to Baghdad, not that that's so much safer."

"I have to admit, I don't like the idea of waiting. Especially on Langley," she said. "Once Abu Ubaida goes operational on this latest attack—and we're talking a week at most—our chance at nailing him and maybe Abu Nazir becomes a total crapshoot."

"What do you want us to do?" Warzer asked her.

For a moment, her eyes searched the walls of the cell as if looking for an answer there. But there was nothing but bits of penciled-in Arabic graffiti, which, except for the occasional invocation of Allah, was amazingly similar to Western graffiti.

"Go back to electronic surveillance on Romeo's family. I gave him money. He'll want to give them at least some of it. I'll be by in a bit to translate," she told Virgil, who got up, still holding the tea, and went out, presumably to a holding cell on the second floor where he'd set up his gear.

"What about me?" Warzer asked.

"Abu Ubaida is here in Ramadi. I can't believe some of these Ramadi policemen don't have snitches. See if you can find out if anyone knows where they're hiding."

Warzer started to get up. She motioned to him. Not sure how to say it, she just said it. "Warzer, do you think these Iraqi police think I'm a whore?" she asked, using the Arabic word, "*sharmuta*." "It's just now, with death so close, there's so little time . . ." She faltered.

He looked away, clearly uncomfortable, then back straight at her.

"Carrie, you're a very beautiful woman. Truly. For these men, you're like a movie star from Hollywood. Someone so far out of reach. But also, our world with women is so different. So yes, maybe, a little like a *sharmuta*. But listen, Captain Dempsey, as a man, I like him. He has courage. But you don't know him. There are rumors. Be careful," he said.

"What kind of rumors?"

"Money," he said, rubbing his thumb against his fingers. "Stories about sales of American equipment, medical supplies, ammunition, refrigerators, all kinds of things on the black market. This war is the biggest gold rush in history for companies. Blackwater, DynCorp, KBR. Everyone is getting rich except the people."

"Do you know this is true about Captain Dempsey?"

"I know nothing. I shouldn't have said anything, except . . ."

"Except what?"

"I like you, Carrie. For me, you are the best of America, so good. About you and Captain Dempsey, I should not speak. Only"—he hesitated—"I think you are very lonely."

She was talking with the police chief, Hakim Gassid, about informants when Virgil came and got her.

"You better come see this," he said.

She followed him back to the cell where he kept his equipment. On his laptop, he showed her two interior scenes in the entranceway and main room of Romeo's family's house.

"This was last night," he said, rewinding the footage, people making gestures and moving backward. Then he started playing it forward, with Romeo coming into the house.

She watched as Romeo came into the entryway and then into the main room. As in most of Ramadi, there was no electricity and the rooms were lit with lanterns and candles. She listened as he greeted his wife and mother and then cradled his children in his arms. Like most Iraqi homes, the furniture was sparse and set along the walls, a carpet on the main room's floor. So far, everything and the conversation seemed normal, except she noticed he kept looking around. At one point, he got up and picked up a lamp and looked at it.

He's looking for bugs, she thought. He knows. Of course he knows. Idiot, she thought, mentally kicking herself. First, he's not stupid, and second, someone, some neighbor or extended family member, must've spotted Virgil, who even on his best disguise day couldn't pass for a Kurd, not that people wouldn't wonder what a Kurd was doing in Ramadi.

She watched him give his wife some or all of the money she'd given him—impossible to tell—and whisper something in her ear she couldn't hear. And in the distance, even on the soundtrack, she could hear gunfire. As they watched, Carrie quietly translated what she could hear.

They watched Romeo go to the side of the room, turn over the corner of a carpet, pull up a board from the floor and take out an AKM assault rifle. He put the floorboard back and started to check the AKM.

The children came back; he talked with them and let them climb over him. The little boy tried to pick up the AKM and Romeo smiled and showed him how to hold it and aim. Then the wife and Romeo's mother took them away, presumably to bed.

Something was missing. What was it? She watched the video intently and then she had it. No nervous tic. He wasn't twitching. It was gone. That miserable son-of-a-bitch liar, she thought. Why did he do it? To gain sympathy in Abu Ghraib? To distract questioners? To help disguise his identity? Or was he just a pathological liar? Everything he said had to be taken with a huge grain of salt. But she knew that already, didn't she?

"No tic. Is that what you wanted me to see?" she asked Virgil.

"Wait," he said, holding up a cautionary finger.

The mother, Aasera, came and made tea and brought him a glass. They talked for a bit about the family. He asked her about Carrie, the American woman, and her Iraqi companion, Warzer.

"I don't trust them," Aasera said. "They pretend to be friends, but they are infidels. Why did you bring them to us?"

"Ama, I had no choice. *Inshallah*, they won't bother us again," he said.

"Take care. I think she is dangerous, this blond *sharmuta*."

"Enough, woman. Stay out of my business," he snapped,

and waved her away. She darted a suspicious glance at him and left the room. As soon as she was gone, he took out his cell phone and began texting.

"Can we get what he's texting and the number he's calling?" Carrie asked Virgil.

"That's not the phone we gave him. Baghdad Station can probably pick it up from Iraqna's cell COMINT. AQI may have their own functioning cell station. Maybe we can pick it up from the Iraqna company and I can get it from them, but it'll take a couple of hours."

"Let's do it," she said, and started to get up.

"Wait," he said, stopping her. He sped the video up so that about an hour had gone by when suddenly, she heard sounds from outside on the video and saw Romeo stand up. His wife, Shada, looked at him and asked who it could it be at this hour. He started to ready the AKM, then put it down on the chair and motioned for her to answer the door. He followed her to the entryway.

As Shada opened the door, four *mujahideen* with automatic weapons, she assumed AQI, burst in past her, followed by Abu Ubaida himself. She recognized him from the *souk*.

"It is late, my brother," Romeo started to say, but Abu Ubaida cut him off.

"You have to come now. He wants to see you," Abu Ubaida said.

"But my family—I promised them I'd stay home tonight," Romeo said, gesturing at Shada and his mother, who came into the room.

"Are you sure you want them involved in this, Walid? He has questions, brother. So do I," Abu Ubaida said as the four men hustled Romeo out of the house. On the video, Carrie could clearly hear the sound of car doors slamming and someone driving away as the two women just stood there, staring at the door. Virgil stopped the video.

"He's blown, isn't he?" Virgil said.

"Yes, but did you hear what Abu Ubaida said?" she said.

"That was him, wasn't it?"

"Hell yes, it was him. Do you realize what this means? He said, 'He wants to see you.' There's only one person who can give Abu Ubaida orders: Abu Nazir himself! We've got 'em both! Both in the same place at the same time! We call in a drone and we can eliminate both of them, once and for all! Virgil, you're a genius!" she said, and hugged him. "Does he still have the cell phone we gave him?"

Virgil nodded. "So far," he said.

"So we can track him?"

"Have a look," he said, opening another window on his laptop and showing her a pulsing dot superimposed on a Google satellite image of Ramadi. It appeared to be on Highway 10 in al-Ta'mim District in the western part of the city, south of the canal.

"Do we know where that is?" she asked.

"I asked one of the policemen. He says his best guess is that it's the porcelain factory. He says it's ruined now because of the fighting, but it used to make sinks, toilet bowls, stuff like that."

"We've got them," she breathed. "We need to call in a strike."

Virgil frowned. "Unless it's a trap," he said.

It was like a slap in the face. Of course, what was she thinking?

"What time was the video showing them coming and getting Romeo?" she asked.

"A little after midnight."

She looked at her watch. It was just after eight A.M. So Romeo had been with Abu Ubaida and also, possibly, Abu Nazir for seven to eight hours. Or maybe not. She had to admit there was also the possibility that Abu Ubaida had split from Abu Nazir and that his comments to Romeo had been a ploy. Abu Ubaida had to have found the cell phone she had given Romeo. That cell phone was still on and Abu Ubaida had to assume it was being tracked.

No question, the probability was huge that Virgil was right. It was a trap. They might have been torturing Romeo this very second, if he wasn't dead already. They wouldn't have to torture him much for him to tell them everything he knew about Zahaba, the blond Arabic-speaking female CIA agent and her Iraqi sidekick. She felt queasy. It would make her al-Qaeda's number one target in all of Iraq. Not to mention, Romeo was her asset, her responsibility. She'd put him into this situation.

Unless Abu Ubaida still trusted Romeo. In which case, there was a chance that Abu Ubaida had been telling the truth to Romeo and they could still kill both Abu Ubaida and Abu Nazir today. Although she had to admit, the way that Abu Ubaida had spoken to Romeo certainly didn't sound like he trusted him. What was it Romeo had said to her about Abu Ubaida in the teahouse? *He doesn't trust anyone. Anyone he doesn't trust, he kills.*

So which was it? Time to decide, Carrie.

If she called in a drone strike, Romeo would die too, along with whoever was with him in the porcelain factory. If it meant getting Abu Ubaida and maybe Abu Nazir, stopping the assassinations and a civil war that could mean tens of thousands of lives, it was worth it. Romeo was collateral damage.

But if it was a trap, it meant they knew they had to stop her. Tracking works both ways; the thought stopped her dead. Had they been tracking her?

"Even if it is a trap, we need to get to the Marine commander and have him order up an attack on the factory," she told Virgil, motioning for him to follow. As she headed for the stairs, she saw Warzer coming up, his face twisted.

"Carrie," he said. "I'm sorry. Truly."

"What is it?" she asked.

"IED. On Highway 11 outside Fallujah. Dempsey's dead."

CHAPTER 31

Al-Ta'mim, Ramadi, Iraq

It was the young Marine, Lance Corporal Martinez, who spotted it. A thin metal tube almost completely hidden under some debris in the middle of the street, just sticking out of the pavement.

"Probably pressure trigger," he said. He had stopped their armored Humvee just two feet short of it. Another half second and they would have gone over it, and that would have been the end of her. They were all living on borrowed time, Carrie thought, wiping her forehead with her sleeve. The temperature was already in the high nineties. She wore an oversized Marine utility uniform with a desert camouflage pattern, her *abaya* and personal things in a backpack she kept next to her on the seat.

They were trying to make their way to the Government Center, where the regional Iraqi Provisional Government, protected by the 3/8 Marines—Third Battalion, Eighth Regiment—were headquartered in Ramadi. She had thought Ramadi was the deadliest place on the planet, but this part of the city was like something out of a World War II documentary. Not a single building was left intact; nothing was functioning, and nothing moved on the streets except a lone skeletal cat walking atop a pile of garbage. Everywhere she looked, there were shattered buildings, the rusting hulks of destroyed vehicles, debris and rotting garbage.

Martinez backed the vehicle up a few feet, then carefully drove around the metal tube, and they continued down the empty street. Virgil and Warzer, in the backseats, scanned the ruined buildings and rubble for snipers, while Carrie, in the front passenger seat, tried to hold it together, her hands trembling.

She had killed Dempsey, she kept thinking. The whole operation was crazy, but with the battle ramping up in Ramadi, Abu Ubaida about to move on Baghdad and all her doubts about Romeo, who was at the least a double agent, sending him down Highway 11 had to have been a suicide mission. If she had been tracking Romeo to get to Abu Ubaida, it was also possible Abu Ubaida might have been doing the same, using Romeo to track her and her team.

Except what else could she do? A pair of assassinations that would launch a civil war was about to start. Romeo wouldn't have lied about it because if it didn't happen, she would have destroyed him and his family just by having the Marines be nice and help them.

There was no choice. She had to get the intel to Langley. Nothing else mattered. Dempsey had been a Marine. He would understand that, she told herself. Only now Abu Ubaida and maybe Abu Nazir were within striking distance of their goal—and Dempsey was dead.

"Where? What happened?" she had asked Warzer, so stunned she could barely breathe.

"According to the Iraqi security force, it was just a few kilometers

before the bridge into Fallujah. That empty stretch of Highway 11 between the Duban Canal and Lake Habbaniya. Something on the road made Dempsey slow down and when he did, they detonated an IED. They said it left a crater four meters deep in the highway. I don't think there was much left." Warzer grimaced.

Oh God, oh God, she thought. And then the question she couldn't help asking.

"Any idea if it was random, or were they waiting for him?"

"No way to know," Warzer said. "It could have just been bad luck."

Except it wasn't. Not when you were playing with a double agent like Romeo, who could feed intel about her, and possibly her team, directly to Abu Ubaida and maybe even Abu Nazir himself. Given that combination, how likely was it that it was random? The conclusion was inescapable.

I killed him, she thought. I am a disaster to anyone who gets near me. Dima, Estes's marriage, Rana, even Fielding, and now Dempsey. Anyone. She felt like crawling into a corner and never coming out. The loss of Dempsey was a physical pain, like someone had stabbed her in the chest. Except she couldn't collapse. Not now, not when everything, the entire war, was at stake. Hold it together, Carrie, she told herself. You can feel sorry for Dempsey and yourself later. You have no choice. No one here does—and neither do you.

They drove past a mosque with a pointed gray metal dome that was oddly intact, then turned up a rubble-strewn street. Up ahead, they heard the sounds of automatic weapons firing, and explosions.

Martinez stopped the Humvee and grabbed the SINC-GARS radio handset. "Echo One, this is Echo Three. We're at Red Zone Alpha," he said. Then he listened and said, "Romeo that. Light the fire, we're coming in." He looked back at the others. "Hang on, folks. It's gonna be like the Fourth of July."

Martinez put the Humvee in gear and they lurched forward. He stepped on it and they began bouncing over ruts and rubble, pointing at a big rectangular concrete building in the middle of a wide open space. In front of it was a high wall of sandbags. That has to be the Government Center, she thought. Every building on the street approaching it was a total ruin, some with what was left of bedrooms exposed, with dangling scraps of bedsheets and broken picture frames on walls.

As they raced up the street, Martinez gunning the Humvee, the buildings suddenly came alive with flashes of weapon fire and the staccato rattle of AKMs shooting at them, bullets pinging on the steel armor plate. Carrie scrunched down in her seat, thinking, There's no way we can make it through this. An RPG round exploded in front of them as Martinez swerved, the windscreen suddenly stippled with shrapnel chinks. A bullet went through the open window, barely missing her face.

At the same time, there was an answering roar from the Government Center as Marines at the sandbag barricades and from the windows and roof of the big building poured withering fire on the buildings where the insurgent fire was coming from. There was the loud percussive boom of a big gun. The wall of a building near them exploded in a hail of brick fragments. The AKM that had been firing at them from that building fell silent.

"That's the Abrams," Martinez said, talking about the big gun. He floored the gas pedal as they barreled toward a narrow gap in the sandbag barricade and shot through. Martinez whipped the Humvee into a radical ninety-degree turn and pulled up in the shadow of the barricade. By the side of the building, Carrie saw the M1 tank, whose big gun had fired the shot at the building. It had probably saved her life, she thought as they got out and ran inside the building.

Even before they got inside, Carrie was assailed by the powerful stench of urine, rotting garbage and unwashed bodies. She could hear the hum of a generator providing an undercurrent to the almost constant sound of gunfire punctuated by explosions. The Government Center was full of Marines, some at window openings, the windows long since gone, firing at the hulks of shattered buildings surrounding the square. A few Iraqi officials, in unpressed suits, moved like ghosts among the Marines, some of whom, despite the gunfire, slept where they were on the hard tile floors. Others stepped around the sleeping Marines as they worked.

One Marine beside a window opening paused from shooting to eat from an MRE while two other Marines came down the stairs carrying a heavy bucket on a pole that, even wrapped with plastic, reeked of fecal waste.

"Sorry for the stink. No running water," Martinez said to them. "Commander's office is on the second floor."

"Thank you, Lance Corporal," Carrie said, heading up the stairs. The Marines stopped what they were doing, looking at her as though she was a creature from another planet. As she continued up the stairs, someone gave a wolf whistle.

She almost responded, but the thought of Dempsey smacked her hard, like pain from an amputated limb. Inside she was nauseous, shaking. Was it her meds? I can't do this, she thought, then realized, There's no choice. I have to. It wasn't just the mission, it was the war itself.

She asked for directions from a couple of Marines on the second floor, who just stared at her, then pointed to an office. A hand-lettered sign taped on the wall read, "Lt. Colonel Joseph Tussey, CO Third Battalion, Eighth Regiment, USMC." There was no door. Carrie, followed by Virgil and Warzer, knocked on the wall and walked in.

Tussey, sitting behind a metal desk, was a trim, medium-sized man, about five eight, his thinning hair cropped in a USMC high-and-tight, his eyes the pale blue of Arctic ice. On the wall next to him was a map of Ramadi with colored pins in it. His look, when they walked in, suggested they were as welcome in his office as a plague of locusts.

"Good morning, Colonel. I'm Carrie Mathison. This is Virgil Maravich and Warzer Zafir. We were working with—" She was about to say "Captain Dempsey" but couldn't get the words out. It was all she could do not to cry like a girl in front of this grim-looking Marine officer.

"What the hell are you people doing in the middle of a battlefield?" Tussey said. "My men don't have time to play nursemaid."

"We don't need hand-holding. But I am going to need a number of your men and some support, including a drone," she said.

"I don't know who the hell you think you are coming in here, but we've got a battle on our hands and the only thing I'm going to allow you people to do is hunker down till we can figure a way to get you the hell out of Ramadi—and my hair. Dismissed," he growled, and started typing on his laptop computer.

Warzer started to leave but Carrie motioned to him to stay. After a minute, Tussey looked up.

"Why are you people still standing here? I said 'dismissed,'" he said, raising his voice.

"I'm sorry, Colonel," Carrie said. "But I'm going to need

some help. At least a couple of platoons or more. And communications. I need secure communications to Baghdad and Langley ASAP."

"Look, Miss whatever-the-hell-your-name-is, get out of my office now or I'll have you locked up. And if you think this shit hole smells bad . . ."

Carrie motioned for Virgil and Warzer to go outside. She waited till they walked out, then came around the desk and stood right in front of him.

"I understand your situation, Colonel, and believe me, I'm not interested in a pissing contest with you. But before you throw us into whatever passes for detention in this dung heap, let me just pick up a radio handset and I'll have General Casey, commander of Coalition forces, directly order you to cooperate with me. Besides, when you hear what I have to say, you're going to want to give me everything you can."

Tussey exhaled slowly. "Well, ladybird, I'll say this: you got balls. Sit down," he said, gesturing at a metal folding chair, and she sat.

"My mission is classified, Colonel. But as of seven hours ago, we located the leaders of AQI, Abu Nazir and Abu Ubaida, the men who are the leaders of the people trying to kill your men this very second. They're west of here, in the porcelain factory in al-Ta'mim District on Highway 10. Give me the forces and we can kill them," she said.

"Just like that?" he said, snapping his fingers.

"Just like that," she said.

"How do you know they're there?" he asked.

"We have a double agent, an officer in AQI, inside. They brought him in to be questioned by Abu Nazir himself. We tracked him by a cell phone we gave him."

"Abu Nazir? *The* Abu Nazir?"

"Yes."

"And Abu Ubaida too? How do you know he's there?"

"I saw him myself in the *souk* yesterday. We also bugged our double agent's house. Abu Ubaida is the one who came to take him in."

"You saw him? In the market? An American woman wandering around like a tourist—and you're still alive?"

"I was wearing this." She pulled her *abaya* out of her backpack to show him. "A woman in an *abaya* is invisible to a lot of men in this part of the world, Colonel. You'd be surprised."

"Possibly." Tussey grimaced. "Seven hours is a long time. They could be all the hell the way to Syria by now."

"Except if they want to interrogate him, it takes time. They're still there."

"How do you know?"

"Because the cell phone hasn't moved," she said, leaning forward. "Come on, Colonel. Give me some Marines. Abu Nazir and Abu Ubaida are smart as hell. Without their leadership, these *mujahideen* shooting at you and your men are clueless. They'll fade away."

"Maybe the cell phone hasn't moved because they left it behind. Maybe your man inside is dead. Maybe it's a trap."

She didn't answer right away but looked at a jagged opening in the wall behind him that had once been a window. It was bright with sunlight, the day getting hotter. The stench from below because of the lack of toilets was indescribable. How the hell do they stay here? she wondered.

"Maybe. Very possible," she admitted. "But Abu Nazir and his right-hand killer, Abu Ubaida, are responsible for the deaths of hundreds of Americans. This is the best shot at them we've ever had."

"Who did you say you were working with as liaison?" he asked.

"Captain Dempsey. Ryan Dempsey, USMC," she said, unable to suppress a quaver in her voice. "Task Force One Forty-Five."

"I know him. Where is he? Why isn't he with you?"

"He was killed this morning. Highway 11 outside Fallujah. I just found out myself an hour ago," she said, her hands trembling. "I have urgent intel to get to Langley and USF-I headquarters and we had no cell or Internet communications. It's my fault. I killed him." She clenched her jaw and had to try to force herself to stay under control. "It's not going to be for nothing."

He stood up.

"Like a Marine," he said, and touched her shoulder with his fist as he walked past her to the map to study the location of the porcelain factory on Highway 10 in al-Ta'mim District. He looked back at her. "How many men does Abu Nazir have with him at the factory?"

"I don't know." She shrugged. "Could be ten; could be a hundred."

"I can't give you a couple of platoons. Truth is, I can't even spare a fire team. But I'll give you a squad. That's two fire teams. Probably lose half of them within two blocks of here," he muttered.

"What about a Predator?" she asked. A Predator drone armed with Hellfire missiles would help even the fight, even if all they had was a Marine squad of eight men.

"That's you clandestine types or the Air Force. If you're such a hotshot with USF-I HQ as you claim, you ought to be able to order one up. But if I were you, I'd hurry. The *hajis* have been stepping up their attacks exponentially. There's something big coming, and soon. Real soon," he said.

The porcelain factory, what was left of it, was a sandstone shell of a building on a big empty lot about a kilometer south of the Ramadi Barrage, the steel and concrete dam on the Euphrates Canal. There was a chicken-wire fence atop a concrete berm with gaps in it that ran all around the factory grounds. The day was hot, a touch of breeze blowing dust in from the desert.

Carrie was with Sergeant Billings, a big Montana ex–ranch hand with shoulders the size of Yosemite's Half Dome, on the ground-floor ruins of a destroyed house across the road from the factory. The sergeant had deployed himself and one fire team of infantrymen with them, facing the factory, and the second fire team behind the concrete and chicken-wire fence on the opposite side of the factory. He had positioned his light machine gunner in an armored Humvee with another Marine as the driver, defiladed in the rubble behind their position. When the shooting started, they were to use the Humvee to block the road to prevent any attempts by the terrorists to escape.

Except where were the *mujahideen*? she wondered. If Abu Nazir and/or Abu Ubaida were in there, there should have been armed al-Qaeda insurgents swarming all over the place. But there was no one. What had gone wrong? Had it taken them too long to get here?

And yet, they were in there. They knew this because Virgil had activated software on Romeo's cell phone that enabled them to eavesdrop on anything being said near it. The range was limited to within a meter or two of the cell phone. And what they were getting was an interrogation.

Virgil had handed Carrie an earbud connected to his laptop so she could listen in. Someone—it could have been Abu Ubaida or even Abu Nazir himself—was asking Romeo questions. Romeo's answers were interspersed with screams.

"This woman was a CIA *sharmuta* whore?" she heard the questioner say. To Carrie, it sounded like Abu Ubaida's voice from the video in Walid's house.

"She never said so, but yes. She implied it," she heard Walid say. It was his voice. She was certain of it.

"What was her name?"

"I don't know. Aieeeee!" Walid screamed.

"What was her name?"

"Aieeeee! Please! If I knew I would tell you. I swear," Walid babbled.

"Don't blaspheme! What was her name?"

"Aieeeee! Please! Aieeeee! I only knew her code name. Zahaba. Please, no more. Please, brother."

"Why gold?"

"The color of her hair. She was a blond. I only knew her code name."

"Describe her."

"American. Long blond hair. Eyes blue. Height about one point six five meters. Slim. Weight, perhaps fifty kilos, not more."

"What did she want?"

"Information about you and Abu Nazir. Anything I could give her, but I told her nothing. Nothing!"

"You lie," the questioner growled, and there was the sound of screaming. It went on for a long time. She took the earbud out. So the interrogator was Abu Ubaida. No question. "Information about you and Abu Nazir," Romeo had said. He could only have been talking to Abu Ubaida.

"What do you think?" she asked Virgil and Warzer, both of whom were lying prone on the ground, scanning the factory across the road with binoculars.

"You're hearing what I'm hearing. They should be there." Virgil grimaced. "But I don't see a damn thing. It's wrong. There's something wrong."

"We took too long to get here. There should be al-Qaeda all over the place. At the least, they should have someone watching the road. There isn't anyone," Warzer said.

"So you both think it's a trap?" she asked.

Virgil nodded. So did Warzer.

"Sergeant?" she asked, turning to Billings, who squirted a brown stream of chewing-tobacco spittle on the bricks in front of him.

"This is Indian country, ma'am. When you don't see the Indians, that's when you gotta worry," Billings said.

"It's unanimous," she said, looking at them. "That's what I think too. We call in the Predator?"

"You realize, if Romeo's still alive in there, he's a dead man," Virgil put in.

Carrie thought about that. About Walid; his wife, Shada; his children, Farah and Gabir, who would be fatherless; his mother. I'm death, she thought. I bring death to everyone I touch.

"Romeo's al-Qaeda. The bastard was dead the minute I met him," she said.

Billings, grinning at that, motioned to PFC Williams, a skinny African-American twenty-year-old who was the radio operator. Williams handed the radio handset to Carrie and showed her where to press the button.

"This is Thelonious One. Come in, Cannonball," she said

into the handset. At her request, they were using jazz code signs.

"Cannonball here, Thelonious One," said a crackled voice via the encrypted satellite link.

"You have a go here, Cannonball. Do you . . . ?" She looked at PFC Williams, who mouthed the word "Romeo." Ironic, she thought. "Do you Romeo?" she said into the handset.

"Romeo that, Thelonious One. Watch yourself."

"Will do. Out," she said, passing the handset back to Williams and putting her arms over her head, scrunching herself down into the rocky floor as low as she could go. Next to her, she sensed the others doing the same. The seconds ticked agonizingly slowly as they waited for the attack.

This wasn't what she'd anticipated when she'd contacted Saul from the Government Center building via the Marines' AN/MRC satellite radio. She'd first tried his office number, but when no one picked up, she called his cell. Checking her watch, she saw it was a little after ten A.M. Three in the morning in Virginia. Saul picked up on the fourth ring.

"Berenson," he said. She could hear the sleep in his voice.

"Saul, it's me," she said.

"Are you where I think you are?" he asked. She assumed he meant Baghdad.

"Worse," she said, and told him her intel and what she needed, including the Predator drone authorization from the USF-I HQ, the U.S. Forces–Iraq, General Casey's headquarters. "Can you stop you-know-who from coming here?" She meant Secretary of State Bryce.

"It might be too late. How the hell did they find out about that?"

"Remember your training story about crabs?" she asked,

referring to something he'd said to their class years ago during training at the Farm, that in a closed intel environment, you had agents crawling over each other like crabs in a basket. "When that happens," he'd told them, "a secret is harder to keep inside than diarrhea."

"Can you stop it?" he asked. She assumed he meant the assassinations.

"Have to. Saul—Dempsey's dead."

For a long moment there was silence on the line. Ask me if I killed him, she thought. Ask me. Finally, he said, "What about you? How're you doing?"

"Good. I'm good," she lied.

"You're a tough girl."

"Saul, I've seen him. With my own eyes."

"Alpha Uniform?" AU, Abu Ubaida. "What about the big guy?" Abu Nazir.

"Just the first. We're close."

"What about your Joe?"

"I don't think he's going to make it," she said.

Her memory of the conversation was suddenly interrupted by a shattering explosion in the factory across the road, sending debris and smoke flying, shaking the ground under them. Seconds later, the factory was hit by a another, equally powerful explosion. Then nothing.

Her ears were ringing, the smell of explosive was all around them and when she lifted her head, all she saw for a few seconds was thick smoke and dust. Through the smoke, she could just make out that the factory across the road was almost completely gone. The roof that had still been on top of the building, the bullet-pocked, crumbling walls—all gone. Nothing was left but pieces of the fence and rubble.

Virgil was saying something but she couldn't hear him

through the ringing in her ears. He stood up and motioned to her to follow. She understood. They needed to get to the warehouse and identify the bodies. See if they could confirm who they'd killed.

After all this, God, I hope we got Abu Ubaida, at least. Abu Nazir would be a miracle. It would make all of this worthwhile, she thought as she, Virgil, Warzer and the two Marines, Sergeant Billings and PFC Williams, jogged across the road, weapons held ready to fire, all of them looking left and right to watch for any *mujahideen*.

They made their way gingerly into the smoking ruins of the factory. Fragments of concrete and porcelain and machines everywhere. Above them, no roof, only the blue sky obscured by smoke. And yet, there was somebody talking in Arabic. At first, she couldn't make out the words. As she moved toward it, she heard the sounds of the interrogation they had been listening to on Virgil's laptop. The interrogator's voice and Romeo's screams. Then Warzer shouted. They went over and she immediately understood. It was the charred, headless torso of a man; by his clothes, an Iraqi. A few feet away, they found the head perched on rubble, scorched on one side, but otherwise intact.

Romeo. In what was left of his mouth, someone had shoved the cell phone. Next to the head, a scorched Sony digital recorder still played the sounds of the interrogation.

"Contact him. Aieeeee! He'll tell you . . . ," Romeo's voice cried out from the recorder.

"Of course he will. What good is that? I need you to tell me."

"But he's—ahhhhhh!" he moaned.

Virgil reached down and shut it off.

"*Ya Allah*," Warzer murmured.

Carrie's mind was racing. Who would tell them what? This

was something new. But what? She went back and touched Romeo's body. Rigor had well set in.

Usually rigor mortis kicked in after four hours or so, but in the heat of Iraq once the sun came up, it would have sped up, she mused. Bottom line, Romeo was likely killed last night around 0200, 0300. Meanwhile, the others looked around, kicking over the twisted steel remains of machines, crunching over rubble, but there were no other bodies.

"What the hell?" Virgil said, taking off his utility cover and scratching his head.

For Carrie, looking at the jumbled debris, there could no longer be any doubt. It was a trap.

"Get out! We have to get out now! Run!" she shouted. The two Marines started back toward the road from where they had come. "No! The other way!" she shouted.

Suddenly, as if by magic, *mujahideen* fighters came up out of the ground from camouflaged holes around the factory where they had lain hidden. In buildings and ruins across the way, scores more *mujahideen* appeared, their AKMs blasting at them. Sergeant Billings and PFC Williams briefly returned fire, then turned and ran after Carrie. As they raced toward the far side, Carrie saw an RPG rocket flash by and she just had time to dive to the ground as it exploded, fragments shredding what was left of a porcelain sink.

The dinging sound of bullets ricocheting off pieces of metal and the steel support posts of a roof that was no longer there ripped through the air around them like metal wasps. She got up and ran on, running like when she was in college, conscious of the others lumbering behind her. There were bullets everywhere. It was impossible not to be hit, she thought.

A machine gun opened up somewhere behind them on the road. Thank God, she thought. The two Marines in the

Humvee were firing at the *mujahideen* who were now coming into the factory after them.

Ahead, she could see one of the Marines from the other fire team in position behind the concrete and chicken-wire fence on the other side of the factory. He was waving them in as the other Marines in his fire team laid down covering fire with M4s, rifle grenades and a light machine gun. From behind she heard shouts and curses in Arabic as the *mujahideen* running into the factory were cut down by the Marines. She was beginning to think they might make it when she heard Virgil cry out from behind her.

"I'm hit!" he shouted.

CHAPTER 32

PFC Williams saved them. He called in the Predator, which was still up there, too high to be seen or heard from the ground. As Carrie and Warzer half-carried, half-supported Virgil till they were able to roll over the concrete barrier by the Marines, Sergeant Billings giving covering fire, the Predator fired its remaining two Hellfire missiles into the buildings from which most of the *mujahideen* were shooting. The sounds of the explosions rolled toward them from across the road.

Once they had come through a jagged hole in the fence, the *mujahideen* who had come into the factory after them were caught in a withering crossfire between the Marine machine gun on the Humvee in the middle of the road and the Marines with them behind the fence.

Carrie watched as more than twenty *mujahideen* raced toward the Humvee from the ruins of the buildings on the far side of the road, only to be cut down by the light machine gun from their position. Thank God Sergeant Billings had the foresight to station his second fire team behind the factory, she thought, taking her first real breath since they'd entered the factory.

Virgil had been shot in the lower leg. The wound was bleeding profusely; it was possible an artery had been hit. Sergeant Billings used his combat knife to slice open Virgil's pants leg and put a tourniquet above the wound, but they needed to get him medical help urgently. A few minutes later, the firing from the *mujahideen* was reduced enough to load him on a Humvee and get him across the canal to Camp Snake Pit, a fire base that was an area of open sand surrounded by sandbag walls, where they bundled Virgil into a Huey helicopter. Carrie went with him, along with one of the Marines, who had also been wounded by fragments from an RPG. There wasn't enough room for Warzer; he would follow on the next helicopter out.

The helicopter lifted up in a clatter of sound and dust, the camp swiftly dropping far beneath them. Carrie sat next to Virgil, who was lying on a stretcher beside the wounded Marine on the floor while a Marine corpsman tended to him. Through the open doorway where a door gunner stood, she could see the sand-colored city and the V-like fork where the Euphrates River divided from the canal below. The helicopter banked and headed high over the river east toward Baghdad.

"How long till we get there?" Carrie asked the corpsman, almost shouting to be heard over the sound of the rotor, the wind from the open doorways tugging at her utility uniform and whipping a few strands of hair that had escaped from under her helmet about her face.

"Not long, ma'am. He'll be all right," the corpsman said, indicating Virgil. "I gave him some morphine."

"How're you feeling?" she asked Virgil.

"Better with the morphine." He grimaced. "Nobody ever says how unbelievably much being shot hurts."

"I'm sorry," she said. "We knew it could be a trap."

"Couldn't be helped. A chance to get Abu Ubaida *and* Abu Nazir. We couldn't pass it up. Too bad about Romeo, though. If you could've still run him, we might've gotten another shot."

"Romeo was a double." She frowned. "He worked against us as much as for us." She leaned closer to him. "I think he was responsible for Dempsey."

"What makes you think so?"

"He gave us actionable intel—and he knew there was no working cell phone service in the city. Field radios have too limited a range and al-Qaeda was besieging the Government Center. He had to figure we'd send someone back to the Green Zone. The clock started ticking from the second we parted in the teahouse."

"So why'd they kill him?"

"I don't know. It's bullshit," she said. "They shouldn't've. They didn't need it to set the trap for us. There's something else. I'm not seeing it."

"We left it too long. We should've hit the factory right after they took him there."

"How? It was impossible to move around the city at night. And we sure as hell couldn't have done it without the Marines. Spilled milk," she said. "At least you're out of it. Your family will be happy."

"My family won't give a shit. Not that I blame them." He frowned. "Carlotta and I separated a couple of years ago. My daughter, Rachel, thinks I'm the worst father in the world. And she's right. I haven't been there for her." He grimaced.

"You'll have some time now. Maybe you can make it up."

"Why? So I can drop them like a hot potato the next time a Flash Critical op comes up? They'd be crazy to let me into their lives again." He grabbed her arm. "People like us, we're junkies. We're hooked on the action. Don't let them do it to you too, Carrie. Get out while you still can. I don't know anybody on the NCS side of the Company with a decent marriage. Why do you think everyone messes around?"

"Take it easy," she said, patting his shoulder. "We do good. Without us, the country's blind. Doesn't matter how strong you are if you can't see."

"That's what we tell ourselves. Listen, Carrie, you didn't kill Dempsey," he said.

"But I did. I really did."

"Because of Romeo? Shit, this hurts," Virgil said, trying to straighten his leg.

"No, Abu Ubaida. He had his suspicions about Romeo and he's smart enough to know we'd try to send someone to Baghdad," she said.

"It's not all on you, Carrie. Ramadi's a battlefield. Dempsey knew what he was getting into. Saul handpicked him for this."

"Maybe," she said, looking out of the open doorway on her side. Below, she could see the sun shining on the miles-wide surface of Lake Habbaniya, like a blue mirror on the desert floor. "What you said before, about everybody messing around. What about Fielding? Is that why he was with Rana? He must've known the risk he was running."

"I don't know why Fielding did—ow!" he cried as the helicopter jolted a little. "I don't know why he did half the things he did. You still going on about that?"

"The way he died, I don't believe it," she said.

"Listen," he said, tightening his grip on her arm. "This place, the whole American mission here, is about to explode into a million pieces. Focus on that. I'm out of it now. You're the only one who can stop it."

She nodded and sat there, holding his hand till the long runway of Balad Air Base came into view.

She accompanied Virgil in a military ambulance to the Balad base hospital, the nearest military medical facility. Once she saw that Virgil was being taken care of, she called Saul from the head nurse's office. It was after three in the afternoon local time, eight A.M. in Langley. Saul was in his car on his way to work. She told him about Virgil so he could make arrangements. As soon as Virgil was stabilized, they would take him to Ramstein AFB hospital in Germany for follow-up treatment, then back to the States.

"Are you operational?" he asked her. Virgil's being wounded must've shaken him.

"Cut the crap, Saul. I'm not some weak-kneed little girl and this is an open line. What about Bravo?" B for Secretary Bryce and her trip to Baghdad. "Can you stop it?"

"Bill and David are meeting with her today." Okay, she thought, breathing a little easier. David Estes and the DCIA, Bill Walden, himself. They were taking this seriously.

"Saul, Romeo is down."

He didn't respond immediately. She heard the faint sounds of a car horn honking on the line. Probably some jackass on Dolley Madison Boulevard or wherever, she thought.

"What about Tweedledum and Tweedledee?" Their respective code names for Abu Nazir and Abu Ubaida.

"No. I'm sorry," she said. What else was there to say? It had to have hit him hard, the first time they'd ever had a shot at both of them together. "On the other matter, I'm sending an Aardwolf." An Aardwolf was a Flash Critical report, the most critically urgent, highest-priority type of communication within the CIA. In theory, when Aardwolf came in, the director of the CIA was supposed to get it within one hour of its receipt at Langley.

"I'll alert Beanstalk," Saul said. If he was pissed at her failure in Ramadi, he wasn't showing it. Beanstalk was Perry Dreyer,

CIA Baghdad station chief. He had given her Dempsey and she had killed him. She wouldn't have blamed him if Dreyer wouldn't give her the time of day now, although if anyone had a clue about how things really were in Iraq and what she'd had to deal with in Ramadi, not the official bullshit the administration was putting out, it would be Perry. "Listen, are you sure it's actionable?"

So Saul *was* doubting her, she thought. It was a fair question, though. She was basing her intel entirely on Romeo, who had been not only a double, but a duplicitous al-Qaeda son of a bitch. Except—she'd seen Romeo with his kids. He loved them and he had to know that if the Marines smothered them with help and money, it would get back to Abu Ubaida and Abu Nazir in a New York minute. Romeo also knew that if the assassination attempts hadn't happened within a week, she'd have known he was lying and would have acted. The intel he'd given her had to be good. The fact that they'd beheaded Romeo and killed Dempsey proved Abu Ubaida knew that Romeo had passed along actionable intel.

Sometime during the long night, before she and her team got to the porcelain factory, Romeo, tortured by Abu Ubaida, had given it up. If Romeo had been feeding her false intel, they'd have roughed him up but would have kept him alive to feed her more garbage and maybe lure her into another trap.

A slim reed, but all she had.

"It's highly actionable. Get everything ready. I'll be in Golf Zulu"—GZ, the Green Zone, Baghdad—"as soon as I can," she said, and hung up.

She said good-bye to Virgil at the hospital and, using her cell phone, tried texting Warzer, hoping he had caught a helicopter ride to Camp Victory, adjacent to the Baghdad airport, and had managed to make it back to the Green Zone.

"how is v?" Warzer texted back, asking about Virgil.

"good. r u back? we shd meet," she texted.

"im back. meet clk twr my district fajr −2." Thank God, she thought, feeling the first sense of relief in days. Warzer had made it safely back to Baghdad.

She remembered his telling her that he and his family lived in Adhamiya, a Sunni district on the east bank of the Tigris. She would have to find out where the clock tower was, probably near a mosque or a main square. Fajr was the dawn prayer for Muslims and the minus two was a little piece of misdirection that meant plus two hours, so they would meet about eight A.M.

She boarded the helicopter a half hour later, munching a Subway sandwich she'd bought from a mini-mall of American fast-food stores like Subway, Burger King and Pizza Hut on base. For most of the servicemen and women living and working behind the blast walls and fortifications of the big American base, it was as if they had never left home; they had no connection to the Middle East at all.

Walking out to the helicopter, she could smell the smoke and see black columns rising from burn pits, where, someone had told her, they burned the base's garbage. It was almost dusk, the helicopter casting a long shadow across the tarmac. Being at this bustling American base made Ramadi feel unreal, like a different universe.

The helicopter lifted off and flew low over Highway 1, south to Baghdad. Traffic on the highway was light as night approached. It was far too dangerous to be on the road after dark. As they flew over the outskirts of the city, she spotted something she hadn't paid attention to on the ground. From the air, Baghdad was the palm tree capital of the universe, the setting sun turning the Tigris River to reddish gold.

CHAPTER 33

Adhamiya, Baghdad, Iraq

Perry Dreyer was waiting for her in his office at the Convention Center. The sign on the door read "U.S. Refugee Aid Service" and was a few doors down from the USAID office where she had first met Dempsey.

Carrie waited at the reception desk while an American woman in her thirties in a neat skirt and white blouse checked out her dirty Marine utility uniform with a big rust-colored stain on the shirt from Virgil's wound, her unwashed face, tangled hair and backpack slung over her shoulder. Go to hell, Carrie thought. You think you're in Iraq, try Ramadi instead of the Green Zone, honey.

The woman picked up the phone, said, "Yes," then, "Come with me," and got up and led Carrie through a big modern office filled with CIA personnel at computers into a large private office, where Dreyer, an intense, curly-haired man in slacks and a plaid shirt and wearing steel-rimmed glasses, seated behind a glass-topped desk, gestured for her to sit.

"How's Virgil?" he asked.

"Good. The bullet hit the fibular artery in his leg, but they were able to stop the bleeding. They're fixing it and as soon as he's stabilized, he'll go to Ramstein, then home."

He nodded, his eyes on the bloodstains on her shirt. "What about you?"

"What about me?"

"No bullet holes in you? Everything good?"

"No, everything is not good. Dempsey is dead, Virgil's out and we lost Romeo. So no, I'm not 'good,' but I'm operational, if that's what you mean."

"Whoa," he said, holding up his hand. "Take it easy, Carrie. You're shooting at the wrong guy. Saul didn't have to sell you to me. I wanted you here. And I was right. What you've accomplished in just a few days back in-country is little short of miraculous. So ease up. And call me Perry."

She slumped in her chair.

"I'm sorry," she said. "Since I screwed up on Dempsey, I've been ready to kill somebody. It just landed on you."

"Dempsey was a casualty. We've taken a lot here—and something tells me we're about to take a lot more. You're going to do an Aardwolf?"

She nodded.

"Good," he said. "I'll give you a computer with a secure JWICS link." He pronounced it "Jay-wicks." The Joint World-wide Intelligence Communications System, or JWICS, was the CIA's computer network, designed for highly secure, encrypted top secret communications. "Maybe it'll finally wake up those idiots in Washington. What about the assassination attempts and the planned attacks? What do you need from me?"

"This new Shiite guy, al-Waliki, the new prime minister."

"What about him?"

"Secretary Bryce is the appetizer; he's the real target. AQI gets him, they've got their civil war. I need to meet with him. We have to protect him."

Dreyer grimaced. "Not so easy. This belongs to State. They're very proprietary. Our fearless leader, Ambassador Benson, has issued orders. No one meets with Waliki but him."

She looked at him incredulously. "You're joking, right? We've got Marines having to live in their own shit in Ramadi, IEDs and headless bodies from Baghdad to Syria, this whole damn country's about to explode and this guy's playing bureaucracy games?"

"He's afraid." He frowned. "The Kurds are ready to start their own country, the Sunnis want a war and the Iranians are making moves with Muqtada al-Sadr and the Shiites to come in and pick up the pieces. Benson's the president's boy. We can't go around him."

My God, she thought. Was it possible that Dempsey and Dima and Rana and even Fielding had died for nothing? To have America lose the war and have so many die because of bureaucracy?

"It sucks," she said.

"It totally sucks," he said in agreement. "When is the attack?"

"My asset thought it was next week, but that was before Abu Ubaida realized he was a double and cut his head off." It reminded her that she'd promised him she'd look after his family. I will, she told herself. But first she had to stop a war.

He took his glasses off and polished them with a cloth. Without them, his eyes were softer, less guarded. "Carrie, this is me—and Saul—asking. When do you think?"

She sat up straight. She had felt grimy and desperately wanting a shower when she came in, but now suddenly, she was feeling wonderful, no fatigue at all. No worries about Virgil or anything. Then it hit her. Was she going on one of her flights? She hadn't taken her clozapine in twenty-four hours. Had it started already? She swallowed hard. She needed to get out of here and take a pill. Meanwhile, she had to focus. The good thing about Perry was that at least, like Saul, she could level with him.

"What everybody forgets, what everybody doesn't realize, is how smart these guys are. Everybody thinks they're a bunch of idiot *hajis* running around screaming '*Allahu akbar*' who can't wait to blow themselves up so they can get to the seventy-two virgins. They think," she said, tapping her temple with her finger. "Strategically. That's what makes them dangerous. We have to also."

"I agree," he said, putting his glasses back on. "Don't hold back. What do you think is going on?"

"I'm not sure, but Abu Ubaida's been pushing the envelope. First Beirut and New York, now here. Why? You could say, he's in the terrorist business; that's what he does. But I think there might be something going on between Abu Ubaida and Abu Nazir. My asset Romeo hinted as much and I had the sense even before," she said.

"What are you saying?"

"There's no evidence to suggest that Abu Nazir was even in Ramadi. When I first interviewed Romeo, he put it out there that Abu Nazir was in Haditha. I think it was a slip of the tongue. Romeo tried to cover it over by suggesting he might be in Fallujah, but I think it was a feint. U.S. forces are all over Fallujah. One thing we should do is get some eyes out to Haditha now."

"Pretty dangerous there," he said, rubbing his hand along his jaw. "What about Baghdad?"

"Let's assume for the moment this whole thing is Abu Ubaida. I know *he* was in Ramadi because I saw the son of a bitch. Put yourself in his place. He has to assume we know about the assassinations from Romeo, so he's only got two choices: call it off—in which case, whatever game he's playing with Abu Nazir or us, he's lost—or he moves up the timetable."

Dreyer leaned forward on his desk. "Best guess: how much time do we have?" he asked.

"What about Secretary Bryce? Have they canceled her trip?"

"Her plane's already in the air. She'll make a stop in Amman to meet with King Abdullah, then here."

"I don't get it. She's walking into a trap."

"The president thinks this meeting with al-Waliki is too important. The administration feels their whole Iraq policy is on the line. Midterm elections in November," he grimaced.

"Are they out of their minds?" She shook her head. "Do they think we're making this shit up?"

"Never mind that. How much time have we got?"

"Forty-eight hours; for my money, a lot less. They're probably moving *mujahideen* into position inside Baghdad this very second," she said. "Perry, I don't give a shit what Ambassador Benson says. Get me a meeting with al-Waliki."

"In order to do that, I need more from you. Specifically, how and where are they going to come at the targets?" he asked.

"That's what I'm going to find out."

"Don't take too long," he said.

Midnight. She woke up bathed in sweat from a bad dream. For a moment, she wasn't sure where she was. It had all come together: Reston, Beirut, Ramadi, Baghdad. The sound of gun-fire in the distance reminded her. She was back at al-Rasheed Hotel, Baghdad.

In her dream, her father had been in the factory in Ramadi. They had cut off his head. He was standing there, covered in blood, holding his head in his hands, and it was saying to her, "Why won't you see me, Carrie? If Mom loved you, she wouldn't have gone away and never said good-bye. She would've contacted you. But I stayed and look what you did to me."

"Please, Dad. I'm sorry, but please. You're scaring me with that head," she cried.

He put the head on his neck and said, "Listen to your dad, princess. How is anyone ever going to love you if you won't talk to the one person who does?"

Right when he said that, Abu Ubaida came up to her in the *souk* with his knife, saying, "Now it's your turn, Carrie. Such a pretty head." And she woke up.

She went to the minibar and opened a bottle of Afnan water. She drained it, then went to the balcony door and looked out at the city and the river. Leave me alone, Dad, she thought. I'll be nice and talk to you when I get back, I promise. But right now, I've already killed too many people and I'm about to kill some more, so please let me sleep. I need it so badly and this crazy disease you gave me doesn't make it any easier, but I guess you know all about that, don't you?

Maybe we both need redemption.

In the morning, back to her Beirut garb of tight jeans, a sleeved top and a black *hijab* over her hair, she met Warzer by the clock tower of the Abu Hanifa Mosque in the Adhamiya district on the other side of the river. After separating and doubling back and forth in taxis between the mosque and Iraqi

University to make sure they weren't being followed, they met at an outdoor table at a *shisha* hubble-bubble café on Imam al-Adham Street. There were few men sitting outside, no one near them. The morning was hot, already steaming, and the air was permeated with the smell of apple- and peach-flavored tobacco smoke coming from inside the café.

"She's still coming?" Warzer said, shaking his head about the secretary of state's visit. "I don't understand."

"It's an election year in America. A lot of things won't make any sense," Carrie said, leaning closer over her coffee. "We need specific intel. How are they going to get into the Green Zone? Where's the attack going to be? Exact time? How are they going to do it? Guns? Car bomb? And whatever we find out, we have to get it soon. I doubt we have more than a day, if that."

"What do you want me to do?"

"There are two Sunni strongholds in Baghdad that AQI might use: here in the Adhamiya district and al-Amiriyah, right near Camp Victory and the airport. Best guess, for the attack on the secretary flying in . . ."

"Of course. They'll use al-Amiriyah. For the other attack, you're thinking from here, from Adhamiya?"

She nodded. "What I need is intel on new people, young men, Salafi-type Islamists from Anbar, just arriving into Adhamiya in the past two or three days, staying with family or friends. Who would know about that?"

"Their relatives. The women in the *souk*." He shrugged.

"I'll take care of that. Who else?"

"Of course." He smiled. "We were just there. The *masjid*. The Abu Hanifa Mosque. Men gossip as much as women."

"Okay, so that's how they launch the attack on the Assassin's Gate. How do they get across the river?" she asked.

"The Assassin's Gate is on Haifa Street, near al-Jumariyah Bridge. Across the bridge?"

"Either that or by rubber raft or scuba. They'll come tonight. But how and where are they going to get to the secretary and the new prime minister?" she asked, then sat up straight.

"What is it?"

"Wait! Right across the street from me!"

"What do you mean?"

"The Iraqi Council of Representatives has their offices and chamber in the Convention Center, where the U.S. has its offices too, just catty-corner across Yafa Street from my hotel."

"But, Carrie, the Convention Center is heavily guarded. How are they possibly going to get in?" he asked.

"Oh, that." She smiled, taking a sip of coffee. "No problem. I know exactly how they're going to do it."

CHAPTER 34

Al-Jumariyah Bridge, Baghdad, Iraq

"Give me some good news, Perry," Carrie said, slumping into a chair in Dreyer's office in the Convention Center, wearing jeans, her black abaya slung over her arm. It was late afternoon, the sun low behind the buildings on Fourteenth of July Street, casting shadows across the soccer pitch, more dirt than grass, that his office window looked out on through venetian blinds. "Do we have an appointment with al-Waliki yet?"

"Not yet. The ambassador's adamant. He says dealing with the Iraqis is like negotiating with a basket of eels. He wants only a single message coming from us. The president supports him. In fact, he's meeting with the new prime minister tomorrow," Dreyer said, making a face.

"Well, the message to al-Waliki is going to be that he's dead! And Benson too! What about Saul? David? The director?"

"They tried and got shot down. It's Benson's show. How much time have we got?"

"Tomorrow. It all happens tomorrow."

"You're certain? What's the probability?"

"Now you sound like Langley," she said. "Ninety-nine percent. Is that close enough for everyone? And as for Benson, if you can't get me, him and al-Waliki in the same damn room, tomorrow's his last day on earth."

"How can you be sure? They're both going to be here, inside the Convention Center. Both well guarded. How are the AQI fighters going to get in?"

"They don't have to get in."

"What are you talking about?"

"They're already inside. They're here now," she said, inclining her head toward the center of the building.

"Meaning . . ." She watched him work his way around to it. "The ISF. They've infiltrated the Iraqi Security Forces. They're going to be killed by the people assigned to protect them," he said.

"According to our guy Warzer, most of the ISF providing security for Iraqi government officials live in trailers or in squatters' apartments inside villas in the Green Zone that were abandoned by Ba'ath Party officials when Saddam fell. They're already here."

Dreyer sat back in his chair and looked at her the way she imagined a basketball coach looked at one of his players who was about to try a three-pointer at the buzzer.

"You sure about this?"

"It's actionable."

"How the hell did you find this out?" he asked.

"As you know and Washington can't seem to understand, the thing about the Middle East is that it's not a region of countries; it's a cockpit of tribes," she said. "Our man Warzer is a member of the Dulaimi tribe from Ramadi; he's a Sunni, living in Adhamiya. He's also not stupid. He can see which way the wind is blowing in Iraq, and right now, it's blowing for the Shiites. We Americans did that—and it scares the shit out of him. So he needs a Get Out of Jail Free card in case it all goes bad—and that means asylum in America. So he needs to make himself as useful to us as possible."

"Get to the point."

"Warzer's been cultivating as a possible asset a fellow tribesman who's a member of the ISF, Iraqi Security Forces, but with some questionable contacts. For me that means there's no way he won't at least know someone in AQI. This guy also lives in Adhamiya. His name is Karrar Yassim.

"I spoke briefly with Yassim's wife. She's scared to death. Scared of the Shiites, the Mahdi Army, and of us. She confirmed what we already suspected: some new additions, Dulaimi *jihadis,* to the ISF guards assigned to protect al-Waliki here inside the Green Zone and the Convention Center. This isn't rocket science, Perry; it's murder. Can you get me that meeting with al-Waliki or not?" she said.

"All right," he said, exhaling and clasping his hands together. "I'll try again."

"Good. Because saving Benson's ass or even al-Waliki is not the most important thing on my mind."

"Oh? What is?"

"Killing Abu Ubaida. This time I'm going to get him," she said.

Through the night-vision binoculars, she watched the *mujahideen* enter the building on Abu Nuw'as Street one by one. The street ran along the east bank of the river and was shrouded in darkness; the entire eastern part of the city was suffering one of the electrical power outages that plagued it daily. They were heavily armed; it looked like mostly AKMs and RPGs, she thought. One of them carried a big tubelike weapon, followed by two men who were carrying something bulky on their backs.

"What's he carrying?" she asked.

"Shit," muttered Colonel Salazar, commander of the Third Infantry Division's Fourth Brigade, charged with primary responsibility for the defense of the Green Zone. "Could be an AT-13 Saxhorn. Russian, dammit."

"What's it for?"

"It's a tank killer." He pulled off his night-vision goggles and looked at Carrie in moonlight reflected from the river, the only light available in the darkened room in the Iraqi parliament building on the west bank of the river, which they were using as an observation post. "I don't like this idea of letting them cross the river into the Green Zone."

"I know, Colonel," she said. "But take them out now and the threat remains, only next time we may not know they're coming. Ten-to-one Abu Ubaida is with them now. You give me a team to kill him and we cut off one of AQI's hands in Iraq. When we kill Abu Nazir, that'll be the other hand."

"You're saying the main attack will come right across al-Jumariyah Bridge tomorrow?"

"I'm not sure what their tactics are. They might send a few men over tonight to take out whoever is guarding this side of the bridge tomorrow. You would understand that better than I, Colonel. But yes, the main attack to breach the Green Zone will be at the Assassin's Gate. Our informant confirmed they were training for that in Ramadi. Watching them go into that building across the river confirms it."

"What about Abu Ubaida? Where will he be?" Lieutenant Colonel Leslie, the colonel's executive officer, asked.

"Either right where we're looking, that building on the other side of the river, or here, the children's hospital on Haifa Street, right next to the Assassin's Gate checkpoint," Sergeant Major Coogan put in, pointing at the map location on his laptop screen, which glowed in the darkness.

"We should just call in the Air Force. Obliterate the damn building," Leslie said, jerking his chin in the direction of the building across the river.

"And how would we know he's dead?" Carrie asked. "That's why I'm here. So when your men kill him, I can make a positive ID."

Colonel Salazar studied her in the moonlight, his cropped salt-and-pepper hair darker than it would have been in the light. He had a no-nonsense, slightly bulldog-type face. Intelligent, Carrie thought.

"All right, Miss Mathison. You know this creep better than any of us. Where do you think he'll be tomorrow?" he asked.

"I think your sergeant major's right, Colonel. The children's hospital. He'll be close to what's happening at the checkpoint and the Convention Center, but not directly in the line of fire himself. Possibly disguised as one of the staff."

"One of the doctors maybe?" Colonel Salazar suggested.

"That's exactly the kind of thing he'd do," she nodded.

"So we'll need you with whoever we put in there to make sure we don't shoot the wrong medico?" Leslie said. "That checkpoint'll be a kill zone, miss. It's going to get pretty damned hairy. I know you're CIA and all, but no offense, are you sure you're up for this?"

"I just got back from Ramadi. I know exactly what I'm in for. And trust me, I won't be going in front. I'll be well behind the soldiers you send in. And, Colonel," she said, looking at Salazar, "please don't underestimate Abu Ubaida. He's not just some raghead; he's smart as hell. And he's only a tenth as smart as Abu Nazir."

"I won't," Colonel Salazar said, eyes narrowed. "At least, thanks to you, for once we have the element of surprise on our side. We're giving you a Special Forces Group unit for the hospital. The best we've got. Who's leading it?" he asked Leslie.

"Captain Mullins. Second Battalion," Leslie said.

"Good man. If anyone can protect you and get this son of a bitch, he will," Colonel Salazar said.

"What about the secretary of state?" Carrie asked.

"Politicians." Colonel Salazar grimaced. "We'll try to keep her at Camp Victory while we sweep the Amiriyah district with enough force to make the insurgents keep their heads down until we settle what's happening in the Green Zone. But obviously, no one, including General Casey himself, can tell her what to do or where she can or cannot go."

"When's her plane due in?" she asked.

"Last I heard, oh nine oh five hours," Leslie said. He checked his watch. "Eight hours from now. Not much time to get everything set up."

"The key is the Assassin's Gate," Carrie said. "I assume you'll have plenty to stop them there? They're going to try to force their way through to the Convention Center."

Lieutenant Colonel Leslie nodded. "Plenty, including a platoon of Abrams tanks and a couple of Bradley APCs that we'll move in behind them. Once they're in the killing zone, they stay there."

She turned to Colonel Salazar. "Colonel, this Russian missile we saw? Would an Abrams tank survive if it was hit with one of those things?" she asked.

"Possibly," he said. "Depends on a number of different factors. Assuming the missile hits the tank, where it hits, the tank's MCD defenses, a number of things."

"What about a Bradley? Would it survive?"

"Not a chance."

CHAPTER 35

Assassin's Gate, Green Zone, Baghdad, Iraq

She spent the remaining few hours of the night on a narrow bunk in a shipping container that everyone called a "trailer," set in a sea of trailers laid out in a grid near the old Republican Palace. Dreyer had given her his trailer while he slept on a blanket on the floor in his office. But she couldn't fall asleep. All she could think of was Dempsey and how he'd looked the first time she saw him, and again that night that they made love at al-Rasheed, and imagine what the IED had done to him and what he must've thought in that last instant. Did he blame her? Damn, he was a good-looking man. Just being near him had made her feel sexy, alive. Would she ever feel that way again? Could she ever even allow it again?

She opened her eyes but couldn't see anything. The trailer was a dark, closed metal box. Like living in a coffin, she thought. She could feel depression moving in on her like a storm on a TV weather map that's heading toward you. She pushed it away. No time for that now. Kill Abu Ubaida first. Then get drunk and let it come, she told herself.

Still, she couldn't sleep. Something didn't fit. What was it?

Suddenly, she sat bolt upright in the darkness. What was it on the recorder in the factory? Abu Ubaida's voice when he was interrogating Romeo. Something about Abu Nazir. What was it he said?

Of course he will. What good is that? I need you to tell me.

Why? What did it mean? Why wouldn't Abu Nazir's word be good enough for him? Why did it have to come from Romeo? Was it just a power trip on his part? She didn't think so. The stakes were too high. Think, Carrie. Think.

I can't, she thought. Clozapine wasn't a cure-all. Oh God, let me sleep. I can do this, I swear, if I can just get some sleep.

By the time she showed up in Dreyer's office that morning, in jeans and a T-shirt, with a Beretta M9 pistol Dreyer had given her, the sun was just edging over the tops of the buildings on the other side of the Tigris. It was going to be another hot day, she thought. Dreyer was already at work on his computer. One look at his face told her the bad news.

"Benson turned us down. I tried. Believe me, I tried," Dreyer said.

"Well, he's not turning me down," she said, heading for the door.

"Carrie, wait!" he shouted. "Technically, we're attached to the embassy. They'll order me to send you back. We need you here. We can't afford it."

She stopped at the door and looked back at him. "I've gotten a lot of blood on my hands since this thing started, Perry. I can't have any more. You do what you have to. So will I," she said, and left.

She hit her cell phone and called the number Sergeant Major Coogan had given her for Captain Mullins, commander of the Special Forces Group being assigned to her by Colonel Salazar. He picked up before the first ring was completed. She told him where she was and what she needed. He said he'd be there in ten minutes.

"Meet me in the prime minister's office. It's on the second floor," she said, ringing off and heading for the stairs. As she started up, Perry Dreyer joined her, followed by three of his staff, young men with M4s.

"If I can't stop you, I guess they'll have to fire us both," he said.

They walked all the way around the big interior atrium to the prime minister's corner office on the Yafa Street side of the building. Two armed Iraqi soldiers wearing the red berets of the Iraqi Security Forces guarded the door.

"Prime minister not in," one of them said in bad English.

"*Salaam alaikum, sadikh'khai,*" Carrie said, greeting them in Arabic as friends. "You're both Shiite, yes?" One of the soldiers nodded. "Of which tribe, *habibi*? Shammer Toga? Bani Malik? Al-Jabouri?" she asked, naming major Shiite tribes of the Baghdad area. She was guessing that al-Waliki, the candidate of the Shiites, would only trust being guarded by fellow Shiites, preferably from his own tribe.

"Bani Malik," the first IFS guard said.

"Of course, as is Prime Minister al-Waliki." Carrie nodded. "I should have known."

"He is of al-Ali of the Bani Malik," the guard said, indicating al-Waliki's specific tribal subbranch.

"We're from the CIA. Sunnis of al-Qaeda are planning to kill the prime minister this morning. No doubt you will die as well. Call your commander to join us and come with us," she said, pushing past him and opening the door. She walked into the large, plush office where the prime minister, Wael al-Waliki, was meeting with Ambassador Robert Benson.

The two men were seated at a small mahogany table. Behind

them, a curtained window, one of the few in the Convention Center, provided a view of the lawn and grounds and beyond the fence to tree-lined Yafa Street and the Al-Rasheed Hotel in the distance. Dreyer, the CIA men and the two Iraqi ISF guards were behind Carrie.

"What the hell is this? Get out—all of you," Benson growled. Spotting Dreyer, he said, "Perry, I gave you strict orders. Are you that interested in committing career suicide? Get out."

"He tried to stop me. This is my idea," Carrie said to Benson, and to the Iraqi prime minister she added in Arabic, "*Lahda, min fathlek*, Prime Minister, but your life is in danger. You must listen."

"Look, I don't know who you are, miss, but this is a direct order. Get out of this room now," Benson said.

"Ambassador, if I walk out, you and the prime minister will both be dead within the hour. So if you want to end my career tomorrow, fine, but I'm not leaving," Carrie said.

"Who the hell is she?" Benson asked Dreyer.

"One of ours, Mr. Ambassador. You need to listen to her. She knows what she's talking about."

"Look, miss, thank you for your concern, but we don't need protection. We're in the well-guarded Green Zone, surrounded by American troops in the most protected building in the Green Zone, not to mention ISF guarding these offices. Your concern is unnecessary," Benson said.

"And with all due respect to you, sir, AQI has infiltrated the ISF and they won't give a shit who you are when they kill you. And if you could pull your head out of your own self-important ass for one second you'd realize that it doesn't matter if they kill you. You'll be replaced. But if they kill him"—she pointed at al-Waliki—"the Shiites go nuts and this whole country erupts in full-scale civil war."

"What is this? Some kind of a joke?" Benson snapped.

"I just came from Ramadi last night covered in blood from one of my guys. Do I look like I'm joking? Right now, we need to get you and the prime minister to a safe location without anyone knowing. We have to do it immediately. Take off your clothes."

"What?"

"You and the prime minister both. We're going to disguise you," she said, and repeated it in Arabic for al-Waliki, then turned to Dreyer. "We need an absolutely safe location within the Convention Center. Someplace the ISF won't look and that can hold at least a half dozen or more U.S. soldiers just to make sure they'll be okay. Any ideas?"

"There are some rooms in the basement under the big round auditorium, the one where the parliament meets," one of the CIA men said. "I heard someone say Saddam's secret police used to use them for all kinds of shit. Drugs, interrogations, rape."

"Charming," Dreyer muttered.

At that moment, Captain Mullins arrived with a squad of soldiers in full combat gear, along with an Iraqi officer wearing the red ISF beret.

"You Carrie?" Mullins asked. He was a small, muscular man, about five seven, with brown eyes that took in everything in an instant.

"Why aren't you at your posts?" the Iraqi officer said to the two ISF guards in Arabic.

"I needed them here. You'll understand in a minute," Carrie told him in Arabic. Then to Mullins, she said, "We need to get Ambassador Benson and Prime Minister al-Waliki to safety. This man, what's your name?" She pointed at the CIA agent who'd mentioned the storage rooms.

"Tom. Tom Rosen," he said.

"Tom will show you where to take them. We need men we can absolutely trust to guard them. How many men did you bring?" she asked Mullins.

"Two ODAs. A Teams. Twenty-four men, not counting me," he said.

"How many can you spare? I need at least three or four," she said. "They, plus our CIA staff can protect them. You've got the extra uniforms?"

One of Mullins's men handed Carrie two pairs of ACUs, desert camouflage fatigues, and two M4s. She gave them to Benson and the prime minister.

"Put these on," she told them. "You'll pretend to be soldiers." She turned to the ISF officer. "We want everyone else in the ISF to think they are still meeting in this office," she told him in Arabic, motioning him closer. "Get fellow Shiites, men you know and trust, if possible from your own tribe. You need to find the AQI infiltrators. As soon as we leave, no one gets in or out of the Convention Center. Any Sunni soldier in this building who joined the ISF within the last three months is suspect. Disarm every one of them and turn them over to us for interrogation. They are not to be harmed, understand? They have critical information."

She turned and translated for Dreyer what she had told him.

"And, Perry, whatever you do, don't let them get rid of them or let them buy their way out. We need intel from whoever they take in as prisoner," she said to Dreyer.

Prime Minister al-Waliki stood and faced her. "You, CIA lady. I won't do this. I can't hide. What if someone sees me dressed like an American soldier? Politically, it would be the end of me," he said in English.

"You have no choice," she told him in Arabic. "Sunni elements of al-Qaeda are already inside the building. If they kill you, Iraq will split apart. There will be civil war. You know this better than anyone, Prime Minister. Then Saddam wins. He may die, but he wins. Put on the clothes for just an hour or two. Stay alive."

Suddenly, the boom of a massive explosion rattled the windows. It was followed by additional booms from a cannon—Carrie was willing to bet from the 105-mm guns of the Abrams tanks—and a nonstop firestorm of small-arms fire. The battle had started.

"They're attacking the Assassin's Gate. Get your pants on," she shouted at Benson. "Hurry!"

The Assassin's Gate was a white stone arch over Haifa Street topped by a domelike sculpture that looked like an ancient Babylonian warrior's helmet. It was about three hundred meters east of the Convention Center and had become one of the major checkpoint entries into the Green Zone. Led by one of Mullins's team leaders, they headed east on Yafa Street, then down an alley behind the buildings toward Haifa Street, the sounds of the battle getting louder and louder the closer they got. In the gaps between the buildings, they could see Iraqis, men, women clutching children, some pushing carts, all running the other way on Yafa Street, fleeing the fighting.

They stopped beside a building, looking out toward a parking lot behind the children's hospital. It was a big open area bordered by bushes. If the insurgents had taken over the hospital, they could be walking into an ambush. The sounds of the battle were very loud, an almost nonstop staccato of automatic-weapons fire punctuated by booming cannon fire. They could see the flashes of gunfire coming from the windows of the children's hospital.

They formed into two A Teams, Alpha and Bravo, and gave Carrie the code name "Outlaw." Master Sergeant Travis, on point for A Team Alpha, signaled that he was going in. A moment later, as he sprinted toward the parking lot, the other team members took up positions behind parked cars to provide covering fire as needed. But there was no fire from *mujahideen* from the windows or from the parking lot. As Captain Mullins had anticipated, everything was concentrated on the Haifa Street side of the hospital, where the battle was taking place.

Although she couldn't see the fighting at the checkpoint from here, she anticipated that Colonel Salazar had turned it into a killing zone. With tanks and troops dug in to defend the checkpoint and more men and Bradleys brought up from behind to box the *mujahideen* in, it was plenty loud enough. What the big blast had been—an IED or a car bomb or something—she didn't know, but it meant Americans had likely taken casualties too.

Warrant Officer Blazell, whom the others called "Crimson" because he came from Alabama, a six-foot-six, shaved-headed, midthirties African-American whom Mullins had assigned to look after her, tapped her on the shoulder and indicated that she should follow him as the team zigzagged across the parking lot, where two A Team members had already taken control of the back door to the hospital.

She followed him, running lightly; the only thing she was carrying was the Beretta pistol. Once they were inside the door, Crimson shoved her to the floor. It was instantly apparent why. Gunfire from everywhere in the building and from outside at the checkpoint echoed in the corridors. There were flashes from gun muzzles and bullets everywhere. The body of a woman, a nurse, her legs spread wide, her *hijab* covered with blood, lay in the hallway.

She followed Crimson, his big body shielding her, and the rest of A Team Bravo as they ran through the hallways, checking rooms one by one. In one they found sick children huddled on the floor with a nurse next to the lifeless body of an Iraqi in a white smock; a doctor, she thought. She didn't see A Team Alpha or Captain Mullins and assumed they had gone on ahead, maybe to another floor. One of the other Bravo team members by the staircase indicated they had cleared this floor and pointed for them to go up to the next floor.

They ran up the stairs and swept into a ward filled with beds, with no one in them. All the children were lying on the floor, where nurses and aides crawled from one to another. Some of the children had been shot with bullets that had ripped through shattered windows and walls on the Haifa Street side of the building. They were crying and screaming, and as she ran she nearly stepped on a small boy—he must have been three or four—clutching his stomach, trying to hold the blood in and shrieking at the top of his lungs: *"Ama! Ama!"* Mommy! Mommy! And she thought, This is hell. This is what it's like.

Someone, an insurgent coming out of nowhere, ran by the doorway, then came back and fired an AKM at them. As Carrie hit the ground, Crimson turned, aimed and fired back in a single fluid motion, killing him instantly, grunting as he did so.

"You okay?" she asked. She couldn't believe how Crimson had done it. He had an incredible natural athleticism and was amazingly fast and graceful for such a big man.

"Bullet. Hit my vest," he said, meaning his Kevlar vest, not pausing. He charged out the door, whirled and fired at someone else in the hallway. She didn't follow. She'd only be in his way; he'd come back for her, she decided, keeping her Beretta ready in case someone else came through the doorway.

She crawled to the wall beside the shattered window and, getting up on her knees, peeked out above the broken shards of window glass at the checkpoint below. It seemed like there was shooting coming from everywhere. An Abrams tank by the checkpoint was blackened and burning; next to it was the shattered chassis of what might have been a car or truck. Car bomb. That must have been the explosion they'd heard at the Convention Center, she thought numbly.

A pair of Abrams tanks, their machine guns blazing, followed by scores of American infantrymen, were moving forward slowly from the checkpoint. A group of the *mujahideen* appeared to have taken cover in a grassy, parklike area on Haifa, north of the Yafa Street intersection, blasting away from behind bushes and trees, although there was also shooting coming from a handful of buildings on both sides of the street, including from the hospital itself, farther down to the right of her.

Behind the *mujahideen* in the park, blocking their escape, were two Bradley APCs, one coming down Haifa Street from behind the *mujahideen*, the other on Yafa, closing in from al-Jumariyah Bridge, trapping the *mujahideen* in the park from all sides. Both Bradleys were firing their guns nonstop. Suddenly, a bullet cracked through the wall right next to her and she dove back down to the floor.

Idiot, she told herself. You want to get killed? She looked around. The rest of the team had presumably gone out of the ward and farther down the hallway, where she could hear the sound of shooting. She stepped out into the hallway and someone grabbed her from behind, his arm around her throat. She cried out and tried to twist her arm so her Beretta was pointing back at him and felt him twist the pistol out of her hand. He was too strong for her.

He dragged her backward toward the stairs, half choking her. Struggling to get free, she jabbed him with her elbow. He grunted as she felt it connect but tightened his hold on her. She couldn't see his face—his sleeve was white; he was wearing a doctor's smock—but she could smell him. A sour smell of sweat and fear. As he pulled her back toward the stairs, she saw Crimson come out of a doorway, heading back looking for her.

"Help!" she cried out. Whoever was holding her put the Beretta to her head.

"*Eskoot!*" he hissed. *Shut up.*

Crimson snapped into a kneeling shooting position with his M4. "Let her go!" he shouted.

"Drop it or I kill her!" the man shouted back. "Put it down now or she's dead!"

Crimson aimed his M4, utterly still.

"Crimson! Take the shot! I trust you!" Carrie shouted.

"I'm warning—" the man holding her started to say.

Crimson fired. Carrie literally felt the bullet pass her cheek and an instant later, the man's arm fell away. He dropped to the floor; she was free. She bent over and took her Beretta from the dead *mujahideen* in a doctor's smock, who lay on his side, staring at nothing, a bullet hole in his forehead.

"Thanks—" she started to say to Crimson.

"Stay with me, damn it, ma'am. Captain Mullins'll kill me if anything happens to you," he said, and, grabbing her hand, pulled her to follow him.

They ran toward the rest of A Team Bravo. They were coming out of an operating room, shaking their heads. She and Crimson went toward them, but one of the soldiers stopped her.

"You don't want to see, ma'am. They were just little kids. Two nurses and kids. All dead," he said. "Believe me, that's a sight that'll stay with you."

"Come on, you sons a bitches," Master Sergeant Travis shouted from the stairway. "We got two more floors."

"Have you seen Abu Ubaida?" Carrie called out.

"We killed eight *hajis*. You can check them later," Travis said.

She followed Travis and the team to the top floor, where a firefight was going on. A team member fired his grenade launcher through an open doorway and the explosion was followed by a rush of team members racing into the ward, their MP5 submachine guns blazing. The sound of shooting was deafening. Travis and a Sergeant Colfax held back. Travis pointed with his submachine gun to a doorway marked "Roof" in Arabic and English. They opened the door and went up a metal stairway to a roof door.

Travis tried the door. It was locked. He took out a hand grenade and motioned to Crimson, the biggest man there. Crimson nodded, set himself and launched a kick that sent the door flying open, with Travis tossing a grenade through the opening the second Crimson kicked it.

They all moved down a step or two on the staircase as the grenade exploded outside on the roof. Travis and the team immediately rushed out onto the roof, where a hail of AKM gunfire greeted them. Carrie hung back in the stairwell, Crimson half in the doorway, blocking her view as he fired. Someone fired or tossed a grenade and the explosion echoed in the stairwell. She heard the stutter of another AKM opening up and heard someone cry out, "I'm hit!"

Crimson aimed and fired a burst from his M4, then another and another.

All at once, the shooting stopped, though she could still hear sporadic gunfire and the single boom of a cannon in the distance. Was that one of the tanks? she wondered. Suddenly, Captain Mullins and two of his men rushed past her and out onto the roof. They spread out on the roof, firing as they moved.

Someone said, "Oh shit."

Captain Mullins called out, "Where's that woman? Outlaw? Get her now!"

Crimson looked at her and motioned for her to come out onto the roof. She stepped outside, the bright sunlight forcing her to squint. One of the team members was putting a bandage on Travis's arm. The bodies of two *mujahideen* were over by an air-conditioning unit and another body in a white doctor's coat lay faceup near the parapet. But that wasn't why Mullins wanted her.

An Arab man in a doctor's white jacket was standing on the parapet at the edge of the roof, holding a toddler wearing just a diaper in one hand and a hand grenade in the other.

"Is that him?" Mullins asked, keeping his MP5 aimed at the man on the parapet. "Abu Ubaida?"

It was the fourth time she had seen him. First in the photo with Dima she'd gotten from Marielle in Beirut, the second time in the *souk*, the third time in the video from Romeo's house. The thrill of recognition was unmistakable. It was Abu Ubaida.

"It's him," she said. "Absolutely."

"You! American *sahera*," Abu Ubaida said, staring at her and calling her a witch. So he recognized her too. "From the *souk*."

"Me," she said.

"I'm leaving," he told them in English. "Anyone tries to stop me, the baby dies. Shoot me, I drop this grenade and she dies."

"You're not going anywhere," Mullins said. The weapons of almost a dozen American soldiers with him on the roof were aimed at Abu Ubaida.

"Then she dies," Abu Ubaida said, pressing the grenade against the girl's body as she squirmed in his grip.

"Let her go," Mullins said. "That's the only way this ends."

"If you want to kill her, it's on your soul. I am ready to die," Abu Ubaida said.

"You won't go to Jannah," Carrie said, speaking of the Muslim heaven.

"I will. It is *jihad*," he said.

"Not like this. This Allah will not forgive," she said, watching him intently. Whatever he was going to do, she could see in his eyes he had decided. But before she could cry out or do anything, he dropped the toddler and tossed the grenade directly at Carrie, and before anyone could do anything, he shouted, *"Allahu akbar!"*—*God is great!*—and jumped off the roof.

The hand grenade came directly at her and Captain Mullins. As it bounced on the roof less than a meter in front of them, Crimson, moving with incredible speed, jumped in front of her and, unbelievably, kicked it like a football. A split second after leaving his foot, the grenade exploded.

The explosion ripped Crimson's leg off at the knee, metal fragments whizzing right at them. She thought she was dead, but Crimson's massive body with its Kevlar vest shielded her even as he crashed like a tree. Captain Mullins and two of his men were hit multiple times by flying shrapnel from the grenade. Part of Mullins's cheek was ripped open, but Carrie was untouched. The toddler sat on the roof by the parapet, screaming loudly, also apparently unharmed.

One of the other soldiers raced over to Crimson, who lay

on the roof, and began working to tie off his leg, bright blood spurting rhythmically from the stump. Crimson's foot, with his combat boot still on it, lay on the roof a few feet away. Captain Mullins, bleeding, also came over as the other soldiers spread out to secure the roof.

Carrie knew she should stay and help, especially Crimson, but she couldn't. Her only thought was of Abu Ubaida. She had to see what had happened. She turned and ran back to the metal staircase, thinking to herself, What kind of a shit am I? He saved my life, twice—and all I care about is the mission? But she couldn't help herself, racing down the stairs to the ground floor and out the door to Haifa Street, knowing that she would think about what she was doing at this moment for years to come, in the long sleepless nights when the clozapine wasn't working. Abu Ubaida was lying on the sidewalk some fifty meters away, the white doctor's jacket he'd been wearing dark with blood in the bright sunlight.

She walked over, her insides trembling. Except for the blood pooling at the back of his head, the man on the sidewalk looked exactly as he had in the *souk* in Ramadi. His eyes stared vacantly up at the sky and she didn't have to bend down to check his pulse to see that he was dead.

Feeling as if someone other than her was controlling her movements, she aimed her Beretta pistol at Abu Ubaida's face. This is for Ryan Dempsey, you son of a bitch, she thought, and ignoring the fact that he was already dead, squeezed the trigger.

CHAPTER 36

Central District, Beirut, Lebanon

Flying over the peaks of Mount Lebanon, approaching Beirut, the city spread out below her all the way to the Mediterranean, a distant blue in the afternoon sun. She hadn't intended to come to Beirut. In fact, she'd been specifically ordered by Perry Dreyer and Saul to get her "ass back to Langley ASAP."

She had gone back to the U.S. Refugee Aid Service, the CIA cover office at the Convention Center, escorted by Master Sergeant Travis, who made sure she was safe every step of the way, insisting on going with her right up to the door of the office before saying good-bye.

"Please thank Crimson for me. I'm sorry I had to leave. He saved my life today. Twice," she told him.

"I'll tell him. You did good today, ma'am."

"Not really. I'm lousy at taking orders. And I was scared to death," she said.

"So?" He shrugged and, giving her a little wave, left.

She went inside the CIA offices and called Saul via JWICS-based Skype with the code word "Home Run," indicating Abu Ubaida was dead, no matter that it was four in the morning in McLean.

"You're positive he's dead? No question?" he said, and despite the excitement, yawned.

"One hundred percent," she said. "It's him. It's over," she said, suddenly sleepy herself. She hadn't slept all last night and it was starting to hit her. Also, the adrenaline that was part of the battle was seeping away and she felt spacey. She needed her pills.

"Unbelievable. Truly, Carrie. That's really something. How do you feel?"

"I don't know. Numb. I haven't slept. Maybe I'll feel it tomorrow."

"Of course. What about al-Waliki and Benson?" he asked.

"Why? Did Benson give the director an earful?" She tensed, imagining Benson demanding her head on a silver platter.

"Matter of fact, he was saying nice things about you. Says you acted appropriately, probably saved their lives. In fact, it made him feel part of the battle. He can't wait to tell his war stories in the Oval Office. Actually had someone take a photo of him with the combat fatigues and the M4 you gave him."

"No shit?" she murmured.

"We understand Secretary Bryce is fine. She's supposed to meet with Benson and al-Waliki later today. They were setting the agenda when you broke up their meeting," Saul said.

"Yeah. After her plane landed, they kept her in a secure bunker in Camp Victory while they made sure all was quiet in al-Amiriyah."

"Listen, Carrie. David wants to debrief you himself. So do I. We need you back in Langley ASAP."

A pang went through her. Was this like before with Fielding? An excuse to put her back in Intelligence Analysis?

"I haven't done anything wrong, have I?" she asked.

"On the contrary, both Dreyer and David are writing letters of commendation for your 201 file. Congratulations. Hurry back, there's lots to talk about—and we do need a full debrief," he said.

"Saul, there are still loose ends. Beirut for one. Abu Nazir's still out there, possibly in Haditha. And there's something else. Something Abu Ubaida said when he was interrogating Romeo—sorry, Walid Karim, that I can't get out of my head."

"Be back in my office tomorrow. We'll go over it all then. And, Carrie . . ."

"Yes?"

"Helluva job. Really. I can't wait to talk to you in person. There's a lot to go over, even though Perry says he needs you there," he said. A warmth shot through her like tequila. Saul was happy with her. She could lap up his praise like a junkie forever.

She'd booked her flight back to Washington, but on a sudden impulse, while waiting in Amman for her connecting flight to JFK and from there to Dulles, she'd changed her ticket and flown to Beirut.

Now, flying over Beirut, she could pick out the landmarks. The Marina Tower, the Habtoor, the Phoenicia Hotel, the Crowne Plaza. It's funny, she thought. Everything that had happened had all started here with the aborted meet with Nightingale in Ashrafieh. It was like a single run, a kind of marathon that just hadn't stopped. In a way, coming back to Beirut was like coming full circle, because this was where it began for her. Not just that night in Ashrafieh, but when she had gone back to Princeton after her first bipolar breakdown, the one that nearly ended her college career and anything resembling a future life.

Two things had saved her life, she thought. Clozapine and Beirut. The two were connected.

Summer. Her junior *year at Princeton. She had gone back to class and spent all her time studying. She no longer ran, was off the track team. No more five A.M. runs. Her boyfriend, John, was also history. She was on lithium and sometimes Prozac as well. They kept adjusting her doses. But she hated it. She felt, she told her sister, Maggie, as if the lithium took away twenty IQ points.*

Everything was harder. And it felt, she told the doctor at McCosh, the student health center, like she was seeing everything through a thick glass. As if she couldn't touch it. Nothing seemed real anymore. Also, she had periods where she was excessively thirsty or she'd lose her appetite completely. She'd go two, three, four days at a time not eating, doing nothing but drinking water. She hardly ever thought about sex anymore. All she did was go from class to class, back to the dorm, thinking, I can't do this. I can't live like this.

What saved her was when one of her professors mentioned a summer program for Near East Studies students: the Overseas Political Studies Program at the American University of Beirut. At first her father wasn't going to pay for it, even after she told him she needed it for her senior thesis.

"What happens if you have a breakdown there?" he asked.

"What happens if I have a breakdown here? Who's going to help me? You, Dad?" Not saying, Remember Thanksgiving? because they both knew what she was talking about and that what had happened with him might happen with her too. What she didn't tell him or anyone was that she was barely hanging on, that she wasn't far off from suicide. Not far at all.

"I need this," she told him. And when even that didn't work, she added, "You drove Mom away. You want to drive me away too, Dad?" Until he finally agreed to pay for it.

And then, coming into Beirut, surrounded by this amazing city and ancient ruins, meeting students from all over the Middle East, walking on Rue Bliss with the other kids, eating shawarma *and* manaeesh, *clubbing on Rue Monot, and when she was almost out of lithium, she made the great discovery. She went to an Arab doctor in Zarif, a small, clever-looking man who looked at her when she told him about the way lithium made her feel and said, "What about clozapine?"*

Just being able to tell someone, finally, how it felt. And it worked. She was almost like the old Carrie, before the breakdown. When she went back to see him as a follow-up and to get a prescription refill, he was leaving on vacation. She asked, "What if I can't get a prescription from another doctor?" and he told her, "This is the Levant, mademoiselle. For money, you can get anything."

That summer in Beirut, where the pieces all came together for her. The ancient Roman ruins and Islamic mosaic art and listening to jazz late at night and the musicality and poetry of everyday Arabic, the Corniche and the beach clubs, the scent of fresh-baked sfouf and baklava, the call of the muezzins *from the mosques, the clubs and the hot Arab boys who looked at her like they could eat her for breakfast, and she knew that whatever happened in her life, the Middle East would be part of it.*

Now, descending to Beirut–Rafic Hariri airport, she wondered if the pieces would come together for her again in Beirut. This never-ending run she had been on since the night of the aborted RDV with Nightingale in Ashrafieh. Because she didn't believe that asshole Fielding had killed himself. And if he hadn't, it meant someone had killed him. Someone still out there. And that like her, an operation was still running.

She took a taxi from the airport. Riding in traffic on El Assad Road past the golf course, the driver, a Christian, telling her about the preparations for Easter in town and how his wife's mother made the best *maamoul*—little Easter cakes made with walnuts and dates and topped with icing, that time of year—in the city. She had him drop her off near the clock tower in Nejmeh Square and walked the few blocks to the CIA's cover office, where she was to meet with Ray Saunders, the new Beirut station chief.

Walking past the crowded outdoor tables of the street café under the old arched portico, she couldn't help remembering the last time she'd been here, to see Davis Fielding, who'd basically told her that her career was over. It seemed a lifetime ago.

She went inside and up the stairs, pressed the doorbell, said who she was into the intercom and was buzzed in. A young American man in a plaid shirt had her wait in a small reception area till Saunders came out and greeted her. Saunders was a tall, thin, intense-looking man in his forties with long sideburns that gave him a vaguely Eastern European look.

"I've heard a lot about you," he said, leading her to Fielding's old office overlooking Rue Maarad. "Frankly, I was surprised to get your call. So was Saul."

"Is he pissed I didn't come straight back to Langley?" she asked.

"He said he couldn't stop you from coming here if he tried," he said, and gestured for her to sit down. "By the way, congrats. I heard about Abu Ubaida. Nice work."

"I don't know what to say. My being here might be a wild goose chase."

"When I told him, Saul said you had a bug up your ass about Davis Fielding's death. Is that what this is about?"

"You know it is," she said. "Doesn't it concern you? If Fielding didn't commit suicide, then whatever reason or operation was the cause is still running. For all you know, you could be a target."

"I'm curious. From what I heard, you and Fielding weren't exactly a love match. Why are you so concerned about his death?" he asked, studying her with frank interest.

"Look, Fielding was a dick and no loss to anyone. He was going back to face the career equivalent of a firing squad at Langley and I'll bet you're scrambling right now to clean up his mess and figure out how badly Beirut Station's been compromised."

"Sounds like a pretty good reason to commit suicide to me," Saunders said quietly.

"Yeah, but you're not Davis. He wasn't principled enough for that. Someone killed him—and I have to believe it has something to do with the actress, Rana Saadi, and Nightingale. That was my op and that means there is a loose end."

He studied her, not saying anything. From outside, a car horn honked, starting a chorus of honking from other cars. The Beirut *cinq á sept* traffic, she thought mechanically.

"That's what I think too. We found something, but I've been working with a handicap," he said.

"What?"

"I didn't know him. You did." He motioned to her to move her chair around to his side of the desk.

"What did you find?" she asked.

"This," he said, indicating his computer screen. It was a hidden-camera video of this very office. Carrie automatically looked up at the joint where the wall met the ceiling where the camera had to be located, but it was too small and well hidden in the molding. The screen showed Davis Fielding sitting at his desk, his back to the camera. Suddenly, he was on the floor, a Glock pistol in his limp hand, a pool of blood spilling from his head.

"There's a three-minute-forty-seven-second gap," Saunders said. "The dead man didn't do it."

"Can you freeze it?" Carrie asked.

"Why? Do you see something?"

She peered intently at the image of Fielding lying on the floor.

"There's something wrong. I can't put my finger on it, but as Saul would say, something's definitely not kosher."

"It's not the angle he's lying at. We had a forensics expert calculate that the body would fall in that position."

"Is that all you've got?" she asked.

He shook his head. "We've got gaps in security cameras in the reception room, the staircase, the front and back entrances to the building. Longer, but all for the same period and on the same night Fielding was killed. Somebody didn't want us to see him."

"How do you know it's a him?"

"Because he missed one," Saunders said, switching the view on the screen. It showed a view from a roof security camera looking down at Rue Maarad beyond the overhang of the portico. "The roof camera's digital recording disc was on a separate circuit. Watch. We've been able to extrapolate from the time gap. This is about forty seconds after the gap ended."

On the screen, a man in a coverall appeared out from under the portico, crossing the street and walking away toward Nejmeh Square. She could only see his back.

"Not much to go on. Assuming that's our killer," she said.

"We found something else. This is from four days earlier, after one A.M."

Another video, same view, appeared on the screen. A man in a similar coverall was caught walking toward the building briefly before he disappeared under the portico. To Carrie's eye, it looked like there was a company patch or logo on the front.

"Go back. What's that coverall say?"

Saunders rewound and froze the image, which, given the darkness and distance, was too fuzzy to get a clear glimpse of either the man's face or the company name.

"Can't you digitally enhance the image?"

"We did," he said, opening another window and zeroing in on the patch. Although still indistinct, the patch read "Sadeco Conciergerie" in French and Arabic.

"Looks like a janitorial service. I'm sure you checked the company," she said.

"Of course. It's our janitorial service all right, but he's not our regular janitor and according to Sadeco, no such person has ever worked there. We black-bagged their offices one night. Went through all their personnel files. They were telling the truth. Whoever he was, he wasn't one of theirs."

"What do your assets tell you?"

"Nothing. Not a damned thing."

"And the Lebanese ISF? Or the police?"

"As soon as they realized who we were, they backed off and referred us to the Interior Minister, who happens to be from Hezbollah. We're dead in the water. Do you have any ideas?"

"Give me prints of the two images: the one of Fielding and the mystery janitor. Oh, and a head shot of Fielding, something easily identifiable."

"What are you thinking?"

"If this guy in the picture, whoever the hell he is, has got something to do with Rana or Hezbollah or Abu Nazir, I'll find him," she said, getting up, passing him her cell phone so he could add his cell number as a contact.

That night, having a margarita at the bar in the Phoenicia Hotel, Carrie took out the print of Fielding's body and tried to spot what was wrong with it. The image had been shot from above, from the hidden ceiling camera, and behind. A body and a gun. What was wrong with the image? For one thing, it wasn't the way she was used to looking at Davis. How was she used to looking at him? She reoriented the image in her mind as it would be if she were facing him. And then she saw it.

Idiot, she told herself. It was plain as the nose on your face. How was it that no one had caught it before? Of course, she told herself. After Fielding, they'd had to clean house at Beirut Station. No one who really knew Fielding had seen this image. She took her cell phone out of her handbag and called Saunders.

"Snapdragon," he answered. His code name.

"Outlaw," she said, still using the name because of Crimson. "Fielding was left-handed," she said, and hung up.

He would see it the instant he went back and looked at Fielding's body with the pistol in his right hand, she thought. Proof positive, if they needed any more, that Fielding had been murdered. But by whom—and why?

The answer, she hoped, was walking right toward her. Marielle Hilal, still redheaded, still pretty in tight Escada jeans and a low-cut top, with enough male eyes on her to give any girl's ego an elevator ride to the penthouse suite.

"What are you drinking?" Carrie asked.

"Whatever you are," Marielle said, sitting down at her table.

A waiter came over.

"Two Patrón margaritas," Carrie told him, and motioned Marielle closer. "The man you knew as Mohammed Siddiqi is dead. Thought you ought to know."

"I heard Rana was killed too," Marielle whispered back.

Carrie nodded. "Also a Syrian named Taha al-Douni, who was running both Rana and Dima. Did you ever meet him?"

"No, *alhamdulillah*"—*thank God*—Marielle said, checking her lipstick and the room to see if anyone was watching them in her compact makeup mirror. As she started to put the mirror back in her purse, Carrie slipped the photograph of the unknown janitor into Marielle's purse as well. "Is anyone still after me?"

"I'm not sure. I need you to do something for me," Carrie said.

"Why should I? I'm already taking a chance meeting you," Marielle said, looking around nervously. There were at least half a dozen men checking them out. No way to know if it was normal male interest or something else, Carrie thought. Except for one. Ray Saunders, putting away his cell phone and nursing a Scotch at the bar.

"Because I'm trying to help you. And because, well . . ." She didn't finish the sentence, a reminder that she knew where Marielle lived.

"I don't like this," Marielle said. "First Dima, then Rana. Their boyfriends. Who's next? Me?"

"Take a vacation till things blow over. Someplace nice. Someplace safe. Where would you like to go?"

Marielle raised her eyebrows cynically. "I've had men try to buy me. This is the first time by a woman."

Carrie put her hand on Marielle's arm. "Listen, if I can solve this, you'll be safe. In the meantime, what's wrong with getting away? Where would you go?" she asked.

"Paris," Marielle said. "I've always wanted to go."

"I'll give you five thousand dollars American," Carrie said. Money she'd gotten from Saunders for this meet. "You can be sipping wine on the Champs-Élysées tomorrow."

"Just like that? Five thousand American? You must like me better than I thought."

"Too many have died over this," she said, a pang going through her at the thought of Dempsey. "I don't want anything to happen to you."

"Makes two of us. So that's it? We're done?" Marielle said, reaching for her purse.

"There is one thing."

"Now it comes. Do you know, *habibi*, I almost believed you. Almost," she said, wrinkling her nose as if something smelled bad.

"I just need one thing. But it has to be the truth."

"And the five thousand American?"

"Put your hand under the table."

Carrie reached into her handbag under the level of the table, took out the wad of hundred-dollar bills and passed it to the other woman.

"I need to count it," Marielle said. Carrie nodded. Marielle added, "How will you know if I'm lying?"

"Because I'll know," Carrie said, and leaned closer. "Go into the ladies' room; make sure no one sees you. Count the money, then take a good look at the photograph I put in your purse. I need you to confirm for me who that man is."

"What makes you think I know this man?"

"Because you do," Carrie said with a lot more conviction than she felt. She didn't have much time in Beirut, and Marielle was the best shot she had. All or nothing, she thought, taking a deep breath. All or nothing.

"I just tell you and then I leave? That's it?" Marielle asked.

"And bon voyage." Carrie nodded.

Marielle got up and said something to the waiter, who pointed the way to the *salle des dames*. Carrie sat there at the edge of her chair, thinking that this was such a long shot. But if she was right, Marielle had to know the unknown janitor.

That night, after the shootout at the Hippodrome and after she and Fielding and Saul had had it out at the safe house, when Fielding had gone back to his Rue Maarad office, he'd had his Beretta with him. Say what you would about Davis Fielding—and God knew she could say plenty—he knew his basic tradecraft. Under ordinary circumstances, he never would have let a stranger into the Rue Maarad office at night.

But that night, with everything that was going on and with him under suspicion from Langley, sitting there on edge, waiting for Saul and the ax to drop, never in a million years would he have let someone in unless he knew them very well, much less let them get the drop on him and kill him with his own gun. Which meant Davis not only knew his killer, he knew him well. And if he knew him, then Rana knew him—and that meant it was possible, even likely, that Dima and Marielle did too.

If not—and with the Beirut police out of it—they truly were at a dead end, she thought, gulping down the rest of her drink. Where the hell was Marielle? What was taking her so long? How long did it take to look at a photograph? She wouldn't try to make a run for it, would she? No, she knew Carrie knew where she lived in Bourj Hammoud with her aunt or whomever the older woman was. Saunders, glancing over, caught her eye. She tried to look more confident than she felt. All or nothing. All at once, she breathed a sigh of relief when Marielle came walking back to the table.

She knows, Carrie thought excitedly. From her eyes, she could tell Marielle had recognized the unknown janitor in the photograph.

"It's very strange," Marielle said, handing her the photo

and sitting back down. "Why is he dressed that way? Like a *bawaab*?" The Arabic word for "janitor."

"Who is he?" Carrie asked, holding her breath. Come on, she thought. Come on.

"It's Bilal. Bilal Mohamad. I'm surprised you didn't know," she said, looking curiously at Carrie.

"Why should I?"

"Everyone knows Bilal," she said, tweaking her nose with her fingers in a sign for cocaine. "He's a *pédé*. A friend of Rana's. Also her American *papa gâteau* certainly knew him. Dima too. You're not just testing me? You really don't know him?"

Carrie's mind was bouncing all over the place like a pinball. She had a name. Bilal Mohamad. A gay man who knew Rana—and according to Marielle, he also knew Rana's American sugar daddy, her *papa gâteau*, Davis Fielding. It struck her like a bolt of lightning. Suddenly everything made sense.

What was it Rana had said about her sexual relationship with Davis when she'd interrogated her after Baalbek? *"At first we did, but now I'm mostly just for show."* It had puzzled her at the time, but now it fit perfectly. Was this what Davis Fielding had been hiding? That he was gay? But why hide? Who gave a shit? Why would he need a beautiful mistress like Rana as a cover so people would think he wasn't gay? And what about this Bilal Mohamad? Why did he kill him? Was Bilal Davis's lover? Because if he was, it would explain why Davis had let him into the office that night.

Davis knew he was leaving Beirut. Probably forever. That was the other dangling thread that had been nagging at her, threatening her theory about the murder. How was it that the very night he faced ruin and the end of his career, his last night in Beirut, was the night that coincidentally someone just happened to drop by to murder him? Before Saul, who was on his way, showed up? Coincidences like that don't happen. Not in real life, they don't.

So Bilal hadn't just shown up. Davis had called him. Probably told him it was urgent, that he was leaving. If they were lovers, Davis had wanted to say good-bye.

Bilal must have dropped what he was doing and hurried right over. It would have been his last chance to silence Fielding before he spilled everything to the Company, before he, Bilal, was in the CIA's crosshairs. Nothing coincidental about it. She needed to get Ray Saunders and Saul to check Fielding's landline and cell phone records.

The pieces finally fit. Once they started digging, she was confident they would find Bilal connected to both Nightingale and Abu Nazir.

"I've been away. What's he do, this Bilal Mohamad?" she asked.

"This and that." Marielle shrugged. "It's Beirut," she said, making a sign for someone sticking cocaine up their nose.

"Where can I find him?"

"Where do you think? Most nights, Wolf," Marielle said. Of course, Carrie thought. A gay bar. "So I should just leave?"

"The sooner the better. Take a few weeks. Enjoy Paris," Carrie said, getting up to leave. "Everyone does."

CHAPTER 37

Minet al-Hosn, Beirut, Lebanon

The gay bar Wolf was on a side street in the Hamra district, close to the American University. By eleven at night, the sidewalk outside was crowded with men in shirts open to their navels with cocktails or bottles of 961 beer in hand. Carrie squeezed through and walked past the bouncer, a big shaved-headed man who stared at her quizzically.

Inside, the club was jammed, hip-hop music blasting, laser lights flashing across a sea of men, some talking, some kissing and groping each other. Along the walls were leatherette benches where slim young men in tight short-shorts gave lap dances to older men with money to spend. Carrie threaded her way through the crowd to the bar. She was the only woman there. Although she spent time looking, she didn't see Bilal Mohamad anywhere.

"What'll you have?" the bartender asked her in Arabic. He was a slim, baby-faced thirtysomething who could have passed for twenty, topless except for a pair of red suspenders holding up tight leather pants.

"Tequila, Patrón Silver," she said, nearly shouting to be heard over the noise.

"Are you lost?" the bartender said when he came back with her drink.

"No, but he is," she said, showing him the photograph of Bilal Mohamad on her cell phone. "Where I can find him?"

"Haven't seen him," the bartender said, moving down the bar to help someone else.

"You looking for Bilal?" a man crowded in next to her said.

"Bilal Mohamad." She nodded. "Any idea where he might be?"

"Who wants to know?" he asked.

"Benjamin Franklin," she said, showing him a hundred-dollar bill.

"You're not Bilal's type, *habibi*," the man said. "Actually, you're no one's type around here."

"Don't be so sure. There are some really sick sluts in Beirut, *habibi*. I might even be one of them." She grinned.

"You *are* a bad girl," he said, tapping her shoulder with catty delight. "The key question, my darling *habibi*, is, does Assayid Franklin have a brother?"

"If he does, how do I know you'll tell me the truth?" Carrie said, taking out a second hundred-dollar bill and sliding both bills toward him on the bar top.

"He's in the Marina Tower. Sixteenth floor. You don't believe me, ask Abdullah Abdullah," the man said, pocketing the money and flicking his finger at the bartender, who came over.

"Are you really Abdullah Abdullah?" Carrie asked the bartender.

"No, but it's what they call me." The bartender shrugged. He motioned her closer. "Are you sure you know what you're doing, mademoiselle?"

"Does anyone?" she asked.

"Bilal has dangerous friends," the bartender muttered.

"So do I."

"No, mademoiselle. There's dangerous and then there's Bilal. He's a psychopath. Trust me, you don't want to go there. If you want coke, hashish, heroin, let me get it for you. Safer. Better quality. Better price too."

"Is he at the Marina Tower?"

"You know the saying 'The only way to get an apartment in Minet al-Hosn is for someone to die'? They're not just talking about availability and money. They're talking about what people are willing to do for such wealth—and what they'll do to protect it," the bartender said.

"I'm a big girl, *sadiqi*. Is he there?"

"I haven't seen him in days. If you're lucky, you won't either," he said, crushing mint leaves for a mojito.

The Marina Tower was a crescent-shaped white high-rise overlooking the waterfront, the lights from the building reflected on the water of the Marina. The lobby was ultramodern and expensive, an advertisement for the tenants who could afford the millions that an apartment here cost. She'd had to argue with Saunders to get him to let her go in on her own.

"We already know that he killed Davis Fielding—and probably others. And that was even before the bartender's warning. And nobody makes that much money in Beirut without either being very dangerous himself or having very dangerous friends," Saunders said in the BMW SUV on the way over. With them were two new Beirut Station operatives, Chandler and Boyce, two short-haired hard-as-nails transfers from the CIA's Special Operations Group, both ex–Navy SEALs, whom Saunders had brought with him from Ankara to help him clean up Beirut Station.

"Chandler and Boyce. They sound like a law firm, don't they?" Saunders had said, introducing them to Carrie.

"More like antique dealers," she'd said, shaking their hands. "Look, don't get me wrong. I'm glad they're here. But we don't want a shoot-out. We want to know who sent him to kill Davis."

"I think we already know. Abu Nazir," Saunders said.

"No, we think we know. That's not the same thing," she said.

"I should do it. Or Chandler or Boyce."

"Better me. I'm a woman. Less threatening, less likely to escalate. And I speak Arabic better than anyone here."

"All the same, the only way you're going in is wired up like crazy. The second I hear something that even smells like trouble, my antique dealers here—and me too—will be blasting in, shooting first and taking names later. That son of a bitch is dead, understood?"

"I get it. I just want to see what I can get out of him first," she said as they parked the SUV on a side street and walked to the Marina Tower parking lot, the building lit up at night with horizontal lines of white light along the balconies, like a stack of curved neon blades.

"I don't think you do, Carrie. Get it, I mean," he said as they approached the parking lot. "If anything happened to you, Saul would crucify me. Possibly literally."

"I know." She looked at Chandler and Boyce. "If you think I'm in trouble, guys, come get me, please." The two men nodded.

Kneeling beside a Mercedes sedan, they did a voice check on her wire setup and readied their weapons and equipment. When they were set, they walked, one at a time, to the back service entrance from the parking lot.

One of the men, Boyce, picked the service-door lock. They went inside to the elevator and took it up to the sixteenth floor. Three of them exited, one of them, Boyce, going up one more floor. He would set up to make an entrance onto Bilal Mohamad's balcony from the balcony of the apartment on the floor above. The other two, Saunders and Chandler, would wait and monitor Carrie from the hallway stairwell, ready to break in to Bilal's apartment at a moment's notice. Her emergency code was anything to do with flowers. The instant she mentioned it, they would come running.

At a signal from Saunders, Carrie went to Mohamad's apartment door—there were only two apartments on the entire floor—and, taking out her Beretta, knocked.

There was no answer. She knocked again, harder. And again. Nothing. All this and nobody home, she thought, annoyed. She put her ear to the door and listened but heard nothing. Then the faint whirr of something electric, like a razor. Looking back at the doorway to the stairwell, which was cracked slightly open, she couldn't see Saunders or Chandler, but she was glad they were there. She took a deep breath and, taking out her lock pick, began working on the lock, trying to remember her training at the Farm.

There was a click; she turned the handle and opened the door, the Beretta ready. She stepped into a large, luxurious main room, brightly lit and with a panoramic glass view of the marina and the sea. The whirring electric sound was louder. It sounded like it was coming from the bedroom. Leaving the apartment door open a crack for Saunders and Chandler, she moved in a shooting stance toward the bedroom. Pushing the bedroom door open with her toe, she stepped in and stopped at the bizarre sight of a boyish-looking man, muscular, presumably Bilal Mohamad, his hair bleached pure blond-white and his body draped in a black plastic garbage bag with his head sticking out, with a gun with a silencer aimed directly at her.

They stood there, frozen. Neither moved a muscle. The oddest thought occurred to Carrie: he was like a male Marilyn Monroe, sexy and lost. And then it struck her that the whirring sound had stopped.

"*Ya Allah*, this is awkward," Bilal said finally in Arabic. "Should we kill each other or see if there's a way for us both to survive?"

"Put your gun down and, *inshallah*, we'll talk," Carrie replied in Arabic.

"Okay, but if you kill me I'm going to kick myself in hell for trusting a CIA agent. You are CIA, aren't you? Idiotic question. Of course you are," he said in English. "American, female, gun. Some idiot's finally figured out that Davis Fielding didn't kill himself. Was it you? Of course it was. They don't take women as seriously as they should, do they?" he said, tossing his gun onto the bed. Now that she was able to pay attention, she noticed that his hands were covered with blood. He caught her looking at his hands. "You came at a bad moment. Another half hour and I'd have been gone," he added.

"What are you doing?" she asked.

"See for yourself," he said, gesturing at the bathroom. "I hope you don't have a weak stomach."

"Don't move. Keep your hands where I can see them," she said, edging toward the bathroom door.

"Of course. You're already nervous. Why wouldn't you be? I don't want you to shoot me by accident."

She risked a quick glance at the bathroom. There was a man's naked body in the bathtub. Its head and hands had been cut off, the head sitting neatly atop the hands at the foot of the tub. The whirring sound she had heard was an electric carving knife, still plugged in to the bathroom shaving outlet.

Feeling nauseous, she sensed motion behind her and whirled back, ready to fire. Bilal had moved slightly, but only to wipe his bloodstained hands on the bedspread.

"Don't move!" she snapped. "Who was he?"

"Daleel Ismail. He always fancied me. You understand. You're an attractive woman. People like us, we can't help it if men fancy us. Poor Daleel. He thought he was finally going to do me. That's the thing about life. You can never be sure if you're going to be the one doing the screwing or getting screwed," he said.

"Why'd you kill him?" she asked.

"Can't you guess? Listen, can I take this plastic off?" He tugged at the garbage bag he was wearing. "It's hot and the idea of dying while wearing this is disgusting. Unless you'll let me continue what I was doing? No?" he said, looking at her. "Well, I'm taking it off then."

He pulled the plastic covering over his head and tossed it onto the bed.

"We don't have to stand here. Shall we have a drink and talk about it like the civilized murderers we are?" he said, walking to the bedroom door and into the main room. "I know you don't trust me. You can watch as I wash my hands. The human body really is a messy thing, isn't it? Amazing that we manage to idealize and sexually fantasize about it as much as we do."

She followed him to the bar, where she held the Beretta on him while he washed his hands in the bar's sink. He dried his hands on a towel.

"What are you drinking?" he asked.

"Tequila if you've got it. If not, Scotch," she said.

"Scotch. Highland Park," he said, checking the bottles behind the bar. He poured them both glasses and gestured for her to join him on twin ultramodern armchairs in the main room.

"What are we drinking to?" she asked.

"To us both still being alive—for the moment," he said, and drank. She did too.

"This Daleel whatever-his-name-is, why'd you kill him?"

"He looked like me. Same size, height, musculature. People sometimes mistook him for me. I don't know why he couldn't understand my not wanting to do him. It would have been too much like masturbation."

Suddenly, she understood.

"You were faking your own death. That's why the head and hands. To make it hard to identify the body. They would assume it was you. What were you going to do with the head and hands? Dump them in the Mediterranean?"

"You see, you are a clever girl. All right if I smoke?" he said, reaching for a cigarette in an ivory-inlaid box on the glass coffee table. "I know what ridiculous Puritans you Americans are about these things. It's okay to be a murderer, but one mustn't smoke." He lit the cigarette, took a deep drag and exhaled.

"What about DNA? They'd find out it wasn't you."

"Seriously?" He looked at her as if she'd suggested that a caveman program a computer. "This is the Levant, not Manhattan. There's no database, no science. The purpose of police work here is to destroy your political enemies, not solve crime."

"Where were you going?" she asked.

"Actually, it was a ridiculous choice. Death or living in New Zealand. Those two are virtually indistinguishable."

"Who were you running from? Us?"

"There really is no limit to American arrogance, is there?

Why be afraid of you? Become infamous with Americans and the worst that can happen is you get your own reality TV show. Can't you figure it out? You don't look stupid; still, people can fool you." He exhaled a stream of smoke at her.

"What about Davis Fielding? You were lovers?"

"He called me. Can you imagine? All those years, using Rana to pretend he was straight, and him thinking he was running her, when in fact, between Rana and I, we milked him for every piece of intelligence in the Middle East. He called to say good-bye, the sentimental idiot. He was as bad a spy as he was a lover."

Looking at him, with his oddly boyish face and white-blond hair, she suddenly understood.

"Abu Nazir. That's why you killed Fielding. He's shutting things down. That's why you're running," she said.

"So," he said, exhaling a stream of smoke at her. "Not entirely stupid. So what's it to be—Carrie, isn't it?" He smiled nastily, sending a bolt of fear through her at the thought that he knew her real identity. She was seeing the real man. Worse, whatever he was going to do, he had made his mind up. She needed to get her people in here now. "You see, I did get everything out of Fielding. So, Carrie, are you going to let me get back to what I was doing and let me disappear? Or are you going to do something ridiculous, like putting me in a cell with those imbecile *jihadis* at Guantánamo Bay?"

"Neither. You're going to work for us now," she said, and, looking around, spoke into the air: "You know, flowers would do wonders for this place."

Bilal sat up straight. "Who am I to spy on? Abu Nazir?" he asked.

She just stared at him. The sounds of Saunders and Chandler running in were combined with the sight of Boyce rappelling down onto the balcony.

"*Ya Allah,* you don't know Abu Nazir at all, do you?" he said.

Reaching under the seat cushion of his chair, he pulled out a nine-millimeter pistol. Before she could react or say or do anything, he raised it and fired a bullet into his head.

CHAPTER 38

Amman, Jordan

"The Roman Theater was built, as you might guess, in Roman times during the reign of the Emperor Antoninus Pius, in years 138 to 161 of the Common Era. In those days, the city of Amman was being called 'Philadelphia.' So you see, the city in America gets his name from our city, Amman," the tour guide, a curly-haired young Jordanian in Oakley sunglasses, told the half dozen tourists clustered around him. They were standing in the highest row of an ancient semicircular stone amphitheater gouged into the side of a hill in the middle of bustling downtown Amman.

Seated by herself in a row about halfway down, Carrie watched as one of the tourists, a bearded American wearing sunglasses and a trilby hat against the hot sun, which would've looked ridiculous on anyone else but on him seemed exactly right, detached himself from the little group and made his way down the stone aisle to where she was sitting.

"What do they say about mad dogs and Englishmen?" Saul said, sitting next to her.

"Why'd he do it, Saul?" she asked. "Fielding. What was

the big deal about being gay? I mean, who gives a shit? And why'd he go to such lengths to hide it? A phony mistress, an expensive one, who opened him to moles, blackmail? It makes no sense."

"You're too young. Davis Fielding went back to the old KGB days, the Cold War, when gays were considered serious security risks. Remember, those Brits from Cambridge who turned out to be KGB spies—Philby, Burgess, Maclean—were all gay. The stuff of John le Carré novels. Back then, the prevailing view was that gays were more susceptible to being blackmailed. There was even a big court case about it. Bottom line, in those days you couldn't be in the CIA if you were gay. It would have been the end of his career. Fielding knew that."

"Come on, Saul. Look at the connections. Rana, Bilal Mohamad, Dima, Nightingale and finally, Abu Nazir. That's some crew. Look how close he let them get. I mean, look at Bilal. How could he?"

Saul smiled.

"What's so funny?" she asked.

"Something my father used to say: 'When a man's penis is erect, his brain is in the ground.' It's a lot funnier in Yiddish." He shrugged.

"So he betrayed his country for a piece of ass? Literally."

"Oldest story in the world. And to be fair, it was unwittingly. He was a fool, not a traitor."

"What about the missing database records? Ours and the NSA's? He wasn't alone."

"Don't go there, Carrie," he said, shielding his eyes from the sun with his hand to look at her.

She had to take a breath on that one.

"Really Saul," she whispered. "It goes up that high? Is that what this is about?"

"No." He shook his head. "It's about friendship, not some gay cabal. Returning favors that go back decades. It's over. Davis is dead."

"So that's it? You've got to be kidding."

"What do you want, Carrie? You plugged the leak. And you even got the son of a bitch who killed him. That's all that matters."

"Except Abu Nazir's been reading our mail for who knows how long. How bad is it?"

"We're still assessing. But after you left Beirut the first time, without telling anyone, Estes and I shut down everything critical going through Beirut Station. When it came to intelligence, Fielding was on a starvation diet—and he knew it, Carrie. He suspected. That's why until you proved otherwise, the idea that he committed suicide was a real possibility. And don't forget the plus side."

"There's a plus side?" she said, raising her eyebrows as she watched the tour guide lead the little group down to the stage's side entrance, where there was a small museum. Except for a pair of tourists on the stage, she and Saul were alone in the amphitheater. So odd to be sitting there in that ancient site within a few meters of traffic and the modern city, she thought.

"Very much so. Right now, Abu Nazir is the most dangerous enemy we have. And you got us the first solid lead we've ever had to getting him. We're still going through Bilal Mohamad's cell phones and other things, but we've confirmed calls to Haditha in Iraq. It wasn't just Nightingale and Romeo. That confirms the intel you provided before; Abu Nazir is in Haditha."

"He may not be there any longer."

"It's a place to start, which is more than we ever had." He turned to her. "We need you to go back to Iraq, Carrie."

She bit her lip. "I lost people there, Saul. Dempsey, Romeo. Virgil wounded, also Crimson. How's Virgil?"

"He's good. He had a chance to see his daughter. He said to say hi. He's anxious to get back. As for Warrant Officer Blazell, a.k.a. Crimson, he's got one of those fancy new prosthesis legs. He's adjusting," Saul said, hesitating.

"What is it?" she asked. She could always tell when Saul was holding back. He'd make a lousy poker player, she thought.

"I'm not supposed to tell you, but you might want to get used to the idea."

"What idea?"

"What you've done, Carrie, is—well, you're in line for a promotion. When Perry Dreyer moves on, we're going to recommend you to be Baghdad station chief. You'll be the youngest station chief ever—and the first woman."

She was stunned. Of all the things she'd thought he was going to say, she hadn't expected that.

"I don't know what to say."

"Well, that's a first." He grinned. "Anyway, Perry's still there. And he wants you back ASAP. So do we. If you can nail Abu Nazir, we can break al-Qaeda's back."

She looked down at the ancient stage. The two tourists had moved on; it was empty. What plays, what public agonies must have happened here two thousand years ago? A station chief with bipolar disorder, she thought. She would be hiding something that could backfire on them just as much as Fielding had.

"Saul, there's just one problem. We missed something."

"Oh?"

"Walid Karim. Romeo. When Abu Ubaida was interrogating him in the factory he said something I haven't been able to get out of my mind. Romeo told him to get Abu Nazir to confirm that what he was saying was true."

"And?"

"Except Abu Ubaida wasn't buying it. Like he didn't trust what Abu Nazir would tell him. He told Romeo that whatever he needed to hear about us had to come from Romeo. Why? Okay, they were rivals, but Abu Nazir and Abu Ubaida were the leaders of AQI. They were supposed to be working together. So why would he say that and why did he kill Romeo? He didn't have to do it to trap us. The recording alone would have been enough. He didn't have to kill him, but he did. Why?"

"Good. Very good," Saul said, standing up. "Now we're getting to it. But first, let's take a walk, I'm thirsty."

They went down the aisle to the orchestra section of the amphitheater and out to the street, past men in red-checked *kaffiyehs* and honking cars to a juice stand with mesh bags of oranges, lemons and carrots dangling from an overhead beam. Saul ordered a cold orange juice, squeezed in front of him. Carrie got a bottle of Petra beer from the refrigerated glass cabinet.

They walked on the shady side of the street, sipping their cold drinks. Out of habit, Carrie checked for tails, but they were clear.

"It bothered me too," Saul said. "Especially why Abu Ubaida killed Romeo. I came to a conclusion, but it's not a pretty one."

Carrie stopped and looked at him. A young woman in a pink *hijab* walked by. They waited till she was out of earshot.

"He was a triple agent, Romeo, wasn't he? No one in this whole thing, not Nightingale, not Rana, not Dima, not Fielding, no one was what they seemed."

Saul nodded. "We're spooks. We lie for a living."

"Romeo was a double agent for AQI and for me, but all the while he was really working for Abu Nazir against Abu Ubaida.

Abu Nazir used Romeo to get me, the idiot, to eliminate Abu Ubaida for him. He couldn't lose. If Abu Ubaida's attack on the Green Zone and assassination of al-Waliki had succeeded, he would have had his civil war and made it impossible for the American effort in Iraq to succeed. If Abu Ubaida's attack failed, no problem. There would have been some damage to us and Abu Nazir would have eliminated his only rival within AQI. Either way he wins," she said.

"That's about it." Saul nodded. "But you're looking through the wrong end of the telescope. Taking out Abu Ubaida was a good thing. You saved thousands of lives, Carrie. American casualties alone would have been horrendous."

"He used us, me."

"We use each other. Crabs in a basket. Sometimes we eat each other," Saul said.

CHAPTER 39

Green Zone, Baghdad, Iraq

Back at Baghdad International Airport. Heat, flies and Demon giving his Route Irish spiel, telling them it was only six miles from the airport to the Green Zone. He recognized Carrie from the last time.

"I see we have a repeat customer. Wasn't it a nice ride in last time, miss?" he called out to her.

"I've been in Ramadi, Demon. Route Irish is pussy," she shouted back to raucous male laughter and a few good-natured catcalls and cheers.

They got into a convoy of SUVs and Blackwater Mambas. Leaving the airport, driving past the "Condition Red" sign and onto Airport Road, riding on the highway into Baghdad, past the blasted palm trees and burned-out wrecks of cars and trucks, she had the oddest sensation.

I'm home, she thought. All my life I've been looking for a place to belong, never felt at home anywhere. Growing up with her father and mother had been like living in a foreign country—how else could her mother have left like that without saying a word?—and incredibly, home had turned out to be here. Iraq. The Middle East. In the middle of a war. As their convoy drove under overpasses, gunners swiveling in unison like dancers to cover them against anyone who might drop a grenade or IED onto one of their vehicles, past Iraqis in cars who had stopped on the shoulder to let their convoy pass by, staring at them unblinking, she realized it was the risk, the game, that she was addicted to.

As if bipolar wasn't bad enough, she had to be an adrenaline junkie too. Or was it something else? she wondered as they made the turn onto the Qadisaya Expressway, thick with traffic. They drove past palm trees and buildings, some pockmarked with holes from rockets and bullets. It's like crossing a finish line; something is ending or beginning, she thought.

Ever since that night in Ashrafieh when Nightingale had tried to ambush her, she'd been on a run, like when she was at Princeton. The longest run ever. Only now it was over. When she was running NCAA, she'd imagined she could run forever. Now she knew better.

Take a breath, Carrie, she told herself. Time for a new run. This time the rabbit she was chasing was Abu Nazir, as the convoy drove through the checkpoint into the Green Zone, past the parade ground and the Unknown Soldier Monument, back to Yafa Street and the al-Rasheed Hotel.

Abu Nazir. What was there about him? Something truly frightening. Men would rather die than face him. Bilal Mohamad was no *jihadi* religious nut and no pushover either. He was truly evil. She had felt her skin crawl just being in his presence. How was it Davis Fielding hadn't spotted it? Or was Fielding so blinded by the sex? Maybe it was like Saul had said: his head was stuck in the ground. But Bilal had wanted to live. He had been calmly chopping up a gay friend of his so that Abu Nazir would believe him dead when she walked in. Yet when confronted with the chance to stay alive, even Bilal had preferred to kill himself rather than face Abu Nazir.

Well, Abu Nazir, the next dance is you and me, she thought grimly.

Walking into the hotel's marble lobby, she was greeted by Warzer, carrying a big bouquet of roses.

"*Marhaban!* Welcome, Carrie. It's good to have you back," Warzer said, handing her the roses.

"*Shokran,* Warzer." She smelled the roses. "Won't your wife be jealous?"

"She would be, if I were foolish enough to tell her. How is Virgil?"

"Virgil is well. He's hoping to come back."

She left her rolling suitcase with the hotel porter and the two of them went outside and crossed over to the Convention Center grounds. Security had improved since she'd been there last; the Convention Center was ringed by concentric layers of protection. In addition to personnel, surveillance cameras and sensors were everywhere, she noted.

She and Warzer presented their credentials to the U.S. MPs at their sandbagged emplacement, again to Blackwater guards and at a third checkpoint manned by Iraqi ISF soldiers at the front entrance.

"How are things, truly?" she asked Warzer as they walked down the open hallway.

"Things are hanging by a thread, Carrie. The Iranians and the Mahdi Army are smuggling in arms and explosives. The Kurds are going their own way. The Americans are caught in the middle—and once Saddam's trial is over and he is executed . . ."

"Is that a foregone conclusion?"

"Absolutely. He will be hung. Very soon now."

"Then what?"

"That depends on Abu Nazir—and also you, Carrie." He smiled.

They were at the door of the "U.S. Refugee Aid Service." They went inside the reception area and she told the female CIA staffer to let Perry Dreyer know she was there and to get her a vase for her roses, which she handed to the staffer. The woman got up and left, then came back and said to follow her.

They walked into a large bullpen of a room where CIA operatives sat at computers or worked on telephones, the space busy with activity. On the wall, someone had posted framed photographs of Ambassador Robert Benson and Prime Minister Wael al-Waliki in their combat utility uniforms. There was one of the station chief, Perry Dreyer, and on a wall by themselves, the photographs of two United States Marines, labeled "U.S. Marines Missing in Action, presumed captured by AQI, Operation Iraqi Freedom."

The first photograph was of an African-American, "U.S. Marine Scout Sniper Thomas Walker. Captured outside Haditha, Anbar Province, May 19, 2003." Three years. A hell of a long time to be held by al-Qaeda, if he was still alive, poor bastard. Probably not a chance in hell he was alive. Haditha, she mused. The last known location of Abu Nazir. Where she was headed next.

The second photograph was labeled "U.S. Marine Sergeant Nicholas Brody, Captured outside Haditha, Anbar Province, May 19, 2003." They'd been taken together. She studied the photograph carefully.

It was an interesting face, she thought.

CHARACTERS

(in order of appearance)

Caroline Anne Mathison, nickname "Carrie," Operations
    Officer, Beirut Station, NCS (National Clandestine Service
    division), CIA (Central Intelligence Agency)

Saul Michael Berenson, Middle East Division Chief, NCS, CIA

Taha al-Douni, codename: Nightingale, Senior Officer GSD,
    Syrian General Security Directorate

Dima Hamdan, codename: Jihan, female agent for March 14
    Group (Christian Maronite); location: Beirut, Lebanon

Davis Fielding, Beirut Station Chief, Middle East Division,
    NCS, CIA

Virgil Maravich, Technical Officer, "Black Bag" expert, Beirut
    Station, NCS, CIA

Fatima Ali, codename: Julia; wife number one of Abbas Ali,
    Hezbollah brigade commander

Abbas Ali, husband of Fatima; Commander of Hezbollah
    "Organization of the Oppressed Brigade"

Frank Mathison, Carrie's father, lives with daughter Margaret in Alexandria, Virginia; former IT systems administrator, Vietnam veteran; current status: unemployed

Dar Adal, Former Senior Case Officer, "Black Ops," NCS, CIA; current status: independent intelligence agent/consultant

Ahmed Haidar, Member Hezbollah Central Council (Hezbollah's inner governing circle), location: Beirut and Tyre, Lebanon

David Randolph Estes, Director of the CTC (Counter-Terrorism Center), NCS, CIA; location: Langley, Virginia

Dr. Margaret Evelyn McClure, née Mathison, nickname "Maggie"; sister of Carrie Mathison; medical doctor; lives and practices in Alexandria, Virginia

James Abdel-Shawafi, nickname "Jimbo," Senior Analyst II/Database Administrator, NSA (National Security Agency), Fort Meade, Maryland

Joanne Dayton, Intelligence Analyst 2, OCSAA (Office of Collection Strategies and Analysis), Intelligence Analysis Division, CIA

Alan Yerushenko, Deputy Director, OCSAA (Office of Collection Strategies and Analysis), Intelligence Analysis Division, CIA

Abu Nazir, real name: unknown; origin unknown; current status: leader of AQI (Al Qaeda in Iraq); location: unknown

Abu Ubaida, real name: unknown; origin unknown; current status: second-in-command to Abu Nazir, leader of AQI (Al Qaeda in Iraq); location: unknown

Mira Berenson, née Bhattacharya, wife of Saul Berenson; born Mumbai, India; current status: Director, Children's Rights Division, Human Rights Watch organization

Bassam Al-Shakran, origin: Amman, Jordan; current status: pharmaceutical salesman.

Abdel Yassin; origin: Amman, Jordan; current status: student at Brooklyn College, Brooklyn, NY

Captain Koslowski, Captain, NYPD Counterintelligence Division, New York City

Sergeant Gillespie, Sergeant, NYPD Counterintelligence Division, New York City

Supervisory Special Agent Sanders, FBI Counter-Terrorism Division, Washington, DC

Tom Raeden, Hercules Team Leader, NYPD Counterintelligence Division, New York City

Abou Murad, fashion photographer, location: Gemmayzeh, Ashrafieh district, Beirut, Lebanon

Rana Saadi, well-known Lebanese actress and model; location: Verdun district, Beirut, Lebanon

Marielle Hilal, Lebanese actress and model; location: Bourj Hammoud district, Beirut, Lebanon

Mohammed Siddiqi, boyfriend of Dima Hamdan; origin: Doha, Qatar

Captain Ryan Dempsey, USMC; current status: Unit Commander, Task Force 145/liaison to CIA; stationed, Green Zone, Baghdad, Iraq

Warzer Zafir, Iraqi national; origin: Ramadi, Iraq; current status: US embassy translator and liaison to CIA

Abu Ammar, see Walid Karim

Walid Karim, a.k.a. Abu Ammar, codename: Romeo; current status: AQI Commander; origin: Ramadi, Iraq

Shada Karim, wife of Walid Karim, mother of daughter, Farah, and son, Gabir; location: Ramadi, Iraq

Aasera Karim, mother of Walid Karim; location: Ramadi, Iraq

Lt. Colonel Joseph Tussey, Commander, Third Battalion, Eighth Regiment, USMC; location: Ramadi, Iraq

Sergeant Billings, Squad Leader, Third Battalion, Eighth Regiment, USMC; location: Ramadi, Iraq

Perry Dryer, Baghdad Station Chief, Middle East Division, NCS, CIA; location: Green Zone, Baghdad, Iraq

Colonel Salazar, Commander, 4th Brigade, 3rd Division, US Army; location: Green Zone, Baghdad, Iraq

Captain Mullins, Commander, 2nd Battalion, Special Forces Group attached to 3rd Division, US Army; location: Green Zone, Baghdad, Iraq

Ambassador Robert Benson, US ambassador to Iraq; location: Green Zone, Baghdad, Iraq

Warrant Officer Blazell, nickname: Crimson; Assistant Team Leader, 2nd Battalion, Special Forces Group attached to 3rd Division, US Army; location: Green Zone, Baghdad, Iraq

Ray Saunders, Beirut Station Chief, Middle East Division, NCS, CIA; location: Beirut, Lebanon

Bilal Mohamad; current status: drug dealer; location: Minet Al Hosn district, Beirut, Lebanon

GLOSSARY

(in alphabetical order)

A Primer on Lebanese Political Groups—Politics in Lebanon is extremely complex—and the penalty for a mistake can be death. This small ancient country whose history goes back to the Phoenicians in pre-biblical times, is divided along deep fault lines of political interests and religious and tribal affiliations. This volatile internal mix is further complicated by interference from outside forces such as Syria, Israel, the Palestinians, and the Sunni-Shiite divide (see page 357), not to mention the United States. In 1975, the powder keg exploded into a brutal civil war that lasted sixteen years (nearly four times longer than the American Civil War). While the Lebanese Civil War ended in late 1990, to this day, the country's political system remains precariously balanced between opposing elements, all armed to the teeth. Governance in such circumstances is nearly impossible. The Lebanese adopted a unique form of government, in which by law, the President must be a Maronite Christian, the Prime Minister a Sunni

Muslim, the Speaker of the Parliament a Shiite Muslim, and the Deputy Prime Minister and the Deputy Speaker of Parliament, Eastern Orthodox Christians.

In order for Carrie to achieve her mission, she must navigate between these dangerous and conflicting groups and interests. In 2006, the period in which this novel is set, these groupings (also described below) included among others: Hezbollah (Shiite Muslims unofficially allied with Syria and Iran), March 14 (primarily Maronite Christians), PSP (Druze), the Islamic Group (Sunni Muslim Brotherhood) and the PLO (Palestinians).

Note: As indicated in intelligence provided to Carrie by one of her agents, Fatima Ali, a.k.a. Julia, the Second Israel-Lebanon War, prompted by a cross-border incident by Hezbollah, will break out in July 2006.

Alawites—A Shiite Muslim religious group, an offshoot of the "Twelver" branch of Shia Islam, primarily located in western Syria. The Alawites began as a sect that followed the teachings of the eleventh Imam, Hassan al-Askari, in the ninth century. In the centuries that followed, they achieved notoriety as warriors. Alawites represent only a small percentage of the Syrian population and might have passed unnoticed were it not that Syria has been ruled for more than forty years by a single Alawite dynasty, the Al-Assad family, who placed Alawites in positions of power. Bassam al-Assad, son of the founder of the modern Syrian state, Hafez al-Assad, was the President of Syria in 2006, the period in which this book is set. As Alawite Shiites, the Al-Assads, father and son, allied Syria with the other two anti-Western Shiite powers in the Middle East, Hezbollah and Iran.

Al Qaeda—The global international militant terrorist organization. Founded in the late 1980s by Osama bin Laden, a wealthy Saudi *jihadi*, in part as a response to the Soviet war in Afghanistan (1979–1989), al Qaeda (the name means "the Base") is a combination militant Islamist terrorist network, stateless military force and a radical Sunni Muslim movement advocating global *jihad*. As Salafist *jihadis*, al Qaeda is intolerant of all persons of other religions or philosophies except strict Salafist Sunni Muslims. This includes intolerance toward other Muslims, such as Shiites, Sufis, or even Sunnis who in their view do not practice a sufficiently strict Salafist Sunni version of *sharia* law. The organization achieved worldwide notoriety for its attack on the World Trade Center in New York and the Pentagon on September 11, 2001. Since then, although it has lost much of its early leadership, it has developed offshoots in other parts of the world, including among others: AQAP (Al Qaeda in the Arabian Peninsula), the Harkat-ul-Mujahideen in Kashmir, AQIM (Al Qaeda in the Islamic Maghreb; North Africa), Jemaah Islamiah (a Southeast Asian Islamist terrorist group), and AQI (Al Qaeda in Iraq).

AQI—Al Qaeda in Iraq; the Iraqi branch of Al Qaeda; the international Salafist *jihadi* militant organization founded by the Saudi terrorist, Osama bin Laden (responsible for the attack on America on September 11, 2001). AQI was founded in 2003 as a reaction to the American-led invasion and occupation of Iraq. It was first led by the Jordanian militant, Abu Musab al-Zarqawi. After his death, in the *Homeland* version of events, AQI was led by a mysterious man with the *kunya*, or nom de guerre, of Abu Nazir. By 2006, when this novel is set, the American war effort in Iraq is under serious attack. AQI has taken over almost all of the vast Anwar Province that comprises most of western Iraq all the way to the Syrian border.

COMINT—Acronym for Communications Intelligence, i.e., intelligence derived from the interception of electronic or voice communications.

GSD—The General Security Directorate; Idarat al-Amn al-Amm; the brutal agency in charge of internal and external security for the Syrian government. In addition to suppressing internal dissent and security threats against the Assad regime, the GSD is deeply involved in intelligence work outside Syria, such as coordinating intelligence activities and information with Hezbollah and the MOIS, the Iranian CIA, both allies of the Assad regime in Syria. It is for this reason that Carrie regards a senior GSD official, such as Taha al-Douni, a.k.a. Nightingale, as a prize worth trying to recruit.

Hezbollah—An Iranian-sponsored Shiite paramilitary and political movement based in Lebanon (see Sunnis versus Shiites on page 357). Founded in 1982 as a resistance movement against Israel in the aftermath of the First Israel-Lebanon War, its heavily armed militia and strong political presence has made it one of the dominant groups in Lebanon. There are certain areas within Lebanon that are completely controlled by Hezbollah, comprising a virtual state within a state. Hezbollah has ties to both Iran and Syria, all of them, Shiite-based. Hezbollah's tactics have caused the United States and Israel to officially classify it as a terrorist organization. Note that Hezbollah is Shiite and al Qaeda is a radical Sunni movement, which makes them rivals, not allies.

The Islamic Group—Al-Jamaa al-Islamiya; the Lebanese branch of the Muslim Brotherhood, founded in Egypt in 1925, whose credo involves a return to a strict Sunni Muslim version of *sharia* law. Although Sunni Muslims, they joined forces with the Christians in the March 14 alliance in order to oppose Hezbollah and their Syrian allies, who threatened to take over all of Lebanon.

Lebanese Forces, Lebanese Phalange, and the Lebanese Front—The Lebanese Front or Front Libanais was formed as a right-wing ultra-nationalistic paramilitary force, primarily consisting of Maronite Christians, designed to represent and defend "Christian territory" during the bitter Lebanese Civil War. Later, the so-called Lebanese Forces, a.k.a. Les Forces Libanaises, were formed as an umbrella group, which fought as the main right-wing Christian militia force during the Civil War. The Lebanese Phalange, a.k.a. the Kataeb Party, was formed in 1936 as a Maronite Christian paramilitary youth organization by Pierre Gemayel, who modeled it after the Spanish Falange and the Italian Fascist parties. The Phalange became an important component of the Maronite Christian Forces of the Lebanese Front during the Lebanese Civil War.

March 14 Group—A predominantly Maronite Christian coalition founded during the so-called Cedar Revolution, a wave of protests that swept Lebanon in the aftermath of the 2005 assassination of Rafik Hariri, the popular Sunni Muslim prime minister. In addition to its political arm, the group also includes the powerful Maronite Christian Lebanese Forces and Lebanese Phalange armed militia groups, as well as political and military support from some additional allies in Lebanon's topsy-turvy politics: Al-Jamaa al-Islamiya, the Sunni Muslim Islamic Group and also the Lebanese Armenian community. Carrie's assumption that her female agent, Dima Hamdan, is a Maronite Christian is in part based on the fact that Dima is a secret agent for the March 14 Group.

Maronite Christians—An early Christian ethno-religious group originating in the Syrian and Mount Lebanon regions. They began as followers of a fifth-century Syrian Christian mystic, Saint Maron, who spent his entire life on a mountain in Syria. Their church is considered an Eastern Catholic Syriac Christian denomination, unique for its liturgy, which is done in Syriac, a dialect of Aramaic (the language spoken in the time of Jesus). Today, Maronite Christians make up one-fourth of the population of Lebanon and form the backbone of the nationalist Lebanese Arab parties and right-wing militias. A powerful force within Lebanon, politically and militarily, they have often been pitted against the Muslims, Druze and Palestinians in the various complex configurations of Lebanese politics. In 2006, the period in which this book is set, they are represented politically and militarily through the March 14 Group (see page 355).

MOIS—The Ministry of Intelligence and National Security of the Islamic Republic of Iran; Vezarat-e Ettela'at Jomhuri-ye Eslami-ye Iran. Iran's foreign secret intelligence service, i.e., the Iranian equivalent of the CIA. Since both Hezbollah and the Assad government in Syria have ties to Iran, it is appropriate for Carrie to assume that her target agent, Taha al-Douni, codenamed Nightingale, would have access to intelligence from both Hezbollah and Iran's intelligence organization, MOIS.

Murabitun—Al Murabitun was started in 1957 by Sunni Muslim followers of Egyptian President Nasser. They opposed the pro-Western policies of Lebanon's then-President Camille Chamoun, a Maronite Christian. They acquired the name Al Murabitun, "the Sentinels," during fighting in the first Lebanese Civil War in 1958. Later, during the long Lebanese Civil War (1975–1990), the Sunni Muslim Murabitun joined with the LNM, the Lebanese National Movement, a coalition of left-wing and socialist forces who had combined with the Druze and Palestinians, all of whom joined forces against the Maronite Christian Lebanese Forces.

Operations Officer—As an Operations Officer, also called a "case officer," Carrie's job is to recruit and run or "handle" agents. These agents, also called "assets," "sources," "Joes" or "birds" in CIA parlance, are typically nationals of the country she is in. Or they may be members of specific groups, foreign intelligence services or other organizations who can provide "intel" or intelligence that is of value to the United States.

Sunnis versus Shiites—The origin of the conflict between Sunnis and Shiites goes back to 632 when the Prophet Muhammad died without leaving a son or heir. Two claimants vied to replace him as the leader or caliph, of the new religion: the Prophet's closest male relative by blood, his cousin and son-in-law, Ali, whose followers called themselves Shiat Ali, the followers of Ali, or Shiites for short; and the Prophet's father-in-law, Abu Bakr, whose supporters, called Sunnis, believed he would be best able to manage the rapidly expanding Muslim empire. Abu Bakr was chosen, creating the initial rift. The split between these two groups became irreparable in the year 680, when Ali's son, Hussein (who was not only Ali's son, but also the grandson of the Prophet Muhammad), challenged what he saw as a heavy-handed Sunni leadership. Ali, his forces outnumbered, was killed at Karbala in Iraq. Many of his male relatives were slain with him. The massacre of the Prophet Muhammad's grandson, along with most of his male relatives, sent shock waves across the Muslim empire that reverberate to this day. It led Shiites to adopt a sense of martyrdom as part of their faith, exemplified as they saw it, in the actions of Hussein, whose sacrifice is still commemorated on the Shiite holiday, the Day of Ashura. Throughout history, while acknowledging that they are fellow Muslims, Sunnis and Shiites have viewed each other with suspicion. The conflict continues to this day, often played out through surrogates, such as Hezbollah (Shiite) and Al Qaeda (Sunni), and in countries with mixed populations, such as Lebanon and Iraq.

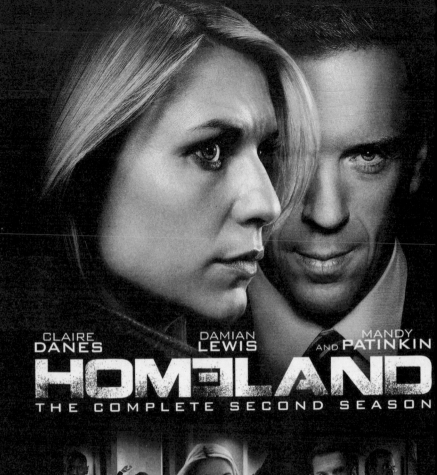

2012 EMMY® AWARD WINNER OUTSTANDING DRAMA SERIES

CLAIRE DANES   DAMIAN LEWIS   AND MANDY PATINKIN

HOMƎLAND

THE COMPLETE SECOND SEASON

BLU-RAY™ AND DVD SEPTEMBER 23R